A Mountain Springs Christmas: A 3-Book Christmas Romance Collection

Copyright © 2024 by Meg Easton

All rights reserved.

No part of this book may be reproduced in any form or by any electronic or mechanical means, including information storage and retrieval systems, without written permission from the author, except for the use of brief quotations in a book review.

This is a work of fiction and names, characters, incidents, and places are products of the author's imagination or used fictitiously. Any resemblance to persons, living or dead, incidents, and places is coincidental.

Cover Illustration: Alt19 Creative

Interior design: Mountain Heights Publishing

Author website: www.megeaston.com

also by meg easton

Romancing the Spy romantic comedies

Spies Don't Fall for Their Asset

Spies Don't Fall for Their Rival

Spiced Chais and Secret Spies

Spies Don't Fall for Their Neighbor (coming 2025)

Nestled Hollow Romances

Coming Home to the Top of Main Street

Second Chance on the Corner of Main Street

Christmas at the End of Main Street

More than Friends in the Middle of Main Street

Love Again at the Heart of Main Street

More than Enemies on the Bridge of Main Street

How to Not Fall romantic comedies

How to Not Fall for the Guy Next Door

How to Not Fall for the Wrong Guy

How to Not Fall for Your Best Friend

How to Not Fall for Your Ex

A Mountain Springs Christmas

The Christmas Pact

The Christmas Bet

The Christmas Clause

Love Started Romances

It Started with a Sunset

It Started with a Note

It Started with a Glance

Silver Leaf Falls romance

Coming Home to Silver Leaf Falls

A Mountain Springs Christmas

contents

THE CHRISTMAS PACT

THE CHRISTMAS BET

THE CHRISTMAS CLAUSE

the christmas pact

one

NOELLE

NOELLE ALLRED HELD her cell phone to her ear, veering to the other edge of the sidewalk as she walked under a mechanical lift that held a man in its basket, draping Christmas lights from one side of Main Street in her hometown of Mountain Springs, Colorado, to the other. She could hear her sister, Hope, on the other end of the line, telling her four-year-old son that he couldn't tie his two-year-old brother to the dog so he could ride him like a horse without falling off. And that they couldn't do it, even if the brother and the dog both acted like they wanted to.

Snow was softly falling from the morning sky, promising to make the lights extra beautiful when they turned them on for the first time tonight. It was something that Noelle used to love, but not anymore. She adjusted her hood so the flakes wouldn't land on her hair, melt, then dry weird on the way to work and make it look like she'd just woken up and hadn't even glanced in the mirror before heading to work.

She shivered and pulled her coat a little tighter.

"I'm back," Hope said, a little breathless. "I had to play the 'Santa's watching' card, and I'm not proud of it. But I also think we avoided a possible concussion in Porter's near future, so I'm working on being okay with it. Back to tonight—what time are you planning to be at Downtown Park for the tree lighting?"

Noelle adjusted the strap of her bag on her shoulder and braced herself for her sister's response. "I'm not going."

"What?! Why not? You've never skipped. Not even for those four years when you were in student housing. How can you not come tonight?"

She took a deep breath and glanced at the shops on Main Street, which all seemed to be trying to outdo each other with their Christmas decorations and window displays. Then she immediately dropped her eyes to the snow falling onto the sidewalk in front of her. "It just doesn't feel right to go with Gran-gran gone." The pain of her loss stabbed her in the heart again, like when the grief had been brand new. She stopped to lean against a building for a minute and just looked up at the snow falling.

Hope was quiet for a long moment, then whispered, "I miss her, too."

Noelle's family was big on Christmas. Actually, that was an understatement. If Christmas was a TV screen, it was the JumboTron at Ball Arena in Denver to her family. If it was a trickle of water spilling over rocks, it was her family's Niagra Falls. If it was a figurine for most families, it was the Statue of Liberty to hers.

And Gran-gran had been the leader of it all.

Noelle didn't say anything more, so Hope filled the silence. "I know it felt that way last year, but that was because she'd just barely passed away. I think it'll be different this year."

But Hope hadn't been as close to Gran-gran as Noelle had been. None of them had been as close. This year felt like it'd be worse in part because she hadn't just passed away. They weren't busy planning a funeral this year, going through all Gran-gran's things, and deciding what to do with them. This year would feel like a regular Christmas, but it'd be missing the most essential ingredient.

"I don't think it will," Noelle said, making herself keep walking toward the bus stop just in front of Downtown Park, a block further down the street. "So I'm just going to skip Christmas this year."

"Skip it? I don't understand."

"You know..." Noelle said, waving her hand around,

trying to encapsulate everything, but realized the motion was pointing out all the decorations on Main Street. "I'm just going to pretend like Christmas doesn't exist."

"You can't just skip it."

"Yep, that's what I'm doing. I am officially done with Christmas. This is no longer the Christmas season; it's simply the winter season. Look—I've got snow all around me just to remind me that's all it is. I'm going to avert my eyes from anything remotely Christmassy." She cupped her hand beside her eye to block out the view.

"Excuse me!" someone called out. Noelle jumped and took a step back as four guys—who had been blocked from her view by the hood of her coat even before she had blocked them even more with her hand—crossed just in front of her, carrying a workshop table for Santa's village that was being set up in Downtown Park for the start of the Christmas festivities tonight.

So much for averting her eyes from all things Christmas.

"There's no way that you, the biggest Christmas lover of all, is done with it."

"No, I am."

She reached the bus stop, which gave her a view of the park that was even worse than her view had been walking down Main Street. A couple of people were working to install the false sides to the big gazebo to make it look like a giant gingerbread house. They would be serving hot cocoa inside during the festivities tonight and at a few other events during the month.

A life-size manger scene was set up on its right, complete with the stable, Mary, Joseph, baby Jesus, a donkey, a handful of sheep, and a shepherd.

To the left of the gazebo, several volunteers were working on getting Santa's village set up, which was a massive undertaking. The village had half a dozen elf houses, red and white-striped street signs, Santa's sleigh, several reindeer, stacks of wrapped presents, and a big outdoor workshop where a dozen elves worked to make toys.

A few more volunteers worked to set up the train tracks and the small working train that would carry the little kids in a circle around the entire workshop. Lighted arches led the way to where the train could be boarded.

And a couple people were stringing thousands of lights on the massive pine tree that stood in the middle of it all. There was so much activity and movement in the park that it kept involuntarily pulling her attention to it. Looking the other direction only meant that she'd be watching people wrap the street lamps on Main Street in garlands.

And not only that, but the bus was late—probably because of the snow. Noelle couldn't exactly keep her eyes closed and still watch out for the bus, so she caught loads of Christmas happenings. No amount of averting her eyes and using her hand as a blinder could keep it all out. And even though her hood was nice and fluffy, it didn't keep out the Christmas music playing for the workers setting everything up.

"Do you really think that you're going to be able to do that?" Hope asked. "While living in Mountain Springs and while being a member of our family?"

Hope was four and a half years older than Noelle, and she was married and had three kids. So they were at very different points in their lives, yet Hope was her best friend. Or, at least they had been as adults, even if they weren't even close to best friends as kids. Now, though, Hope was the person she could share anything with.

Noelle sighed and rubbed her forehead. "It might take a lot more work than I was anticipating. Why did I have to slide on that ice and make my car inoperable right now, of all times?"

She'd bought her car three years ago for her birthday after falling instantly in love. She was the cutest car, not too big, and was the perfect Christmas red. She'd named her Elfie right on the spot.

The only bus stop that would take her from Mountain Springs through the canyon to Golden was right in the middle of everything. And to get to it from her house, she had to walk right down Main Street, so there was no avoiding it all. If she had her car, she could take a wide drive around downtown. She could find a path between her home and work where she could bypass it all.

"I might be skipping all the Christmas festivities, but I'm still going to buy presents for everyone. So there's no way I can afford to fix Elfie anytime soon." People were important, even if Christmas wasn't for her anymore.

"So, what are you going to do?"

She shrugged and squinted through the snowflakes on her eyelashes and all the falling snow to see if the bus was close. "I've decided I need to get a side job so I can save up enough for the repairs. Lots of places are hiring temporary help at this time of year, right?"

"Yes," Hope said, dragging out the word. "Lots of places. Like places where people do their Christmas shopping."

"I hadn't thought of that." Noelle shivered and switched her phone to her other hand so she could put the one that had been holding it in her pocket. "What am I going to do? I can't just wait until after Christmas to get a second job. I don't want to wait that long to get it fixed, and that's when businesses are least likely to hire."

"I don't know, but I'll keep an ear out for you."

She perked up when the bus lumbered around the corner, heading her direction. "Thanks, sis. My bus is here, so I've got to go."

"We'll miss you tonight!"

"I'll miss you, too."

But she wouldn't miss the big reveal when they turned on all the lights and everyone ooh-ed and ahh-ed over the big tree and everything else they were setting up. Nope, not one bit. All of that excitement and anticipation for Christmas had left with Gran-gran. She turned her back on all of it—the decorations, the people setting it up, the Christmas music—and climbed into the bus.

She took a seat in the middle right as a Christmas song came on the radio. The six people seated in the back started singing along to it like they were carolers standing outside someone's house, bringing joy and all that. Noelle pulled her hood a little tighter around her ears and tried to pretend like it was just winter. That's all they were doing—singing winter songs.

She could do this. She could one hundred percent skip Christmas this year.

two

JACK

AS JACK MEADOWS neared his sister Rachel's small house, he could see that the eight inches of snow that had fallen during the day covered her driveway and walks. Even though Mountain Springs was only a thirty-minute drive through the canyon from his home in Golden, it included a two thousand foot climb in eleva-tion. He sometimes forgot how much more snow that meant that his sister got than he did. Snowplows had cleared the roads, thankfully, so he parked in a mostly clear spot in front of her house.

He responded to a few urgent work emails on his phone, then got out of the car, pulled on his hat and gloves, and opened his trunk. This time of year, he always kept good boots in his trunk for days like this. He traded his dress shoes for the boots, wishing he was wearing something other than suit pants, and tucked them into his boots. He would have to remember to leave a pair of jeans at his sister's for times like these.

Then he trudged through the snow and entered her garage door code. He grabbed the snow shovel, switched on the outdoor lights, including the Christmas lights, and then went to work shoveling the snow from the sidewalks and driveway and piling it on the already two-foot-high pile of snow in her grass.

His mind was on work as he shoveled, which wasn't different from any other time of day. He loved having his own ad agency, but it definitely took every bit of his focus while he was awake. And remembering the dreams he'd had last night, he had to admit that his laser focus didn't really sleep when he did.

Eventually, he finished, stomped off his boots, and traded them back for his dress shoes. Then he pulled his car into the driveway, just in case the snowplow needed to come by again while he was inside—the skies didn't look like they were quite done covering the world in white.

As he walked toward Rachel's front door, he marveled at the Christmas lights on her house and trees. A neighbor must've put them up. He and Rachel never once had Christmas lights growing up. He wondered if she had asked for help or if a neighbor had just felt extra Christmassy and wanted to spread it to others.

He used his key to unlock the front door. The moment he had it open, his five-year-old nephew Aiden shouted "Uncle Jack!" and raced toward him, launching himself into the air as he neared, clinging to him like a starfish. Jack gave the kid a tight hug. Their golden retriever, Bailey, had followed right behind him, giving a single bark before panting, wagging her tail.

"Hey, buddy! How are you doing?"

"Good," Aiden said as he slid back to standing on the floor. He grabbed Jack's hand and pulled him toward the open kitchen and family room. "Momma and I were hoping you'd come. She's extra sick today."

Oh, no. He should've left work early. When they got to the family room, he saw Rachel sitting in the recliner, looking pale and weak—worse than when he'd seen her yesterday. He immediately went to her side. He knew that this round of chemo was a tough one, but he hadn't expected her to look quite so sickly.

"Why didn't you call or text to let me know you weren't doing well? I would've gotten off work earlier and brought food."

She reached out for his hand, so he gave it a squeeze. "The—" Her voice came out like a squeak, so she cleared her throat. "The neighbors brought dinner over."

Aiden jumped onto the couch next to his mom in a sitting position, bouncing as he landed. "It was chicken soup and the best cornbread muffins ever."

"Oh yeah?" Jack asked.

Aiden nodded.

Jack looked at his sister. "Were you able to eat?"

She nodded. "Some. Today's just been a rough day."

"What do you think about moving into my apartment in Golden for the next little while? Then I could respond more quickly and help more." Maybe he should get her a live-in nurse.

"I don't know anyone in Golden," Rachel said, "and I've got a good support system here. Plus, I wouldn't want Aiden to not be able to go to school here—it's where all his friends are. My church here organized everyone to bring food for the next few weeks, and they come to check on me often. I feel well cared for."

He nodded. "Do you want me to move in here for the next little while?" It would definitely require some significant adjustments, but he was willing to do whatever would help.

"I do!" Aiden said.

But Rachel chuckled softly. "No. We really don't have the space. But do you mind helping me to my room? I'm just feeling a little weak right now."

Jack scooped her up and carried her into her room that was just off the family room. She felt lighter than the last time he'd had to carry her, and it worried him.

It must've shown on his face because she said, "Stop thinking like that. I'm going to make it through this."

He nodded.

"I'm not just saying that to make you feel better. I feel it in my bones that I'm going to make it through this just fine. I'm sure I'll have to wade through a lot of tough days along the way, but I'll make it to the other side of this challenge."

He could see the truth of her words in her expression.

He set her gently on her bed. Aiden leaped onto the bed and pulled the covers over his mom, making sure to tug it over her shoulders, straightening it out like it wasn't his first time. "You all comfy, momma?"

"Yes, because you're so good at this." He grinned, and she gave him a hug.

Jack turned to leave, but Rachel said, "No, stay. I'm exhausted, not sleepy. Tell me about work."

He nodded and took a seat in the chair near her bed. "Well, December's always super busy, of course, since that's when everyone wants to advertise the most. Many of the companies we work with have had their ad campaigns in the works for months, and we're just in the final stages of actually running the campaigns.

"We still have smaller companies coming to us last minute, though, looking for smaller campaigns to be thrown together quickly. But I've got a good team, and they handle the extra work well."

"You've done great things with your company. I'm proud of you."

"Thank you." Jack didn't have parents—Rachel had taken over that role when they'd both died when he was fifteen. So hearing that from her made his chest swell. He guessed it would've felt the same as if it had come from a parent.

Then she asked the question about work that he'd known she'd most wanted to hear about when she first asked. "And how is Noelle?"

He looked down, shaking his head, but still smiling just at the mention of her name. "She's good. Like always."

"When are you going to get around to asking her out already?"

He took a deep breath. She knew the answer—she'd asked the question plenty of times. "Still never. Because I'm still her boss."

Jack had a good friend and an acquaintance who each dated employees in businesses they owned, and neither turned out well. His friend's relationship had created a lot of office drama that really caused problems for the better part of a year. His friend had been lucky.

For his acquaintance, there had been office drama, indeed. But the bigger problem had been a bad breakup that caused cascading issues that had eventually brought his entire company down. Jack had eight employees whose livelihood depended on his company staying strong and doing well, and he felt the weight of that responsibility exquisitely.

"Such a shame." She turned to her son. "Aiden, why don't you get your snowflake collection to show Uncle Jack?" Aiden hopped off the bed. "Make sure you gather all the ones you made, not just the ones in the box. Get the ones on your bed and on the kitchen table and counters. Coffee table, too."

Rachel watched the door until Aiden was out of sight, then turned to Jack. "I have a favor to ask."

"Anything."

"I want you to take Aiden to do Christmassy things this season."

"Okay, ask me for anything but that."

She swatted him on the arm. "I'm serious, Jack!"

"Come on, Rach. You know I'd do anything for you. But Aiden doesn't need a Grinch making him hate Christmas, too. I can't think of anyone who would be worse at it than I would."

"He needs this. I want him to have the kind of Christmases that we never had."

"And you've been giving it to him every year. One Christmas isn't going to make or break his feelings about Christmas."

"So, what..." She raised an eyebrow. "It takes an

entire childhood of going without it to turn someone into a Christmas-hating Grinch?"

"Pretty much."

"Five years old is the most magical age to experience Christmas, and I don't want him missing out on that just because I'm sick." She paused for a long moment, then added, "Jack, it's important to me."

November and December were his busiest months at work, and he had to put in so many hours a week during those months to accomplish all that he needed to. But how could he say no to his sister's request? Especially when it was important to her?

He took a deep breath. "Okay, I'll make sure he experiences a fun Christmas." He couldn't guarantee it'd be him helping Aiden, but he'd make sure Aiden didn't miss out on a single thing.

She gave him a weak smile. "Thank you."

When Aiden came back into the room, his arms wrapped around a box that was almost too wide for his five-year-old arms, Rachel said, "I need to rest for a bit. Why don't you have Uncle Jack help you hang those up?"

Aiden nodded, and they both left the room, pulling the door closed behind them. Aiden set the box on the coffee table, then went to the kitchen and returned a moment later with a spool of kite string, a roll of tape, and a pair of scissors. After setting them down, he headed back to the kitchen, grabbed one of the chairs at their small table, and hefted it into the family room area.

"Mom says we can't put up the Christmas decorations until she's feeling a bit better, but we can put up these."

Jack hadn't even noticed that they didn't have decorations up. His lack of prickliness at first walking into the room should've tipped him off to their absence.

Aiden patted the stack of snowflakes he'd made from cutting folded paper. "I've been making these for a really long time. I'm talking for a really long time. Like, at least ten days. I want to hang them from the ceiling so it'll look like it's snowing in here. I know they aren't really Christmas decorations, but there's always snow at Christmas, so it's kind of like Christmas decorations."

He much preferred thinking of them as simply a winter thing.

They cut lengths of string, taped one end to each snowflake, and then Jack climbed onto the chair to tape them to the ceiling. Aiden started singing a song he was making up as they went along about hanging them up. Jack was having fun. He liked hanging out with his nephew.

But then Aiden said, "I know! We should be listening to Christmas music instead of me singing!"

And then his nephew turned on the music, and a song about jingle bell time being a swell time filled the room, and Jack felt his hackles rise. The longer they worked and the more Christmas songs played, the more Grinch-like Jack could feel himself becoming. He just had too many negative feelings attached to Christmas from his childhood to ever enjoy the season again.

He taped a snowflake string to the ceiling, and Aiden said, "It needs to go that direction like this much." He held his hands about six inches apart.

"It's fine where it is," Jack snapped.

He immediately regretted the words, even before seeing Aiden's reaction to being barked at.

"Aiden, I'm sorry. I shouldn't have spoken sharply— that had nothing to do with you. It needs to go this direction, you said?" He pulled the tape from the ceiling and moved it to the right. Aiden nodded, so he stuck it in the new spot.

There was no way he could be the one to help Aiden experience the joy of Christmas. Jack couldn't be around anything relating to Christmas without feeling cranky, and no matter how hard he could try to hide it, it was bound to rub off on Aiden. He could never do the holiday justice for a five-year-old who was so wide-eyed and expectant of the season.

He needed to find help.

three

NOELLE

NOELLE SAT around the conference table in the marketing meeting with her boss and her seven coworkers, talking about the ad campaigns they had running for clients and new ad campaigns they had coming up, taking notes about everything that had to do with her job as the copywriter. Assignments were made, deadlines were given.

And then, at the part where her boss, Jack, who was standing with his tablet in his hand, would typically wrap up the meeting by asking if anyone had any questions, he shifted from one foot to the other and then glanced down at the tablet. Then he placed it on the table and looked out at them, putting his hands in his pockets and looking a little uncomfortable.

The uncertain body language seemed out of place for

a boss who was always very professional and busi-nesslike and instantly made everyone pay a little more attention.

"I need some help outside of work for a project unre-lated to work, and I'm wondering if any of you might be interested in the job. You would be paid—"

Noelle's hand shot into the air.

Jack glanced at her, pausing his sentence only momentarily before forging on. "—time and a half, and it would be eight to ten hours a week until the end of the month."

Noelle raised her arm as high as it would go as her brain started doing the math without her even telling it to. That would probably be everything she needed to get her car fixed, and it wouldn't involve working in a retail environment that would practically be exploding with Christmas. If that wasn't a giant Christmas miracle dropped right at her doorstep, she didn't know what was.

Winter miracle, she mentally corrected herself. Fortune smiling down on her. Divine intervention.

It would be so nice to drive her car again!

"Okay," Jack said, nodding at Noelle, "it looks like we have one person interested. Is anyone else?"

Noelle looked around the conference table. A couple of people looked thoughtful, but most looked uninter-ested or maybe even overwhelmed with work and the holidays. Lennox looked like he was considering it for a moment, then changed his mind. Bridget seemed to turn her nose up at just the thought of working more hours. She could probably put her arm down. Jack got that she was very interested.

"And that was our last item of business. Noelle, do you want to come to my office, and we'll talk more about the job?"

As she grabbed her stuff and walked to his office, her mind ran with possibilities of what the job might be. It wasn't spending extra time doing her regular job—he'd made that clear. It couldn't really be organizing files or anything like that, either, since he said it was unrelated to work. Whatever it was, overtime pay was something she couldn't pass up.

Why was it that walking into Jack's office made her feel like she was being "called on the carpet?" It was a funny expression, mainly because most of the building was carpeted, but Jack's office wasn't. His was modern and sleek, like it belonged in a magazine. A couch sat on one side, which should've made the place feel homier, but it didn't. It was leather with angled lines, and even though it had a small rug in front of it, even the carpet had clean lines and a short pile.

Poster-sized images of award-winning ads they had created hung framed on the walls, along with the awards, scaled to the same size. The only personal item in the room was a framed picture on his desk, but it faced him, not the side of the desk she was on. She always wished she had the guts to pick it up and look at it—to get a glimpse into what was important enough to him to be the only thing he deemed worthy of entering his workspace.

Everything was neat and tidy and organized, too, which was so at odds with their work in a creative business. No one else's desks here looked so orderly. It made her uncomfortable. Out of her element.

"Have a seat," he said as he shut the door behind her and went around to sit at his desk.

She took a seat on the leather chair, which, for the record, wasn't soft, even though it was padded. How she hadn't totally blown her interview in this same room a year and a half ago was beyond her. She'd felt just as out of place back then.

It didn't help that her boss was intimidatingly good-looking. He had those strong shoulders that looked so incredible in a suit. In the few times she'd seen him just wearing a dress shirt without the jacket, they'd looked even more impressive. Dark hair, dark eyes, strong jawline—he had it all.

Anyone would agree that he was a very beautiful man. But he had a stiff exterior that hid what he was like on the inside, and he never cracked. They all knew what kind of a boss he was—a very fair one—but no one knew what he was like outside of work, and he never gave any clues.

"I'm going to cut right to the chase here, Ms. Allred. My sister has Acute Myeloid Leukemia."

Noelle gasped.

"She's convinced she'll make it through, but she's been going through the most intense part of treatment right now and is pretty sick. She has a five-year-old son —my nephew, Aiden. Do you have any experience with kids?"

Her brows drew together. Was he looking for a babysitter? Why would he ask work colleagues for that kind of help when he could go to a site or app for care-takers? She hesitated. "I do. I have nine nieces and neph-ews. Two of them are five-year-old boys."

He nodded. "Good. My sister said that Christmas is a magical time for five-year-olds, and she doesn't want him to miss out on any of it just because she's sick. She asked for assistance in providing him with a magical Christmas. What I would need you to do is to help give that to him."

Noelle immediately stood. "I'm sorry; I can't."

Jack looked shocked by the abrupt ending of the negotiation. He stood, too. "Why? Is the pay not good enough for something like that? I can offer you more."

"It's not that. I just can't."

He cocked his head slightly. "I assure you, Noelle, that my nephew's a good kid."

"I am sure that he is. But I'm sorry—my answer is no." She didn't want to turn down something that had seemed like such a gift and an answer to all her problems. But there was no way possible that she could do what he was asking. And the longer she stayed in this room, the more he would think he might be able to talk her into it. "Now, if you'll excuse me, I've got a lot of work waiting for me."

Then she turned and walked out of his office, not even glancing back to see the look on her boss's face. She had always prided herself on being the one willing to take on any extra work whenever he asked, so her response was probably rather unexpected for him.

She really did have a lot of work to do before the end of the day, so she got herself in the ad copy mindset and focused deeply. She started with the copy for a group of ads showing the "perfect" stocking stuffers, and she was on fire. Sometimes, coming up with the right words to go with an ad image felt like an uphill climb when the hill was covered in thick molasses, making each step exhausting work. But other times, like today, the words came like running downhill with a breeze at her back.

After an hour of working so focused on the ads, she could feel her brain power waning, so she took a break to work on other tasks and give her creative juices time to recharge. She refilled her water bottle, sat back down, got comfortable, nudged some papers aside to make room for her water, then opened her email. The top one was from her boss, with a subject line that read *Extra hours*. She sighed and clicked on it.

Noelle,

I sincerely think that you're the best person for the job to help my sister and nephew. I really hope you'll reconsider.

Jack

Nope. That wasn't going to happen. She was super bummed that it wouldn't work out, but it very much wouldn't. So she clicked *reply* and typed, *I am sorry. I really wish I could help you, but I can't.* Then she clicked *send* and forced herself to work on writing ad copy for their "Gifts for the guy who has everything" campaign.

All through the rest of the afternoon, though, working *didn't* help her forget about Jack's request. Not only about how badly she needed the money or how much she just couldn't make herself do anything Christmassy to get it, but also about the pleading look that had been on her boss's face when he had asked. This was his company, and he was passionate about it. That had come through in so many staff meetings over the year and a half she'd worked there. She had seen plenty of impassioned pleas for them to pour their heart into specific projects or to put in extra hours when they had too many great clients needing their services at the same time.

His plea for his nephew had been different. It wasn't that it had been more sincere—that wasn't it. He was sincere about everything he did. She couldn't quite put her finger on what the difference was, though.

Regardless of what had been on his face, the fact remained that she couldn't do what he was asking. It just wasn't possible.

So it felt even worse when she got a text from Jack after she'd left work for the day, just as she was walking from the office to the bus stop.

> Jack: You have now mentioned twice that you "can't" help my nephew—never that you don't want to. Can I assume that means that there's an obstacle standing in your way that you can't get around? Is there something that I can do to help overcome the obstacle?

Noelle wasn't even sure how to respond. Could she pretend that she hadn't seen the text and answer once she had time to think about how to reply? Yeah, probably not—her phone was set to show when she'd read a message. She really needed to change that. She took a deep breath and clicked reply, then just dumped out her thoughts.

Noelle: It's more of a mental obstacle than a physical one. Although I did just slip on ice and slide my car into a pole, ruining the front corner just enough to make it un-driveable, so I guess it's also a physical one.

Noelle: But really, the far biggest issue of the two is the mental obstacle. So, no, there's not much you can do.

She touched send, then had a moment of freaking out that she just told her boss that she had mental obstacles. And suddenly, she couldn't handle seeing what his response might be to a declaration that was far more personal than she had ever been with her boss. Even admitting that she was having car troubles was out of the ordinary. So she hurried and shut her phone off before his response could come in and pushed her phone into her bag.

Then she reached in and pushed it further to the bottom. Underneath everything. Where a response wouldn't feel like it was trying to break free. But then she felt the metaphorical weight of the phone, which now only had the faux leather of her bag between it and her lap, so she moved the bag to the empty seat next to her.

She got off the bus, made the walk back to her apartment—on sidewalks now shoveled clear of snow, thankfully—and went into her apartment before she looked at her bag, trying to decide if she wanted to take her phone out of it and turn it back on.

It was the fact that she knew Hope would be calling that made her grab the phone and power it on. She didn't want to go to the event tonight, but she did love her sister.

No missed calls from Hope yet, which was unusual. But there were definitely two texts from Jack. She realized that she'd forgotten to get her mail, so she grabbed her keys and headed back down to the mail room, looking at the phone as she went, trying to work up the courage to swipe on the notifications. She unlocked her mail box, then hovered her finger over the messages for a long time before mumbling, *You're being a wimp*, then swiped to open the texts. She looked down at the phone in one hand, grabbing her mail with the other.

> Jack: I will pay for the repairs on your car. And while it's in the shop, I'll get you a rental to drive. As far as the mental obstacle, I don't know if I can do anything for that, but I'm hoping this will help...

The following text was just two pictures. The first was of a young boy who she guessed was his nephew. He looked like he was about five years old and was holding a snowflake cut from folded white paper, grinning at the camera. He was adorable, and she found herself smiling back at him. He kind of reminded her of her nephews.

The second picture was the same boy, sitting on the lap of someone who looked frail and like she wasn't feeling well. She guessed it was Jack's sister. That one made her heart hurt.

But so did thoughts of doing Christmas stuff with the boy. So she swiped out of the app before closing and locking her mail box. She had no idea how to respond.

As she walked back up to her apartment, she pushed her phone into her pocket and started looking through the mail in her hand. A package sat on top of some bills and junk mail. It was slightly smaller than a book but also thicker. It was some kind of box wrapped in brown paper. It was addressed to her, but there wasn't a return address.

Curious, she turned it over to the backside but then quickly turned it back as her brain interpreted what her eye must've caught. The postmark was from North Pole, Alaska. She sucked in a breath, staring at the postmark with disbelief. For as long as she could remember, her Gran-gran would send her a letter "from Santa," and the postmark always said North Pole, Alaska. The home of Santa Claus.

She'd figured out that Santa wasn't real when she was seven (which was bound to happen with three older sisters who already figured it out but didn't do all they could to keep the secret from her because she wasn't the youngest). When she'd gotten the letter from Santa that Christmas, she'd announced to Gran-gran that she no longer believed in Santa.

Gran-gran had just smiled, winked, and said, "I'll never stop believing in the magic of Christmas."

And then, when Noelle was eight, a letter from Santa still came, still with a postmark from North Pole, Alaska. They still kept coming, in fact, every year since then. One even arrived "from Santa," postmarked by the North Pole post office last year. Noelle had received it just two days after Gran-gran's passing.

She was still holding her breath, like letting it out might disturb the magic, and the box would vanish. But then, suddenly and with all the speed she could muster, she ran up the three flights of stairs as fast as she could. Her keys shook in her hands as she tried to unlock the door. But she finally got the key in and turned, opened the door, and raced to dump the rest of the mail on her table.

Then she grabbed a pair of scissors from her kitchen junk drawer, forced herself to take the time to remove her key from the front door and shut it, then she took slow, deep breaths and forced herself to be calm.

Ever so carefully, so she wouldn't damage the brown paper, she sliced into the tape just enough to break it and unfolded the wrapping.

Inside was a metal box, with her name painted in her gran-gran's fancy handwritten script across the top. She ran her fingers across it reverently, like it was made of the most precious gems.

Maybe this was nothing. Maybe her parents knew she would struggle this Christmas, so they sent something to the North Pole post office to have it postmarked and sent back to Noelle.

But somehow, she knew it wasn't. With trembling fingers, she lifted off the top of the box.

Inside was a stack of cards on thick cardstock. She picked up the first one—it was a scene painted with watercolors of the tree lighting in Downtown Park. She recognized Gran-gran's style immediately. And among the people painted in the scene, she recognized Gran-gran by the red coat she always wore. Noelle stood next to her. She turned the card over and saw Gran-gran's flowing script that had gotten the tiniest bit shaky over the years.

Start off the season by experiencing the magic in Downtown Park.

Every year.

She laughed once, covering her mouth with one hand, tears starting to fall from her eyes and run down her cheeks. Noelle's entire family always went to the tree lighting, but she and Gran-gran always stuck together like glue while they were there. All that magic she'd ever experienced in Downtown Park had been with her.

One by one, she went through the stack of at least a dozen cards. Each one had a scene painted of one of the traditions they did together, with the description written ever so carefully on the back. Each one of them said *Every year* at the bottom. She could feel her Gran-gran's presence with them all. She swiped at the tears that were running freely down her cheeks so they wouldn't fall onto the cards.

The pain of missing Gran-gran stabbed at her, but it was somehow a blunted stab this time. She could feel her presence with every card. Almost like she was with her as she looked at them.

She got to the last card, but there was no note or letter at the bottom. Where had these come from? And how did they get mailed from the North Pole a year after Gran-gran's passing?

Picking up her phone and dialing Hope with one hand, she picked up each card again, looking it over, overcome by the feeling that Gran-gran was in the room with her.

"Hello?" Her sister's voice sounded strained.

"Whatcha up to?" She tried to make her voice sound normal and happy.

"Wrangling kids into their car seats before we head over to the tree lighting." Noelle couldn't entirely trust her voice to come out normal. When she didn't immediately respond, Hope said, "Are you okay, Noe?"

Noelle nodded, then sniffed. "I got a package from Gran-gran."

"You—" Then, with her voice sounding further away from the phone, she said, "Honey, will you get this?" Then she was back. "You got a package? From Gran-gran? How?"

"I don't know. Hope, I need you to be one hundred percent truthful with me. Did you send this?"

"No."

"Do you know who did?"

"No. How? How did you get a package from Gran-gran?"

"I don't know. It's a metal tin containing cards she painted."

"And you're sure they're from her?"

"I'm sure." She looked at a card that showed Noelle

and Gran-gran shopping for Christmas presents together. "She was definitely the one who painted these."

"But how did they get to you?"

Noelle shrugged again, even though she knew that Hope couldn't see it. "They came from North Pole, Alaska."

Hope gasped. "I want to see these. We've got to get to the tree lighting soon. Can I come over after I get the kids to bed?"

Noelle told her yes and ended the call, then just stood for a long time at her kitchen table, staring at the impossible cards and the words *Every year* at the bottom of each one. It was like she came back to give her a message. Like she knew just how badly she needed it.

After a long moment, Noelle wiped the tears from her cheeks and picked up her phone. Then she took a deep breath and went into Jack's message and touched the picture of Jack's nephew, enlarging it to the size of her screen. Then she swiped to the following picture of the boy and his mom.

She looked back at the box of cards. Did Gran-gran know that Noelle would quit Christmas once she was gone, and this was her way of making sure that didn't happen? Because the message seemed clear that Gran-gran still wanted all their traditions to happen every year, regardless of whether she was present or not. Like she knew that Noelle, specifically, needed to continue the traditions.

She rubbed her nose. Did her gran-gran somehow know that there was a little boy who needed her to do it, too?

Could she do it? What if she felt the pain of Gran-gran's absence so strongly every time she tried to do the things on the cards?

Maybe there was only one way to find out. She picked up her phone and texted Hope.

Noelle: Will you swing by and pick me up on your way to the tree lighting? But don't judge the state of my face.

Then, without even glancing in the mirror to see the damage done to her makeup and exactly how red and puffy her eyes and nose were from the crying, she grabbed her coat and keys and headed downstairs to meet her sister and her family.

four

JACK

JACK THANKED the man he'd been talking to on the phone, assured him that he'd be in touch soon to give him a detailed advertising plan, and hung up. The man owned a small business that made miniature games that were perfect for stocking stuffers, and he needed a last-minute Christmas campaign. Jack's company catered to small businesses who weren't big enough to have their own marketing department, so he was used to getting last-minute panicked requests for help.

Still, though, most years didn't usually have nearly this many last-minute calls.

He finished typing his notes about the company's needs and budget, added them to their list of projects for the month, added them to the agenda for the team meeting later, then pushed his notepad aside and ran his hands through his hair.

And then, because it had been so close to the front of his mind ever since the meeting yesterday, he started thinking about how he'd asked Noelle to help his nephew experience Christmas. The panic he'd been feeling ever since Noelle had sat in his office and turned down his request was returning in full force, too.

He worried that he wouldn't be able to find anyone else to help. And, really, he didn't *want* anyone else to help. He would be entrusting his nephew—his favorite little guy on the planet—with this person, so he needed to know and trust them. And in his gut, he knew that Noelle was the best option.

Plus, he'd talked to Rachel about Noelle enough that he knew Rachel would trust her, too, even though they'd never actually met. He hoped he hadn't been totally out of line by asking her to reconsider more than once, but he'd been desperate. He assumed he had been, especially since Noelle never texted back after he'd sent pictures last night.

He glanced at the clock on his wall—ten minutes to nine. He needed to catch Noelle as soon as she came into the office today and apologize for his unprofessionalism. He always worked hard to keep his attraction to her a secret because he was her boss, which meant that a relationship with her was utterly impossible.

Yet, he'd let himself cross that line of professionalism just because he cared about his nephew. He needed to rein it in. To come up with a Plan B. He never should've gone to any of his employees with a request that was so personal. Just because they were the people he knew the best and cared about and trusted the most was no excuse.

Especially because he'd already known that the line of professionalism was most challenging to keep with Noelle. She wore all of her emotions on her sleeve, so it was easy to tell how she was feeling at any given moment. And, with the singular exception of being tight-lipped about why she didn't want to help out with Christmas, she was usually pretty free with her thoughts and opinions and fears, doubts, hopes, everything.

She didn't seem to have much of a line at all. When he'd first hired her, he hadn't liked that she didn't just keep things professional. But over time, he'd grown to love it. It had helped him to get to know her so much better than he'd have ever gotten to otherwise.

But that was precisely why it was a problem. She made him feel comfortable around her. Like they were friends when they very much were not. So sometimes, he forgot there was a line. Like last night, when he'd texted her, begging for help. *Twice.* They were boss and employee, and that was all they could ever be. It was virtually the only thing he didn't like about being the boss.

But it wasn't like he could just do everything his sister hoped he would do all by himself. Not only was this his busiest month of the year, but he didn't have the slightest clue how to help Aiden with Christmas. A happy, "full" Christmas wasn't something he'd ever experienced himself. Rachel might as well have asked him to build a rocket ship and hop in it with Aiden and go show him the universe.

He glanced at the clock again. It was still several minutes before nine, but Noelle usually arrived a few minutes early. It was time to go apologize. He put his hands on his desk and was just standing when she appeared in his doorway. Her blonde hair was the perfect amount of curly, and she was wearing an ice blue blouse with navy jeans, ankle boots that he loved on her, and dangly silver earrings that brought out the sparkle in her eyes.

No smile this time, though, which was unusual for her. He had definitely crossed a line yesterday. She held a single piece of paper, and he really hoped it wasn't a resignation letter.

"Listen, Noelle. I need to apologize for—"

"Did you find anyone?"

The question—and the interruption—took him by surprise. He looked down, moved a paper on his desk with a single finger, then he put his hands in his pockets and met her eyes. "No. I've still been hoping that you'll take the job."

He couldn't believe he had just said that since he'd already decided against it. It was the concerned uncle side of him speaking, and he shouldn't have let it take over.

Noelle took another step into his office and closed the door behind her. "Okay, I'm just going to lay it all out here, even though it makes me feel awkward. But there are conditions, and you need to know them before accepting my help."

She might still be willing to help? He held his breath, waiting to hear more.

"My gran-gran died a year ago, and she was the most important person in the world to me. Everything Christmas-related I did with her, so everything about Christmas is now entwined with missing her. I didn't want to have anything to do with Christmas without her here, but apparently, she has other plans for me."

Other plans? He raised an eyebrow. He was curious but didn't want to say anything, afraid it might make her stop talking.

"I need to know why you don't want to do this yourself. You clearly love your nephew."

He gave his standard answer. "I don't have time."

"And?"

He should've known that she'd see right through him. And that she'd be okay crossing the line to push for a deeper answer. But he wasn't about to share the whole tale of his childhood, so he was going to keep his response short. He cleared his throat. "Growing up, Christmas wasn't a happy time of the year at my house. I don't know how to make it different for Aiden."

Noelle studied him for a long moment, and he wondered what she was seeing. She didn't seem to be judging him, though. She just seemed curious. He thought he was keeping his face relatively impassive, but judging by her expression, she was seeing more than he meant to show.

She stepped forward and placed the paper on his desk. He didn't dare take his eyes off her to look at it.

"Okay, I'll do this under one condition. I decide what we're going to do. It'll be stuff Aiden will love, of course. And I'll be all 'Happy, happy Christmas' around Aiden, even if I'm not feeling it, but you need to be that way, too, even if you're not feeling it. I'll plan everything and get anything we'll need, which will ease the time commitment on your part and take away your worries that you don't know what to do to give him a good Christmas." She pointed at the paper. "That's the schedule, and I expect you to be present for at least half of the events."

He liked this commanding side of her. He kind of

wished that she was like this all the time. He picked up the paper and glanced at it. There were half a dozen things listed, along with specific dates of when they would happen.

His eyes flew back to hers. "Some of these things are in Mountain Springs. Is that where you live?"

She nodded.

"That's where my sister and my nephew live."

She smiled—the first one he'd seen from her since she walked in. He looked back down at the list, his brow crinkling.

"There are family things on this list. *Your* family things." He wasn't sure what he thought of that. Would it be awkward for Aiden to be with a family he didn't know? Would it be awkward for Jack, as well, since he would be required to attend most of these outings, too?

"My family is big and welcoming and crazy about Christmas. In the extreme. My dad, in particular, would keep Christmas decorations up year-round if he could. And they like to celebrate *big*. It'll be the perfect place for Aiden to experience Christmas." She nodded at the list. "Those are my conditions, and the things on the list aren't negotiable."

He glanced through the list again. "The final say is up to my sister, Rachel, since Aiden is her kid, but as far as I'm concerned, we have a deal."

Noelle smiled big and held out a hand, so he shook it.

"Okay, but get an answer soon because the first one on the list happens tomorrow at two."

He managed to hold off the smile threatening to overtake his face until she turned on her heel and walked out his door.

NOELLE

NOELLE WENT BACK to her desk, let out a huge breath of relief, and collapsed into her chair, sinking into the backrest. She wasn't confrontational or demanding, so she was pretty proud of herself for pulling that off with her boss. But it had been exhausting.

Bridget was just setting her things down on her desk for the day and looked down at her watch. "It's nine oh one. It's way too early to be that tired. Especially on a day when we've got to make something like *Lump of Coal Breath Mints* sound like a good stocking stuffer."

Noelle laughed and sat up in her chair like normal. "It's days like today where we really get to prove how good we are at our jobs." And that was one of the reasons why she loved her job. How boring would it be to work at a big ad agency where they only had to make things like jewelry and sweaters sound like good gifts?

She opened her bag and pulled out the metal box she'd gotten from Gran-gran, placing it on her desk, right in front of her keyboard. Then she took off the lid and pulled out the card she'd already placed on top of the stack—the one with the little painting of the two of them making a snowman in Downtown Park.

And, really, today wasn't a *bad* day. For starters, it was Friday. She put the card, snowman painting facing forward, leaned against her monitor. As long as Jack's sister was on board with her's and Jack's Christmas pact —and the expression on his face told her that he thought she would be—she was going to get Elfie fixed, and she was going to honor Gran-gran's wishes. It might not be the easiest way to do either, but she at least had a plan and having a plan felt good.

ON SATURDAY AFTERNOON, she pulled up to the address that Jack had texted her—the address to his sister Rachel's house. He'd kept his word. She was driving a rental car, and he'd told the shop to charge him for the repairs.

As she walked up to the small home, she decided that the Grinch-ness that Jack had must not be a family thing, because it looked like Rachel had quite a few Christmas decorations and lights outside her house.

Jack answered the door, wearing a dark gray t-shirt and jeans. For the record, he looked every bit as amazing in jeans and a t-shirt as he did in a suit. But it was so strange seeing him not dressed up for work. It was a peek into his personal life that she hadn't seen before, and it felt wrong. Like looking through the pictures on someone's phone without permission or going trick-or-treating as a kid and knocking on the door of a house that you didn't realize belonged to your teacher.

A young boy wearing socks but no shoes came racing down the hall—Aiden, she assumed—with a golden retriever at his side. He skidded to a stop on the hardwood floor and held out a hand, beaming, like he was proud of himself for knowing how to greet someone for the first time. "Hi. I'm Aiden. And this is Bailey."

Noelle shook his hand. "Hello, Aiden." She nodded at the dog. "Bailey. It's nice to meet you both."

Jack closed the door behind her. "Come meet my sister." He put his hand on the small of her back just long enough to give a gentle nudge toward the hallway, and the touch sent an unexpected thrill up her spine.

She walked down the hallway with him, Aiden skipping ahead of them, toward a combined kitchen, dining room, and family room. His sister sat in a recliner in the modest room, looking even sicker than she had in the picture Jack had sent. But she was smiling and looked happy as they walked to her.

"Rachel, this is Noelle. Noelle, this is my sister, Rachel."

Rachel reached out both hands and enveloped her hand. "Thank you for coming. It's so good to meet you! Jack has told me a lot about you."

Jack flinched like he was panicked that his sister shared that. But why would he care? Of course, he would tell his sister about Noelle. She would be hanging out with her son a lot over the next few weeks—Rachel would naturally want to know about her.

They chatted for a few minutes while Aiden pulled on his snow boots, coat, hat, and gloves, then he and Jack drove to Downtown Park in his car, and Noelle drove in her rental. She made it out of her car and to the sidewalk in front of the park first, holding a couple of square buckets that she'd found handy for whatever sculpture they made. The sun was shining brightly, making everything look crisp and new and not nearly as cold as it actually was.

People were standing on the sidewalks and on the pathways they'd shoveled in the park itself, waiting for the event to start. They'd had a good snowstorm earlier in the week and a second one last night. The weather had been a little warmer for both, so the snow was nice and good for packing. Some years it had been so cold that the snow was nothing but powder, which was great if you were skiing, not so great if you were trying to make a snowman.

She spotted her sister, Hope, with her family and waved. She could see her sisters Becca and Julianne with their families, too, and her youngest sister, Katie, with her parents. Seeing them just made all the memories of being at this event over the years flood back in. Of course, the memories included all the family she saw here, but she and Gran-gran always worked on the same snow sculpture even if the rest of them didn't, so her memories included her, especially.

Right out in the middle of the park, they'd created a canoe one year. It looked like it was floating on the snow, and they'd made a snowman inside holding two big sticks like they were oars going down into the snow. And over by the nativity, they'd once made two dozen snowmen that were each about a foot and a half high with little black circular rocks for the eyes and a little bigger one for a mouth, all looking like they were a choir singing. One year, they'd even made a sculpture of a person making a snow angel.

And the whole time, Gran-gran had made jokes, and they'd laughed until their guts hurt, and Gran-gran made her feel like the most important person in the world.

She could feel her emotions rising as she saw Jack

and Aiden get out of Jack's car and start heading in her direction, so she tamped them down. It had sounded like a good idea to follow Gran-gran's wishes and still celebrate Christmas when she'd gotten the cards and when Jack had been asking for help, but now that she was actually here, she was questioning that choice. There were just so many memories tied up in these activities that she wasn't sure she could do it.

But Aiden looked so cute, all decked out for the snow, and he had such a massive smile on his face. And Jack was looking pretty fine in his coat, gloves, and hat. More than fine.

She was taken aback by the thought. *He was her boss.* And not just a regular boss, but an "always keep things professional" boss. The kind that made you not even stop to consider how good-looking he was because it wouldn't be professional. But this wasn't the office, he wasn't wearing a tie, and somehow it made it so much easier to see just how attractive he was.

She cleared her throat as they neared. "So, Aiden, have you ever done this activity before?" He shook his head. "Everyone divides themselves into teams as small or as big as they want. When it's time to start, they say go, and then we've got forty minutes to make whatever we're going to make. After, we'll get hot chocolate in that gazebo that looks like a gingerbread house, then we can check out Santa's village."

She pointed toward the life-sized nativity. "Some people make animals around the manger." Then she motioned toward Santa's village with the train going around it. "Some people make elves or other Christmassy things over there. Some people make funny snowmen, and some people make things that don't really have anything to do with Christmas at all. One year, someone made a pretty impressive dragon. What do you think we should make?"

Aiden pondered it for a moment, tapping a finger on his lips, the most serious expression on his face. Then he raised his finger into the air. "I think we should make a chair."

Jack looked at Noelle, his eyebrows drawn together, then looked back at Aiden. "A chair?"

"Yeah, like a big, padded comfy chair that anyone can sit in. And we should put it right over there so whenever someone sits in it, they can look at everything. Oh, and we should have a snow dog that looks just like Bailey sitting up beside the chair. And there should be a footrest."

"You've got it, buddy." Jack chuckled and ruffled the big pom on the top of Aiden's hat like he was ruffling his hair, and it was definitely the cutest thing she'd seen all week. And she'd seen her six-year-old niece trying on her Mrs. Claus costume for her school play, so the competition had been tough.

They went and found a spot and chatted as they waited for the organizers to say it was time to start. She'd kept her focus mainly on Aiden and asking him questions, but since he liked to also answer for Jack, she'd found out that Jack loved playing Uno, hated the color brown, and wished there was a good Thai restaurant in Mountain Springs.

She'd also met Quinton, a dark-haired kid with a blue and orange coat who was one of Aiden's friends from school. The two had talked rather animatedly about what they were each going to make.

They started building the snow dog sitting tall on his hind legs first, scooping the snow with their arms and pulling it to where they needed it. After they made the general shape of the dog, they started shoveling the snow with their hands, pushing it into the dog, and the more they did, the more the blob of snow began to look like an actual dog. Jack seemed to know just how to press the snow in hard and smooth it out with his glove, using the tip of his gloved fingers to scrape in details. He might not have had a lot of experience with Christmas growing up, but he had clearly had a lot of experience playing in the snow.

And he was so good with Aiden. He showed him how to do all of the things and let Aiden take over so much of it. It was clear that Aiden adored his uncle, too. Doing things together like this didn't seem to be a foreign thing. Which was strange because with as professional and terse as Jack always was at work, she hadn't really pictured him being good with kids.

She hadn't pictured any of this, really. Not too far into making the comfy chair, they had to start filling the buckets to bring the snow from a little further out. The more they worked, the more she saw the mask of professionalism fall from Jack. He looked like he was actually enjoying himself. Truthfully, she hadn't known it was a mask.

He was laughing and joking with her, too.

She bit a finger of her glove to hold it as she pulled it off, then she took out her cell phone and snapped a few pictures of the two of them working. Purely for Rachel's and Jack's sake. Not that she was going to go home and stare at them and think about how very good-looking her boss was and how completely adorable he was with his nephew.

Not that she could allow herself to fall for him, though, no matter how attractive or adorable or funny or very not-stuffy he was. Even if he wasn't acting like her boss right now, he was still her boss. She hadn't seen or heard anything about coworkers not being able to date anyone they worked with, but no one had dated anyone from the office the whole time she'd worked there. That could've been at least partly because there was a small dating pool available, but even if it wasn't said, everyone probably assumed they couldn't just by having Jack as a boss. It seemed like the kind of thing he wouldn't be okay with.

As they neared the end of the time limit and, thankfully, the end of their project, Jack kept stopping to take his phone out of his pocket, frown at it, and then type something. She knew he hadn't wanted to be there at all, so a part of her wondered if he was just laying the groundwork for skipping out early. He would probably break the news by saying there was some kind of emergency and was working on making it more believable.

"Alright, buddy," Jack said. "I think it's time you tested this chair out to see how it feels."

Aiden sat down in the chair made of snow, his arms on the armrests, sitting in it like a king sitting in his throne, then put his feet up on the little ottoman they'd made, and he leaned back and surveyed the park and everything going on in it. He reached out and put a hand on the snow dog's head beside the chair, giving him a little pat.

Then, with an entirely satisfied look on his face, he declared, "We did good work."

Both she and Jack smiled at the cute boy. It felt good to see him so proud of his idea come to life.

Then, just as they blew the whistle to stop, Jack pulled the phone out again and frowned at it. Then he put it back into his pocket and bent down to Aiden's height. "Listen, buddy. I've got to go."

"But we haven't gone around to see what everyone made yet. And we haven't gone on the train around Santa's village."

"I know, and I'm sorry. Do you want to stay with Noelle and do those things?"

Aiden looked up at Noelle and smiled, nodding enthusiastically as he turned back to Jack. "But I'm still sad you have to go."

"I'm sad, too. I'll make it up to you, okay?"

Then Jack stood up, and as the righteous indignation that had been building inside her since he'd first started taking his cell phone out built to a crescendo, he said, "Are you okay to finish up here and take Aiden home after?"

Aiden's friend Quinton came over just then, excitedly talking about his family's creation, so she took the moment while he was distracted to pull Jack aside a bit. "So you're only sticking around for the wintery part and then coming up with an excuse to leave for the more Christmassy part of the event? You know, you're not the only person who is struggling with this."

Jack just looked at her, not saying a word, the muscle at his jaw clenching. She tried to stand tall and interpret the look on his face, but it was pretty impassive, and she was wincing inside pretty hard. She wasn't the kind of person who just stood up to her boss and told him that he was doing things wrong. She was the kind of person who got an assignment and did it cheerfully. She didn't know what had come over her.

Jack turned and left without a word.

She was the only one of them getting paid for being there—an amount per hour that she wouldn't be able to get anywhere else—so maybe she should quit her judging and silent complaining. And definitely quit the out loud complaining to him.

She put a smile on her face and held out a hand to Aiden. "Are you ready to go look at what everyone made?"

He put his hand in hers. "Yep. We need to start with Quinton's. They made a robot wearing a Santa hat!"

As they walked around and saw all the snow creations that had turned out great and the ones that hadn't turned out so great, she felt terrible. Not only from the myriad of memories of Gran-gran that caused a new wave of grief to wash over her but because she felt bad about how she'd spoken to Jack.

After Aiden had gone on the train, went with her all through the village to see all of the elves working hard to make presents and get them wrapped and loaded onto Santa's sleigh, then went on the train another two times, they took off their gloves and headed over to the gazebo to get hot chocolate. They had just gotten their cup of sweet and warm goodness, holding on to the curved part of a candy cane while they stirred the chocolate, when her phone buzzed.

She pulled it out of her pocket and saw that it was Jack. Probably calling to say that he didn't think it was appropriate for her to talk to him like that, which would be totally fair. She answered, and before he even had a chance to say anything, she said, "Jack, I need to apologize. I—"

"Are you two still at the park?"

"Yes."

"Good. My sister started doing a lot worse after we left, and I had to take her to the hospital. It's probably going to be several hours before we can leave."

Noelle's stomach dropped, and she felt even worse.

"I've spoken with the mom of his friend Quinton. Do you remember meeting him?" He was back to being Boss Jack, not Playful Jack.

"I do."

"Keep an eye out for her—they're going to take Aiden home with them. They'll stop by Rachel's and grab his bag, then he'll sleep over at their house. Can I speak to Aiden for a minute to let him know?"

She held the phone out to Aiden. He set his hot chocolate down on the ledge of the gazebo and cradled the phone in both hands as he held it to his ear. She couldn't hear what Jack was saying and only heard a long line of "Uh-huh. Uh-huh" coming from Aiden. Then, "And mommy will be okay?" followed shortly by, "Will she call to tell me goodnight before bed?" and "When will I get to see her?"

Her heart was breaking for the poor kid.

Then Aiden said, "Okay. I love you, Uncle Jack." Then he handed the phone back to Noelle. "He wants to talk to you."

She put the phone up to her ear and said, "I shouldn't have been so quick to judge you when I knew I didn't have the full story."

He was quiet for a long moment. She was about to pull the phone away from her ear to see if either she or Aiden had accidentally hung up when he said, "Keep calling me out whenever you think I'm not doing the right thing."

She was too dumbfounded to make actual words come out of her mouth but did manage to make a sound somewhat resembling an "Oh?"

"It's a skill not enough people utilize because they worry it might make someone mad. And it might do exactly that. But don't let it stop you."

"Um, okay." The word came out as more of a question than she'd intended.

"And Noelle?" His voice was lower than usual, and her name sounded different from how he normally said it.

"Yeah?"

"Thank you for staying with Aiden."

She hung up the phone and looked up at the ceiling of the gazebo, knowing that she was in trouble. She had worked for Jack for a year and a half and hadn't once gone home thinking thoughts about how attractive he was—inside or out. Yet, she knew she'd be going home thinking about him today.

And that was very bad.

six

JACK

JACK KNOCKED on the door of what he was pretty sure was Noelle's parents' house in Mountain Springs. The address seemed right. So did the decorations. Although most homes in the neighborhood had Christmas lights on their houses and a tree or two, this house was, by far, the one decorated the most. Noelle had said that her family was enthusiastic about celebrating Christmas, but he still hadn't imagined it to this extent.

Lights outlined the house and windows and covered the dozen trees and shrubs in the front yard. The decorations rivaled the ones that had been in Downtown Park during the snow sculpture competition—the nativity and Santa's village both included.

Aiden ran through the snow and wrapped his arms

around one of a set of three giant Christmas tree bulbs that were nearly as tall as him like he was giving it a hug. "Look at how big they are!"

Aiden stomped the snow off his feet as they walked to the front door and then knocked. A girl who looked like she was about seven years old answered and invited them inside. A black lab was at her side and gave a single bark of a welcome, and Aiden immediately reached out and pet his head.

The girl pointed to a living room that was just off the entryway and said, "You can put your coats in there."

They both shrugged off their coats and added them to the pile on the couch. Jack asked the girl for Noelle, and she said she was in the kitchen before skipping past a living room and into a family room he could see from the doorway.

They followed her and the dog and entered an area filled with people and Christmas decorations, Christmas music playing overhead. They were at the back of a family room that was open to a kitchen, with the most enormous dining room table he'd ever seen separating the two rooms. A twelve-foot tree rose to the ceiling in the family room, and about ten little kids played with toys in the open area in front of it.

A few adults were in the family room area, too, sitting on the couches holding a toddler or on the floor with the kids or standing, bouncing a baby. The rest of them were in the kitchen area, which was a hive of activity.

Aiden tugged on Jack's shirt, not taking his wide eyes off the rooms full of people, so Jack leaned down.

"*All* of these people are Noelle's family?" he whispered.

"I think so. I know she has four sisters, and I think three of them are married and have kids." There were definitely four people he could guess were her sisters in the kitchen, but six women were about the right age. And, taking a quick count as he looked around, there were enough spouses for five people. So maybe there were more than just siblings here. There were literally a dozen little kids, from babies to possibly seven years old, and he saw a couple who were an age that he could only assume meant they were her parents.

"How did they get so many?"

"I don't know, buddy."

A pack of three kids, all boys, two who looked Aiden's age and one maybe a year younger, were building a tower out of something that looked like magnetic tiles. One of them got up and came over to Aiden. "Want to come play with us?"

Aiden looked up at Jack, and Jack nodded, so Aiden ran off to join them. One asked what his name was, and that was all it took for them to become friends. Aiden was helping them, a big grin on his face.

Noelle spotted Jack from where she stood in the kitchen and wiped her hands off on an apron she had tied around her waist as she made her way to him.

"Hi! I'm glad you could make it. Come on, let me introduce you to everyone." Then she grabbed him by the hand and pulled him past the family room and the dining table to where the bulk of the people were working on getting all the gingerbread parts ready in the kitchen, and he tried to ignore how it felt to have Noelle's hand in his.

"Hey, everyone, this is my boss, Jack. And that little guy over there playing with the boys is Aiden." Then, rapid-fire, she introduced everyone to him. He quickly caught her sister's names—Becca, Hope, Julianne, and Katie—since he'd heard them before, but the rest of the names were lost the moment she pointed to the next person and said their name. He did catch that two adult males were cousins, and two of the women she'd pointed at were their spouses. The names didn't stick, but he did remember which ones were sisters, and he kind of caught which spouses were married to each other.

"Oh, and while we're all here," Noelle said, "does anyone know anything about who sent me the box of Christmas activity cards that Gran-gran painted?"

Everyone shook their heads, a few with eyebrows raised, but they all looked like they didn't know what she was talking about.

"No? Come on. It had to be one of you. Sent to the post office in North Pole, Alaska first, to get the postmark?"

"Honey," her mom said, "you might just have to accept that you'll never find out how it got to you."

But Noelle swung around and pointed at the guy who he was pretty sure was married to Noelle's sister, Hope. "None of you are lying, right? Cory. You helped a lot in cleaning out Gran-gran's painting room. It was you, wasn't it?"

Cory held up both hands. "Noelle, I swear to you, if it had been me who had found a box she left with your name on it, I would've just handed it to you back in January when we cleaned everything—I wouldn't have gone to the work of saving it for all these months and then shipping it to the North Pole first."

"Yeah, you totally would've. It was no one? Really?" Noelle sighed.

"It sounds like the verdict is in," Noelle's dad said, grinning as he looked around the room at everyone. "It's a Christmas miracle."

Everyone laughed, but Jack didn't quite understand why.

Noelle leaned into Jack. "Every Christmas season, my dad declares at least one thing—but sometimes up to a dozen things—a 'Christmas miracle.' It has pretty much become its own tradition now."

"All right," Katie said, clapping her hands together, "now that that's settled, who wants to be interviewed for our annual Christmas Eve video?"

One of Noelle's brothers-in-law raised his hand, and Noelle nodded toward the kitchen counter. "Want to help me fill icing bags?"

He nodded and followed her through the crowd of people, who had all gone back to doing whatever jobs they had been doing before they paused for introductions. Noelle lifted a big mixing bowl from the stand, placed it on the counter, and then used a rubber spatula to scrape around the edges. Then she pulled toward them a stack of triangular-shaped bags that he could only guess were made of silicone and lifted the top one from the pile.

"We just need to drop in one of the tips and make sure it's in the spot at the bottom just right, then we'll fill them maybe half full. Do you want to hold or fill?"

"Hold." Definitely. He didn't have a clue what they were doing.

So he held the bag open as she scooped a bunch of the frosting onto the rubber spatula and put it into the bag, kind of wiping it off against the edge of the bag. Then she went for a second scoop.

It was awkward work, and it required them to stand close enough that the sides of their bodies were touching, their arms trying to occupy the same space. He kept things very professional at work, so there had never been a situation where he'd been this close to her before, and he found her presence intoxicating.

She took the bag from him and moved her hands around the outside, probably trying to get the frosting in the right place, then twisted the top and added a clip to it. He picked up the next bag and put the icing tip into it, just like she'd shown him.

"How is Rachel doing?"

He looked over to meet her eyes, which were definitely green and not hazel. This close, he could see the facets in her eyes and the darker rim around the outside that was almost a navy blue. He'd always thought that her eyes were bewitching, but they were even more so when he was this close.

"She's doing okay. Much better than she was Saturday night or even yesterday." It had touched him that she had sought him out at work this morning to ask how she was doing after her hospital visit.

"That's good to hear. You must be worried about her all the time. I bet that's stressful."

It was. No one had ever really acknowledged that before. He hadn't even really acknowledged that stress— he'd only ever thought about the worry he had.

They continued to work, filling bags. On one, he must not have been paying enough attention to the bag because one side folded in just as Noelle was putting the icing in, getting it on the part of the bag that was supposed to be on the outside. They both jerked forward to fix it, and the rubber spatula got knocked out of Noelle's hand, which they both tried to catch. They managed to keep it from falling to the counter or the floor, but icing got on his hand, her arm, and a bit had taken to the air and landed on Noelle's cheek.

Noelle laughed and reached for a roll of paper towels, and he found himself chuckling. She pulled one off the roll and handed it to him. He cleaned off his hand, then got a second paper towel and said, "Here, let me get the part on your cheek."

He found himself holding his breath as he wiped the frosting from her skin, his face just inches from hers. And she seemed to be holding her breath, too, as whatever this was passed between them. A heat. A spark. A connection. Something. And he knew it wasn't just him who was feeling it.

He dropped his hand and set the paper towel on the counter as she cleared her throat and turned back to the icing bags.

All of the adults who weren't currently holding a child in their arms helped to get all the correct gingerbread pieces placed at each spot at the table, with the icing and candy for decorating spread evenly throughout. Then everyone started finding seats around the table. Jack and Noelle found a spot with Aiden right between them.

It was a bit overwhelming seeing so many family members around the big table. He was pretty sure his parents each had a sibling or two, but honestly, they had never talked about them. Neither of his parents had grown up with close families. It had only been the four of them until he was fifteen, and then it was just him and Rachel until Aiden was born. Aiden's father had never even been in the picture. So all of this? It was a little too much.

"I don't get how this makes a train car," Aiden said, holding up two rectangle pieces of gingerbread. "There aren't even any wheels."

"See that table over there?" Noelle pointed at a large side table against the far wall with a Christmas village set up. "There's a train track that goes all around it. The wheels are over there—what we're making looks kind of like a box. We'll put our gingerbread train cars on top of the wheels over there, and then the train can actually go around the track."

"Cool! And does this gingerbread man go inside it?"

Noelle smiled. "No. That's for you to decorate then take home and eat."

Jack watched Noelle help Aiden as he worked on his own train car. He loved how patient she was with his nephew and how well she explained how to make the box and helped hold some pieces but let him do all the parts he could do on his own. It was sweet. He knew Rachel couldn't give Aiden all the attention he needed right now and knew how happy it would make her to know her son was so well cared for. It made him happy, too.

Once they had their train cars made and were decorating them with the candy and icing, Aiden let out a long exhale. "I wish my mom was here making these, too."

Noelle set down her icing bag. "How about we take lots of pictures? Then you can tell her about every single bit of it when you get home and show her the pictures, and she'll feel like she was here."

Aiden nodded his head enthusiastically. Jack probably should've thought about taking pictures on his own. Noelle pulled out her phone and took a few pictures, then Aiden turned to Jack and tapped his arm. "You get some on your phone, too. Get a selfie with me, you, and Noelle."

Jack held his phone out to get all of them, but Aiden apparently wasn't happy with Noelle being the furthest away from the camera, so Aiden turned to Noelle and said, "Come over here and squish your face right between mine and Uncle Jack's."

Noelle's face reddened a bit, but she got out of her seat and positioned her face right between him and

Aiden. Close enough that he could smell her peppermint shampoo and feel the buzz of energy that seemed to be fueled simply by their being so close.

When everyone finished their creations, they all headed over to the table with the Christmas village and placed their train cars on the mechanical wheel base set on the tracks. With his parents gone when he was fifteen, he'd always felt like he had to spend all of his extra time doing things that made money. Even after his company became profitable, he never slowed down to do something like this. He hadn't even felt like he should come to this activity tonight because there was so much more work to do back at the office. Noelle had only said that he had to be at half of the activities, so this had been one he had definitely planned to skip.

But after missing half of the last event, he decided that he didn't want Noelle thinking he couldn't keep his word. At least he was pretty sure that was his entire reason for coming tonight. Or maybe he just hadn't been willing to admit that other feelings about Noelle played a role in the decision. Regardless of the reason, tonight had felt refueling, somehow, which totally surprised him. He wouldn't have guessed that would be what he'd be feeling at this point.

Once everyone's train car was on the tracks, Noelle's dad turned the train on, and Aiden watched in wonder as the train went all around the village, carrying the train cars that they had just made.

Jack looked at Noelle, and they both shared a smile. But he knew that his smile wasn't just about seeing Aiden's wonder. It was also about Noelle herself. He'd already felt attracted to her more than he was okay with, but now he felt a deepening attraction to her that scared him.

This woman was going to be the death of him. She was as off-limits as they came since not only was she his employee, but she was currently his employee times two.

seven

NOELLE

NOELLE SAT down at her desk at work, and before she got started on the day's work, she pulled out her tin of cards from Gran-gran and started shuffling through them. When she came across the scene painted of the two of them making a snow creation in Downtown Park, she smiled and put it back in the tin. A little acknowledgment of having finished that part of what Gran-gran had wanted her to do.

Then she came across one of them decorating the boxcars for the gingerbread train. That one made her insides smile, too, just thinking about the look on Jack's face as he had moved in close to wipe the frosting off her cheek and the feeling—almost an electricity—that passed between them. Seeing him help Aiden was so sweet, too. She couldn't believe that she had worked with this man for a year and a half and hadn't had a clue about who he really was.

And now that she had caught a glimpse of it, she could feel herself falling for him. Which wasn't a good idea *at all.* But still, she'd take that smile he gave her as they saw Aiden's face at seeing the train go around the Christmas village any day. All day, any day.

"Look at you being all smiley," Bridget said, and Noelle jumped, not even realizing that her coworker was at her desk, let alone watching her. "Dish. Tell me what's new in your life."

Noelle immediately thought of Jack, but she wasn't about to say anything about him to Bridget. Instead, she said, "I don't know. I guess it's just because I'm finding the Christmas spirit again after losing it a year ago."

"Aww! That's so sweet! Do you know who else is finding their Christmas spirit as well?"

"Who?"

"Our boss."

Noelle's eyebrows rose, and she glanced toward the hall that held Jack's office.

"Do you remember what a Grinch he was last year?" Bridget asked. "The biggest Grinch you've ever known, right? He always wants to work more at Christmas and gets even more surly whenever he sees Christmas decorations on people's desks and stuff like that."

"Oh." Noelle glanced back toward Jack's office. "I

had just assumed that he had something hard going on in his life last year."

Bridget shook her head. "This is my third Christmas here—he's like that every year."

Lennox must've been listening in as he was typing something into his computer because then he swiveled his chair around their direction and said, "I can confirm that it's an every year thing. I don't know what's changed in his life, but I was the first person here this morning, and I actually heard him whistling a Christmas tune."

"No way," Noelle said.

Lennox shrugged. "I'm not even kidding you. But I know you won't fully believe it until you've checked it out for yourself."

She really did want to experience it because it made her insides flutter, just thinking that she maybe had something to do with it. The fact that he was changing his opinions about Christmas enough that other people were noticing was kind of a big deal. And, okay, her insides fluttered just thinking about Jack himself. So she grabbed her notebook and stood up.

She walked to just outside his office, still out of sight but close enough to hear if he was whistling. He wasn't; he was on the phone with someone, saying, "No, I haven't even had a chance to shop yet. This is our busy season, and I've been spending any extra time with Rachel and Aiden." There was a pause for a moment, then he said. "I know. I don't know why I'm procrastinating."

Now she just felt like an eavesdropper, so she turned to go back to her desk, but then just as quickly did a u-turn and headed to his open doorway.

He saw her and held up one finger, letting her know to stay and wait. Which she did while also scrambling to come up with a question to ask him to justify standing in his doorway with her notebook. She probably should've thought of that before leaving her desk.

He finished the call and then hung up. Then his eyes met hers, and he said, "Good morning. Did you need to talk to me?" His professional mask was back up. It had been almost jarring yesterday morning, after spending Monday evening with the real Jack, but today it just felt normal.

"Yes, I was looking at the info sheet for the Samurai blenders at Copperstone's but didn't see where it's going to be advertised."

"Oh. I apologize for missing that." He glanced at a paper on his desk. "Facebook, Instagram, Pinterest, and Google Ads."

She nodded, wishing that she'd thought about grabbing a pen, too, so the notebook in her hands would actually have a use. She drummed her fingers on the back of the notebook, trying to decide if she wanted to ask him or not. Then she took a step forward.

"Did I hear you say that you haven't done your shopping yet?"

Shopping was one of the activity cards that Grangran had painted. She'd had such a fun time decorating the gingerbread trains with him, so why not do the shopping one with him, too? She was just so drawn to him. Being around him had awakened feelings for him that she hadn't known she had, and she was curious about just how strong those feelings were. And she really wanted to see more of what he was like outside of the office.

He nodded.

"Do you want to go shopping with me today? Maybe it won't seem like such a hurdle if we do it together."

It felt weird asking him that in the office since it was such a professional space, not a personal one. And this felt like a very personal ask. But they'd had so many personal moments over the past week that it also felt okay. Like she was asking him as a friend, not as an employee.

Okay, a friend with maybe some very more-than-friends feelings going on.

He studied her for such a long moment, though, that she worried she shouldn't have asked. The tightening of his jaw she saw probably meant that he was annoyed.

But then he gave a curt nod. "Okay."

"Okay? Really? All right. Um, does right after work

sound good? Then I won't have to drive all the way back to Mountain Springs first."

"Right after work is good."

She might have been reading more into his expression than she should, but when he said that, his eyes sparked with something and the corner of his mouth tugged up just the smallest amount. The two together gave her the impression that, regardless of his apparent quest to remain impassive, he was actually happy about going with her.

She smiled all the way back to her desk. She was going to go shopping with Jack. Just the two of them. She pulled out her cards from Gran-gran and leaned the shopping one against her monitor.

And then she wondered for probably the fiftieth time since Monday how it had been for him to walk into her parents' house and see her big, noisy but loving family. What had he thought of it? Had he liked it or wanted to run far from it?

"What happened in there?"

Noelle jerked out of her thoughts at Bridget's question. She'd been lost in her own thoughts so much that she hadn't been paying attention to the fact that there were others around her, and she was apparently broadcasting her feelings all across her face. She needed to stop thinking about Jack at work!

Thankfully, she remembered what she had gone to

his office for before she'd gotten distracted with asking him to go shopping. She cleared her throat. "Well, there was no whistling, but I did hear him talking about Christmas shopping, and he didn't sound totally upset about it."

Bridget raised an eyebrow. "I'm impressed. I wonder what made the Grinch change his ways."

Lennox set a stack of papers on Bridget's desk and put a hand up to his mouth and stage-whispered, "Maybe it is a *who*, not a *what*."

Bridget gave Noelle a look of curiosity so strong she was sure she would suggest they investigate. So Noelle gave the most disinterested shrug she could manage while having Jack on the brain and turned back to her work, trying desperately not to show all over her face her hope that maybe it was actually because of her.

NOELLE SAT on a bench in the main hallway of the mall, glancing down the short hallway that led to the front doors, sipping the last of the cup of wassail she'd gotten from the kiosk next to her. She hadn't planned to get one, but she'd arrived early, and the smells of cinnamon, ginger, nutmeg, and apple cider that had filled the air had just been too much to resist. Even though it was a scent and a taste and a tradition that would forever be inextricably tied to Gran-gran and made a fresh wave of loss wash over her.

She let herself feel the feeling. To let herself miss Gran-gran. But she didn't allow herself to think about her—she wasn't about to start bawling in the middle of the mall, right before her boss met up with her.

She tossed the empty cup into the garbage receptacle just as Jack walked through the front doors. He was still wearing his slacks and light blue button-down, but he'd lost the jacket and tie and had the first couple of buttons unbuttoned. She tried not to stare, but good golly, how had she managed to work with this man for a year and a half without having even a tiny crush? Maybe it was because now that she knew more about who he was and had seen a bit of his heart, he was even more good-looking.

And that smile he gave when his eyes met hers had her knees buckling. It was just a slight one tugging at his lips, but his eyes smiled, too, and it told her that he was glad to see her, even if it was in a mall at Christmastime.

"Hi," she breathed as he neared. Then, realizing how breathy the word had come out, cleared her throat. "Are you ready to tackle this?"

He took a deep breath and looked out at the copious Christmas decorations surrounding them. Towering Christmas trees filled the open area, with giant nutcrackers standing at attention around them. Archways of lights and garlands led into the hallways in all three directions. Reindeer were grazing in fields of puffy cotton snow. Every pillar was wrapped like a giant candy cane, and every kiosk was transformed to look like it belonged at the North Pole.

"I'm pretty sure that if we handled getting the ad campaign for Lelepali Luminaries up and running, we can handle this."

Noelle laughed. That campaign had nearly killed them all before they made it to the end. She didn't think he entirely believed that they'd make it to the end of this, but she'd get him there. "Who do you need to buy for?"

"I've already ordered something for the employees, so just Rachel and Aiden and a couple of friends. And Rachel asked me to pick up some things for her."

"Do you know what you want to get any of them?"

He shook his head. "Rachel gave me her shopping list, but for the gifts I need to get, no."

"Well, I have some ideas for Rachel. There's a store that'll be perfect down this way." As they walked down the giant candy cane- and garland-lined hallways, she couldn't stop thinking about his list. It was such a small group of people to shop for. Her own list was wonderfully, ridiculously, overwhelmingly long. Then she realized something about his list that he hadn't mentioned. "No gifts for parents?"

"No. They passed away."

"Oh." The words felt like a stab. Why had she brought it up when he hadn't mentioned them? "I'm so sorry. I shouldn't have asked."

"It's fine. It was a long time ago. They were in a car together when they got in a terrible crash."

"Was it at Christmastime?" She wondered if that was why he seemed to really dislike the season.

He shook his head. "Summertime." She didn't think he would say anything more—and she definitely wasn't going to ask—but after a long pause, he spoke again. "My parents didn't get along great, so they seldom went places together. But they had gone to an outdoor concert and crashed on the way home. I was fifteen, and Rachel was eighteen. She had just graduated from high school, and the courts allowed her to be my guardian. So for a long time, it was just Rachel and me. Until Aiden came along, of course."

Noelle stopped outside of the store she had been leading them to. "And Aiden's father?"

"He's never been in the picture."

She nodded. She'd guessed that had been the case. As they walked inside, she said, "My Aunt Sharon went through chemotherapy a few years ago. I remember that she was really grateful to have a silk sleep mask that she could use during treatments. Oh, like those over there.

"And if you want to get her some fuzzy socks or a really soft blanket, this would be a good store for that.

Maybe even an electric blanket. And there's a great store just a little further down where they have some moisturizers to die for. My aunt had complained about dry skin a lot. And lip balm. Some comfy sweats. Maybe some ginger candies for nausea—I bet we could find some in a candy store or something. Oh! A HEPA air purifier might be good, too." She paused. "What?"

He was giving her a strange look that she couldn't quite interpret. She liked what it did to the corners of his mouth and the brightness of his eyes. Even the slight tilt to his head. But had no idea what it was.

He lifted one shoulder in a shrug but kept those bright eyes on her. "You're really good at this."

She might have blushed. But she hated blushing, so she waved off his comment, commanding her body to do the same, and said, "You haven't seen anything yet. Wait until you witness my ability to find the exact clothing size needed when there doesn't appear to be any. It's legendary."

It wasn't legendary—it just happened sometimes. Why did she say that? She was probably going to get a chance to back up her words with action on this shopping trip, and it was going to be embarrassing when she failed.

He selected a sleep mask and an unbelievably soft electric blanket that would make even the most workaholic insomniac snuggle up and fall right asleep. As they were in line to pay, he said, "Tell me about your grandma. You said she was the most important person to you? And the reason why you took the job to help Aiden?"

All the feelings of loss that she'd been suppressing while being in this mall at Christmastime came rushing back to her at once. She knew she had to get a handle on them quickly or she'd be a sobbing mess. That was very much not how she wanted this shopping trip to go.

She swallowed hard. And then, instead of focusing on how much she missed her right now, she focused on the great memories they had together.

"Gran-gran was ... my person. The one who got me. You met my three older sisters—Becca, Hope, and Julianne—at my parents. They're each just under a year and a half apart in age, but because of when their birthdays fell, they're only a year apart in school. Which meant that they went through a lot of the same milestones very close to the same time. Sports, dance lessons, starting to date, school dances, getting driver's licenses, deciding on a college, and all those kinds of things. They just took a lot of attention, and all three of them needed a lot of it at the same time.

"I am three years younger than them, and Katie is three years younger than me. She got a lot of attention from my parents, too, just by being the youngest. And I was kind of ... forgotten. Not purposely," she quickly added. "My family isn't like that. I just kind of got lost in the middle of it all."

Jack nodded, his face looking thoughtful, but he stayed quiet, waiting for her to continue. But then it was their turn at the register, so she held off on her story until the items were paid for, in a bag, and they were heading out of that shop and onto the next one.

"Gran-gran was a middle child, too, and she knew entirely too well what that felt like. She always made me feel not forgotten. Important. But not only that, we just got along really well. Like from the moment I was born. She always used to say that we'd been best friends in heaven and that I sure took my sweet time coming to earth so she could get her BFF back."

Jack chuckled. It was a good sound. And it made her realize how good it was for her to talk about all of this. As much as she thought that doing things like this that she used to only do with Gran-gran would be painful, doing them with Jack was actually helping her heart. Like it was nourishing it and allowing it to heal.

"She loved Christmas more than anything, so of course, I did, too. And we did a lot of Christmas traditions together. The cards I got from her were the things we used to do together, painted by her. I still have no idea how they showed up on my doorstep, but I know that she wanted me to continue doing them."

"Well," Jack said, giving a nod to what they were

doing together, "I am very grateful that your gran-gran sent them to you." The look on his face was sweet and playful but also had something more, hiding just below the surface. A longing, maybe?

Whatever it was, it was beautiful and made her stomach flutter.

eight

JACK

"SO, these cards that your gran-gran sent you. Was shopping on one of them?"

She glanced at him as she led him toward a toy store. "It was."

He shouldn't ask. But hearing more about these cards helped him know her better, and he desperately wanted to know her better. It was a need that he knew was dangerous, but they were here, and she seemed to really enjoy talking about her gran-gran. So he wanted her to keep talking, knowing full well that the more he got to know her, the harder it would be for him to be around her and not pursue a relationship.

"What were your traditions around that? Because if your gran-gran wanted you to do that, maybe we should."

He was expecting a quick response, so when it didn't come, he glanced over at her. She seemed hesitant. He didn't know if it was painful or because she didn't want to do it with him. Maybe she needed to do it with her own family. He shouldn't have asked.

But then she said, "Are you sure?" like she didn't think he would want to.

"Of course."

He shouldn't have worked so hard to talk her into doing any Christmas activities with Aiden. He had his own issues with Christmas, so he should've respected that she had hers. He probably wouldn't have pushed if he hadn't already been so drawn to her. But he'd been drawn to her for so long and had kept it all in check for a year and a half. Why could he not seem to now?

They stepped just inside Taheny's Toys, and she picked up a bucket of slime that was big enough that it took both hands. And that was when he noticed that her cheeks were a bit pink. Was she embarrassed?

"Do you promise not to laugh?"

So she *was* embarrassed. He nodded, a smile already tugging at his lips.

"As we shopped, we wrote bad ad copy hooks for the items we saw."

His eyebrows rose, and a chuckle of disbelief escaped his mouth before he could stop it. "As a kid, you did this?"

"Yep. The dorkier the ad copy, the better. Gran-gran had a job in marketing, and writing bad ad copy made me want to become a copywriter. Growing up, no one else my age even knew what ad copy was or what the job of a copywriter entailed, so it was kind of a special thing only between Gran-gran and me."

"Huh. So that's why you're so good at it."

She turned the bucket of slime around in her hands. "Are you saying that writing bad ad copy made me good at my job?"

"Don't tell me it didn't help you recognize good ad copy." He nodded at the slime. "What would you write for that?"

She studied it for a moment, then, in a voice he could only describe as an announcer's, said, "It's ooey. It's gooey. It's stretchy. It's slimy. And if you get this for your kid this Christmas, then by New Year's you'll know just how many objects in your house a three-pound bucket can stretch to cover."

He laughed, and they went into the store and started walking down the aisles. They made their way through the store, getting the things Rachel had asked him to pick up. He also found a few toys that he wanted to give to Aiden and got those, too.

All along the way, one of them would pick up a toy and say some bad ad copy in the same announcer voice that Noelle had first used. He held up a bin of Legos and said, "We could target parents and say, 'Want to level-up your ability to find sharp pieces while barefooted in the dark? Get the one thousand piece set for your overly-enthusiastic child.'"

Noelle found a stuffed elf that looked more like he belonged in a horror movie than on a shelf. "Think you've been getting too much sleep lately? Put this creepy toy in your kid's room, and you'll never have that problem again."

He laughed and pointed out an electronic drum set that was on display and fully worked, much to the thrill of all the kids in the store. "Did your brother buy your kid a xylophone last Christmas? Buy his kid these drums. It's the ultimate one-up he'll never be able to top."

"Oh, and then we could do an ad with all the noisy toys on it, and the ad copy could say, 'Think you might want noise-canceling headphones for Christmas? Trust us: you do.'"

He was pretty sure he had never had as much fun in a toy store before, not even as a kid. He definitely knew it was worlds above every other Christmas shopping experience he'd ever had.

She picked up a toy doll. "Do you want kids?"

"I like Aiden. I wouldn't mind having some kids for myself sometime. I just haven't found 'the one' yet." Not that he'd been looking. But he was suddenly curious about her. "You?"

"Of course. I just haven't found 'the one,' either."

He picked up a box containing a race car track but didn't really look at it at all. He needed to prod. To find out more. And the only way he could think to do that was to offer more himself. "I've just always kind of assumed that marriage isn't for me. I never looked at my parents' marriage and thought, 'I want that for me some-day.' Not that I'm against marriage—I know there are plenty of good marriages out there. I guess I've just never had a lot of faith that it'd happen for me." His issues weren't deep, but they were still there a bit.

She was silent for a moment. Maybe taking in what he'd just said, or perhaps trying to decide if she wanted to share anything. He hoped she did. "Have you ever gotten to the point of talking about marriage with anyone you dated?" Okay, that was really pushing for personal information. He couldn't believe he'd asked it.

She shook her head. "Not really. A few had gotten a little more serious, but I think I knew long before we broke up that it wasn't heading toward marriage. I do look at my parents and think, 'I want that for me.' I just haven't found my person. The one who will look at me the way my dad looks at my mom."

Was it wrong that he suddenly desperately wanted to be that person for her? Yes. It very much was. He forced himself to break eye contact with her and set down the box. "We should probably go pay."

She nodded. He didn't know what was going through her head just then, but he could tell that it was a lot. He needed to lighten things up a bit.

As they walked out of the store, arms laden with bags, they got away from the noise enough to hear the Christmas music filling the halls. He never listened to Christmas music by choice, but he still knew the song right away—*The First Noel*. "Oh, hey, it's your song."

"I love this song! When I was little and would see 'noel' everywhere at this time of year, I would always tell anyone who would listen that they spelled it wrong."

Jack chuckled. "Did it ever bother you to have a name that was linked to a holiday season?"

"No, because I was born on Christmas Eve. My birthday is super entwined with Christmas, so it feels right that my name would be, too."

"I'm guessing that having a Christmas Eve birthday didn't help with feeling forgotten."

Noelle laughed a big hearty laugh that people didn't do in public nearly often enough. It made him smile. "No. But it has its perks, too. One year, when I was probably five, my dad had just finished reading us the poem *The Night Before Christmas*. At the end, he said the words, 'Happy Christmas to all, and to all a goodnight!' and Becca shouted, 'Happy birthday to Noelle,' and like they planned it, but they hadn't, everyone else shouted, 'And to Noelle a good night!'

"Every year since, as my family gets together for Christmas Eve, someone will randomly shout out 'Happy birthday to Noelle,' and everyone else will stop what they're doing and shout back 'And to Noelle a good night!' My nieces and nephews especially like it."

"That's actually pretty sweet."

"Yeah. What about your name? Does it come with anything significant?"

He shrugged. "I was born in January. A frigid January, as the story goes. My dad wanted to name me Jack Frost because he thought it would be funny. I'm not really sure you should choose a baby's name based on what you think is funny, but that's my dad for you. Thankfully, my mom wouldn't let him. Their compromise was to name me Jack with the middle initial F."

"If it helps, my parents didn't give me a middle name, so my full name is Noelle Allred. Whenever I have to sign my initials, I have to put 'NA.' Like I'm writing that it's just not applicable to me."

He laughed. "Weirdly, that does help. My last name helps, too. Meadows is a word with very springtime connotations, so it kind of undermined my dad's plan. I never knew if he wanted to name me Jack Frost in hopes that I would be the sprightly character of myths or if he named me that because he thought I was the Bringer of

Cold. On days when he was sober, I liked to think it was because of the sprightly character. On days when he was drinking and was an ornery cuss—which was most of the time during the holidays—I was sure it was the Bringer of Cold."

"Is that why you don't like Christmas?"

He had told her the story to be funny but hadn't thought about how much it would bring out the negative parts. "Yeah. Every Christmassy thing that my mom tried to have us do, my dad always turned into a big blowup. So everything Christmas-related is very tied to memories of my dad being at his worst and making all of us miserable."

She was quiet for a long moment, and he was sure he was going to get pity from her, which he very much did not want. He also really didn't want to talk about it anymore.

Instead, she asked, "Have you ever heard of exposure therapy?"

"You expose yourself to your greatest fear to get over it, right?"

"Right. So, I had a deathly fear of heights. If it was because of some traumatic childhood experience, I know nothing about it. But it was there regardless. When I was in high school, I got a job at a ski resort in Nestled Hollow. I thought I'd just be making hot chocolate in the lodge, seeing cute guys, stuff like that."

"I think I can see where this is headed."

"Yep. For an entire snow season, I was assigned to be the lift operator up the mountain. Every single day I had to ride the tram to the top, and I was terrified—pulse racing, heart pumping, hyperventilating, all of it. I was so convinced I was going to die. But by the end of the season, not only was I still alive, but I wasn't afraid of heights anymore. I think it has something to do with the emotions tied to the event. So instead of terrified feelings being tied to heights, it turned to safe feelings being tied to it, since I was safe every single time."

"And you think I should do that with Christmas?"

Noelle shrugged. "Well, right now you've got some pretty negative feelings tied to it, so you hate it. But if you were around Christmassy things a lot and had positive feelings tied to it, those feelings would overtake the negative ones." Then she said, almost in a whisper, "Maybe we both need that."

He looked at her for a long time, not quite knowing how to respond.

She must've switched from thinking about how much she needed it to thinking about how much he did because the next time she spoke, her voice wasn't a whisper at all. It was full of confidence. "When I took the side job to help provide Aiden with Christmas experiences, I told you that you needed to come to half of the activities. I think you should come to all of them."

He met her eyes. Could he commit to that? He was probably at the halfway mark of attending Christmas events right now and could easily bow out of the rest of them. If he agreed, then not only would he be facing more of a holiday he'd hated for his entire life, but he'd be spending a lot more time around Noelle.

The exposure therapy for Christmas might just work to turn it into a holiday he loved. But exposure to more of Noelle might just make him fall more in love with her, too. And he knew just how dangerous that would be to his heart.

But still, he found himself nodding and saying, "Okay, it's a deal."

nine

NOELLE

NOELLE PULLED up in front of her parents' house in her own car. It was so nice to have Elfie back! It wasn't as nice as the rental she'd been driving, but it was great to feel "home" again in her car. She opened the back door to let Aiden and his dog, Bailey, out. Aiden immediately grabbed Bailey's leash and ran across the lawn, weaving between all the lawn decorations, to where her family was congregating around the hot chocolate before the hayride, excited to introduce his dog to her parents' dog, Captain.

Noelle went around to help Rachel out of the car, but she was doing well enough that she was out before Noelle even got there. She looped her arm in Rachel's like they were sisters, so she was right there if Rachel needed any help.

They walked through the mostly tramped-down snow, around the nativity and the giant ornaments. Rachel looked to where Aiden was making himself at home with Noelle's family. "Thank you so much for all you've done for Aiden. You've gone well beyond everything I was hoping for him."

Noelle looked at Aiden, too. "He's a cool kid. I've enjoyed every moment of it. And I'm so glad you're feeling well enough to join us for the hayride! It's one of my favorite traditions, and if you're going to experience one, this is it. It was my gran-gran's favorite, too."

Rachel smiled as they made their way across the snow-covered ground. "From what little I've heard of your gran-gran, she sounds like she was a pretty cool person."

"She was. I was kind of worried about today because it was one of our favorite traditions, but I'm doing better than I thought I would. Last year, celebrating felt like we were just ignoring that she was no longer with us. This year, though, it feels like we are honoring her by continuing the traditions she loved."

"It sounds like that's what she would've wanted." Rachel smiled and gave her arm a little squeeze. "Thank you for including me."

Based on the Christmas decorations in Rachel's yard, Noelle figured that she actually did like the holiday. She probably hadn't been able to celebrate it much at all, though. "Do you think it might make you nauseous? We do go pretty slow, but it's sometimes a little bumpy."

"I'm doing pretty good today, actually. I think I'll be okay."

Noelle grinned and led them toward the table filled with hot chocolate supplies where all of her family was congregating.

This year, she was even more excited about the hayride. Not only was Jack coming, but Rachel was there, too. Which meant that she'd be able to get some more info about Jack.Now that she was seeing his personal side and finding out more and more about him, the more she wanted to know. She felt like she was stranded in the desert, and information about Jack was a jug of cool water—she just couldn't get enough of it.

It didn't take long after Noelle introduced Rachel to her parents and sisters and their spouses and kids that Rachel was chatting with her and her sisters like they had known each other their whole lives. And it didn't take long for Noelle to start picturing her as a sister-in-law.

Stop that, she chided herself. *Nothing is happening between you and your boss, so stop setting yourself up for heartbreak.*

And then Jack pulled up in front of her parents' house and got out of his car. When his eyes found hers, he wore an expression that had her whispering out loud,

"Or maybe I'm wrong." Because the smile on his face felt like it was just for her. It quirked up on one side just slightly more than the other, and his eyes were all soft and warm, and it made her stomach flutter and happiness wash over her. And gosh, he looked good even in a wool coat, gloves, a hat, and a scarf.

His eyes stayed on her as he walked around the lawn decorations and across the snow, only leaving hers for a moment while he went up to Rachel, gave her a hug, then gave a nod toward the hot chocolate. She nodded, then his eyes were immediately back on Noelle's. So, of course, she took a couple of steps to the hot chocolate table.

"Hi," he said, and it felt like so much was loaded into that single word.

"Hi," she breathed back, practically melting. Then, realizing that her dad was at the hot chocolate table, ladle in hand, she cleared her throat and said, "Would you like some hot chocolate?"

Jack nodded. "I'll get some for Rachel first."

Aiden noticed that his uncle had arrived, so he came running over from where he'd been playing with his new friends, Bailey at his side. Her dad ladled up hot chocolate into four cups, and Noelle helped Aiden make his—mixing in chocolate chips and a massive scoop of whipped cream—while Jack added caramel and a pinch of sea salt to Rachel's.

Then she and Jack started making their own. She reached for the spoon in the raspberry jelly, her favorite hot chocolate mix-in, at the same time as Jack reached for it, their hands bumping. "You like raspberry in yours?" No one in her family liked it. Well, except for Gran-gran.

He looked at her, surprise on his face. "You do, too?"

The biggest shock, though, was when they both reached for the cayenne pepper next.

"No way," Noelle's dad said. "I thought Noelle was the only person on the planet who liked raspberry and cayenne in hot chocolate."

Jack gave her that smile she loved that quirked up more on one side. "I've always thought she had impeccable taste."

"Corbin," Katie said to Becca's husband as she pulled her phone out of her pocket. "Are you ready for an interview?"

As the two of them headed away from the crowd and the kids running underfoot for a bit, Noelle and Jack took Rachel's hot chocolate to her.

Her mom came over at the same time and said, "Rachel, we're so glad to have you here! And if you're feeling up to it and don't have other plans, you should join us for Christmas Eve dinner. It's Noelle's birthday, too, so we always have a big celebration. We would love to have you."

Rachel looked like she was touched to be invited and said she would attend if it was at all possible, and it looked like she really meant it. Jack looked happy to be asked, too. This might end up being her favorite birthday / Christmas Eve ever.

Her mom motioned to the truck that had two flatbed trailers connected to it like a train. Both had hay bales arranged in a rectangle, with bales stacked two high in the middle for backrests so that people could sit on all four sides on each trailer. They had already laid blankets across all of them so they wouldn't be itchy. "I want to make sure you're in the spot that's going to be most comfortable. I know that chemo can make you really nauseous; which spot do you think will be best for keeping that at bay?"

"Oh, um, probably facing the direction we are driving. Maybe on the second trailer?"

Her mom winked. "I'll get it ready for you."

Then they all headed toward the trailers and found seats. Noelle's mom had put extra padding in the spot where Rachel would be sitting, and her dad told all the little kids they couldn't jump around on that trailer. Rachel seemed to love having Noelle's parents fawn over her. She glanced at Jack. He was watching Rachel, too, seeming to love seeing her love it.

"Okay, how this works," Noelle said as she leaned over Jack, who was sitting by Rachel, "is that we drive around and look at all the lights. But every once in a while, we'll stop at a house, jump off the trailer, then all go up to sing Christmas carols."

Then her mom turned on the Christmas music and her dad, who was sitting in the driver's seat of the truck, pulled it gently away from the curb. They started heading down the street, the chill in the slight wind causing all of them to pull their hats on a little tighter and to reach for the extra blankets piled on the top of the middle hay bales. Jack stood up and grabbed one of the blankets and placed it over Rachel and Aiden, tucking it in at their sides. Then he grabbed a second one, sat down, and wrapped it around himself and Noelle.

Was it wrong to snuggle into him? Because it was so cold, and he was so warm, and the blanket was kind of pulling them together a bit. Plus, he smelled divine. She took in another deep breath just to smell the sweet pine scent again, even though the cold burned her nose.

His hand was on his leg, but his pinky rested up against her thigh. As they drove past all the beautiful lights people had used to decorate their houses and yards, his finger moved, hesitantly at first, brushing so slightly against her jeans, sending thrills up her spine. It was the slightest touch, but it felt monumental.

She hesitated a very long moment, then decided to just take a gamble and reached for his hand. She heard him suck in a breath like she had surprised him, but then he entwined his fingers in hers as the music played and the lights sparkled, and a light snow drifted down from the sky.

"Hey, Aiden," Katie said as she took a seat next to him and Bailey. "Are you going to dress this cute dog of yours up for the pet costume parade?"

Aiden looked to Noelle. So she nodded and said, "You bet we are. My gran-gran and I used to dress up her dog Daisy every year—it's so much fun."

He grinned and turned back to Katie, so she said, "Can I interview you for the video I'm putting together to watch on Christmas Eve?"

"Yes!" Aiden said, pumping a fist. "I was hoping I'd get to be in it!"

With her phone aimed at Aiden, Katie said, "What's your favorite part about Christmas?"

"Being with my mom." He paused for a moment, then he added, "And making decorations, like the snowflakes that are hanging from our ceiling. And doing all of the activities with Uncle Jack and Noelle."

"You're new to this hayride," Katie said. "Tell us about how you're joining us this year, so when we watch this when we're old and gray, we'll remember why."

"Well," Aiden said, settling against the hay bale at his back, his voice ringing out loud and clear, "I heard my mom telling Uncle Jack that she wanted me to do fun Christmas things, and he got Noelle to help. At first, my mom wasn't all the way happy about that, but only because we hadn't met Noelle yet.

"*But* Mrs. Sowards brought us over a meal one night. They thought I was in my room, but I was actually sitting under the kitchen table. And I heard Mom tell Mrs. Sowards that she was glad that Jack asked Noelle for help because Jack has been more smiley since he started hanging out with Noelle.

"And," Aiden said in a whisper loud enough that everyone on both trailers heard—and probably her dad, too, since he had his window rolled down, "she thinks he's pretty much in love with her. You know, the kind of love where there's kissing and marriage and sneaking food off each other's plates."

Noelle felt Jack stiffen.

Rachel gasped. "Aiden!"

"What? I whispered it, so they didn't hear."

Then Rachel turned to her and Jack. "I am so sorry. And I didn't say anything about the kissing and plates and marriage thing. That was all him."

There was an uncomfortable, awkward silence. But also, it came with a feeling of hope.

Her dad must've either heard Aiden or sensed the tension because he pulled over to the side of the road, giving everyone something else to think about.

"Hop off for a caroling stop!" her mom called out,

and everyone threw off their blankets and got off of the trailer, the two dogs included.

"Are you coming?" Noelle asked Jack.

He shook his head. "I need to stay here and help my sister."

Rachel didn't look like she needed help, but if she had been Jack, she would've stayed behind, too. She got off the trailer and grabbed hold of the hand Aiden wasn't using to hold Bailey's leash and walked with everyone else up to the porch of their neighbor's house.

She took one glance back at the trailers as Hope knocked on the door and saw Jack straightening Rachel's blanket and making sure it was tucked in around her so the cold couldn't get in. It was so sweet that he was so protective of her.

After a rousing rendition of "Silent Night," where the dogs joined in and did their best to sing, too, they headed back to the trailer. This time, Jack didn't sit close enough that their legs touched. He didn't reach out with a pinky to brush her leg, and he didn't take her hand in his. She felt the loss keenly. That hope Aiden had given her felt a little less potent.

As they turned down another road, Rachel said, "Hey, my friend Amy lives in that house up there on the left. She has brought me so many meals while I've been going through chemo."

Noelle's mom, who was riding in the closer trailer,

called out to her dad, "Stop at that blue house on the left."

Before Jack got any other ideas, Noelle said, "I'll stay with Rachel this time—it's your turn to go up and sing."

He shook his head. "I don't—"

But Rachel interrupted with, "Will you tell Amy I said hi?"

Noelle was close enough to see the muscle in his jaw working, but then he gave a nod and called out to where Aiden was now sitting with Noelle's nephews. "Come on, buddy. Let's go sing."

Aiden and Bailey both leaped off the trailer and ran around to take Jack's hand before walking up to the home. Noelle watched them, impressed that Jack was willing to go, even though he had such bad associations with Christmas, he didn't sing, and he probably didn't know Christmas songs very well.

"What's Jack like at work?"

Noelle scooted closer to Rachel so they could talk more easily. "Very professional and closed off. He doesn't get personal, ever."

Rachel laughed. "I wondered if that was what he was like since he always seems so concerned about professionalism. Well, that and the fact that he always goes to work dressed in a suit. But outside of work, he's sweet. Thoughtful. Fun."

She had seen a lot of that over the last couple of

weeks. It was a side of him she was growing to love. "What was he like as a kid?"

Rachel looked up like she was thinking about where to start. Then she said, "When our parents died, he hit a bit of a rebellious stage. Which I totally understood—it was such a hard time. I was eighteen, and suddenly I was his guardian, and I had no idea how to be the mom of a fifteen-year-old. I had mothered him a lot all of his life, but this was different.

"And it wasn't that he was rebelling against me—it was more that he was mad at the world because so many things had been stacked against us. He just stayed out past curfew, got some questionable friends, started dressing differently, things like that. I knew it was likely just part of the grief process and how he dealt with it. But I was so worried for him and didn't know how best to help.

"After a few months, there was a night when he'd left with friends and hadn't been in the best headspace. Before, he'd missed curfew by an hour or two. That night, it was four hours past, and I worried myself sick every single second of those four hours. By the time he got home, I was a complete wreck.

"He came home and saw exactly what that night had done to me. I swear, he stopped being rebellious right then." She snapped her fingers. "Like flipping a switch. He somehow figured things out and pulled himself out of it. I think he realized that he was piling even more stress on me when things had already been hard enough for both of us.

"But he'd always been a sweet, thoughtful kid. When we were little, our dad would drink a lot and get verbally abusive. Just mean. Sometimes physically mean. We learned to just stay away whenever he was drinking. Our mom dealt with it by closing herself off and shutting down, so Jack and I had to rely on each other a lot. Since I was the big sister, I acted like the mom when our mom wasn't.

"When we were small and putting ourselves to bed, he *always* thanked me for taking care of him. I've never known anyone to be as grateful as he is. One night, after he thanked me, he said, 'But there's no one taking care of you.' There wasn't. And I really felt it, you know? I nearly started bawling right then and there just to have it acknowledged.

"So from that night on, he always told *me* a bedtime story, so I'd be taken care of, too. He made up his own before he was old enough to read and did a mix of reading stories to me and making up stories as he got older. I swear that was what made me survive our childhood. I'm lucky to have him as a brother."

Noelle's eyes were misting at hearing how his childhood was and how sweet he was through it. She looked over at where he stood at Amy's porch, holding Bailey's leash in one hand and holding Aiden, who was perched on his shoulder, with the other hand.

"He's going to make a really good dad someday."

Rachel nodded. "The best."

Noelle tried not to imagine him being a dad to their own kids. She knew how dangerous that kind of thinking was.

Yet, a part of her still imagined it anyway. And it must've been showing on her face because when Jack and everyone else came back to the trailers, he was giving her a curious look like he was trying to interpret her expression.

And this time when he sat down, he pulled the blanket around them snugly, so she cozied right into him.

When they made it through all the lights in town and back to her parents' house, everyone started saying their goodbyes. Jack had planned to take both Rachel and Aiden home, but Aiden said, "Can I *please* ride back with Noelle? She has windows that you roll down by turning a handle instead of pushing a button!"

Okay, her little Kia Rio was not that old—it just happened to have manual windows. Hearing Aiden talk about it made it sound like it was several decades old.

"It's freezing out here, buddy," Jack said, his hands deep in his pockets, shivering a bit as he said it. "You shouldn't be rolling the windows down."

"I only roll them down when we're at a stoplight, so no wind blows in. Noelle said it was okay. Please?" he said, dragging out the word to the full extent his lungs could manage.

Rachel and Jack both looked at Noelle as if asking for permission. So she smiled at the adorable kid. "Sure thing, kiddo."

True to his word, he only rolled down the window when they were stopped. But it was at every stop sign and stoplight on the way home. At least they were already used to the cold temperatures.

After getting Aiden and Rachel inside their home and saying their goodbyes, Jack walked her out to her trusty car.

He leaned against Elfie, which made her smile. It meant that he wasn't planning to leave super quickly, and she was in no way ready for him to go. "Thanks for making me come tonight. I actually rather enjoyed it."

She grinned and stepped a little closer to him. She didn't lean against the car—that thing was freezing cold—but she got within a foot of Jack's warmth. "Are those negative feelings about Christmas changing yet?"

This time, he reached out for her hand. And, even though they were wearing gloves, the feel of his hand in hers still sent shivers of happiness up her. "They are. I think they started changing before I even noticed it."

His voice was low and gruff, yet with the perfect

amount of smoothness, too. It was mesmerizing, and she just wanted him to talk to her with that voice all night long. It didn't even matter what he said—it could be his to-do list for tomorrow, and she'd still be enthralled.

He gave her hand the slightest tug. An invitation to come closer if she wanted to, but still slight enough that she could pretend she didn't notice. But it wasn't like she was going to ignore it. She stepped even closer, her leg pressing against his. "I am more than happy to keep helping with that exposure therapy. You're coming to the Santa Mystery Hat thing tomorrow, right?" They were so close that her words came out as a whispered breath in the crisp night air, the words making little puffs of warmth in the cold night air.

"Of course," he breathed, his lips just inches from hers.

Her eyes searched his, trying to unravel everything he might be thinking, and his eyes searched right back, probably trying to guess what she was thinking, too. She could search his eyes all night long and not tire of it.

And then a car drove past, and whatever spell they had been under was broken in an instant. Jack stood up straight and said, "We shouldn't. I'm your boss."

"Yeah," she said, acknowledging the part about him being her boss, wishing it hadn't sounded like she was also acknowledging the "we shouldn't" part.

He gave her hand a squeeze, then said, "I'll see you tomorrow night?"

She nodded as he opened Elfie's door, then she gave him a smile as she sat in her seat. At least they had tomorrow.

JACK

THE ENTIRE DAY, Jack had been thinking about how he'd almost kissed Noelle last night. A part of him wished they had kissed—he so wanted to. He had wanted to for the past couple of weeks. For the last year and a half, actually.

But a more significant part of him was terrified that he'd come so close to very nearly kissing her. She was his employee. He was her boss. Kissing Noelle wasn't on the table.

Since it was a Saturday and he wasn't hurrying to get off work, he told Noelle that he would pick Aiden up for the Santa Hat thing because he wanted to check on Rachel. When he walked into their house, though, Aiden didn't come running to leap onto him to give him a hug.

Rachel poked her head out from the back of the

house and held a finger to her lips, motioning for him to be quiet. As he got closer, she whispered, "Between the hayride last night and sledding this afternoon with Quinton's family, he was tuckered out. We just ate, and he fell asleep at the table just a few minutes ago. I'm sorry I didn't realize how tired he was before you drove all the way here."

"It's no problem." He walked into the kitchen and saw his little nephew slumped back into his chair, soundly asleep. He was glad he came; he would've hated for Rachel to have had to try to carry him into his room. She might have been doing better the past few days, but something like that would've been too much.

He scooped Aiden into his arms and carried him to his room, placing him on his bed and pulling the covers up to his shoulders. Then he gave his hair a ruffle and stepped out of his room, carefully pulling the door closed behind him.

He was surprised at how disappointed he was that they wouldn't be going to the activity with Noelle's family. He was actually starting to really like those celebrations so much more than he thought he ever could.

He looked around Rachel's kitchen and family room area. "Since I'm here, what do you need help with? I can clean or do dishes..."

Rachel shook her head. "No. I'm pretty tuckered. Since Aiden is asleep this early, I'd like the chance to go to sleep this early, too." She paused. "But you should still go to the activity."

He should. He told Noelle he would be there, and he didn't want to let her down. And he had agreed to the exposure therapy thing. But they had also very nearly kissed last night. He had been so successful at keeping things professional with her for so long, and last night, he came so close to completely failing. Could he even trust himself to be with her more?

"You told her you would go," Rachel said in a stern voice. "You should keep your word."

Rachel knew him well enough to know exactly what to say to get him to go. He really didn't want to go back on his word. The part of him that had wished he had just kissed her last night celebrated.

The other part was going to have to be on high alert.

When he arrived at Noelle's parents' house, Noelle seemed genuinely sad that Aiden couldn't come. The two of them appeared to have bonded more strongly than he would've guessed.

"Okay," Noelle's dad said, holding a Santa hat by the white fur trim and shaking its contents, "we've got six teams and six papers inside. Two for the dinner, two for the entertainment, and two for the decorations. Are you all ready for this?"

Everyone cheered, and Jack looked around. Noelle and her four sisters were each standing with their spouses—a date for Katie—and had their kids with them. It seemed that each sister was a team with her own family, so the sixth team must be her parents and Captain, who was sitting upright at their feet, clearly thinking he was on the team to beat. Jack was glad he hadn't skipped coming—it would've left Noelle in a team by herself.

Noelle rubbed her hands together, eyes on the Santa hat, seeming full of anticipation at what they would draw out. It made him smile. Her dad took the hat to Hope, and she drew out a paper and then said out loud, "Dinner."

"Let's hope that Katie doesn't get the other 'Dinner' paper," Noelle said, apparently kicking off the smack-talk portion of the evening.

"Hey, I heard that," Katie said. Then, after a pause, she added, "But really, even I'm hoping for that."

Noelle leaned in close to him, and he tried to ignore the way it kicked his heart rate up a notch. "If we get dinner, we have thirty minutes from the time we leave the house to the time we get back to shop for food. We'll have twenty dollars, and we'll have to buy ingredients that the *other* team will use to make a meal. The challenge is to buy things that in no way will go together. We'd have thirty minutes to cook once we get back."

His eyebrows rose. "Let's hope we don't get that one, then."

Her dad took the hat to Becca next, and she drew out one and said, "Entertainment!" and her three older kids pumped their fists.

He leaned in and whispered, "What's that one?"

She kept her eyes on the Santa hat but whispered, "Each team will have fifteen minutes to gather props and costumes from anywhere in the house. Then they give what they collected to the other team. Then each team has forty-five minutes to come up with a skit using those props and costumes and practice it."

Wow. Her family really did the high-pressure activities here. He felt completely out of his league.

Then her dad brought the hat to Noelle, and she drew out a paper. "Yes! We got decorations!"

She was so excited that it made him smile.

She leaned in and said, "Okay, they'll have a list of things we need to get, and we'll have forty-five minutes to get them. Then, when we get back, we'll have fifteen minutes to decorate a small tree with what we collected."

That didn't seem too hard. He could do this.

Katie and her date drew out the other "Skit" paper; Julianne, her husband, and her two kids were going to decorate the second tree; and Noelle's parents drew the other "Dinner" paper.

"Okay," her mom called out, "you've got five minutes to huddle and come up with a game plan. When you hear the horn, your timer for the games starts!"

Noelle grabbed one of the papers her dad held out, then grabbed Jack's hand and pulled him into the living room that was right next to the front door as the rest of the family scattered to different locations. A tree that was probably two and a half or three feet high and already had lights on it sat on a table in the middle of the room.

She put her hand on it. "Our challenge is basically a scavenger hunt for items to decorate this tree. We have to get something that fits each of the items on this list. The more creative, the better, since everyone votes on which team wins."

"What's at stake?"

"Bragging rights and a trophy. Whoever wins it keeps it for a year and proudly displays it. The next year, they have to give it up to whoever won that category. And Jack? We really want to win."

He smiled, loving this competitive side of her. He glanced at the list of five items. "We can probably go to that craft store on Main Street and get all of this."

She shook her head. "We can't get more than one thing at any one place, and we can't spend more than ten dollars total. So it has to mostly be things that are free or that we can ask someone for." She gestured to a little table. "We have a hot glue gun, scissors, tape, markers, um, it looks like a couple of hole punches—one a circle and one a square—but we don't have time to get too crafty. We need to keep it simple. And come up with a theme.”

Okay, maybe they didn't get the easy one. He was *definitely* out of his league.

Noelle tapped a finger on the list. “Something edible… What kind of food would make a good decoration? Gumdrops are too small… Oh! I saw holiday pretzels at the convenience store just right out on Center. They were shaped like stars. Maybe we can do a theme around that.”

Jack nodded. Okay, some direction. He had no idea what to do with the direction, but it sounded good.

“Something sparkly or shiny… Hmm. And something red or blue. That one's easy enough—we could always get a roll of ribbon at the craft store to glue to the back of the pretzels to hang them with. Then we need something found outside and some kind of garland.”

Yep. Totally out of his depth.

And then an idea hit. “Something outside—I saw a giant pine tree two houses up. I bet there are pine cones under it still. Maybe we could get some for decorations or…Oh. Maybe if we get five"—he grabbed the markers and laid them out on the table like he was making a big asterisk—"we could put them like this and glue the inside right here to make a star.”

“That's genius!” Noelle said, grabbing his arm and

making him feel pretty proud of himself for thinking of it.

"Now we just need something sparkly or shiny and some kind of garland. What goes with stars? We can't just have the entire tree be stars. Planets? No. Moons? No." She shook her hands out. "I can't think of anything that goes with stars. What else is in the sky?"

As soon as she said that, all he could think of was helping Aiden to hang all the snowflakes he'd made from the ceiling of their family room. "How about 'Snow under the Stars' for the theme? Maybe we can cut out snowflakes."

"Ooo," she said. "I like that. Okay, we need something sparkly or shiny. I know that the craft store has sheets of paper that are a shiny silver. Maybe we can make the snowflakes out of that. It's thicker paper, so we won't be able to be too intricate with them, but I think we can make it work."

"That's two things from the craft store, though."

"Sixty seconds!" Noelle's mom called out from somewhere else in the house.

"Eek! You're right. We've got to move fast. Um... Oh! The woman who lives on the corner makes handmade cards. She's bound to have ribbon—let's ask her. What are we going to do for a garland?"

"Maybe something with the snow theme? Like

tissues or something?" It sounded stupid, but it was the only idea he had.

"Oh! Tissue paper. We could get white—it's everywhere and super cheap. There's an antique store next to the craft store, and they use it to wrap up breakable trinkets. We could try there. We could cut the sheets like big snowflakes and then, I don't know, tape them together into a long garland and then bunch it with ribbon."

A loud horn sounded.

"Huddle time is up!" Noelle's mom called out. "You have sixty minutes from right now to be back here to present what your team has come up with!"

Noelle grinned at him, her eyes lit with excitement. It was coming so strongly off her that he was feeling it himself. "Are you ready?"

He nodded and grinned back. They both slipped on their coats, then she grabbed his hand and pulled him outside. They raced to the neighbor with the pine tree first, knocked on the door, got permission to take "as many pinecones as you'd like—feel free to take them all!" and grabbed seven, just in case. Then they ran just as quickly to the house on the corner.

A woman who was probably in her seventies answered the door, and when Noelle explained what they were doing, she said, "Of course, dear! Come into my craft room. No, don't take off your shoes—you've got a race to win!"

In less than two minutes, they had a roll of ice blue ribbon in their hands, and they were racing back to where his car was parked. He dumped the pine cones onto the floor behind his seat, then they got into the car, and he headed toward the convenience store.

Luckily, they had the pretzels in stock. Noelle picked up two big bags of them and put them on the counter.

Jack's eyebrows drew together. "Why two?"

"Because Aiden is going to wake up tomorrow morning and realize he slept right through this activity, and he's going to feel bad. I figured I could take a bag over to him tomorrow and hang out with him for a bit so he won't feel like he missed so much."

Jack just stared at Noelle. They were in the middle of a race against the clock, trying to win a prize that seemed really important to her, and she was stopping to think of someone who was vastly important to him? It touched him in a way that left him speechless.

She put her credit card back in her pocket, grabbed the bag from the cashier, and said, "Come on!" and they both raced out of the store.

When they were in the car and driving toward the craft store, he asked, "So who would you be on a team with if Aiden and I weren't coming this year?" He came so close to not attending this once he found out that Aiden wasn't.

She was quiet for a long moment before she

answered. Then she cleared her throat and said, "I don't know. But it kind of requires six teams. This event has evolved over the years—before everyone started getting married and having kids, we used to do it with cousins, aunts, and uncles. Their families have grown, too, so they do their own versions of it now. For as long as I can remember, Gran-gran had always been my teammate. We didn't do it last year since we were planning a funeral, so this was the first year without her."

He felt an acute pain from what had almost happened. What if he'd just stayed at Rachel's and helped out around her house and not come at all? He felt sick just thinking of how it would be for her to face this first event without her gran-gran and have to do it without a teammate.

He could feel the emotions coming from her as she, too, likely thought about what the night would've been like if he hadn't come. Maybe if he and Aiden had never planned to come, she would've asked one of her cousins or a friend to join her. He was glad it was him here, though.

"What was your favorite time when you pulled *Decorations* from Santa's hat?"

She chuckled at whatever had just come to her mind, and he was glad it was a happy memory. "One year, Gran-gran and I decided to do a 'snow globe' theme. We got these little balloons that were see-through and poured some glitter inside, and then pushed in little random objects we found outside before blowing them up. We had thought it was the most genius idea ever until we put them on the tree and a good half of the balloons popped when they made contact with the pine needles. We were both laughing so hard, I don't think we even finished decorating it before the horn sounded."

Her story made him smile. Their lives growing up were so different from each other. He was glad she had memories like that.

"I'm worried that we aren't going to finish everything," Noelle said. "It's going to take a while to cut out all the snowflakes and glue ribbons to all the ornaments, so we need to get back as quickly as we can. I know where the paper is at The Crafty One. Do you want to run into Trove of Oldies and ask for the tissue paper at the same time?"

He said yes just as he turned into a parking spot, coming to a stop way too quickly, and they both jumped out of his car and ran into their stores. There must not have been too many people in line at The Crafty One because she actually beat him back out to the car. The woman at the Trove of Oldies register had wanted to hear all about the scavenger hunt, but still, it hadn't taken too long.

Then they drove back to Noelle's parents' house. The whole time they were in the car, he tried to think back to the last time when he'd done anything as fun as this and was coming up blank. Surely a race to gather supplies wasn't the highlight of his life.

He glanced over to where Noelle sat with such an intense look of determination on her face. Maybe it was less about what he was doing and more about who he was doing it with.

They parked, grabbed the supplies, and headed into the house. After they dumped all the supplies on the craft table, Noelle pulled out her phone. "Thirty-two minutes! I think we just set a record!"

It was a good thing they had twenty-eight minutes left on the timer instead of fifteen because his hands weren't used to doing stuff like this. They started with the pinecone and made the star for the top of the tree before realizing that they didn't have a way to make it stay up there. Noelle gasped, then ran out of the room. Moments later, she returned with a triumphant smile on her face, holding an empty toilet paper roll. "We'll just hot glue it to this, and then we can just slide it down over the top branch."

Surprisingly, it worked. They cut snowflakes out of the big tissue paper next, which wasn't easy. Then, side by side, they laid out the snowflakes on the floor, corners overlapping, and taped them together, and started bunching them and tying the bunched part with ribbons. They were working so closely that their shoulders were nearly constantly touching, their hands brushing each other with every ribbon they tied. And every time they did, it sent a new feeling of euphoria through him.

The same thing happened as they cut ribbons, glued them to the back of the star pretzels, and then cut little snowflakes from the shiny silver paper. It was too thick to fold and cut like Aiden had, so they quickly used the square and round hole punches to make it look as close as possible to snowflakes.

Then they went to work putting all their decorations on the tree. As they hung the garland, they pushed some of the lights through the holes in the thin paper, making it look like moonlight spilling over fresh snow. It amazed him how well they worked together, seeming to anticipate each other's moves, working so much more quickly than he could've guessed.

They got the final pretzel stars and silver snowflakes hung on the tree just as Noelle's mom called out, "Five-minute warning!"

Noelle turned to him, her breaths coming fast, a look of wonder on her face. "We finished with five minutes to spare! Can you believe it? And look how amazing our tree is!" She gave him a hug, and he gave her a tight squeeze back.

They both turned to admire their handiwork. He had to admit he was impressed that they could decorate the tree in the amount of time they had and make it look awesome. He felt taller just looking at it.

"We've got time," Noelle said. "Maybe we can get a few more lights to show through the garland."

They both leaned in, hands working together as they moved around the tree, this time without the sense of urgency that had driven them for the past hour. This time, he just reveled in being so close to Noelle, being so in sync with her.

On one particularly tough part, where the tape made the garland bunch up weird, they were both leaned in close, both of their hands bumping each other as they worked, and Noelle turned her face from the tree to his. He looked over, too, their faces barely a couple of inches apart. He could feel her quiet breath, smell her shampoo, which smelled remarkably like gingerbread, and see the longing in her eyes.

She was so beautiful. He'd known it for a long time. But now he understood how much of her beauty came from the person she was on the inside, shining through for all to see.

She bit her bottom lip, and his eyes were immediately drawn to those lips. Those lips that he'd imagined kissing a million times over, stopping himself each time. Then he saw her eyes shift to his lips, too.

Then, after a quick breath, Noelle's hands flew to his face, her palms resting against the sides of his face, her fingertips in his hair, and her lips were on his. He let out a slight groan, and they both straightened to standing as he put an arm around her waist, pulling her closer.

Her lips moved against his with the same sense of urgency they had felt while decorating the tree. A need to hurry before time ran out.

There's time, he thought. *We have time.*

And, just like they'd been in sync all evening, she seemed to be in sync with his thoughts, too. The sense of urgency seemed to flee, and she relaxed into the kiss, her fingers slowly skimming along his cheeks, down his neck, across his collarbone, her hands coming to rest on his shoulders.

A tiny voice said that he shouldn't be kissing her. But a much louder voice, one that only spoke in emotions, told him that this was perfect. She was perfect. Kissing her was perfect. That part of him exploded with hope, adoration, happiness, peace. A dream a year and a half in the making coming to life.

He was here with Noelle. And if he wasn't mistaking the emotions she seemed to be pouring into this kiss, she felt about him the same as he felt about her. Heat radiated through him, a lightness in his limbs, a tension-free calm spreading out from his chest.

"Time's up!" Noelle's mom called from the kitchen.

Noelle pulled away ever so slightly, and he traced kisses along her jaw, then paused with his lips just brushing her ear and whispered, "I think that means we should stop."

She sighed and sank into him, her body pressed against his, a hand resting on his chest, filling him full of light and heat. "There should be a trophy for *that* because I'm pretty sure we just won."

He chuckled softly. "I think we did."

As he heard the footsteps of walking adults and racing kids heading back to the central kitchen and family room area from all the places in the house they'd scattered to, that quiet voice inside him whispered just barely loud enough to be heard, *But you're her boss.*

He ignored it as, hand-in-hand, they headed into the family room with everyone else.

eleven

NOELLE

NOELLE GOT into her car Monday morning to go to work and blasted the *Christmas All Day* station, singing along to it. Christmas music just didn't sound the same in the rental car she'd been driving. She patted Elfie's dash. It was so good to have her back.

Christmas was five days away. Christmas Eve—and her birthday—was Friday. She loved her job, but it was still exciting to have a break coming up.

She took her usual detour to bypass driving through Main Street. She still hadn't recovered enough from Gran-gran's passing to drive down it with all its Christmas decorations yet—it still flooded her with too many emotions to handle first thing in the morning—but she was making progress. She only had four days of work this week before they were off for Christmas break, and she was determined to drive down it by Thursday morning.

And, because she hadn't gone a full five minutes since Saturday night without thinking about the kiss she and Jack shared, her mind went there again. All night long, they had worked together so well. So many times, they'd brushed hands, shoulders, knees. So many little touches from working so closely together, yet every one of them had sent thrills right through her.

As they were working on putting the final touches on their tree, he just looked at her with the sweetest expression. Like there was nowhere else he would rather be and no one else he'd rather be with. Like he was just soaking in the moment of being with her, and it mirrored what she felt so much that she'd wanted to kiss him so badly.

It had taken a lot of guts to make that move because she hadn't been sure how he would respond. The moment he put his arm around her waist and pulled her close, a weight had lifted from her, and she just sank into his kiss. It had been so sweet and wonderful and full of more emotions than she could even name.

She jerked out of the memory at the sound of her phone ringing. Glancing at the console, she could see that it was her sister, Hope. She pressed the button to let the car answer the phone. Elfie might not have power windows, but the manufacturer must've known how much she'd need Bluetooth.

"Hi, sis!"

"Hi! Okay, I just got Makelle off to school, and Porter and Weston are quietly eating breakfast, which means I have about a four-minute window of calmness here. Tell me about this weekend! You and Jack were looking pretty cozy. Did he kiss you? Because I got the vibe that he wanted to kiss you."

"I kissed him."

Hope squealed. "I knew it! When? How was it?"

"When we were decorating the tree, and it was *amazing*. It was like everything all night had been building up to it. Actually, everything from the moment he showed up to the hayride Friday night. We had just been on the same page so much the whole night, and I could tell that he wanted to kiss me as badly as I wanted to kiss him. It was magical. Like nothing I've ever experienced."

Hope squealed again, and she wasn't even a squealer. "That's how it was the first time Cory and I kissed. Tell me more. Was there a second kiss?"

"No." She'd tried to not sound disappointed when she said the word, but it came out anyway. "It just started seeming like we weren't on the same page so much after that. Like he was pulling away."

"Maybe he just didn't like the food. I mean,

Julianne's team's chicken tortilla soup was pretty... interesting."

Noelle chuckled. "True. But I think it has more to do with him being my boss; I know he was worried about that. I was hoping that he'd kind of decided that it wasn't such a big deal. But I don't know, maybe I was wrong. And it wasn't like he was dropping any big hints that he's not okay with 'us.' It was more subtle things. Things I might not have picked up on if we hadn't been so in sync."

"Ooo, that's tough. Weston! We don't put fistfuls of Cheerios and milk in people's hair." She heard a few sounds of dishes moving and a grunt, probably as Hope pulled Weston out of his high chair, then heard the water run. "Keep talking. I'm listening."

"I just think I probably shouldn't have let my heart get so involved. I never thought that would even be an issue when Jack asked me to take this side job, so I was kind of blindsided by my attraction to him. I should just back away as quickly as possible."

"Maybe you should," Hope said, which she was totally not expecting, especially after the squeals.

"But my heart got involved with his nephew, too. I went over there yesterday after church to give him the star-shaped pretzels, and we just hung out and played. He's just such a cute kid. And I think he'll be sad, too. He has really loved playing with everyone's kids."

"Oh, yeah. That's extra tough."

"And I just can't stop thinking that when Christmas is over, Jack is going to go back to just being my boss, and Aiden is going to go back to being a kid I never see because it wasn't like I had seen him even once during the first year and a half I worked for Jack. And I'm not sure I can handle either of those things, Hope. Especially not the part about Jack."

"So, what do you want to do?"

"What do I *want* to do? I want to spend time with him outside of work every single day and then kiss like we did on Saturday night."

"Okay, so what are you *going* to do?"

"I don't know. We texted a bit yesterday, but even his texts seemed more distant."

"Maybe you should talk to Becca and Corbin since they've both worked in human resources."

"Maybe." She pulled into a parking spot in front of work. "I just need to put him out of my mind. I need to back away. Amazing kiss, amazing night, amazing man or not, I just need to back away before I get my heart in any deeper." She took in a long breath, then blew it out in a huff. "I just need to focus on being grateful that I have Elfie fixed, and I'm driving her again. That was what I did all this for in the first place. Mission accomplished."

"That sounds like a plan. Good luck with it!"

After Noelle went inside the building and set her bag at her desk, she pulled out her lunch container and headed to the break room to put it in the fridge.

As soon as she stepped through the doorway and saw Jack pouring himself a cup of coffee, she knew her plan was destined to fail, and no amount of luck was going to save it. It wasn't like she had started falling for him, and it was no big deal because she was actually bungee jumping and was going to get pulled back to the starting point at any minute. She had already fallen entirely. The parachute had been deployed, she'd landed, and there was no going back.

"Hi," she breathed, a smile spreading across her face.

A beautiful, perfect, joyful smile filled his face, too. How had she not been falling for this man from the moment she'd started working here?

The second he'd switched from his natural reaction at seeing her to a logical, thought-out worry was evident on his face. She knew that something along the lines of "I'm the boss, so this isn't appropriate" was churning in his mind. But she could also see hints of something else. The same longing that she was feeling. She wanted to tell that part of him to stay strong. She really wanted it to win.

"Good morning."

"How was the rest of your weekend?"

He opened his mouth like he was going to give the

answer that first came to mind, but then he shut it again. Then he said slowly, pausing after every word or two like he was choosing his words with great care. "It was... good. I can't say it came without worries."

Oh, no. He had definitely been spending a lot of time thinking about the boss/employee thing. In an attempt to keep things light, she put on a big smile and said, "It sounds like you need a night of Christmas fun to keep your mind off your worries."

He just studied her, not responding, and she could see the care in his eyes. Then his eyes shifted to the door behind her, and he turned back to his coffee. Noelle turned around just in time to see Lennox, who had strode into the room, falter in his step as he looked between the two of them, trying to decipher what had just been going on.

Noelle acted like nothing was out of the ordinary and opened the fridge, putting her lunch inside. "The meeting's at two-thirty, right?" There. She'd just made it sound like that's all they'd been talking about.

Jack nodded, then gave Lennox a nod and said, "Good morning," then walked out of the break room.

Lennox clearly hadn't bought her "Let's talk about the meeting" cover. Probably because the meeting was always at 2:30 on Mondays.

He glanced at the doorway Jack had left through then back at Noelle. "So, what was that about?"

"Just an issue with a client and my part in it." She didn't mention that Jack was the client. And she definitely didn't say that her part in it had been falling in love with him.

Since she'd thrown herself under the bus with the comment, Lennox seemed to buy it. He grimaced. "That's no fun. Good luck."

That was twice in less than twenty minutes she'd been wished luck on something that needed more than luck. It wasn't like Jack was going to stop being her boss, and it didn't appear that her heart was going to stop wanting a relationship with him.

twelve

JACK

JACK WENT BACK into his office, shut the door behind him, set his coffee on his desk, then ran his fingers through his hair. The moment Noelle had walked through the doorway into the break room, his entire body had filled with happiness. Like it had forgotten all the time he'd spent worrying over the past day and a half. His body just felt more alive whenever she was in the same room.

But Lennox's reaction to catching them in the teeniest tiniest bit of a moment together was precisely the reason why it was so wrong to have fallen so fully for Noelle.

He knew Friday that he'd stepped over a line in the sand that he'd drawn for himself. He'd known then that the smart thing to do—the responsible thing to do—would've been to call things off then. Yet he didn't.

And then, during Saturday's activity, there had been no time to think—just time to react as they raced through the scavenger hunt and made everything they needed for the tree. There hadn't been time for the logical part of him to keep shouting that he was making a wrong choice. He was usually so good at self-discipline. How had he let himself get into a situation with such considerable consequences to his heart?

And now that he was looking back, he realized he had been brushing over that line and redrawing it for a couple of weeks. Opening himself up more and more to Noelle.

He sank into the chair behind his desk and couldn't stop thinking about the way Noelle's face had lit up when she walked into the break room. And what it did to his stomach to see the woman he'd been falling in love with for the past year and a half having such a joyful response at seeing him.

Which made him think about the look she'd had on her face right before she had kissed him. He wanted to experience seeing that look on her face every day.

But then, like all the emotions had been standing in line to see him, the moment that one stepped away, the next one he'd experienced that night stepped forward. After their kiss, he and Noelle had joined the rest of her big family to see the results of everyone's Mystery Santa Hat offerings.

And as he stood, surrounded by all of them, he thought about how much he'd been falling for Noelle's family, too. They were everything he had grown up without. Rachel and Aiden meant everything to him. He never would've guessed that his heart had room for a family that big, but then they went and surprised him, too, and showed him how much he actually needed them. He saw it in Rachel's face during the hayride and Aiden's every time they did anything at Noelle's parents' house.

And all of that scared him. Because he was still Noelle's boss, which meant that he *couldn't* have a relationship with her.

All through that night, the emotions within him battled. He sat at Noelle's side as Becca, Corbin, and their four little kids performed a sweet version of the first Christmas, with Joseph wearing a colander as a hat, Mary wearing a Superman cape, a shepherd wearing a bedazzled scarf instead of robes and holding a stuffed bear instead of a sheep, a wise man wearing a suit coat that was so long on her that it dragged on the floor, a second wise man wearing swim goggles and arm floaties, and baby Jesus constantly climbing out of the giant mixing bowl that was supposed to be the manger. The wise men placed gifts of gold, frankincense, and myrrh at baby Jesus's manger, but were actually a mixing cup, a microphone from a preschooler's karaoke machine, and a lint roller that baby Jesus kept trying to put in his mouth.

And then they watched as Katie and her date reenacted the scene from the movie Elf when he sang, "I'm singing! I'm in a store, and I'm singing!" Her date played the part of Buddy the Elf, and Katie played the roles of Jovie, the store manager, and several people in the store, hurrying to change costumes and props with each line.

Laughter had filled him as they watched both skits, loving sitting next to Noelle and being with all her family. Yet, sadness that it all was going to go away had quickly fought with that laughter.

He'd been so proud of their tree when they presented it. With as overwhelmed as he'd felt by the task, it had turned out well. Of course, Hope's family had turned theirs into a "family tree," with each family member hand-drawn by their kids, and had taken home the trophy. Still, though, he'd been impressed by the tree he and Noelle had made.

There had been a lot more laughter—and plenty of *Eww!* and "Gross!" and even a few people said "Yum!" as they ate the creations from the two teams who had pulled "Dinner" from Santa's hat.

Julianne, along with her husband and two kids, had made chicken tortilla soup that definitely had chicken in it, and he guessed some taco seasoning, but the rest of the soup looked like it was maybe four different kinds of canned soup mixed together. Their dessert was an Oreo cookie topped with a dollop of Cool Whip, topped with a single blueberry. It was kind of weird, but not too bad.

Noelle's parents had made a stir fry with a strange collection of vegetables and a meat that was definitely *not* chicken. His guess was canned tuna. They'd made an apple crisp that was pretty impressive, especially considering that the topping seemed to be made out of a mix of crushed potato chips, Fritos, and Doritos.

And he'd experienced it all with Noelle by his side. During it all, things were slightly awkward between them and didn't have the same easiness they had gained during their previous activities. He knew it was all coming from him because grief at the impending loss battled with contented happiness all night long. Yet, he still longed to spend every moment with her. Even knowing that every minute spent with her was going to make calling it all off even more difficult.

He stood up and paced in his office, trying to come to terms with what he needed to do, especially when such a large part of him was fighting every bit of it.

But if Saturday night hadn't let him know that he needed to end things, Sunday night did. He'd gone over to Rachel's for dinner and to check on them, and Aiden couldn't stop talking about how Noelle had come over and played with him and how much fun he had.

Somehow, he hadn't thought through how much hiring Noelle would affect his nephew. Of course he'd get attached to her. Who wouldn't? How could he not have realized that?

He was in deep. They all were. He needed to end things before it got any worse.

thirteen

NOELLE

NOELLE'S WORKLOAD of last-minute ad copy changes for the final days of Christmas advertising was huge. She spent all morning intensely focused on them, then hit it again hard after lunch. By two, her brain was mush, so she leaned back in her chair and ran her hands over her face.

Then she opened her desk drawer and pulled out the tin of cards from Gran-gran. She ran the tips of her fingers over the scene Gran-gran had painted of the two of them standing in front of the little tree they'd decorated with balloon snow globes, half of them popped, holding their stomachs from laughing so hard.

It was a great memory.

So was Saturday night's.

If Gran-gran had been there, she would've been

hooting and slapping her knee and wiping tears from her eyes from laughing so hard at the skits. During the dinner, she would've been giving commentary on the meal like she was a food critic at a Michelin-starred restaurant, saying how delectable everything was. And she would've said that the tree she and Jack decorated should be on display in the White House.

She carefully placed the card back in the tin and put the one with the pet costume parade leaning against her monitor. The painting on it was of when they had dressed Gran-gran's dog, Daisy, up as a Christmas tree with a star on her head. They were going to do something similar tonight with Aiden's dog, Bailey. She had already dropped off at Rachel's and Aiden's house a big piece of green felt, colored pom-poms, ribbon that looked like it could be used as a garland, and her hot glue gun.

Bridget rolled her chair over to Noelle's desk. "Remember how I didn't have a clue what to get my mom for Christmas? Well, her little dog apparently decided she was mad about something and took it out on my mom's favorite lap blanket. So I went to that store in the mall with all the comfort items and got her the softest blanket I've ever seen."

"Oh! Jack got his sister one of those blankets! I couldn't believe how soft it was."

Bridget cocked her head to the side, a mix of confusion and something else on her face. Suspicion? "You went shopping with Jack?" She paused a moment, then added, "Is that the after-hours job he was asking for a volunteer to take in the meeting a couple of weeks ago?"

Noelle nodded. "Well, actually, it was all about doing Christmassy things with his five-year-old nephew, Aiden. His sister is sick and can't do it herself. But since he hates Christmas, he wanted help."

Bridget nodded slowly.

She hadn't meant to keep it a secret from her coworkers. They just hadn't asked, and she hadn't thought to bring it up. But she fully intended to keep the kiss a secret. But even though she would've had no problem talking about it last week or the week before, she felt weird talking with Bridget about it now, especially because of all the feelings she was having about him.

"How's that going?"

"Good!" Her voice came out bright, just like she'd hoped. She hoped it came out with zero guilt, too. "He's a super cute kid. He's helped me to reconnect with Gran-gran."

"Aww. That's so sweet. Then I'm glad it was you who agreed to help."

Noelle really didn't want the conversation to continue, just in case she asked any tough questions. So she said, "Have you created the images yet for the Ducasse account? I'm having trouble coming up with ad copy for them and could use some inspiration." The topic change totally worked, and she did a mental fist pump.

BY THE TIME she got everything together that she needed for their staff meeting, most of her coworkers had already headed to the conference room. Arms full of papers, notebooks, and her tablet, she headed down the hall leading to the meeting. Jack stood outside of the door, greeting people as they entered, like he always did, standing tall and looking so incredible and professional in his navy suit. It was such a different look than what she saw him wear outside of work, yet he was every bit as attractive both ways.

A wide smile spread across her face at seeing him. She expected a similar return smile from him, but instead, he just gave a nod and said, "Noelle."

She walked into the meeting and found a seat, wondering if he was losing interest or if he was just so much better at hiding their relationship at work than she was. She hoped it was the latter because a forbidden relationship was kind of exciting. That, and it made her heart hurt to even think that he wasn't interested.

Which was stupid, because she'd already decided to back away and keep her heart protected.

He was acting so distant all through the meeting, though, which made her start questioning everything. He'd always been distant at work, so that part wasn't entirely unusual. He just hadn't been quite so distant since she started seeing him outside of work to help with Aiden.

And then, completely unbidden, their kiss popped into her mind. He had definitely been on the same page as her during that kiss. They had definitely connected on a new level Friday and Saturday. Seeing him acting like nothing had happened—even if that was the way he should be acting while at work—made her realize just how much she'd fallen for him.

She was the last one to gather her things at the end of the meeting, and as she passed by Jack at the door, she said, "Are we still on for the pet parade tonight?" After seeing how he'd been in the meeting, she'd started to wonder if they were.

"Aiden is really looking forward to it."

She nodded, wondering exactly what that meant. She had gotten about three steps down the hall when he said, "Noelle, can you meet with me in my office at four?"

She turned and said, "Sure," then headed back to her desk.

There was still a lot she needed to get done by the end of the day. But at least half of her brain was constantly wondering why he wanted to see her in his office. Should she be excited because he was going to sneak a kiss when no one in the office was looking? Or should she be worried that his acting distant was a foreshadowing of what was to come?

At four o'clock on the dot, she knocked on his office door, and he immediately opened it, then closed it behind her. He motioned to the couch that sat against one wall—the one she'd never seen him use. So she sat down and studied his face. There was no "I'm about to kiss you like we kissed Saturday night and make your entire week" look on his face. All that was there was a seriousness. A sense of determination.

"I have...worries. About"—he glanced at the door—"Saturday night. Worries about myself, I guess. I don't think it's a good idea for me to be around you outside of work."

Just the thought of not seeing him outside of work made her feel like she was going to crumble. She could talk big with Hope, and she could even talk big to herself and mostly convince herself that it was for the best. But the fact remained that she had completely fallen for him. Enough that it sounded miserable to not have him in her life outside of being her boss.

Okay, Noelle. Think about this logically. He said he was worried about Saturday, so the kissing her part. He hadn't mentioned all the other days. "Let's just assume that Saturday happened because Aiden wasn't there. He'll be there tonight, so it'll be just fine."

"I don't think it'll be fine. Aiden's presence hasn't stopped me from wanting to be around you yet."

So he was interested in her. Somehow, though, the knowledge of that made this all even more heartbreaking. Could he not get over the fact that he was her boss? She swallowed hard and tried to be strong. "I can take Aiden to the pet costume parade tonight without you." That was what their original pact had been, anyway.

He shook his head. "I don't think that's going to work, either. I'm sorry. I know tonight is important to him, so I'll help him make the costume for Bailey and take them to the costume parade. But I think we should mark our agreement as fulfilled. I will still pay you the amount we agreed upon, of course, but your help is no longer needed."

JACK

A MASSIVE WEIGHT seemed to be dragging Jack down as he drove from Golden to his sister's house in Mountain Springs. All he wanted to do was bury himself in work, sleep, run a few miles, or do anything else that would keep him from having all of his thoughts directed at Noelle and how he'd ended things. And to keep his mind off how his heart was aching at the thought of things going back to the way they'd been before he'd asked for her help.

If they could even go back to that.

But he knew how much tonight meant to Aiden, and he wasn't about to go back on his word to him. When he walked into Rachel's house, Aiden did his customary run down the hallway and leaped onto him, giving him a starfish hug. He hugged Aiden back, then set him back on the floor. "Where's your mom?"

"In here," Rachel said, her voice sounding weak.

He walked into the kitchen to see her carrying a bowl to the sink, looking like she didn't have the energy to even stay standing long enough to get to a chair. He rushed to her side. "Are you okay? What do you need? Do you need me to take you to the hospital?"

She shook her head. "I'm just so tired today. That's all."

"Then you should sleep. Do you need anything before going to bed?"

"No. But I was going to..."

He put an arm around her back to support her. "I know. But do you think you have the energy for that?"

She sighed, seeming resigned. So he scooped her into his arms and carried her into her bedroom, and placed her gently on her bed. "Where's your phone?"

"On the table, I think."

Aiden had followed them into the bedroom, so he asked him to run out and get his mom's phone. When he got back, he laid it on the nightstand beside her. "Just sleep. Don't worry about anything. Aiden and I are going to have a great time tonight. I'll wake you up when I bring him back home and get him to bed."

"Are you sure you don't need anything right now?"

"I'm sure."

"Call or text me if you do need anything, okay?"

She nodded. He gave her hand a squeeze, and Aiden pushed into the space between them and gave his mom a tight hug. "I'll tell you all about the parade later, okay?"

She kissed Aiden on the forehead, and Jack led him out of the room.

The two of them looked at the bag of supplies that Noelle had dropped off that they somehow had to make a dog costume out of. He was already feeling lost without Noelle and was hoping that Rachel would be feeling great and could give them some direction.

"Well, buddy," he said, "it looks like it's up to us to figure this out."

"When is Noelle going to get here?"

This was the question he'd been dreading. "She's not going to be here. I'm sorry."

Aiden let out a breath that made his chest sink and his shoulders slump. "Will she be at the costume parade?"

He shook his head. "I don't know."

They moved the coffee table in the family room off to the side then emptied the bag's contents onto the floor. The little colored puffs were obviously meant to be ornaments, and the ribbon, he was guessing, was probably a garland. Oh, and there was a hot glue gun; he plugged that into the outlet and put it on the coffee table. He was glad he found out how that worked on Saturday night.

But the two foot square of green felt? He didn't have a clue what to do with that.

"Well, where do you think we should start?"

"Noelle didn't tell you how we make it?"

He shook his head. He hadn't even thought to ask.

Aiden tapped a finger on his lip, thinking, a mannerism that always made Jack smile. Aiden grabbed hold of the felt and turned it, smoothing it out. "We should make it a diamond, like this, instead of a square. Maybe this point at the top can be the top of the Christmas tree, then these points at the side can wrap around onto Bailey's stomach."

He was impressed at the kid's ability to figure this out. "Come here, girl," he said to Bailey, and the dog walked right over to him like she was all-in on this project. He and Aiden laid the fabric on Bailey's back, and Aiden pressed the sides down and held them in place under Bailey's stomach. Okay, that could work.

"And then maybe we should just cut this bottom point off," Aiden said, marking it with his hand, "so it's flat, like the bottom of a tree."

He nodded and spread the fabric out on the floor. He handed the scissors to Aiden and said, "Do you want to do the honors?"

Aiden grinned and started cutting as Jack drew a line with his finger just ahead of Aiden's cut. It was an extremely jagged line, but Christmas trees were like that, anyway. And Aiden was so proud of it.

He looked at the ribbon and pom-poms, then to the glue gun. "This glue gets really hot, so I think I better do that part. Do you want to just choose an item, I'll glue it, then you point where to put it?"

Aiden nodded, and they went to work. Aiden hadn't exactly had the same picture in his mind as Jack did about how the ribbon should go on, but he let him make it his own. In the end, the ribbon went in wavy lines in three crisscrossing directions, and pom-poms were stuck everywhere.

Aiden sat back on his heels, surveying their work, and grinned. Then he put out a fist, and Jack bumped it with his.

Then he looked down at his hands in his lap. "I really wish Noelle had come. I miss her."

"I do, too, buddy." So much.

Aiden nodded and reached out to scratch the top of Bailey's golden head. "Do you want to try this on? Stand up, girl."

Bailey complied, and they laid the fabric on her a second time. It looked better than Jack thought it would. But then Bailey barked and wiggled her back in excitement, and the tree costume fell right off.

"It needs to connect," Aiden said. "How do we do that part?

"I don't know," Jack admitted. They couldn't exactly use hot glue to glue it into place without endangering Bailey or one of them. Plus, he didn't know if they'd be able to get the costume off after that.

"Can we tie it?"

Jack tried, but it wasn't quite long enough for a knot. He also had the idea to pull off one of the pom-poms and glue it to one point underneath and cut a slit in the other point to use it as a button, but he'd apparently used way too much glue on the pom-poms to be able to remove one.

"I really miss Noelle," Aiden said again.

"She made stuff like this look easy, didn't she?" He hadn't fully appreciated that trait of hers until just then. He looked down at his watch. They needed to leave within the next minute or two if they wanted a chance of being there in time.

"Oh!" Jack said, bunching the fabric at Bailey's stomach in his hand. "We could just use a rubber band to hold it like this! Do you know if you have one?"

Aiden jumped up and ran to a drawer in their kitchen and started rifling through it. "What about this?" he asked, holding up a hairband.

"Perfect."

Bailey was remarkably patient as they tried with the costume once again. The hair tie worked, and the outfit looked like it might stay in place for a bit. Hopefully for long enough.

"Okay, run and get your shoes and coat on. I'll get Bailey's leash."

Ten minutes later, they pulled into a parking spot at the community center and ran with Bailey and her costume to get inside. Pets dressed in all kinds of Christmas costumes and their owners were everywhere, and Jack had to work to keep Aiden and Bailey at his side while he checked in. Then someone led them to a room beside the gym to get Bailey's costume on.

It was less easy getting the hair tie holding the costume on this time around because Bailey was so excited to be around all the people and other dogs who shared the room. But eventually, they managed to, not long before someone came in.

"Okay, listen up. You're Dogs Group Two. I want you all to file in behind me. I will lead you through the parade route, and then you'll be free to come back here to get anything you left behind, or you can join the folks sitting to watch the parade."

She led them back to the gym, where everyone sat in the middle of the room while all the dogs paraded around the perimeter. Instead of looking at the other dogs, every minute that his eyes weren't on Aiden and Bailey, they were scanning the crowd for Noelle, desperately hoping to catch even a glimpse of her.

But they made the circuit around the room, and he couldn't see her at all. They found seats and sat down while Aiden told Bailey over and over how good she did and how proud he was of her.

Maybe Noelle was bringing her parents' dog to the show. His mind raced with all the things he could say to her and what it would be like seeing her. He wondered if they were ever going to be able to get things back to the professional relationship they'd had before.

And he spent plenty of time cursing himself for ever letting his feelings take the driver's seat. She was his employee, and he'd decided long ago when he first started being attracted to her that he was never going to let anything happen. And then he did and ruined everything.

He shouldn't have been surprised, though. How could he not fall in love with her by spending time outside of the office with her? Still, he should've made different choices. He owned the company, so it wasn't like he could stop being her boss.

His heart leaped when he spotted Noelle's parents walk into the gym with their black lab, Captain, at their side, dressed as Rudolph and pulling a tiny sleigh. It took a bit for them to make their way around all four sides of the gym and to where he was sitting, but when they got close, he stood up and went to them to say hello. They said hello to Aiden and Bailey, too, and said how much they liked her costume.

"Is Noelle here?" Feelings of hope were caught in his chest.

But they both gave sad shakes of their heads. Then her mom said, "Her gran-gran had a little tan and white terrier named Daisy, and Noelle and Gran-gran used to work together on a costume and dress her up every year for this event. Daisy passed not long after Gran-gran did —this is our first Christmas without her. Between that and…" She didn't say whatever came after the "and," but it was clear that she meant Jack ending things earlier today. She cleared her throat. "Well, it was just too much."

He closed his eyes for a quick moment. He'd stopped things right before an activity that was probably already so difficult for her. He didn't want her to feel bad and wished he could go to her and comfort her without making things worse. "Is she okay?"

Her dad lifted a shoulder in a shrug. "Not yet, but she will be."

Her mom reached out and gave his hand a squeeze, looking at him like she was trying to impart something to him. Courage? Hope? Forgiveness? He wasn't sure. All he knew was that it wasn't a look of harsh judgment like he deserved. "It's good to see you, Jack, Aiden, Bailey. I hope we get to see you around again soon."

As they turned and left, he suddenly remembered their Christmas Eve plans, which also happened to be Noelle's birthday plans. He, Aiden, and Rachel had all been invited to the big dinner and celebration. It hadn't hit him until just now that he was ruining Rachel's and Aiden's Christmas Eve plans, too. And he ended things with Noelle just days before her birthday.

He'd gotten them all into quite a mess, and he had no idea how to get them out. He ran his hands over his face.

Aiden tugged on his coat. "Why is Noelle not okay?"

"It's just been a really tough couple of days, buddy."

He nodded like he understood. Then he said, "Well, then we should do something to make things better."

"I know. I just wish I knew how."

NOELLE

NOELLE ROLLED over in bed and looked at the clock on her phone. She really needed to get up and get ready for work. Could she call in sick? No. She'd sent an email to everyone at work—all eight of them, including Jack—to say that she was ill on Tuesday, which she never did. She loved her job too much for taking time off. But her heart hurt enough that she definitely hadn't been well enough to go in.

She still felt like she wasn't.

She had thought of letting everyone know that she was sick yesterday, too, but her workload was too big to skip a second day. And since today was the final day before Christmas break, she really had to go in. She couldn't leave all of her work for her co-workers. So she forced herself to get out of bed and to get ready.

She knew she had promised herself to drive down Main Street by today, but she just couldn't. Not now.

Her birthday was tomorrow, and she was going to be twenty-six. She had kind of figured that she would be married by now. Maybe even thinking about having a kid. Not still single. And the first guy she had been interested in for quite a while was completely unattainable.

Not that it was a reason for being sad about her age or thinking she hadn't accomplished things. She probably wouldn't have even thought about it at all if it wasn't for the fact that she had fallen for Jack so entirely and wanted him in her life.

HER WORKDAY ENDED up mostly being the same today as it had been yesterday. She'd tried to pretend that everything was fine, but everyone seemed to know that she wasn't okay. And it wasn't just Bridget and Lennox who had noticed. She had mostly managed to avoid Jack at work, but apparently, he had been pretending that everything was fine and failing at it, too, because everyone was talking about it.

And although they weren't saying anything, they were definitely putting two and two together and realizing that her and Jack being simultaneously *not fine* probably meant that they weren't fine because of each other.

Noon rolled around, which meant it was time for their Holiday Sendoff celebration. They all headed into the conference as their catered meal was brought in, and everyone prepared to socialize before taking off work and doing whatever it was that they were doing for the holidays. She couldn't avoid Jack there.

They all took seats around the big conference table that they usually had meetings at like it was a big family dinner, both Jack and Noelle pretending to be fine. But there was a tension in the air surrounding everyone.

After they all dished up their food, she attempted to lighten the mood by saying, "How about we go around the table and tell our favorite something. Like our favorite holiday song or holiday movie."

"Or our favorite person to spend the holiday with," Lennox said, clearly attempting to decipher the situation.

"No," Jack said with enough authority that it left no room for negotiation.

"Oh...kay," Lennox said. "Favorite movie, then."

As they went around the table, saying what their favorite movie was, Jack looked across the table at her with a longing that matched her own.

If they felt the same way about each other, it was

stupid that they should both be miserable and apart. She pulled out her phone and texted her sister, Becca.

Noelle: Can I come over after work and talk with you and Corbin?

Becca: Of course! Come at 6:00 if you want dinner, 7:30 if you want ice cream.

NOELLE PUT a spoonful of ice cream in her mouth and savored the candy cane-flavored goodness as Corbin got their one-year-old out of her high chair, and Becca used a cloth to wipe all the ice cream off their three-year-old's mouth before he ran off to be crazy with their two older kids. Then her sister and brother-in-law joined her at the table in their beautiful home, the halls fully decked, Christmas music playing over the speakers, each of them finally getting to their bowls of ice cream.

Corbin got a scoop of ice cream on his spoon, then looked at it for a moment and said, "I'm guessing you're here about your boss," before he put the ice cream in his mouth.

Becca added, "And you're wanting our opinions on dating him since we've both worked in human resource departments."

"Wow, you guys are smart."

"That's why they pay us the big bucks," Becca said, winking.

"Okay, then, I have a question. Is it illegal for a boss to date an employee?"

"Illegal?" Corbin asked. "No. But it might be against your employment contract and could get you fired."

"It's not in my employment contract. So couldn't we just date?"

"What does he think about it?" Becca asked.

"He thinks we shouldn't. Like it's an ironclad law that shouldn't be broken. But I know that he really wants to date—I can see it in the way he looks at me. And I want to date him, so I just don't think we should let obstacles stand in our way."

Becca's eyebrow rose. "Does he seem like the kind of guy who would go against his beliefs to get what he wanted?"

Noelle let out a long breath. "No. Not even a little bit."

"Overcoming obstacles in a relationship is a good thing. So is respecting what's really important to the other person. He obviously cares a lot about his company—and he should! He's got what? Seven employees?"

"Eight."

"They all depend on him to make good choices for his company. He depends on it, too."

"I just don't see how our dating would be bad for the company."

"Okay, look at it this way," Corbin said. "If the two of you dated and fell in love and didn't keep it a secret, how would all of your coworkers feel about it?"

She thought about it for a moment. It had been a natural instinct to keep things with Jack quiet at work. Was it because she didn't believe her coworkers would be thrilled to know that they were dating? Both Bridget and Lennox had acted a little wary at the slightest hint that there was something between them.

"And how would you feel when you got a raise or a promotion or anything like that—maybe something you had been working hard for since the day you started working there—and everyone assumed that you only got it because you were dating the boss?"

Oh. Yeah, that wouldn't be awesome. She hadn't thought about that.

"Jack is smart to have strict rules for himself about dating one of his employees," Becca said. "Just think about breakups—they can get messy. And if they do, they can take a company down. But not only that, it can be nearly impossible to keep away from the appearance of favoritism. Even if someone is determined to not show favoritism, it can creep in without them even noticing. And that can greatly affect the morale of all the employees."

Noelle leaned back in her chair, stunned. She hadn't thought about any of those things at all. Ever since Jack had told her the story about how he'd never looked at his parents' marriage and felt that he wanted that for himself someday, she had kind of assumed that he was letting fear stop him. She covered her face with her hands. "I judged the situation so wrongly."

Then she sat up straight, dropping her hands from her face. "And I was the one to kiss him. *I* initiated that. The hand holding on the hayride, too. He had said that he couldn't get involved with me after the hayride, but I ignored that and still kissed him the next day."

Becca reached out and gave Noelle's hand a squeeze. "There was a lot you didn't know at the time. You can't beat yourself up for that. Plus, I think he might have been letting his heart take charge a bit, too."

"Maybe." She ran her spoon through and through her ice cream, making designs in the partially melted cream but not really seeing them. "But I do have the power to change things."

Corbin cocked his head to the side. "Are you talking about your job? You *love* your job."

"I do. But if you think about it, it all comes down to one question: which do I love more—my job or Jack?"

sixteen

JACK

JACK WALKED INTO THE OFFICE, unlocking doors and turning on lights as he went. Yes, it was Christmas Eve. No, he hadn't planned to work. But there was work here he could do, and he couldn't be at home all day, thoughts of how many people's Christmas Eve he'd ruined running on a loop.

Or how he had managed to find the perfect woman, the only one he'd ever imagined having a life with, the one who made his entire being happy to be alive, yet lose her just as they were getting started.

Or how he wanted to spend every single occasion with her—extraordinary or ordinary—but he had closed himself off from celebrating Christmas Eve and her birthday with her.

Or was he just not looking deeply enough for a solution? He wandered through the main office area, running his fingers along each of the desks as he meandered. Maybe he could hire a manager to run the day-to-day business, and he could take a step back. Could he give all of this up? Not be a part of it all? Could he find someone who would care about the business as much as he did? And if he did, could he pay them as much as they would be asking?

As he was thinking through the logistics, a thought popped into his mind. *Even if you did, you would still be her boss.*

A frustrated growl escaped his mouth. There had to be a way. He couldn't experience a glimpse of what life would be like with Noelle and then just live life without her. She had changed him. Now that he knew what was possible, he knew he couldn't turn his back on her. He had to find a way.

He turned to head back to his office, then stopped at Noelle's desk. A single hand-painted card was leaning against her monitor. He picked it up to get a closer look—it must be one of the cards she'd received from her gran-gran. He couldn't believe she'd left it there over the break. A woman—probably her gran-gran—was with someone who had to be Noelle. Christmas decorations filled the background of the scene. Noelle held in front of her a big cupcake with a lit candle on it. Her cheeks were full of air, her lips making an O as she was preparing to blow out the candle.

He turned the card over.

Only the most special people are born on Christmas Eve. You celebrate the day with all you've got!

Every year.

He put the card back and went into his office.

An hour later, not only had he not come up with a solution, but he had barely made a dent in the emails he was trying to get through. His senses went on high alert when he heard what he thought was a door opening. None of his employees worked today, and the building's cleaning staff wasn't in, either.

He was just standing up to go check on everything when Noelle appeared in his office doorway. "I thought I might find you here."

"Noelle. Why are you at work today?"

She stepped forward and held out an envelope. "I just came to give you this."

He took it from her hand but didn't so much as glance down at it—he didn't want to take his eyes off hers. "What is it?"

"My resignation letter."

Oh, no. Had he messed up so badly that he made her want to quit? "You know I can't accept this."

"I need you to."

He swallowed, afraid to ask the question but needing to anyway. "Why?"

"Because I think I might be in love with you."

He was too stunned to move.

"And I think that you might have been feeling the same things over the past few weeks, too."

"I've been feeling them over the past year and a half." The words were quiet. He couldn't believe they actually came out of his mouth.

Her eyebrows shot up. "*A year and a half?* Why didn't you ever tell me?" She paused. "Oh. Right. Because you are my boss." She gave a single nod like maybe pieces in her head were clicking into place. "Which is exactly why I need you to accept my resignation. Because now that I know what it's like to have you in my life, I don't want you to ever not be in my life."

Emotions pricked at his eyes. "I can't ask you to do that." He set the letter on his desk.

"Ahh, but you're not asking me, so it's okay."

"It's not, Noelle. You can't just quit your job for me. I'll—"

"Jack," she said, stepping forward and putting a hand on his forearm. "I appreciate you being all chivalrous and wanting to fix this, but you can't. It's *impossible* for you to fix this. Sure, you could be the one to quit, but then I would still be out of a job, and so would the seven other people who work here. Or you could change who you are as a person and ignore your rules about dating an employee, but I don't want you to change. I love you exactly how you are."

She took another small step forward. "But it's not impossible for me to fix it."

He looked down at the envelope on his desk, running a finger over the corner of it. He hadn't expected this at all and was so not mentally prepared for it. "You're the best ad copywriter that we've ever had."

"But I'm not the best one there is, so you're going to find someone else, and they're going to be awesome. Now here are the terms of my resignation. I'm not giving a two-week notice because I don't want to wait that long to see you again. But feel free to hire me as an independent contractor for two weeks to cover my job while you find someone new if you'd like. I'll be my own boss then, so there won't be any boss/employee anything going on."

He chuckled and shook his head, looking down at the ground. Could this really work? And if it did, would he always feel guilty that she had to leave because of him? "So you haven't started looking for another job yet?"

"Um, it's Christmas Eve."

"What if you don't find something?"

"Jack, I've been copywriting since I was old enough to talk. I'm going to find something quickly. Trust that I'm strong enough and capable enough to make this choice."

"I've seen you work, and I've seen you play. I know that you're more than strong enough and capable enough."

She smiled, and there was something else behind it. A playfulness. A confidence. Maybe even adoration. "You've got my resignation letter. It's up to you to choose whether to accept it or not. I'll know your answer by whether or not you show up for Christmas Eve dinner tonight."

Then she turned and walked to the doorway. She stopped right before going through it and turned her head just enough for him to see her cheekbone. "But tell Rachel and Aiden that they're welcome to come whether or not you do."

And then she left, and he stood there in the middle of his office, grinning so big it made his entire body happy.

seventeen

NOELLE

NOELLE FINISHED SPOONING the seasoned panko breadcrumbs on the brie-stuffed mushrooms, then glanced in the direction of the front door for the fiftieth time. She wasn't only glancing when she heard people come in or out anymore—she was glancing every time she thought of Jack, which was about every four seconds, apparently.

"Ugh," Makelle, Hope's six-year-old daughter, said as she tried to turn the strips of pie crust dough into a lattice but kept getting mixed up on which one should be pulled back for another one to be laid down beneath it. "This is so hard!"

Noelle wiped off her hands on her apron. "Would you like some help?"

Makelle held up her hand like a stop sign. "No. You

can't help with your own birthday cake! Besides, my mom says it's good to struggle because that's what helps you to grow. And I really want to be taller because this girl in my class, Trisha, has me beat, and she's not even nice. Don't worry—I've got this."

Noelle chuckled and glanced in the direction of the door again. Still no Jack. The place looked amazing, though. The big tree in the family room never looked better. Garlands were hung over every doorway, every side table and the mantle was decorated, the gingerbread train was moving around its tracks, Christmas music was playing over the speakers, and all of her family was surrounding her.

She should feel like she had everything she needed. But there was a particular pang of longing. A hole that wasn't filled. And that hole was Jack-sized.

"He'll come," Hope said as she reached around Noelle to grab the tray of mushrooms to slide them into the oven. "He has to."

She set the timer on the oven and took a breath. Based on their conversation in his office earlier today, she knew he would come. So why was she so nervous that he wouldn't?

"Happy birthday to Noelle," her five-year-old niece, Sadie, shouted out.

A chorus of voices shouted in return, "And to Noelle, a good night!"

Noelle grinned, held onto her Santa hat with *birthday girl* stitched into it, and took a slight bow as Sadie giggled.

Noelle went over to the big dining room table and helped Julianne to set it. She loved setting the table for this meal because they used the special white Christmas plates with the red rims, the white tablecloths, the red napkins with the red and white striped rings, the fancy crystal goblets, and the greenery down the center of the table that she and Gran-gran had picked out together.

She wished she hadn't left the cards from Gran-gran at work. She wanted them home with her, especially over Christmas. She'd realized she'd forgotten them at the end of work the day before and had meant to grab them when she'd gone to give Jack her letter of resignation earlier today, but she'd had so many other thoughts in her head then that she'd forgotten. And it wasn't like she could've just gone back at that point and seen Jack again after the way she left things.

The doorbell rang and her seven-year-old niece, Erika, jumped up to go get the door. She heard adult shoes stomping off snow, so she hurried over to the side of the family room by the stairs so she could see down the short hallway to the front door.

It was Rachel and Aiden, brushing snow out of their hair and off their coats before they stepped inside. She stood on her toes and peered around them but didn't see

Jack. Erika said, "You can put your coats right there," and pointed to the couch in the living room, then she skipped back to the family room.

Noelle gave Aiden a hug. "Oh, I'm so glad you two came!"

"Me, too," Aiden said, then added, "Santa is coming tonight, *and* it's even snowing!" Captain had heard them come in, too, and was wagging his tail. Aiden gave the dog a big hug around the neck, then ran to join her nephews.

Then she gave Rachel a hug. "You look like you're feeling pretty good."

She smiled. "It's been a good day."

Noelle swallowed and couldn't put off asking any longer. "Is Jack not coming?"

Rachel gave a little shrug. "I think he's planning on it. He was still at work last I talked to him, so I told him a neighbor was heading this direction and could give us a ride. I'm sure he'll be here soon."

She nodded and walked with Rachel into the family room.

"Whoa! This place is magical," Rachel said as she looked around in wonder.

Noelle looked around, too, with fresh eyes. It really was. She was lucky to be able to spend her Christmases here.

Rachel looked at her and must've been able to sense

her nervousness because she put a hand on her arm and said, "He'll come."

She nodded and went to help the others with the last-minute preparations in the kitchen. But by the time they all sat down to eat, Jack still hadn't come. She was starting to believe Rachel's and Hope's encouraging words a little less.

The sound of people chatting and the excitement of Christmas Eve filled the air as everyone passed around the plates of maple bacon Brussels sprouts, prime rib, mashed potatoes, stuffed mushrooms, and baked vegetables. But next to Noelle was an empty seat, and she felt that emptiness deep in her soul. Jack's absence made her realize exactly how much she longed to have him at her side and how much she enjoyed every minute of being around him.

Why wasn't he there? Did he decide he didn't want to be? Did something happen to make him not be there? Would he have told Rachel if he wasn't going to come, or was she just as clueless about the situation as Noelle was?

He had seemed that he wanted to accept Noelle's resignation and date her when she'd laid her heart out for him earlier today. She should've just waited for his answer then, instead of letting everything come down to tonight. Then she wouldn't be dealing with all this nervous anticipation right now.

"Happy birthday to Noelle," Porter shouted.

Everyone else replied with "And to Noelle, a good night!"

She grinned at everyone, even though she wasn't feeling it. Now that she'd experienced having Jack in her life, it no longer felt right to not have him there.

As they were all finishing up the meal, she saw Rachel, seated two chairs down from her, pull out her phone. She held her breath, hoping that it might be Jack and that Rachel would immediately turn to her with news.

But instead, Rachel just set her phone down and turned back to her conversation with Corbin, who sat on her other side. Noelle's shoulders slumped a bit as she exhaled and pulled out her own phone, checking to make sure that there weren't any messages that she hadn't felt come in. There weren't.

She turned to Aiden. "What do you hope Santa brings you for Christmas?"

"Paper," Aiden said while driving half of a Brussels sprout on the end of his fork around his mashed potatoes like it was a racetrack.

"Paper?"

"Yeah. I used all we had making snowflakes, and I want to make some more."

She chuckled. "You're a cool kid, Aiden."

Corbin stood up and put his napkin on the table. "I

just realized that I forgot something we need for dessert. I'm going to go get it."

Everyone looked at him in confusion.

"It's Christmas Eve," her mom said. "You're not going to find a place that's open. What did you forget? I'm sure we can come up with something or do without."

He shook his head as he headed toward the front door. "No, it's important. We really need it." And then he rushed into the living room, and a moment later, they heard the front door open and close.

Noelle pushed some of her own food around her plate. She just wasn't feeling so hungry.

"Is everyone done?" Katie asked. "I'm super proud of this year's video, and I can't wait for you all to see it!"

Everyone carried their plates to the kitchen and cleaned them up, then went to the family room side of the room and piled on the couches and floor, leaning against the sofas and legs. As everyone snuggled into each other, Noelle felt the loss of Jack even more, even though she had a nephew on one side of her, a niece on the other, and two nephews on her lap. She would give anything to be able to snuggle into Jack right now.

The video started with a screen saying *An Allred Christmas*, then went to her mom, who was standing in the kitchen, with everyone working on their gingerbread train cars in the background. "One of my favorite things about Christmas is family. You are all a huge part of what makes this holiday so special."

Then her dad, obviously on the night of the Mystery Santa Hat activity, said, "I love you all. I want you to know that. I also want you to know that I still plan to take home the trophy tonight for Best Meal. That spot on our mantle has gone too long without a trophy, so we plan to give it all we've got."

A few of her siblings, siblings-in-law, nieces, and nephews told a few things about their favorite Christmas things or things they loved about this year, then it cut to Aiden. "And I heard Mom tell Mrs. Sowards that she was glad that Jack asked Noelle for help because Jack has been more smiley since he started hanging out with Noelle. And she thinks that he's pretty much in love with her. You know, the kind of love where there's kissing and marriage and sneaking food off each other's plates."

Everyone in the room laughed and commented and clapped at Aiden's clip, and Aiden beamed. Noelle's face flamed just as red now as it had when she'd heard Aiden say it during the hayride.

Then the video cut to Jack, and she sat up straight. "I didn't know you interviewed Jack!" It looked like it had been filmed the night of the hayride, too. She wasn't even sure how it had happened without her noticing. It was when they were at her parents' house, but she wasn't sure if it was before they had left or after they'd returned.

"It's hard for me to express how much I appreciate you all opening up your home and your traditions to Aiden and me and Rachel. This has all been unlike anything I've experienced. I grew up with all celebrations at Christmastime being non-existent. I thought I was fine without any of that because it was just the way things had always been. And I *was* fine.

"I didn't know how much I had needed things like this—family, traditions, acceptance—until you showed it to me and healed a part of my heart that I hadn't known had been broken."

Tears were falling down Noelle's face, and Weston turned from where he sat on her lap and said, "Are you sad?"

Someone passed a tissue down the couch to her, and she took it and dabbed at her eyes.

"I have loved seeing how much joy all of your traditions brought into Aiden's life as well. And I have loved seeing Rachel's face when Aiden tells her all about it. I know it has meant the world to her to know her son got to experience so many wonderful Christmas traditions. I will be forever grateful for you all."

The tears were streaming now, and she heard more than a few sniffles from everyone else. Now Tommy had turned in her lap to watch her with concern on his face, too.

The front door opened, and twenty heads all turned in unison to see who it was. "All right," Corbin said, "I got what we needed for dessert!"

And then he moved to the side, and Noelle saw Jack standing at the door, stomping the snow off his boots. He carried a couple of packages in one arm and a bouquet of beautiful red, green, and white flowers in the other, and she desperately wanted to be next to him.

As she extricated herself from her niece and nephews and the kids sitting on the floor who were using her legs for a backrest, Jack had made his way to where her mom had stood to welcome him. He handed her the flowers and said, "These are to say thank you for hosting tonight and for inviting us."

She thanked him and gave him a hug, then Corbin took the two packages from him and set them on a side table.

Then Noelle got free, stepped between what seemed like a dozen legs outstretched on the floor, and breathed, "You came" as she finally reached him.

He looked at her with the softest, sweetest eyes and said, "I wouldn't have missed it for anything. I got slowed down a little bit on the way here—a car slid through a traffic light and crashed into me."

Noelle gasped, grabbed hold of his arms, holding

them out, and stepped back a bit, checking him over for damage.

He let out a soft chuckle. "I'm okay. The people in the other car are okay. The paramedics checked us all out and gave us the green light to head home. Our cars, not so much. But the people are okay." He smiled. "It looks like it's my car's turn in the shop while I drive a rental."

She wrapped her arms around him in a hug, so overcome with emotions that he was okay. And he was here. But then she heard the slightest *oof* of air escape him, and she pulled back. "Oh! You're injured."

"I'm okay. I'll probably be feeling it a bit in the morning, but I'm okay." He reached for her hand and tugged her a little closer.

She gazed into his eyes, trying to decipher what he was thinking, especially after hearing what he'd said during the hayride. "I saw your interview in Katie's video."

"Oh yeah?"

Noelle nodded.

"That was for your family. There's more I wanted to say to you."

She leaned in a bit closer like she was being pulled. "Like what?" Her words came out a little breathier than she'd intended, and his eyes shifted quickly to all the people she knew were behind her before they came back to her eyes.

She should probably offer to take him into the living room or something so they could have a private moment. But he was here, and he was safe, and he was looking at her with those amazing eyes of his, and she didn't think she could move her feet if she tried.

"Like how much I love that when you really smile, you get a dimple right there. Like now. And the way your eyes crinkle when you're amused. And when you bite your bottom lip ever so subtly when you're thinking or considering something new. And how you raise your left eyebrow slightly more than the right just before you share a brilliant idea.

"And the way you cock your head just slightly to the side when you hear someone talk about something that happened to them or when you notice someone is down, right before you jump in and do something to help. The way you look out for others. The way you put your all into everything you do.

"You are always so open with your emotions and your life, which has been both a blessing and a curse for me because it means that I've been falling in love with you every day for the past year and a half."

She blushed and looked down. Had he really noticed all those things about her? What had *she* been doing at work all this time? Except for the last few weeks, when she'd been hyper-observant of everything about Jack, she felt like she'd spent the year and a half before that being remarkably *un*observant and not nearly good enough for this man, despite all the kind words he said about her.

Then, like he could read her mind perfectly, he said, "I wasn't showing you the same courtesy you were showing me."

Her eyes flew up to meet his.

"I have kept myself professional and closed off at work because I think I should be." He took a deep breath. "A lot of people get an idea about who someone is and have a hard time seeing anything differently. Thank you for being willing to see beyond the only face I ever showed at work, even at times when I really didn't want you to see beyond that. In these past few weeks, it has felt like you could see straight to my heart."

His eyes were looking at her so earnestly, his voice slightly gruff, like the emotions behind what he was feeling were coming through. She felt all those emotions, too. "I haven't ever had anyone be that way with me. To see past the things that most people would see and be judgmental about, then not go any further.

"But you were never judgmental. You saw the real me, and, probably without even realizing what you were doing, you gave me permission to be the real me. I'm grateful for that because it has made me feel like I could open myself up to love. And I can tell you that I've never been as happy in my life as I am when I'm around you."

He gave her a smile that was sweet and soft and made happy fluttering in her chest.

"And I think I might be in love with you, too." He smiled that smile that she had seen so often over the past few weeks. The one she loved so much because it felt like it was only for her. "In fact, I'm sure of it."

She grabbed him by the front of his coat with both hands and pulled him in close. "You, mister, are one very amazing man, and I'm sure I'm in love with you, too." Then she pressed her lips against his. She wanted him to wrap his arms around her and maybe even lower her into a dip and kiss her like he had in the living room when they'd been decorating the tree.

But she knew that her entire family was currently right behind her, probably all leaning forward with rapt attention. So she pulled back quickly and grinned at him, a giddiness filling her to the brim.

Then she turned to face her family, which apparently gave them permission to stop watching in utter silence because a cheer went up from the entire crew, and they all stood and swarmed them in a giant, lopsided, very crowded group hug.

A few minutes later, they were all seated around the table. The seat next to her that had been empty at dinnertime was now filled with a man who had at one time seemed like a Grinch, yet now it was her own heart that felt like it had just grown three sizes.

Someone turned the lights out, and her mom carried a piece of caramel apple pie on a plate toward her, the candle in it glowing brightly in the darkness as everyone sang happy birthday to her.

At the end of the song, Sadie shouted out, "Be sure to make a wish!"

She smiled at Jack. "I did, and it already came true."

"Well, if that isn't a Christmas miracle," her dad said, "then I don't know what is."

Noelle chuckled, then blew out the candle.

JACK

IT HADN'T MATTERED that Jack had spent twenty-seven Christmases not ever experiencing a Christmas Eve that he enjoyed. In a single night, tonight had made up for all of them. Aches from the car crash and all.

After the festivities had started to die down, Noelle had grabbed a thick blanket off the back of the couch and motioned for him to follow her out to the back patio. He'd picked up the present he'd brought for her and followed her into the snowy night, setting it on a small table. He would follow her anywhere.

They had been standing at the edge of the patio, blanket wrapping them both, for a good twenty minutes, watching the snow softly fall, their breaths making little puffs of clouds. The moonlight shone across the snow, giving everything an unearthly, magical glow.

She looked up at him from where she was snuggled in at his side. "I thought this Christmas would be terrible. Thank you for making it the best." Then she leaned her head against his chest, and he just wanted to stay like that forever. It didn't even matter that it was cold or that his back still hurt from the wreck.

"Oh!" She said, turning in the blanket he held around the two of them so that she was facing him. "You brought out a present for me!"

He chuckled and removed the blanket from around the two of them before placing it around her shoulders and walking to the small outdoor table shielded from the snow and picking up the package.

He leaned in close to her and whispered, "Happy birthday," before placing the package in her hands.

"Oh. It's heavy."

She set it back down on the table and started carefully opening the wrapping paper to reveal a plain brown box. She looked at him in question, then lifted the lid and gasped.

She pulled the snow globe out of the packaging and held it up to admire it. The globe itself was set in a red lantern-shaped housing. It had a small motor that constantly set the water inside in motion, and with its interior light, the swirling glitter looked as if the snow was falling like it was just beyond the roofed patio where they stood.

She didn't seem to have any words, so he stepped in close, pointing out the figurines in the globe—it was of the two of them, decorating their snow and stars Christmas tree during the Mystery Santa Hat activity. "I figured that since your gran-gran and you had made a snow globe-themed tree that snow globes were important to you. I found someone who custom makes these, and she was more than willing to do an extremely rushed order."

She brushed her fingertips along the curved glass. "Jack," she breathed, "this is incredible. It's our own little scene!"

He smiled at the look of wonder on her face, thrilled that she liked it as much as he hoped she would.

He placed a kiss on her temple. "And I hope we have many more in our future together."

She carefully set the globe back into its packaging, then turned and brought her chilly hands to his face, letting the blanket fall to the patio floor.

Her kiss earlier had been quick and sweet. When she kissed him this time, she seemed to pour everything into it. Her kisses were soft and tender. When he put his arms around her and pulled her in close, she wrapped her arms behind his neck, her kisses became something more. A thank you, a promise, an acceptance of everything that he was.

From somewhere around at the front of the house, they heard jingle bells ringing, and Noelle broke the kiss just enough to whisper against his lips. "That would be my dad."

A sound erupted from the family room, just beyond the closed patio doors, and, keeping their arms wrapped around each other, they turned to look. All the kids were running around, grabbing things, all the parents were standing up, and everyone started hugging each other.

"We should probably go back inside," Jack said, but not before placing one last kiss on her cheek, just in front of her ear.

As soon as they opened the door, Aiden came rushing up to Jack. "Santa is nearby! We need to get home and get to sleep because he's going to be coming really soon!" The excitement coming off of Aiden was palpable and contagious. Rachel was right—he was at the perfect age for Christmas. He was glad that Rachel had pushed Jack to help Aiden experience it all.

"Okay, buddy. Get your shoes and coat on, and make sure you've got all of your stuff."

Then he turned back to Noelle. "I don't want to leave." He leaned in close enough that his lips were brushing her ear and whispered, "But I've got to go be Santa."

"I don't want you to leave, either. But I am going to enjoy picturing you doing that tonight." Noelle gave him a smile that made his chest soar. "You go. We've got forever ahead of us."

He gave her one last smile and kiss. "We do."

epilogue

NOELLE

One Year Later

Noelle stood by all the coats piled high on the couch in her parents' living room, picking up one at a time and handing it to its owner as everyone said their goodbyes to each other.

"Happy birthday to Noelle..." Aiden shouted out.

And then everyone else joined in the chorus, "And to Noelle, a good night!"

She smiled, just like she always did whenever anyone did that on her birthday. Especially when it was Aiden. The kid she now got to call her nephew. That made her smile even bigger.

Once they all made it outside and she and Jack were splitting off to head to his car while Rachel and Aiden veered off toward theirs, Aiden turned and called out, "We'll race you back to our house!"

"No," Rachel said, "we will drive the speed limit or under on the way back to our house. We don't want Uncle Jack to get in a Christmas Eve car crash ever again."

"Right," Aiden said. "Don't speed, Uncle Jack. And don't wreck."

Jack chuckled, then saluted Aiden. "You've got it, buddy."

As they pulled away from her parents' house, Noelle said, "I wish we could've been in our new house by Christmas. It would be fun to have Rachel and Aiden sleeping over at our place this year."

That had been their original plan. But owners of the home in Mountain Springs that they were buying had a delay on the house they were building, so now they weren't going to be able to close on their home until mid-January.

Jack reached out and entwined his fingers in hers—something she would never tire of feeling. "It's okay. This Christmas already has enough firsts—we can save *First Christmas in our new house* for next year."

"True." And the house they were buying was so perfect for them and so beautiful, and so close to both of their families. It was worth waiting for.

"This year," Jack said, his eyes darting to hers for a

quick moment before watching the road again, "is the first Christmas where I get to call you my wife."

"The first Christmas where I get to call you my husband. And the first Christmas where everyone on the hayride actually went to the church for our wedding instead of going caroling."

Noelle smiled at how perfect it had been. Her favorite activity led to her favorite day of her life.

Jack gave her hand a squeeze. "The first Christmas while you've been working at Anderton Advertising."

She had found the job quickly after she had quit working for Jack. And much to her surprise, she loved it. She thought she'd never find a place she loved as much as working for Jack, so it definitely eased the blow of not continuing to work for him.

"And the first Christmas where they put you in charge of planning the holiday party. And put you in charge of a million other things once they found out what a rockstar employee you are."

She chuckled. He always made her sound like she was more impressive than she was. Anderton's was a much bigger ad agency, so she often met with clients personally, which she still wasn't entirely used to. It made her wish he was there to introduce her to each new client because he always made her sound like she was capable of taking over the world. It gave her a boost of confidence every time.

"And," she said, dragging out the word, "this is the first Christmas where you had to be worried about the boss/employee relationship with Jess." Jess was the woman who had taken over her position after Noelle had quit a year ago today. As she was training her, she quickly became her best friend, so Jack hadn't quite gotten past having to navigate the waters of socializing with an employee outside of work hours.

"Yeah," he said dryly, "thanks for that."

She laughed heartily just hearing his tone. Then she gave his hand a squeeze. As they turned onto Rachel's street, she said, "It's our first Christmas seeing Rachel so healthy after being declared cancer-free."

Jack's smile seemed to fill his whole face.

"You really like that one, don't you?"

"I will never tire of seeing her so healthy. Ever." He pulled into her driveway just as Rachel pulled into her garage. "This is our first Christmas taking home the trophy for the best dinner."

"And I can't wait to put that trophy on our new mantle."

"Even though it's a trophy of the world's scariest-looking elf wearing an equally horrifying Christmas sweater?"

"Especially because it's of the world's scariest elf and horrifying sweater."

As they were both walking up to the front door, shivering in the cold, he said, "First Christmas where we know we'll be leaving the next day to go honeymoon in warm, sunny, not-at-all snowy Cancun."

Noelle moaned in anticipation. "I can't wait to soak up all that sun."

Before Jack opened the front door, he put an arm around her waist and said, "First Christmas where I get to say happy birthday to my wife." And then he planted a sweet kiss right on her lips.

Once they got inside, Aiden gave Jack his usual running starfish hug, then hugged Noelle, and they both pet Bailey as she nuzzled in between them all. They helped get Aiden to bed, read him the book *The Night Before Christmas*, then put out the presents when they knew he was asleep. After saying goodnight to Rachel, they got ready for bed and headed into the living room, where an air mattress was already blown up and waiting for them.

They shifted to get situated, bouncing each other on the air mattress with each tiny movement. Then, covers pulled up to her chin, Noelle lay her head on Jack's shoulder, snuggling into him. She turned her face toward his. "First Christmas where I get to wake up on Christmas morning right next to you."

He kissed her forehead and said, "Here's to many more firsts."

the christmas bet

one

RACHEL

RACHEL WALKED past the Christmas tree in the main area of the company offices and down the hall to the managing editor's office.

Since the door was open, she stepped in and plopped the book she'd been carrying down onto her friend Courtney's desk with a thunk, landing it right next to the figurine of Big Foot wrapped in Christmas tree lights, wearing a Santa hat. "I'm in. The bet is on."

For as much as she'd fought even reading the book in the first place, her chest was light and her heart was racing as she thought about actually committing to the bet. She'd wanted to let Court know all day, but their next magazine issue was a double, which always made their December workloads insane. She'd been scrambling all day to get the most urgent things done.

Courtney's eyes traveled from her computer screen to the book to Rachel's face before her hands got all fluttery and she picked up her desk phone. She pressed a speed dial button before putting it on speaker phone and placing the phone back into its cradle. Normally, when Courtney was behind her desk, she was the picture of professionalism—her clothes perfectly pressed, her brown hair in a bun, her expression exuding confidence, competence, and poise. But right now, she looked much more kid-at-Christmas than Managing Editor at *Memories not Dreams* magazine.

Of course, once Court stepped out of the office, she typically showed off the part of her personality that had bought the Christmas-obsessed Sasquatch sitting on her desk.

The moment Rachel heard the word "Hello?" come from the phone's speaker, she knew that Courtney had called their friend Lucy.

"Have you left for the day yet?"

"I'm in the middle of leaving—just stepped off the elevator. Why? What's up?"

Courtney looked at Rachel, excitement in her eyes. "Come back up. Rachel just said yes to the bet."

Rachel crossed her arms and rolled her eyes as Courtney ended the call. "This is not that big of a deal."

Court stood and made her way around the desk. "Yes it is, and you know it."

Okay, yeah, she knew it. Saying yes to new things was far outside Rachel's comfort zone and wasn't going to be easy. Maybe she was just saying it wasn't a big deal to make herself believe that she could do it. That it wasn't going to be so hard.

Courtney picked up the book, *A Year of Yes*, and ran a hand over the cover before meeting Rachel's eyes again. "So you read the whole thing?"

"I did." It had taken her an embarrassing amount of time to finish. Her son, Aiden, was only six, so by the time Rachel saw him after work, he was dying for her attention. As a single mom, her to-do list was always a million miles long, so it wasn't like she could just sit down and read during daytime hours. And by the time she finally fell into bed at night, she often only got a paragraph or two read before she fell asleep with the book still open.

But for a book that suggested doing something that was the very opposite of her nature, she *wanted* to do what it suggested and say yes to new experiences. On her own, though, she knew it was something she'd never convince herself to commit to, so maybe it was good that her friends were pushing her.

Lucy hurried into the office and shut the door behind her. She was panting, like she'd run the whole way, her dark bob of hair a little messier than normal, her eyes wide with excitement. "You're going to do it? I can't believe that you sat at the desk next to mine all day and didn't say anything!"

Back when Rachel was the office assistant instead of a graphic designer, she had become good friends with Lucy. It had thrilled her that she got to sit next to Lucy once she'd taken on her new job. As impossible as the task sometimes seemed as a single mom, Rachel tried to be on top of everything in her life. By contrast, Lucy was the definition of a "hot mess," which was, admittedly, rather refreshing to be around. It kept Rachel feeling balanced, somehow.

"I don't get why this is such a big deal for you two," Rachel said. She got why it was a big deal for herself— just not why her friends wanted her to do it so badly.

Courtney and Lucy shared a look before Court said, "You need everything... controlled. So this kind of thing is just a bit unusual for you."

"Oh, come on. I'm not *that* bad." Right? They didn't live in her head so they didn't really know how much she liked things organized and predictable. It couldn't be that obvious to others.

Lucy's eyebrow rose. "You sewed dividers into your purse."

"Okay, that's not controlling. That's *practical*."

Lucy folded her arms. "And you put labeled tabs on each divider like it's a filing cabinet."

"If the three of us raced to see who could grab a

fingernail file out of their purse the quickest, who do you think would win?"

Courtney didn't even answer. She just said, "And let's not forget the Daily List on your phone."

Oof. That felt like a shot straight to the list. That thing was important and needed to be defended at all costs. "I have a lot to stay on top of. If I didn't have everything scheduled down to the minute, it wouldn't all get done."

"And then there's the Monthly Plan," Courtney said.

Lucy pointed to Courtney. "Oh, and the Yearly Plan."

"Okay," Rachel said, holding her hands up, begging them to stop before they started talking about her house cleaning list or her closet organization. She'd always loved being organized. But after what felt like a very long, grueling fight with cancer before her last scan six months ago showed no cancer, when practically everything had been out of her control, she craved being in control now more than ever.

And, okay, she had been noticing lately that it maybe wasn't always the best mindset to have, especially because she didn't want Aiden to miss out on things. Which was the only reason she was entertaining her friends' bet. "Can we get back on topic?"

"Yes," Courtney gave a single nod. "Like I mentioned when I first gave you the book—*months* ago —I think a year of saying yes to things is too much.

Baby steps are good. Are you ready to have a Christmas Season of yes?"

Rachel swallowed down her worries. "Yes."

"You don't have to say yes to the same thing more than once. This is all about trying new things and opening yourself up to new possibilities. If you try something and hate it, you're not obligated to say yes again."

Rachel nodded. That was good. She could do this.

"So you'll say yes to *everything* this Christmas?" Lucy asked like she was trying to get her to swear under oath or something.

"I mean not everything. I still have to be a responsible parent."

Courtney cocked her head. "Do you, though? Hear me out. Let's say Aiden wants dessert for dinner. Is saying yes one time going to be the worst thing ever and doom him to an adulthood of not being a productive member of society?"

Okay, okay. Perspective. That was what was going to get her through this season. Looking at the big picture. Because she wanted to say yes to more things. To live a bit more spontaneously. But she still wanted to be responsible.

"And you don't have to say yes to anything dangerous," Lucy said. "Like if a man dressed in a dark hoodie says, 'Hey, you should walk down this shadowy, sketchy alley and I'll sell you a knock-off Prada Galleria Saffiano

Double-Zip Tote Bag for fifty bucks,' you don't have to say yes to that."

"So I can say no to being ax murdered. Got it."

"And who knows?" Lucy said. "Maybe one of those yeses will bring you to the man of your dreams." She wagged her eyebrows.

That thought was laughable. "Do you really think now is the right time? When I'm so busy I can't even seem to fit in something as quick as putting in earrings in the morning?"

Lucy lifted a shoulder in a shrug. "Love is like Jell-o. There's always room for it."

Courtney clapped her hands once. "We need stakes! I can't believe we forgot the stakes. What happens if you don't follow through, and what happens if you do? We can't just have a bet for a bet's sake. There has to be consequences."

The three of them stood there in a circle—or, really, a triangle—looking at each other.

"If we were guys," Rachel said, "we would already have this part figured out."

Lucy raised a finger like she was pointing at the light bulb that just went off above her head. "I've got it! If you stick with it and say yes to everything that isn't dangerous—"

"—at least once," Court cut in.

"—then we will give you a day of pampering to die

for. If you don't, then we drive to the Wal-Mart in Littleton, go to the middle of the store, and you have to belt out Whitney Houston's *I Will Always Love You* at the top of your lungs. Deal?"

"And we get to film it," Courtney said.

Rachel bit her lip. Could she commit that fully? She really couldn't sing. At all. But that day of pampering did sound pretty glorious. And she really wanted to be more spontaneous, so maybe having something as motivation like belting out a song that no one other than Whitney Houston or Dolly Parton could pull off might be just what she needed.

Her eyes went from Courtney to Lucy, back and forth, as she tried to decide if she could. Then she tried to shake all her fears out of her head and let herself make the crazy choice. "Deal. The bet is on!"

As soon as Court's and Lucy's cheers died down a bit, she said, "And guess what the first thing is that I'm saying yes to? Getting that wreath at The Home Improvement Store that Aiden was begging me to buy. I've already called the babysitter to see if she can stay a few minutes longer."

Courtney gave Lucy a look before turning her gaze back to Rachel. "I see you're living large already."

It *was* living large. For her. She glanced down at her watch. "Oh—I've got to go! I am so behind schedule!"

WHEN RACHEL GOT to the last stoplight before Main Street, she pulled up the Daily List on her phone. She had so much to do. Being a single parent was hard all year, but it was especially hard at Christmastime. She took a deep breath. She could be a good mom to Aiden and still get everything done.

When the light changed to green, she turned onto Main Street. It wasn't completely dark yet, but the lights that draped overhead from one side of the street to the other were on, and all the Christmas decorations in front of the shops were lit with their own lights. It reminded her that she hadn't managed to get her decorations up yet.

It was on her Monthly List, though. She had it scheduled, so it would happen.

She parked, grabbed her purse, and glanced at her watch as she speed-walked into The Home Improvement Store. Since she already knew right where the wreath was, she could just hurry to the aisle, grab one, race to the self-checkout, and she'd be pulling into her driveway not too much later than the time she'd told Bria, the sixteen-year-old who picked Aiden up from school and stayed with him until Rachel got home. Aiden was going to be so excited when she showed up with the wreath that seemed to speak to his soul.

Once she was inside the store, she turned right down the main aisle. This was no Home Depot or Lowe's—Mountain Springs wasn't big enough for that—but they sure tried to be. She passed by the aisle of electrical supplies, past plumbing, past the paint department, and then turned the corner to seasonal.

The display of wreaths with the colorful bulbs and bells sat at the end of the aisle, and a man's cart was literally caught up in them. It looked like he'd maybe turned a corner, gotten stuck on one, then the other wreaths took the opportunity to join in on the fun.

The man was good-looking, too. He was wearing a light blue polo shirt and dark wash jeans, both of which fit him extremely well. His hair was a wavy auburn and one lock curled down just above his very frustrated expression. It was actually kind of endearing, seeing him covered in Christmas like that. Maybe Lucy wasn't so off when she said that the Season of Yes could bring a man into her life. She was going to say yes to helping him out of the mess.

She headed toward him to help just as he tried to free his cart from the decorations. The rest of the display came down on him, covering him in wreaths, their bells jingling up a ruckus and causing not only everyone nearby to stop to watch, but even brought people from other aisles to see what was going on. A woman with a toddler in the cart stopped, and the toddler put both hands over his ears to block out the noise.

The poor guy's face was reddening and the harder he tried to break free from the holiday embellishments, the worse it seemed to make things. She was maybe a dozen feet from him when the man seemed to summon herculean strength and shouted "Stupid Christmas decorations!" as he threw his arms out, sending wreaths flying.

One of the wreaths came straight at her, like a missile targeted on her. She ducked, covering her face with her arms, but it still hit her right in the forehead before falling to the floor with a tinkling clatter. It hadn't hurt at all—the clanging sounded so much worse than it actually was. Bulbs clinked and bells rang, but the thing was fairly light-weight.

She picked up the wreath. It was *not* a stupid Christmas decoration, and his saying so made him so much less attractive. If she was going to meet a guy in her Season of Yes, it wasn't going to be this guy. After growing up with a dad who hated everything to do with Christmas and wouldn't let any of it into their home, she wasn't interested in a Grinch.

No matter how good he looked in that polo.

"I'm sorry," he said. He looked like he was going to

take a step toward her, but the mound of wreaths surrounding him stopped him.

She just held up the wreath and nodded. "Thanks."

Then she turned and headed toward the registers and away from the Christmas-hating man.

two

NICK

NICK WALKED out of The Home Improvement Store with barely a sliver of dignity intact. He opened his trunk, put in the gallons of primer and the bag of painter's tape, tarps, spackle, and the wreath inside, then shut it and got into his car. He couldn't believe all that happened during an innocent trip to the hardware store. He ran his hands over his face, let out a long, slow breath, then picked up his cell phone.

The background image on his phone was a picture of his wife, Clara, that he'd taken just two weeks before she'd passed away. He'd been on a business trip and just like he and Clara did every business trip, they'd video-chatted at night.

She'd already taken off her makeup and had her hair pulled up in a messy bun— something she only did in the evenings—and she had loose strands framing her face. She'd looked beautiful. He'd snapped a screenshot so he'd always have it, not knowing that it would be one of the last times he'd ever video chat with her.

Like he did whenever he felt like he needed to talk to Clara, he swiped to the last page of apps on his phone, a page with a single icon, so he could see more of her face. It kind of felt like he was actually video chatting with her, and hopefully, anyone walking by would assume he was on a video call, not just that he was talking to his dead wife.

"Hi, Clara. I'm in Mountain Springs right now, and I don't know if you've ever noticed when we've visited your parents before, but the home improvement store is actually named *The Home Improvement Store*. Those are the exact words on the building. So when you're talking to someone and say, "Bye, I'm going to the home improvement store, they don't know if you're saying it in lowercase or title caps."

He chuckled. "But since you grew up in the next town over, and I doubt that Nestled Hollow has their own home improvement store, you probably already knew that. But if that's the case, then we should've laughed about this together before now.

"I've told you that I hope that in heaven you get to watch what's going on down here like it's a TV show. If you do, I hope you were watching what just happened in there and that you were busting a gut from laughing so hard at it. Because if nothing else, I want someone to be able to laugh about it."

She probably laughed. She was probably chuckling about this conversation, too. He shook his head. "But Clara, I was kind of a jerk in there. I felt like such an uncoordinated fool, and everyone was watching and the cursed jingle bells just wouldn't stop jingling. I shouted something negative about Christmas decorations, but I'm ninety-something percent sure I didn't swear. And I should get some kind of gold star for that because I really wanted to swear—it was that bad. And then I sent a wreath flying and tagged some poor woman right in the head with it. I felt awful."

He paused for a moment and looked down Main Street at all the decorations each store had out for Christmas. Colorado Springs—where he and his six-year-old daughter, Holly, had lived until just recently—put on a pretty good display of Christmas, but nothing like Mountain Springs did. Even though Mountain Springs was probably one two-hundredth of the size, this town went all out.

He looked back at the image of Clara. "You always made Christmas so magical. I don't think I ever fully recognized all you put into it. Now that it's all my job, I realize that I have no idea how to do the same. I was at the store getting paint supplies for the new house and figured I'd just take a little stroll down the Christmas aisles to see what caught my eye. And Clara, I barely turned onto the first aisle and the decorations practically attacked me."

Now *he* was laughing at the ridiculousness of it all. He scratched his forehead with his thumb. "Anyway, I just wanted to say that I miss you. Holly misses you. Last Christmas I was still so buried in grief that I did a terrible job at making Christmas good for Holly, but I want you to know that this year, I'm going to find a way to make it magical for her. I even bought one of the wreaths after I extricated myself from them, so I've taken the first step. If you can, maybe jingle some bells near me now and then. I'll consider it you cheering me on."

He gave her one last smile, then turned off his phone and pulled out of his parking space. His last "video call" with Clara was a week ago, as he told her that he and their daughter had moved near Clara's parents as she had always hoped. Well, technically they were living *with* her parents at the moment, but the house he'd bought was just a block away.

In the week since they'd moved to Mountain Springs, he'd fixed the plumbing and some electrical issues on the new house and started cutting and installing baseboards and trim. Before long, he'd be able to paint and replace some flooring. He didn't care how hard he had to work, he would have the house ready for him and Holly to move into before Christmas.

He pulled up at his in-laws' home, which had lights on the house and trees and a manger scene out front, even though December first wasn't until tomorrow. The house he'd bought was still completely empty and didn't have a shred of Christmas decorations, so he was glad they could stay with Ben and Linda for a bit so Holly wouldn't be missing out.

When opening the door, he was immediately greeted by the smell of pot roast and... was that baking cookies? As much as he wanted to finish getting his new house ready, he couldn't deny that Linda's cooking was a huge perk of staying with them. When he got to the kitchen, Linda was at the island counter, decorating sugar cookies with Holly, and Ben was sitting at the kitchen table, reading on his tablet.

Their rough collie intercepted Nick on his way to his daughter, her long fur bouncing as she ran, then she gave a single bark, so he used both hands to scratch her head before making his way to Holly. He hugged his daughter from the side, careful not to mess with the bag of frosting in her hands. "What are you two up to?"

"Well," Holly said in her best cooking channel voice, "we decided that cookie cutters are very common, so it was up to us to use our creativity and decorate the cookies more uniquely."

It always made him chuckle when his daughter used that voice. Maybe because the words always sounded like they came from someone older than six, even if the tone didn't.

"So instead of an ordinary bulb for the circle ones, we added a marshmallow to the top of this one—doesn't he look like a melting snowman? And we decorated this one like a wreath. And see this one? We think it was supposed to be a sweater, but we turned it upside down and made it a kid throwing their arms up on Christmas morning because they're so excited."

"I love them all. Nice work, Hollybear!"

His daughter's hair was light brown, like his wife's, but it had his curls. He kept his hair fairly short, but he sometimes wondered if his would be as curly as his daughter's if it was as long as hers.

Linda slid an odd-shaped cookie—a bell, maybe?—across the counter to Holly. "Sweetie, why don't you make a surprise decoration on this one for your dad? Grandpa and I just need to talk with him for a minute. Anything goes. Make it as creative as you'd like. Just keep lassie-dog from stealing any."

"Grandma, her name is Rosy!"

Nick glanced between his in-laws. Why did he suddenly feel like he was in trouble? Nick kissed the top of Holly's head. "I'll be right back."

He followed Linda into their front room, where both

Ben and Linda took a seat in the armchairs. He suddenly didn't feel like sitting, so he just leaned against the display table in front of the window, arms folded, facing them.

Ben and Linda both looked at each other, then Ben said, "We might as well just say it. We think you should start dating again."

Nick sat up straighter, putting his hands on the table at his sides. "What?" Of all the things that ran through his mind that they might want to talk to him about, that was the furthest thing away. "Why?"

Linda leaned forward a bit, too. "I don't think that Clara knew she was going to die last fall, but she must've sensed it on some level because she mentioned a few things she wanted to have happen if she did pass away before us. One of them was you getting remarried."

Nick knew that. Clara had mentioned it to him, too. He'd laughed it off at the time, saying that it wasn't going to happen so she would just have to live forever. But Clara had said, "No, I'm serious—Holly needs a mother, even if it can't be me, and you need a wife." It had been too hard to think about, so he'd just put it out of his mind.

"Your daughter needs a mom," Linda said, echoing his thoughts of his conversation with Clara so close that it was eerie. "As time goes on, she'll need one more and more, not less."

"Are you saying that you don't think I'm doing a good enough job trying to be both parents to her?"

"That's not it at all, son," Ben said. "You're doing everything you can. That's helping. The dog is helping. We are helping."

"But there's not a whole lot that can replace a mom in a little girl's life," Linda finished.

He knew that. He did. But he loved Clara, and he couldn't imagine loving someone else like that again. "I don't think I'm ready."

"I know," Ben said. "It's hard to imagine that you'll ever be ready until you meet the one who will be your next love. You might think you can never love again, and then you'll meet your Linda." He reached across the space between the two armchairs and squeezed his wife's hand.

Nick had almost forgotten that Ben had been married before. He'd known that Ben's first wife had died in a car wreck after they'd been married only a couple of years. Before they'd had any kids. He just hadn't thought about it in a long time. But Ben was right—Nick wasn't sure he could ever love again. It just felt… weird to even try to imagine it.

"For about a year when Clara was about Holly's age," Linda said, "Ben worked overseas and only came home once a month for that full year. Now, I know it's not the same experience as having a spouse pass away, but I did often feel like I was single parenting." She paused for a long moment, then said, "and I know how lonely it got."

Her words hit him in the chest pretty hard. He felt busy all the time trying to balance work and home life. He always felt like he wasn't doing enough as Holly's only parent and as the only adult taking care of all the things they and their home needed. But as busy as he was, there still seemed to be plenty of time for him to feel those pangs of loneliness very acutely.

"You've got a fresh start here," Linda said. "You're no longer living in the home you shared with Clara, so—"

Nick shook his head. "No. Now I'm living in the home she lived in as a junior and senior in high school and with the parents who raised her."

"That's just temporary," Linda said. "You know, I can set you up with someone if you'd like."

"I am not having my *deceased wife's mom* set me up on a date."

"*I* can set you up with someone," Ben said. "A couple of guys I work with have daughters—"

"Why are you two even okay with the thought of me dating again? You should be freaking out that one day I might 'replace' your daughter."

Ben shook his head. "No one can ever replace Clara."

At least they agreed on that.

"Remember when the two of you got married?"

Linda asked. "Ben told you 'Welcome to the family,' and I said that I now consider you my son?"

Nick nodded. He'd choked up at the time.

"That didn't change just because Clara is no longer here. We still love you like a son, which means that we care about you and want what's best for you. Holly is our only grandchild, and we want what's best for her, too. You staying single forever isn't what's best for either of you."

They both kept quiet for a long moment while Nick let their words sink in. Objectively, he knew that they were right. If a friend were in his position, he would suggest the same thing. But seeing someone else go through losing a spouse and going through it yourself were two different things. He never could've guessed all the emotions that would hit him along the way.

Besides, how was he supposed to just find someone who would be okay with marriage being tied to motherhood of a six-year-old? And how was he going to find someone who was going to instantly be a great mom?

"You and Holly are all we have left," Linda said. "And we want you both to be happy."

Even though there was a wall between him and it, Nick looked in the direction of the kitchen, where he could hear the muffled sounds of a Christmas song that Holly was singing loudly, Rosy doing her best to bark backup. He always tried to do what was best for his daughter and do it all by himself. But maybe doing it all himself wasn't actually what was best for her.

And what about what was best for him? He no longer even knew what that was. He definitely didn't have that figured out.

He looked back at Linda and Ben. "Okay, I'll think about it."

Ben nodded once. "Good man. Now give me a hand and pull me up, will you?"

RACHEL

RACHEL OPENED her front door and called out, "I'm home!" She'd barely set her things on the small table by the door when Aiden came running down the hall toward her, their golden retriever, Bailey, hot on his heels, the babysitter close behind.

As he neared, he leaped into the air and landed on her, giving one of his patented "starfish hugs." Her son was getting bigger all the time—and faster—so she had to make sure her feet were firmly planted or he would knock her over. But after that year of being too weak for his starfish hugs, she wasn't ever going to ask him to stop.

"Hey, buddy! Guess what I got on the way home?"

He slid to the ground, so she turned and grabbed the

bag from the table and pulled out the wreath. Aiden looked at it with the same sense of wonder and admiration he'd had when they'd seen it in the store together, but this time, his expression also contained amazement at it being in their house. He ran a finger across one of the red bulbs, then turned to show it to Bria. "Isn't this the best wreath you've ever seen?"

"It sure is."

Aiden looked up at Rachel. "Can we hang it up right now?"

"Of course!" She opened the front door again, then lifted him so he could place it on the hook himself.

When she set him down, he stood back, admiring it. Then he turned his grin on her. "Thanks, momma!" Then he gave her a tight squeeze.

She didn't have a lot of money to spend on frivolous things, but this had been a good choice. Her Season of Yes was off to a good start. She grabbed her purse and the book off the table, and as they headed back toward the family room and kitchen, she said to Bria. "Thank you so much for staying later."

"No problem." Then, as Aiden raced into the family room with the dog, Bria added in a low voice, "He didn't have the best end to his school day. He was pretty upset when I picked him up."

Rachel set her things on the counter and thanked

Bria for letting her know before the girl grabbed her keys and headed out the front door. She opened the door of the fridge and looked inside as the exhaustion of the day started setting in, wishing she'd see a fully prepared meal just magically waiting for them. Maybe she would have to work some more meal prep into her Weekly Plan.

At least she had the meal planned and it was a fairly easy one. She pulled out the half of a rotisserie chicken, a package of tortillas, some grated cheese, and a jar of barbecue sauce. The barbecue sauce was key because if she used it, she could sneak in quite a few diced bell peppers without Aiden complaining, and she had a partial red one and half a green one.

As she gathered everything, Aiden told her a story about his friend, Quinton, and a small hill at school where the fields gently sloped down to the playground. "And we figured out that if we lay on our backs and lift our legs like this," he said, lifting one knee and wrapping his arms around it, "then we can slide down the hill on the snow! Did you hear that? We used our *coats* as a *sled!* It was the greatest thing ever. And then all the other kids saw us doing it and so they started doing it, too, and we basically started a new thing. I bet if we could be out there at the same time as the fourth and fifth graders, they'd be doing it, too."

Every day when she got home from work, Aiden told

her about his day at a million miles an hour, barely stopping to take a breath, and all she could do was nod and show the right facial expression. There was no space to even comment until he got enough of it out.

She dumped her armful of ingredients on the counter, then Aiden said, "Hey, can I help?"

"Always."

He stepped up on the stool, washed his hands, then scooted the stool to the counter she stood at.

As they worked and his stories paused without mentioning the end of the day, she eyed him. "How was the rest of school?"

His little shoulders dropped immediately. "Not all the way great."

That was a new thing Aiden was doing lately that she loved. Everything was related to the word "great." He was "extra great," "kind of great," and "mostly great"—how much changed, but the word "great" was always there.

"You want to tell me about it?"

He let out a huff and turned on the stool so he was facing her. "I know you told me to be nice to the mean girl because she's new and hasn't made friends yet, but she just makes me so mad!"

"Aiden, what happened?"

"I was nice to her *all* day. And she was being nice to

me, too. Then, right at the end of school, none of that even mattered. Miss Goodrich said she needs parent helpers to make the chimney and living room for our Christmas program for when we all say *The Night Before Christmas*. And momma, guess what? In class today, I only messed up on one line!"

"Good job, buddy." She gave him a high five.

"When the bell rang, I went up to my teacher and said that you could make the set."

A bolt of panic struck her. "Me?"

Aiden nodded. "I told her that you design things for your job, that you're the best at it, and that you can pretty much make anything. But Holly had gone up to talk to Miss Goodrich, too, and she said that you *weren't* the best and that her dad could do it better."

She didn't know Holly's dad at all or anything about what he could or couldn't do, but just thinking of her very full Monthly Plan made her guess he probably *could* do it better. Besides, what did she know about making set fireplaces? Not only did she not have tools for that kind of stuff, but she wouldn't have a clue of how to even start. Her design skills began and ended with digital creations.

"As sweet as it was to say all those nice things about me, honey, that seems like a really big job and will take lots of parents' help. This should probably be headed up by someone who's done this kind of thing before. Maybe Holly's dad knows what he's doing."

"Mom, did you hear what I said? She said that you weren't the best!"

She was probably right. "I know, honey. It's okay. Her dad is probably pretty good at that kind of stuff."

Aiden turned back to the roasted chicken and started pulling off chunks of meat with a little more force. "But she's trying to get him to take over everything."

Rachel pulled out the cutting board and knife and started dicing the chicken. "Holly hasn't even asked her dad about it yet, so you don't know if he even can. And honey, I don't know if *I* can. I'm working so many extra hours and trying to get ready for Christmas…"

Aiden brought his hands together, pleading. "Please, Mom? Please say yes." He hopped off his stool and went to the table to grab a paper. Then he came back and put it in her hand.

She looked down at the flyer that now had chicken fingerprints at the top and started reading about the program and how they could use volunteers. The mom guilt was getting heavier and heavier with each passing moment. But she also knew that she couldn't take on much more than she already had on her plate.

She glanced over at Aiden, who was still looking at her with hopeful eyes, the chicken in front of him all but forgotten. As she studied his expression, she tried to guess what was behind his insistence that she help. It was probably because of last Christmas. She had been going through the most intense parts of chemotherapy during the holiday season, which made her unable to do their normal traditions.

And beyond that, since she had changed job responsibilities a few months ago, she'd been working more hours to try to get her feet on the ground. Aiden was only six. He probably just wanted assurances that she would be around this year to make the season special.

But was volunteering for a project so big—a project she had very little experience with—really the right way to do it? It was such a huge commitment, and if she dropped the ball at all, it would impact a lot of people.

She glanced at her phone and could picture her Daily List and her Monthly Plan. They were already so full. The words "no," and "I'm sorry" nearly came out of her mouth.

But then she spotted the book half tucked under her purse. It hadn't even been two hours since she'd made a bet with her friends that she'd live a Season of Yes. This was exactly the kind of thing the bet was supposed to get her to say yes to.

She took a long, slow breath, and then turned to her son. "Okay, I'll tell Miss Goodrich that I'll help with it. And we'll make it awesome."

"You're the best!" Aiden said, wrapping his arms around her waist in a tight hug.

She hugged him back and smiled at him, knowing full well that she now had chicken handprints on her back.

NICK

NICK TOOK a bite of the roast beef as he watched his mother-in-law and daughter work on decorating the last few cookies. When he'd told his work that he wanted to move to Mountain Springs, they had been gracious enough to allow him to work from home four days a week. As a software developer, it was a fairly easy job to work remotely.

But they still wanted him to come in one day a week to meet with clients and his team and to coordinate with quality assurance. Those days were the hardest, because his commute was an hour in each direction on a good day, making his work day so much longer. Linda, Ben, and Holly might've already eaten when he got back from in-office days, but having a warm meal that he didn't have to prepare waiting for him when he returned was a luxury that he was going to miss when he and Holly moved into their new home in a few weeks.

"And," Holly said, dragging out the word, "done!" She held up her most recent masterpiece, which looked like Mrs. Claus with a hand up, waving. Nick was pretty sure that the cookie shape was intended to be a mitten, with Mrs. Claus's arm as the thumb.

"Nice!" Nick said. "I give this one fifty-seven stars."

Holly tilted her head. "Out of how many?"

"Fifty."

She pumped a fist. "Yes! I knew I'd get over on this one!"

As Nick walked over to the sink to rinse his plate, he asked Holly, "Want to go to the new house with me tonight to patch some holes in the walls? We can go on a hunt to find every last spot that needs fixing."

"You know it," she said before hopping down from the bar stool she'd been kneeling on. "I'll go get my stuff."

Holly was nothing if not a seeker of adventure. Of course, she was in.

Linda watched as Holly skipped out of the room, then turned to Nick. He worried for a moment that his mother-in-law was going to bring up something more about starting to date again, but instead, she said, "That will be good for her. Just so you know, she came home in a mood. The cookie decorating distracted her, but you should probably still ask about it."

Nick's attention flew to Linda as his chest tightened. "Do you know why?"

She shook her head. "Something at school. She said she would only tell you, but if I had to guess, something happened with that same boy."

THE NEW HOUSE was only a block away, but he, Holly, and Rosy still drove there. It was very cold, very dark, the sidewalks looked very slippery, and his trunk had more things than they could carry in a single load, including several gallons of primer. Besides, it was a little too chilly for the dog's paws.

When he opened his trunk, he grinned at Holly. "I know we aren't planning to decorate for Christmas until we move in, but what do you say we get a head start?" He pulled from its bag the wreath with the bulbs and bells that he'd bought and showed it to Holly.

She took the wreath in her hands, looking at it in awe. Then she ran with Rosy, the dog's yips of excitement matching Holly's, and she reached up, standing on her tippy toes, stretching her arms way up, to get it hooked on the nail that was pounded into the wooden door.

The look Holly gave him as she grinned back at where he stood by the trunk and the happiness on Rosy almost erased the bad memories of getting attacked by the blasted things in the store.

Well, maybe not *almost*. "Partially" was a better word.

Once they had all the supplies carried inside, Holly stood beside him in the family room with her hands on her hips, staring at the wall, just like he was. Except for the tools and supplies that seemed to be multiplying in the home the more days he worked on it, the place was empty and every sound they made echoed off the walls and hardwood floors.

"Okay, what we're looking for are holes like these." He stepped up to the wall and ran a finger over a nail hole, then he pulled a putty knife from the tool belt he wore. "To fix it, we just put the corner of this into the Spackle and get a little on. We only need about this much. See? Then we just push it into the hole, like this, and then lay the knife flat to scrape off the extra. Got it?"

Holly nodded, her eyebrows drawn together in serious focus.

"Okay, you try this one." He moved the step ladder just in front of a second nail hole, then handed her the putty knife. It wasn't too difficult a task for her, and based on the proud grin she gave him when the hole was no longer, she was going to love what they would be spending the next hour or so doing.

Plus, he figured it might help her get more invested in the new house and claim it as home. He was sure it wasn't easy for her to leave the home she'd spent her entire life in. He'd grown up not being exposed to home improvement stuff at all, but Clara had. Her parents were quite the DIYers, so when he and Clara had bought their first house, Clara had total confidence in picking up a saw, a hammer, a wrench, a drill, and a million other tools, and he wanted Holly to be exposed to the same thing.

He put a roll of blue painter's tape on her arm like a bracelet and told her to start filling holes and if she found anything bigger than the tip of a pencil to tear off a piece of the tape and stick it to the wall right by the hole. And then when she was finished, she could start filling the finishing nail holes in the baseboard that he'd installed yesterday.

As Holly filled a second hole that she'd found and he worked on patching a bigger hole beside the fireplace, he asked, "So, what happened at school today?"

The nice thing about Holly was that she was always willing to spill whatever was on her mind, no coaxing needed. All he had to do was open the gate.

She held up one finger as she concentrated on scraping the excess spackle from the wall, then turned around to face him, fists on her hips, getting a dab of white spackle on her pants where the putty knife in her hands bumped up against it.

After opening her mouth to speak, she closed it, then took in a deep breath. "Remember how you're always saying that it's important to help people? Especially the ones who really need it?"

He nodded slowly, wondering where this story was going that ended with her being upset.

"Well, I want you to remember that you always say that because I'm about one minute away from asking you to help my school make a living room for our program." His eyebrows rose, and Holly stayed quiet for about five seconds before saying, "Will you help make a living room for my school?"

"You want me to make you... a living room?"

"Not a real one, Dad! A fake one. With a fireplace with an opening big enough for Santa—a first-grade one — to crawl out of, with stockings hanging on it. Those can be real. And then, I don't know, a chair and a rug or something."

"Hollybear, I'm not sure I can—"

"You've got all the tools. You can use that saw you've been using for the baseboard and that other saw that's more growly and we can buy paint and I don't think it'll be too hard for us."

"I know. But there's a lot of work I've got to finish on this house so we can get moved in before Christmas."

"This is important, Dad!" Her face was so full of emotion that it surprised him.

He set down his mud pan and drywall tool then lifted her off the step stool and sat on the plastic drop cloth-covered flooring with her. "Okay, okay. Talk to me about why it's so important to you that I do it."

She gazed at the window that didn't have any blinds or curtains. With as dark as it was outside, all it showed was a reflection of the mostly empty room. Then she met his eyes. "Remember that kid I told you about?"

"The one who said he could make the best paper snowflakes?"

She nodded. "My teacher said she needed parent helpers to make the set for our Christmas program, and I was going to tell her that maybe you could help because you're fixing up an entire house. But Aiden beat me up there and he said that *his* mom would be best at it. Can you believe he said that? Like my mom couldn't do all that when she totally could have!"

"Oh, Holls," he said and pulled her in for a hug, wrapping his arms around her little shoulders. It couldn't be easy losing a mom at such a young age.

"So I told him that you'd be better at it than his mom is." Her words came out muffled against his shoulder.

He pulled back. "Holly."

"I know. I wasn't 'winning friends and influencing people,' like grandpa Ben always says I should, but *please*, Daddy. Please make the living room for us. I know it's not the same as mom doing it, but I have to show Aiden that he was wrong about her. Please?"

Nick wanted to help her. He knew he needed to do more to fill in the gaping holes left by a parent who had passed. And he wanted to do everything he could to help her not be so sad that her mom wasn't there for all of it. Could he even do this, though? Add one more thing to a long list of things to finish before Christmas?

He could. He could somehow find a way to make it all work and be awesome for his daughter when she needed him to be.

"Okay."

Holly sat up straighter, her eyebrows raised in hope. "You'll do it?"

He nodded, and she wrapped her little arms around him in a hug, which made him feel pretty great. He might not be able to give her all he wanted to, but he could give her this.

When she pulled back from the hug, she said, "I miss Mom. Can I video chat with her on your phone?"

He looked at her, confused. Holly understood that her mom was gone.

Then she gestured to the phone at his waist. "You

know, the picture you have of Mom on your phone. I've seen you talk to Mom on it."

Heat rose to his cheeks just knowing that his six-year-old caught him talking to a picture. He pulled out the phone. "You know it's not really her."

"I know. But it helps, right? It seems like it helps."

He swiped to the last page of apps and handed the phone to Holly. "I think it does."

"Hi, Momma," Holly said while looking at the screenshot, her voice full of emotion that grabbed his heart. "I miss you. We are in our new house, just fixin' things up. Check it out." She turned the phone around, so she was basically showing the picture to the walls. "And Dad's even letting me help search out all the nail holes and fill them. Mom, I'm making them practically disappear!"

She showed the picture of the tool she was using, then she turned the phone back to face her and said, "I know you're watching over us, and I think you'll really like watching us in this house. Well, I better get back to work! Love you lots and lots, Momma."

She pressed the button to turn off the screen, then handed the phone back to Nick and said, "You're right. It does help."

Holly went back to her job of filling the nail holes, this time in the baseboard, humming a tune she was probably making up. It amazed him how quickly she could bounce back from such strong emotions.

As they worked, Nick couldn't seem to get what his in-laws had said out of his mind. Now seemed as good a time as any to bring it up with Holly.

"So," he said, spreading the last of the joint compound on the hole repair, trying his best to act nonchalant, "your grandparents think I should start dating again. How do you feel about that thought?"

Holly shrugged.

"Come on. You always have an opinion about everything. What's your opinion about this?"

She was quiet for a moment, tilting her head as she slowly moved the putty knife over the baseboard. Then she turned around to face him. "Mom said you should."

"She did?" He wondered if Clara had told Holly and her parents to prepare them, just like she had with him, or if she had only gone to them after he'd brushed aside her request like it could never actually happen. Maybe she knew he'd need outside encouragement to someday date again.

Holly nodded. "She said I'd need a mom, even if it couldn't be her."

"And how do you feel about someday getting a new mom?"

"I think," she said, dragging the words out like she was trying to figure out her thoughts as she went, "that she wouldn't really be my mom, so it would be kind of weird." She bit her lip for a long moment. "But maybe it would be nice to have someone who is *like* a mom, you know? Someone else who can love me and help take care of me. It might be weird. But maybe I'd like it." She pointed the putty knife in his direction. "Only if she's nice." She waited another moment before asking, "Would it be weird for you, too?"

Holly wasn't always perceptive, but when she was, she never shied away from asking the hard questions. Questions he didn't have the answers to.

"I don't know, Hollybear. Maybe we'll just have to figure all this out as we go along."

He looked down at the gold band still on his ring finger and wondered if it was maybe time to retire it.

five
RACHEL

RACHEL PARKED in the nearest parking stall and hurried into the school. She had told Bria not to worry about picking up Aiden since she planned to be there the moment that class got out. Instead, she had to call the school to get a message to Aiden's teacher that she would be fifteen minutes late. She thought she'd be able to get off work early enough, but then a client had an issue with the layout of an ad that was super urgent, and there she was, looking irresponsible to her child's teacher.

She turned down the hallway that led to Aiden's classroom and saw him standing in the hall outside his door, arguing with a girl she could only assume was Holly. Not that they were being loud enough for her to hear what they were saying, but their rigid postures and clenched fists at their sides said that it wasn't exactly a pleasant conversation.

She hurried down the hall, but before she reached them, Miss Goodrich and a man came out of the classroom.

"Whoa," their teacher said. The woman was probably in her late thirties and for spending all day with a couple of dozen six-year-olds, was always dressed immaculately and her hair was always pulled up neatly. She was the most organized person Rachel had ever met. "What is going on here?"

The girl pointed at Aiden and said, "He's being mean" at the same time Aiden pointed at her and said, "She's being mean."

"Okay, I think you both could use a moment to cool down while I talk with your parents. Follow me."

The man stayed in the hallway, and as she neared, they met gazes. So he was the girl's dad who Aiden said was trying to "take over" the project. Somehow, she hadn't put two and two together and imagined he'd be present at this meeting to talk about the project, also. She gave him a small smile of commiseration that their kids' attentions were currently being redirected to avoid them fighting, making it feel—at least to Rachel—that she and Holly's dad were getting called to the principal's office.

As the teacher got the kids seated at desks away from

each other, working on a word search paper, Rachel tried to figure out why the man looked so familiar. She didn't have time to figure it out, though, before the teacher rejoined them in the hall.

"Rachel," Miss Goodrich said, "this is Nick Stewart, Holly's dad. Nick, this is Rachel Meadows, Aiden's mom."

She suddenly realized why the man—Nick—looked familiar. He was the guy trapped in the Christmas wreaths at The Home Improvement Store. *Great.* She would be working on a Christmas set piece with a Christmas hater.

Nick looked like he was about her age, fairly tall, nice build. He had auburn hair that was long enough on top that it showed that it had a slight curl. It was a color she didn't see often on a man but went so well with his skin tone. And his eyes were striking. They were the color of the sea on a cloudy day, with a rim of darker blue, leaning toward teal. And right now, she was seeing the concern in them.

Miss Goodrich brought her hands together in front of her. "You probably already know that your kids aren't getting along with each other so well."

Rachel nodded.

"I've been worried that Holly isn't making new friends," Holly's dad said. "I thought kids forgave each other like two seconds after a disagreement and then were practically inseparable."

Miss Goodrich lifted one shoulder in the slightest shrug. "And maybe they'll get to that point. But I think other issues are going on that's stopping that."

Rachel could guess what Aiden's issues were. And they were probably all related to it being Christmastime and the fact that she was so sick from the cancer and treatments last Christmas.

"I've pulled them aside separately to try to get to the bottom of the issue. There might be multiple issues, but it seems like the big one is jealousy. And a bit of insecurity."

Rachel's eyebrows shot up and she pulled back in surprise. Nick's reaction mirrored hers. "Jealousy?"

"I hope I'm not offending either of you by saying this, but I do think you need to know." She turned to Rachel. "Aiden doesn't have a dad, right? He isn't in his life?"

Heat crept up Rachel's neck and she hoped she wasn't blushing. It was just a fact. A fact that rarely embarrassed her. But she normally wasn't in the position of talking with a teacher about an issue with her usually sweet, thoughtful son and getting called out on it.

She cleared her throat. "No. He never has been."

She was pretty sure that Nick just stole a glance at her ring finger.

Miss Goodrich held out a hand like she was presenting Nick. "And Holly has a dad who's always there for her."

The revelation shocked her even more than the jealousy comment did. Aiden's dad had never been in the picture. Aiden did have an uncle who he loved and who was great with him, though. She had always promised her son that she would find him a dad someday, but he had never even mentioned being sad that he didn't have one. Between that and the fact that Rachel had grown up with a dad who wasn't the nicest guy even when he wasn't drunk, it had somehow never occurred to her that Aiden would feel that loss.

Yet Rachel knew that dads were important and made a big difference in a child's life. She knew he needed one, but she hadn't realized he had gotten to the age where it had become so important.

She *did* want to find someone and get married. She *did* want him to have a dad. But like so many things as a single mom, it just never really fit into her plans.

Miss Goodrich turned to Nick. "Holly's mom passed away, right?"

Rachel sucked in a breath as a pang of sadness hit her. She found herself glancing at Nick's ring finger and the gold band that was there. He seemed to sense Rachel's gaze on it because he twisted it around his finger somewhat self-consciously before he pushed his hands into the pockets of his pants.

"Yes. Just before Thanksgiving last year."

Miss Goodrich gestured to Rachel. "And Aiden has a mom who does everything with him."

Nick shot Rachel a glance before looking back at the teacher. "You really think that's why they've been fighting so much?"

She nodded. "I do. I'll keep helping all I can at school, but I just wanted you two to be aware in case opportunities come up at home where you can discuss it with your child."

Both she and Nick nodded. She wondered if his head was as full as hers was right now.

"Now come in," Miss Goodrich said as she waved them into the classroom, "I got both of your papers saying you are willing to help with the set, so let's talk about the project."

Aiden and Holly joined the three of them at the table in the back of the room, and Miss Goodrich talked about their Christmas program. Rachel kept glancing at her son, trying to guess what was going on in his head, and had to force herself to focus on what his teacher was saying.

Miss Goodrich said that several parents had filled out the request for help form. Parents had offered a padded armchair and a rug for their stage living room, and some parents donated cash, so they should have enough for the supplies they needed to make the fireplace.

"Neither of you has a Santa costume that will fit a six-year-old, do you?"

She and Nick both shook their heads.

"That's okay; we'll get that taken care of. So all we need the two of you to do is to make a fireplace and chimney about four feet wide and about eight feet tall."

Rachel gave Nick a smile, mentally crossing all her fingers that this guy knew the first thing about making a large fake fireplace because she sure didn't.

APPARENTLY, what they needed was to have all four of them go to The Home Improvement Store and get a four-by-eight-foot piece of plywood and several two-by-fours, which Nick arranged with the store to have delivered to his house before the four of them set off to shop for the other supplies. Aiden and Holly wanted a brick fireplace, and they found some 3-D Styrofoam brick panels that looked like real brick and were lightweight enough that they wouldn't make the project unmanageably heavy.

"Okay, construction adhesive…" Nick said after he turned the cart onto an aisle with dozens of options. Rachel scanned the columns of products, trying to land her eyes on anything that said construction adhesive but finding nothing.

Holly picked one up, her eyebrows drawn together, and looked at her dad. "This is caulking, right?"

"What's caulking?" Aiden asked, tripping over the unfamiliar word.

Holly turned to him. "After you put in the baseboards, you squirt a line of this along the top of it and smooth it out all pretty. It makes that little space disappear."

Aiden turned to Rachel. "Disappear?"

"Not disappear," Rachel said. "It just hides it."

"Some of these are just used for one thing," Nick told both kids. "Glue or caulking. But some, like these over here, can be used for both."

Rachel just watched as Nick, crouched down on the balls of his feet, answered all of both kids' questions. He answered so patiently, too, even though the kids seemed to be in a competition for who could ask the most questions. And she watched Aiden's face as he ate up every single word that Nick said. Aiden hadn't even shown any kind of interest in home improvement or construction-type stuff before, so it wasn't like he finally had someone to answer his questions.

But who knew? Maybe he hadn't shown any interest because he hadn't been exposed to it before. He did enjoy doing crafty things—maybe this was just a bigger version of that passion. Or maybe he was just showing interest because Miss Goodrich had been right in guessing that Aiden wanted a dad in his life.

She tried to think back to her second impression of Nick—she'd already decided that she was going to pretend the first impression with the wreaths hadn't happened—when she'd hurried down the hall to where Aiden and Holly were arguing earlier. Had she noticed then just how attractive he was?

Yeah, she'd noticed. So maybe it was how adorable he was, crouched down and talking with her son that made her heartstrings stand up and take notice. This was her Season of Yes. She should say yes to being attracted to this man. It was practically part of the bet, right?

The man grabbed two tubes of what must be construction adhesive and tossed them into the cart with the panels and some screws they'd added along the way. Rachel took the break in conversation to ask what she'd been wondering on and off for most of the shopping trip. "What do you do for a living?"

"I'm a computer programmer. I help make the software used for many online courses."

"Software? I assumed you worked in construction." Especially because the first time she'd seen him, he'd been at a hardware store.

He laughed. It was a nice sound—the kind that made her chest feel instantly lighter. "No. Don't mistake my ability to explain caulking to a couple of six-year-olds for expertise. I know just enough to be dangerous."

"You're not dangerous, Daddy," Holly said, walking alongside the cart with one hand on it. She looked at Rachel. "He's not—he's really careful. We got a new house and he's redoing everything in it. It'll be all done just in time for Christmas."

Rachel raised an eyebrow. "It sounds like you know a lot about this stuff."

"My dad was in the military," Nick said. "And although we lived on plenty of bases all over the world that really could've used some home improvement, we never did any ourselves. But my in-laws practically built the house they live in, so my wife, Clara, grew up helping with every project imaginable. When we bought our first home—a place that had seen better days—Clara and I did all the work of fixing it up ourselves. I learned as I went."

He glanced down at his wedding ring, seeming... uncomfortable, was it? Self-conscious? Rachel couldn't quite tell. Either way, this was clearly a guy who was still grieving, and Season of Yes or not, she had no business checking out how nicely those shoulder muscles filled out his t-shirt.

"Look, Dad!" Holly said, pointing. "The wreaths! Let's turn down that aisle."

Nick chuckled as he rubbed the back of his neck.

"Uh, that aisle is dangerous to take a cart down." He shot a glance at Rachel. "Sorry for the other day, by the way."

She hadn't realized that he'd recognized her from that brief interaction. She figured his mind had only been on freeing himself from the wreaths. They were all hanging nicely on their hooks now. "I'm glad to see you and the wreaths both made it out of the tussle unscathed."

"Well, I wouldn't say *entirely* unscathed. My ego left here looking like it had been in a fight with an alley cat."

The expression on his face was adorable, and she couldn't stop looking into those striking eyes.

Nick cleared his throat. "So, when are you free to start working on this?"

Rachel opened the flap of her purse as they walked and pulled out the planner from the "records" tab. She glanced through the things they had coming up—and there were a lot of them—and only saw one opening over the next few days. "We are available tomorrow."

Holly put her hands together, pleading. "Aiden has a dog."

"Bailey," Aiden said.

"Can they please bring her, too? Then Rosy will have someone to play with."

Nick looked at Rachel and she nodded, so he told Holly yes. Then he scratched down his address on the note paper they'd been using as a shopping list and handed it to her. "Tomorrow it is."

Okay, tomorrow. She wrote it down in her planner. And since he was right next to her, she didn't write down what she knew she should—a reminder to not notice how attractive he was or what a good dad he was.

Of course, that ring on his finger was its own reminder that he was every bit as unavailable as if he was actually married.

six

NICK

NICK SANK onto his bed and adjusted the pillow against the headboard so he could sit up comfortably. It had been such a long day, and he was exhausted. But Clara's parents had gone to bed and Holly was asleep and he was finally able to crash in this temporary room of his. He opened his phone and flipped to the last page of apps so he could see Clara's picture and smiled back at her.

"Remember that conversation you had with me a month or so before you passed away where you said that if you ever died that I should remarry quickly so I wouldn't be alone and so that Holly would have a mom?" He gazed up at where the corner of his room met the ceiling for a moment before looking back at the phone. "I'm sorry I completely blew you off at the time.

You probably needed me to say that I understood instead of just saying that your death wasn't ever going to happen.

"I like to think that you had the same conversation with Holly and with your parents to prepare them, too, because that's the kind of thing you would do. If part of the reason why you told them was because I had ignored your plea, I apologize." He shook his head. "But between your parents, Holly, and Holly's teacher, I got your message loud and clear this week."

He shifted the way he was holding the phone so he could pull his wedding ring off his finger. Then he held it up between his thumb and pointer finger and just looked at it for a long moment.

He shifted his gaze back to the phone. "I think maybe it's time I stop wearing this. Actually, today it felt like it was time to stop quite a while ago, and I've probably been ignoring that, too. I'm hoping that seeing me take this off and taking the first step to moving on is making you cheer. I mean, in a way, it feels good to be making this step finally."

He paused for a long moment, not sure what to say. "At the same time, though, I don't know how I feel about it. I can definitely say there's not any cheering going on over here." He shrugged. "But somehow, it also feels right, if that makes any kind of sense. Even though I know this is what you wanted, it's still hard. Just know that I'll never stop loving you, okay?"

He twisted in the bed to pull open the drawer of his nightstand and placed the ring inside before pushing it closed.

"Goodnight, Clara." He turned off his phone and the lamp before readjusting the pillow and lying down, staring up into the darkness, praying that he could make it through everything that lay ahead of him.

NICK WAS glad that today had been a remote work day instead of one where he had to drive to the office. The day had been full of both meetings and deep focus work, but it meant that he was able to finish early enough for him and Holly to grab a bite of dinner before heading over to their new house with Holly's dog, Rosy.

When he heard the knock on his new door, he answered it, letting in a gust of freezing wind blowing with it the powdery snowflakes that covered everything. Rachel, Aiden, and their golden retriever were all shivering in the light of the porch, so he said, "Come in, come in."

"Hey," Aiden said, "you've got the same wreath on your door that we have on ours!"

Aiden shrugged out of his coat and handed it to his

mom, then he and their dog raced through the foyer and into the big kitchen, dining room, and family room where Rosy was barking her own hello.

"Welcome to our home that we don't even live in yet," Nick said. It felt weird to welcome guests into a home with no furniture—just empty, echoing spaces. He didn't have a coat rack or even a chair to put their coats on, so he added Rachel's and Aiden's coats to his and Holly's on the railing leading to the upstairs.

Rachel looked all around the area. "I love what you've done with the place."

"I've heard that a minimalist look combined with sawdust and accents of construction tools is what's in this season."

"I work at a magazine, so I've got some contacts. I think I'll have to put in a call to see if we can get HGTV Magazine to come spotlight the look."

He chuckled. "I've been told that I have the magic touch when it comes to home decor."

"I can tell by the wreath you chose for your front door."

His face immediately heated just thinking of their first interaction, before he'd known who she was and when he'd been trapped under an avalanche of the things. Luckily, though, she wasn't looking at his face. She put her hand on the trim that went around the opening into the living room. It hadn't had any until a couple of days ago. It still wasn't painted, but all the nail holes were filled and sanded and everything was caulked.

"Seriously, though, this looks incredible." she walked into the living room, glancing around at all the work he'd done. "You learned all this just by trial and error?"

"Well, in all fairness, the bulk of the errors happened at the previous house." The kids and the dogs were both racing around the open spaces. They sounded happy and occupied, so he asked, "Would you like the grand tour?"

Rachel appeared interested in the idea, so he took her up the stairs first. Maybe because he was eating up her praise and he'd put in a lot of work on that staircase and railing. As she looked around at the room that would be Holly's once they moved in, he said, "It's good to see you again when I'm not trapped under a mountain of Christmas decorations or when we aren't being called out by a teacher."

"Neither of us got after-school detention, so I say we call it a win."

He smiled at her. It had been a very long time since he'd last flirt-bantered. It was nice to know he could still do it, even if he was a little rusty.

The sounds coming from downstairs seemed to instantly turn argumentative, so they hurried back to the family room. Holly and Aiden were having a heated discussion about which parent was more creative.

"Whoa," he said. "Why am I hearing so many angry voices?"

Aiden turned to Rachel. "She said that since we are making the fireplace here, it means that her dad won. That he's the best at this kind of stuff."

Nick was so embarrassed that Holly was acting like she was. He loved that she had a spitfire personality. At least most of the time. He didn't love seeing it aimed negatively at others. He was going to have to have a good discussion with her about this later.

"I was just defending your honor, Dad."

"Hollybear, my honor doesn't need to be defended. Our guests *do* need to feel welcomed, though. How do you think you can help with that?"

"Are you trying to be grandpa, Daddy? Because sometimes 'winning friends and influencing people' doesn't feel like the most important thing. Letting someone know when they're wrong is."

"Holly!"

She took a deep breath and blew it out slowly. "You're right. Now isn't the time to point out that Miss Goodrich says she tells us when we got the wrong answer because that's how we learn. Now's the time to work together."

He rubbed a hand across his forehead. It was at times like this he wished Clara was still there. They could figure out how to help Holly together, instead of him trying to figure it all out by himself and constantly worrying that he was doing it wrong. He wanted to pull her aside right now and talk to her about everything. But he also didn't want to make the situation more awkward than it already was for Rachel and Aiden.

Before he could even open his mouth, though, Holly turned to Aiden. "I'm sorry for what I said."

Aiden tapped a finger on his lip, then smiled and said, "Thanks. Me, too."

Holly may be a spitfire, but she was always quick to apologize. He'd never been so grateful for that trait of hers.

Quickly after, Rachel got both kids turned around and looking down at the plywood. It lay right in the middle of the mostly open space. Since this was the biggest room in the house and most central, it was where he kept all of his construction supplies and tools, but he mostly had them on a tarp near the wall by the fireplace and out of the way.

"So," Rachel said, "the fireplace is at the bottom, with the mantle about halfway up, right?"

Aiden nodded. "Yep! And we need to cut open the middle part because a kid in our class"—

"Zach S."—Holly cut in.

"—is going to be Santa Claus, and he needs to come from behind it, like he came down the chimney."

Rachel grabbed the tape measure from his supplies

and sat down on the floor with her legs crossed. "Well, then, it sounds like we need to figure out how tall that opening needs to be for Santa to climb out of it." She extended the tape a good three feet, then held it measuring from the floor up, and had both kids walk beside it, crouched, so she could measure.

Since the wood they were working with was only four feet wide, the logical width of the opening was two or two and a half feet wide, and if they were doing the mantle halfway up, the logical height of the opening was about three feet high. That would leave enough space to do the faux bricks surrounding it.

They could've figured that out even if the kids weren't present. But Rachel was telling them how many inches high they were as they crouched past the tape, and both of them were going past it time and time again, trying to get lower, the dogs participating right along with them, the kids' laughter building with each pass.

The sound made his heart happy in a way he hadn't felt lately. Like a tiny little piece of it was fused back into place.

No, it was more than that. The more he watched, the more he realized the feeling came from knowing a piece of *Holly's* heart was fusing back into place. He knew that leaving their old home was the right choice and that Holly was excited to move close to her grandparents. It was still hard, though. It was the only home she'd ever known. It was where her friends were, and she was apprehensive about making new friends.

But he'd assured her that she would. Every day after school over the past two weeks since they'd moved to Mountain Springs, he'd ask if she'd made any friends that day. The only kid he ever heard about was Aiden and how much they *weren't* becoming friends. Finding out from Holly's teacher that she was struggling because Clara was gone had just pulled at his already frayed heart.

He studied Rachel as the kids and the dogs went around and around. The smile on her face was open. Full of Joy. Her green eyes sparkled and her dark hair fell in big waves down to her shoulders, framing her face. Watching her help the kids turn from anger to happiness was mesmerizing. *She* was mesmerizing.

Eventually, the kids fell to the floor, exhausted from laughing, but they still managed to laugh and squirm more once the dogs started licking their faces. Rachel turned to him and grinned. "I think three feet will do it."

"Thank you," he said, and it was the most genuine *thank you* he'd given in a long time.

She smiled back at him, and he had to admit it did something to his stomach. Something rather unexpected.

He and Rachel lifted the piece of plywood onto two saw horses, putting it closer to waist height, and she measured the wood three feet from the bottom in a couple of places, marking each. He placed his framing square against the side of the plywood so he could make sure the line they were making would be perfectly parallel to the base. Then he held it down with his left hand so he could mark the line with his right.

As soon as he put his hand on the square, his ring looked conspicuously absent. At first, he thought that maybe it just looked that way to him, since he'd spent the last nearly eight years always seeing it there, but Rachel seemed to notice every bit as much.

Enough that it felt like a tangible thing in the air between them, begging for a comment from him. He cleared his throat. "It was time." He watched as the expression on Rachel's face changed, but as much as he studied it, he couldn't guess what she might be thinking.

He hadn't noticed what Holly was doing, since she was on the floor behind him, playing with the dogs, but she'd apparently had a great vantage point for witnessing the exchange. She reached forward and patted him on the leg.

The perceptive kid had noticed the lack of his ring within moments of seeing him this morning. He'd told her that it was hard to take it off, but that he knew he should. She'd said, "It doesn't mean you don't love Mommy still. It just means that you know she's in heaven, and we need to keep on living here." He'd been worried about telling her, yet she'd been the one to share wisdom and reassurance with him.

Sometimes it felt like Holly had the insight of someone well beyond her years, then she would show the maturity of someone exactly her age when she played the whole "my dad can beat up your dad" card with Aiden. The girl was a walking dichotomy, and he loved her fiercely.

Before long, he and Rachel had the opening cut. Pretty quickly after that, they'd figured out how to use the two-by-fours to construct a frame on the back of the fireplace to make it freestanding. They'd even had enough wood left over to create the mantle and get it screwed to the plywood. And it had all generated enough small leftover pieces of the two-by-fours that the kids were having a blast using them like building blocks.

It had taken a lot of back-and-forth discussion and lots of measuring and math to decide how to make the piece. He and Rachel stood next to each other, grinning at the very plain fireplace. Both Holly and Aiden crouched down and climbed through the fireplace opening, just to test it.

Rachel turned to him. "We did good work."

His smile was big as he nodded. "We did."

Before they started, he'd wished that Clara was there to help him figure it all out, because she'd always been crafty. But what he'd experienced that evening with

Rachel had been rather remarkable. Neither of them had known what they were doing when they started, but together, they figured it out just fine and the results were pretty great. *Everything* he was feeling was pretty great. It was nice to experience that specific sense of teamwork again that could only come when two people figured things out together.

The kids were now playing something with the extra wood pieces that seemed to be a mix of the floor is lava and follow the leader, all while chanting the lines of *The Night Before Christmas* that they'd memorized.

He turned to Rachel, hoping that he could manage to take a leap of faith without crashing and burning at takeoff. "Holly and I have a few Christmas traditions of going to holiday outings, but most of them were tied to our old town. Well, except for my in-laws' ugly sweater party. We've got a fresh start here, and we decided that we need a few new traditions. Do you have any suggestions?"

He wasn't asking Rachel on a date. The last time he'd asked someone on a first date was ten years ago, and he wasn't quite ready to take a leap that big. But he also knew that it would only take about one more day to finish the fireplace, and he wanted to see Rachel again.

Rachel's entire face had brightened when he mentioned Christmas traditions, but then she seemed to hesitate. He held his breath as he waited for her response. It was fine if she just recommended a town event that he and Holly could attend or told him about a Christmas activity. He hoped that she would take it as an opening to see each other again.

She bit her lip and looked at Aiden, thinking. Not thinking, like she was coming up with a list of things to suggest, but thinking like she was trying to decide something. She clearly understood that his question was an opening.

He continued holding his breath.

Then she turned back to him. "Yes."

"Yes?" He wasn't quite sure what that meant.

"The snow sculpture activity in Downtown Park happened last week, but they're still there. And there's Santa's village, a manger scene, a gingerbread house with hot chocolate, the works. Aiden and I planned to go tomorrow. Would you like to join us?" Her expression was uncertain, but he could see the hope behind it, too.

He grinned. "We'd love to."

seven

RACHEL

RACHEL WAS JUST SAVING all of her work in Photoshop, Illustrator, and InDesign—yes, she'd managed to use all three today—and closing out of her many open tabs in her browser when her desk phone rang. A second phone started ringing on Lucy's desk in their shared cubicle. They both picked them up and said hello at the same time.

"I'm so glad I was able to catch you both," Courtney said in her professional, *I'm on the clock* voice. "It is Wednesday, which means it's been one full week since the bet officially started and we need to do a check-in. Will you both please meet me in my office promptly at five o'clock?"

Rachel glanced at the clock at the bottom of her computer screen. That gave her five minutes to wrap up.

"Yep. For once, I'm actually finished with everything on time."

She glanced at Lucy, whose eyes were on her screen in a frantic focus and whose desk was a mess of printed magazine layouts, sketches, post-it notes, and a half-eaten bag of peppermint bark. "I'm not finished, but I can come back... Do you know what?" She leaned back in her chair. "This all can wait until tomorrow. See you at five!"

They both hung up and Rachel organized the few papers she had on her desk and put some items into tomorrow's Daily List on her phone. Then she and Lucy headed to Courtney's office.

Court was focused on something on her iPad, but she glanced up long enough to wave them in and say, "Take a seat."

And then, like Courtney's internal clock knew right when the work day ended, she turned off the iPad screen, set down the pencil, and grinned at Rachel. "Okay, it's been a week since we made our bet, and Lucy and I want an update. Will we be pampering you or experiencing a concert put on only by you?"

Lucy rubbed her hands together. "We want to know everything you said yes to."

"And if you said no to anything."

Rachel took a deep breath, trying to think back over the past week. They had texted in the group chat enough times that they had already been updated on much of it, so she tried to think of the things she hadn't already shared. She probably should've been keeping a list on her phone.

"I think Aiden's onto me. So far, he's asked for a later bedtime, to put a tree he made out of Legos as the topper on our Christmas tree—yes, we have a tree on top of our tree now—to skip doing his reading homework one night, and to wear all of his clothes inside out to school one day. I think my saying yes to that one was what tipped him off. He learned pretty quickly not to ask for the same thing twice."

"He never asked for ice cream for dinner?" Courtney asked. "Such a shame."

"No, but he did talk me into getting ice cream and eating it outside in the snow. I think I still have a touch of frostbite on my lips." She touched her lips and for some crazy reason, Nick popped into her mind.

"And you said yes to everything?" Lucy asked.

"Yep."

"Okay," Courtney said, "but that's saying yes to Aiden, which wasn't exactly the point. What else did you say yes to?"

"I already told you that I said yes to helping with Aiden's class Christmas program and that I said yes to making a four-foot by eight-foot fireplace to use as a set piece." They still looked impressed by that one, which they should be since she had never done anything like that before. "Oh, and I think I said yes to a date tonight."

"What?" Courtney said, getting out of her chair behind the desk and coming around to sit on the edge of the desk in front of Rachel, right as Lucy said, "For real?"

"Okay, you don't need to act so shocked. Plus, it's not really a date."

Courtney folded her arms. "Explain."

"I'm working with the dad of one of Aiden's classmates on that fireplace, and we are getting together with our kids."

"Divorced?" Courtney asked.

"No. Widowed."

"Oh! A single dad!" Lucy said. "My heart just melted like snow on a warm spring day."

"I don't know," Rachel said, fiddling with a piece of lint that was on her skirt. "His wife passed away more than a year ago, but up until a couple of days ago, he was still wearing a wedding ring." She looked at her friends. "Do you think that's a bad sign?"

Courtney cocked her head. "I think that's the sign of a guy with the capacity to love someone deeply. Where are you going?"

"To Downtown Park to see the snow sculptures and Christmas village."

Lucy wagged her eyebrows. "I heard that if you both

wear Santa hats when you walk under the arch to the train that goes around Santa's village, you'll fall in love."

Rachel chuckled, shaking her head. "Yeah...My six-year-old told me the same thing. He also believes in Santa Claus."

TONIGHT, Rachel said yes to Aiden wearing his Santa hat to the park. But because she also didn't want her kid to freeze to death, she said yes to him wearing it on top of a knit hat that would actually keep his adorable head warm.

As they got out of the car and walked to where they could see Nick and Holly waiting by the manger scene, she laughed out loud when she saw Nick's hat—it was knit, like all of theirs were, but his was red with fluffy white around the base and a white pom on top. She loved that Christmas was in his heart enough to do something like choosing to wear a knit Santa hat in public. A lot of guys might have been embarrassed. She wondered if he had any idea how attractive it made him.

Not that the guy needed any help in that department. He even looked attractive in a winter coat and boots. And the fact that he was holding his little girl's hand made her heart get a little melty, too.

"Hi," she said as they reached them, not meaning for

her voice to come out nearly as breathy as it did. Maybe that was a side effect of a melting heart. She cleared her throat like maybe it was the cold or something that had caused it, but by the way the corner of Nick's mouth pulled up just a bit, he didn't buy it. "Should we go check out the snow sculptures?"

They had only looked at a single sculpture together —a couple of carolers—before Aiden and Holly ran to the next one. It was a giant Santa head and shoulders as if he was a mythical beast rising out of the ground. As the kids raced on to one that looked like it was probably supposed to be Snoopy lying on top of his dog house, Rachel said, "We might think we've lost them for a bit, but I'm betting they'll come back to pull us to look at a dozen different sculptures before we're done."

Nick laughed as they meandered through the sculptures filling the open area of the park. "I expect nothing less."

Nick stopped walking to watch their kids gaze in wonder at a sculpture that looked like a miniature log cabin with Santa at the chimney, so she took the moment to sneak a peek at him. Those striking eyes of his were crinkled at the sides from smiling and he looked so thrilled that the two kids were getting along. At least, they were for that exact moment.

She noticed his hat again and was suddenly very curious about his childhood. As they started walking through the sculptures again in the same direction the kids were heading, she asked, "What was Christmas like for you growing up?"

He looked up a bit and gave a slight shrug. "Pretty typical, I guess. Tree, stockings, a special dinner, a present we could open on Christmas Eve that was always pajamas, presents Christmas morning."

Everything she had craved as a child. "I need to hear more about the Christmas Eve pajamas. Matching or not?"

He chuckled and scratched at the stubble on his jaw. "Always one piece—the kind with feet that zips up. And always matching for all of us, my parents included. For as many people who have the Christmas Eve pajamas tradition, ours was probably a bit more unique just because of the fabric.

"One year, it was reindeer. And I'm not talking pictures of reindeer on the fabric, I mean it was like a reindeer costume. There was even a hood with antlers. Another year, there were these green fringe pieces hanging down that made us look like Christmas trees. One year, it was elves, another, gingerbread men."

He chuckled again. "One time, it was the words 'You'll shoot your eye out,' with a pair of glasses as the O's, you know, from A Christmas Story. My dad loved that movie. There was a flap in the back of those pajamas. Oh, and one year, they were covered in Christmas lights that glowed in the dark. I think it prepared me for my future in-laws' ugly sweater party."

She was trying not to listen with her mouth dropped open in awe and longing. "Your family sounds fun. Do you see them often?"

He shook his head. "Not nearly as often as I'd like. Since my dad was in the military and we moved all around, it kind of gave everyone wanderlust. We are spread all over the world now, so we only get together during the summer every other year." He glanced over at her as they stopped to watch the kids check out a snow sculpture of a man sitting on the actual park bench. "Have you moved much?"

"No. My wanderlust is limited to travel, which I guess is to be expected when you work for a travel magazine. We've lived in Mountain Springs since Aiden was a year old."

"So you didn't grow up with all this?" He motioned to the entirety of everything in the park.

"Nope. I grew up in Erie."

"And what was Christmas like for you? What kind of traditions did you have?"

She shrugged. "We only had one. Well, two, kind of. The second was because of the first. My dad hated Christmas, so we couldn't celebrate it at all unless we wanted him to be even more cranky than usual, and he was very cranky about everything at Christmastime. He probably had his own trauma related to the holiday, but it wasn't like I was going to ask about it.

"My mom had no issue with the holiday, but she reacted to my dad's 'seasonal irritability' by kind of checking out. When she was present, she would leave a Dove chocolate on my pillow. It wasn't Christmassy, so we didn't risk setting off my dad, but the first time she gave me one, she told me that doves represent peace, so it was my little piece of peace for when our house wasn't peaceful. I lived for getting those little chocolates on my pillow."

She glanced at Nick to see that he was watching her with a curious expression. She didn't know how she felt about his focus being on her so intently. Looking back at where Aiden stood a couple of dozen feet away by a sculpture of Santa and Mrs. Claus, she said, "I think I've pointed out doves enough around Christmastime that Aiden thinks they're practically magical. Well, he pretty much thinks all of Christmas is magical. It has always been one of my number one goals for him.

"A few years ago, I found some Christmas tree dove ornaments. They have real feathers on them with little clips where their feet are so they can clip on a branch. I got half a dozen of them. Aiden loves them so much! He always spends a lot of time at the tree each year, petting the doves with a single careful finger."

She glanced again at Nick, and this time, he was

looking at her with something different in his expression. A softness, for sure. But there was something else behind those eyes that she couldn't quite name that made her insides react in a way that she hadn't felt in a while. Was she so date-starved that a soft look would impact her so much? And why did she suddenly not know how to react?

She broke eye contact and said, "Wow. The kids haven't pulled us over to them even once. Should we be concerned?"

Nick nodded in their direction, where they were whispering something to each other, giggling. "Clearly, yes. That's the look of two kids plotting something."

The kids ran toward them, racing around a circle of miniature snowmen whose stick arms made it look like they were holding hands, and stopped right in front of her and Nick.

"Can we go on the train now?" Holly asked.

"Sure thing," Nick said.

Holly grabbed Nick's hand and Aiden grabbed Rachel's, and the two kids pulled them toward Santa's village and the kid-sized train that ran all around it. As they neared the arch where everyone lined up to ride on the train, Aiden stopped and said, "My hat is getting itchy," and took it off. "Will you wear it on your head?"

"I can hold it for you," she offered.

He shook his head. "No, it has to be over your hat."

Rachel looked over at Nick. It was clear by the look on his face that he hadn't heard the legend that said if you wear a Santa hat when you walk under the arch leading to the Christmas train that you'd fall in love. Based on the way Aiden and Holly were sharing looks and still giggling, Aiden had let Holly in on that little piece of knowledge. And Holly's dad was conveniently already wearing a Santa hat.

She took a deep breath. Of course, *she* didn't believe the myth, but Aiden did. Would wearing the hat give him false hope? Or would not wearing it take away a bit of the Christmas magic that he and Holly were feeling? It was obviously important to them.

She was suddenly picturing Courtney and Lucy standing there, reminding her that this was her Season of Yes and this choice counted.

It was not that big of a deal. She smiled at Aiden and said, "Okay, put it on me."

She crouched down and he struggled for a moment as he tried to fit the kid-sized Santa hat not only on an adult-sized head but on a head that was already wearing a knitted hat. Eventually, he just kind of balanced it there and she stood back up, trying to hold her head level so it wouldn't fall off. Both kids were so happy they were practically dancing. It was the right decision.

The giggling intensified as they walked under the arch. At least they were getting along.

There weren't too many people at the park right then, so it didn't take long before it was Aiden's and Holly's turn to get on the train. Nick had his phone out, ready to take pictures before Rachel even got a chance to pull out hers. They both took a few pictures, then Rachel just watched as Nick started videoing the train ride. She loved how attentive he was as a father. Between growing up with her dad, losing both of her parents, and then having Aiden at age twenty-four, she'd gathered quite the list of requirements for a future husband, and many of them had to do with how the guy might be as a dad.

Maybe that was why she dated so infrequently. It was hard to find someone who would be a great husband and a great dad, and who would be willing to step right into the dad role from day one. Why did she have to find someone who seemed perfect, but was still grieving his late wife?

Because it had been a very long time since she'd looked at a guy like she was now looking at Nick and felt such a strong attraction. The guy's nose, cheeks, and the tops of his ears were red from the cold, yet he was in Santa's village with his daughter, looking like he was loving every minute of it.

Courtney's words, "I think that's the sign of a guy with the capacity to love someone deeply" echoed in her head. That was what she was seeing—a man loving his daughter deeply.

The train was coming back around for its final time, and a few of the kids waiting to get on bumped into her in their excitement, pushing Rachel right into Nick. He wrapped his arms around her to steady her and keep her from knocking them both down.

"I got you," he said in a low tone. His voice, so close to her ear, her chest against his, his arms wrapped around her, sent warm shivers through her body. She stood frozen for a moment, so shocked at all the emotions coursing through her that she couldn't move.

"Mom!" Aiden shouted as he leaped off the train, not even looking over at her, his eyes glued to something by the gazebo that had wall panels to make it look like a gingerbread house. "I found a dove!"

Rachel mumbled "Thanks" to Nick, then straightened herself up to standing and not pressed into his embrace, her cheeks feeling not quite as cold as they were. She grabbed the Santa hat that had fallen from her head to his shoulder, then hurried to catch up to Aiden as he was making a beeline to the gazebo.

"I knew I'd find a dove here!" Aiden said as she caught up to him. The decoration was new—it was slightly bigger than an actual dove and was perched on a post right next to the gingerbread house. Aiden took off his gloves and reached down into his pocket to pull out a small, wrinkled, folded piece of paper.

"Is that your Christmas list?" Rachel asked him. "I thought you wanted to go give that to Santa."

Aiden shook his head as he worked the paper into the claw of the dove. "It's a Christmas *wish*."

She wasn't sure what the distinction was in his mind, but if she had to guess what was on it, it was a request for more paper. Her little crafty boy could never seem to get enough paper.

Nick and Holly caught up with them just as they turned and nearly bumped into Rachel's brother, Jack, as he came out of the gazebo with his fiancée, Noelle.

"Uncle Jack!" Aiden said, jumping up to give him a starfish hug before sliding back to the ground.

Rachel introduced her brother and Noelle to Nick and Holly. The entire time that Jack and Nick made small talk and shook hands, with Nick's focus entirely on Jack, Noelle's was on Rachel. She raised her eyebrows, grinning, and mouthed, "He's cute."

Rachel smiled, knowing that it wasn't just her who noticed. Of course, the more she got to know Nick, the cuter he became. Between today and working on the fireplace with him, the man had practically stepped up a good seventeen spaces on the attractiveness scale.

Noelle gave Rachel a questioning look that she knew meant "How serious are the two of you?" and Rachel loved that she instantly knew what Noelle was asking. For almost her entire life, she'd only had a brother. But after Saturday night, she'd finally have a sister. Well, technically a sister-in-law, but that was every bit as good. She couldn't think of a better gift her brother could give her.

Rachel gave a slight shrug, and Noelle seemed to understand that she wasn't quite sure what was going to happen between her and Nick and that it was much too early to try to pin a name to anything between them.

Aiden was talking to Holly, and Rachel finally tuned into what he was saying. "And there are so many things to put in the hot chocolate, and we get to go to the wedding on a hay ride and it's the best! It's so much fun and one of my favorite things about Christmas. And," Aiden said, puffing his chest out, "I even get to carry the rings at the wedding."

The more Aiden talked about how great everything was at an event that Holly wasn't invited to, the more Holly's expression became closed off and sour. She crossed her arms and looked at the ground, but also looked like she really would've just preferred kicking Aiden in the shins.

"Aiden," Rachel said, putting her hands on his shoulders and turning him toward the activities going on in the park, "maybe we should focus on everything here instead."

"Oh, hey," Noelle said, seeming to have a gift of

understanding what was going on between the kids, "you two should come to the wedding!"

Rachel shot her almost sister-in-law a look. She and Nick weren't even dating. This tonight wasn't even a date. Inviting him to a wedding where she and Aiden were the only people he would know meant that Noelle was basically setting the two of them up on a date. Asking while they were both present made it extra awkward to say no. But she was pretty sure Noelle didn't even feel bad about that.

No, it wasn't a date. Jack and Noelle were just inviting them to an event that was also going to be attended by a lot of family and friends.

"You should," Jack said. "We had a couple of people cancel because they are nervous about the weather, so we've got the space."

"No, we couldn't," Nick said. "This is your wedding, and you don't know us—"

"—Yet," Jack said.

Noelle nodded. "And that's why you should come. You're new in town, right? It'd be a good way to get to know people." She smiled at Holly. "And I bet Holly will love it."

Nick looked at Rachel like he was trying to see what she thought about it all. What was she even feeling? Nerves? Awkwardness? A thrill at having a reason to see him again in just three days? Anticipation? Excitement?

Worry that she was putting herself in a position to become even more attracted to a guy she shouldn't be attracted to? She was pretty sure she was feeling it all.

And, of course, she was right in the middle of her Season of Yes. That meant she *had* to say yes, right? She smiled at Nick. "Yes, you should come. It'll be fun."

Hopefully, it would turn out better than her purchase of the atrocious sweater they'd come across that Aiden thought she should buy because it "looked so cute."

eight

NICK

NICK STOOD in front of the closet doors that were made of mirrors in the guest room where he was staying at his in-laws' house. The mirrors were dated monstrosities that had startled him more than once when he walked past them at night when the lights were off, but they were sure helpful while he was getting ready.

His fingers kept fumbling as he was tying his tie, making him restart. What was he doing, going to the wedding of a couple he'd barely met, just because the groom's sister was the mom of one of the kids in his daughter's first grade class?

That wasn't why he was nervous, and he knew it. He was nervous because that mom was someone who made his heart beat faster every time he saw her. His breath catch. His chest floated like everything that had been weighing him down was suddenly lighter. As he was sitting at the desk in this cramped room, writing code or working through lines of code, trying to find exactly where an issue was, Rachel's smile started popping into his head. But not just every smile—the smiles she gave him, specifically. He was starting to crave those.

He glanced over to the wooden chair at the edge of the closet where Holly was sitting as she waited for him to get his suit coat and tie on. "Do I look okay?"

Holly stood up on her chair and motioned him over, so he walked up to her. She reached out and straightened his tie and then brushed her hands over his shoulders. "You look beautiful, Dad. Oh, wait. For boys, it's *handsome*, right? Rachel is going to see you and her eyes are going to bug out because you look so handsome."

He looked back at the mirror. Was that why he was so nervous? Was that what he wanted— for Rachel to see him and like what she saw? Yes, it was, he realized. So why did he feel so very not ready? Maybe because it had been so long since he'd been in the dating pool that he'd forgotten how to swim. He felt like he was in the shallow end, thinking someone really should put arm floaties on him before he waded out any further.

"Now this is the part where you tell me that I look like a beautiful princess."

He smiled at his daughter as she twisted from side to side on the chair, her poofy ankle-length dress swishing out as she did. "You look like a beautiful princess, Hollybear."

"Thanks!" she said and leaped off the chair. "Now let's get there already."

They said goodbye to Ben and Linda. Yes, they'd encouraged him to start dating, but it didn't make it feel any less weird to see them right before meeting someone who was not their daughter. It wouldn't be too much longer, though, before he would be finished with the renovations at the new house and he and Holly could move in.

They pulled up to the address that Rachel had given him, which was apparently the bride's parents' house. Strings of Christmas lights lined the house and lit up all the trees and shrubs. Santa's village and a manger scene decorated the lawn, and a couple of dozen people milled about all the decorations, kids chasing each other around everything. A truck with two flat-bed trailers loaded with bales of hay covered in blankets sat parked in front of the house.

Holly put her hands on her cheeks. "It's just so magical!"

They got out of the car, and Holly ran ahead, her golden dress bouncing below her blue winter coat, and Nick scanned the crowd for Rachel. He found her talking with a small group of people and started walking toward her. She was wearing a plum-colored dress coat and tall boots, the bottom of her dark green dress visible below the coat, and her dark hair pulled up all fancy. She looked stunning standing there in the middle of the snow and the Christmas decorations.

It took a moment before she glanced in his direction. The moment her eyes landed on him, her expression—the one that spontaneously appeared before she even would've had a chance to choose it—looked a lot like elated happiness. Something washed through him at seeing it. He wouldn't have been able to describe it, but it made his chest swell to know he evoked that reaction in her.

She was still smiling when he reached her and she said, "I'm so glad you two came. We are going to be loading up soon. Should we get some hot chocolate, first?"

Holly and Aiden both seemed to materialize at their side just then, almost like they knew the hot chocolate was coming. Rachel led them to a table filled with different hot chocolate mix-ins where Noelle's dad was pouring hot chocolate into cups with a ladle and handing them out.

As they were choosing their mix-ins, Holly asked, "Are these all the people that are coming to the wedding?"

Rachel glanced out at the crowd. "No—the hay ride can't fit everyone at once. This group is just us and

Noelle's parents, siblings, and their kids. Extended family will be arriving in a bit, and they'll ride over in the second group. Everyone else will just meet us at the chapel."

Holly's eyes grew as Rachel listed off who was coming, but all Nick could think was that they were in the wrong place. Everyone there was only close family. They were a last-minute addition, and it wasn't even a real date.

Not long after they got their hot chocolates, he heard a ringing and everyone's attention went to the bride and groom—Rachel's brother, Jack, and his soon-to-be wife, Noelle, whom they'd met three days ago. They stood at the top of the sloping yard, near the house. Jack was dressed in a fine-looking tux, and Noelle wore a white wedding dress with a white fur-lined coat that looked kind of like a cape and went all the way to the ground. They were both grinning and holding champagne glasses filled with hot chocolate.

"We want to thank you all for coming," Jack said. "It means a lot to us."

Noelle smiled. "This is not the most traditional start to a wedding, we know, but we wanted to celebrate with you in a way that we most love celebrating."

Jack said, "Noelle was my employee a year ago when we last had this hot chocolate and hay ride activity, and I had some pretty high walls up. It was sitting on that second trailer right over there when I first let those walls come down for a minute. It felt appropriate to have this lead to our wedding."

"Cheers!" Noelle said, holding her hot chocolate up high.

Everyone else held theirs up and shouted "Cheers!" right back.

They all took their hot chocolates with them and climbed onto the trailers, the bride and groom sitting on hay bales stacked two high on the first trailer, facing everyone.

Aiden initially sat down next to Rachel, but in true six-year-old fashion, only stayed there for about five seconds before he jumped up to sit next to the woman Nick had figured out was Noelle's mom. So Nick took the opportunity to sit right next to Rachel. The story Jack told about this hay ride was pretty sweet. It surprised him that he was suddenly wanting the same thing to happen to him.

Someone started Christmas music playing, and Rachel motioned to a woman who was videoing everything with her phone and leaned in close to him to say, "That's Noelle's sister, Katie. She interviews the family at the Christmas activities and makes a video to show on Christmas Eve."

She continued, telling him who all the people were on both trailers, but there were so many names and he was so distracted by her nearness. The peppermint scent of her hair. The feel of her warm breath against his cheek.

Holly had been right when they pulled up. There was a sort of magic here.

His attention, right along with Rachel's, went to Aiden as the boy said to Noelle's mom, "So what do I call you after Uncle Jack gets married?"

Mrs. Allred cocked her head. "Call me?"

"I'll get to start calling Noelle 'Aunt Noelle,' but I don't know what I'm supposed to call you."

"Well, technically, we still won't be related."

Aiden frowned, his eyebrows pulling together. "No, we have to be related. Won't you be my grandma-in-law or something?"

The woman chuckled as she put an arm around Aiden and pulled him into her side. Then she told him a story about how where she grew up, they referred to found or adopted family as hanai and said that they were hanai now. "So, as hanai, what would you like to call me?"

Aiden pointed at the boy on her other side, who looked about his age. "Tommy calls you Grandma. Can I call you that, too?"

"You sure can."

Nick stole a glance at Rachel and saw the most elated smile on her face. It must've meant a lot to her that this family that was soon to be her brother's was also claiming them.

On Nick's other side, Holly tugged on his coat sleeve, then she got to her knees so she could whisper in his ear, trying to surreptitiously point to Noelle's mom. "If you and Rachel get married, will I be able to call her Grandma, too?"

The question caught him off guard so much that he was almost too stunned to answer. He hadn't thought Holly would've connected so many dots with him and Rachel, and he wasn't sure if he should be worried that she was starting to form connections with her friend's uncles in-law.

"Um, I don't know, honey. I guess we should wait and see." It wasn't the best answer, and he knew it. But he hadn't prepared himself for questions like that.

"WOULD YOU LIKE TO DANCE?" Nick asked, holding a hand out to Rachel, who was seated at a table.

He soaked in the smile she gave him as she set down her drink and stood, putting her hand in his. When they reached a good spot on the dance floor, he put one arm around Rachel's waist and held her hand with his other, just like his mom had taught him and his siblings all those years ago at the army base in Fort Leavenworth, Kansas.

As they moved to the music, so in sync, he reveled in the feel of her in his arms and felt himself fall for her just a bit more, like he had been all night.

Shortly after they'd arrived, he and Holly went with Aiden and Rachel, where Rachel and Katie were prepping Aiden to be the ring bearer. As they told Aiden about how special and important his role was and what exactly he needed to do, Nick could see Holly getting surlier and surlier.

He understood that Holly felt bad that Aiden was getting so much attention and was being assigned a cool job and Holly wasn't. But the groom was someone very important in Aiden's life and Holly had just barely met the guy.

Holly getting upset and jealous seemed to happen a lot lately, which told Nick that she was struggling to adjust to the big move. And since she didn't know anyone well except for Aiden, she was kind of taking it all out on him. He was about to crouch down to Holly's height and talk to her about it. What he'd say, exactly, he wasn't sure. It wasn't like anything he could say would make her less jealous in the moment.

But before he could, Rachel turned to Holly. "And I have a huge and important job I could use your help with."

Holly perked right up, all signs of dejection falling from her demeanor. "You do?"

Rachel nodded and took her by the hand to a small table by the doors that led into the chapel. It held the guest book and a basket of something. She told Holly that they wanted all the guests to toss rose petals as the couple came back down the aisle after getting married and that each guest needed a pouch of roses. They'd be coming soon, and she wanted her to hand one to each guest.

He was sure that the plan had been to just leave the basket on the table for each guest to pick up their own, but by the time Rachel finished talking with Holly, Holly was convinced that her job was the most important one of the entire wedding. He'd watched Rachel as she'd pulled off the magic, feeling his chest warming, his heart being tugged, that she would care so much for his daughter. What she had done had completely changed how the evening was likely to go, and he was so grateful to her for it.

But his feelings hadn't stopped at gratitude. He'd fallen some more. The kind that left his stomach whooshing.

He'd sat next to her during the wedding ceremony and watched as she'd beamed at her son, walking up the aisle in his little suit, acting so proper yet with a wide grin on his face, and he'd had the thought *When Clara said she wanted me to get remarried, this was the kind of person she was imagining.* And he fell for Rachel a bit more.

It was just Jack and Noelle and the officiant at the front of the room, which felt so perfect for the venue and the crowd. They'd both written their own vows, which made practically the entire chapel start reaching for the tissues. When Rachel's brother said, "I had always hated Christmas and thought it was impossible to get past it," Rachel grabbed Nick's hand. He gave it a squeeze as Rachel sniffed, dabbing at her tears with a tissue in her other hand.

"You came along and changed everything," Jack had said. "I spent most of my life figuring that I would never find 'the one.' Then you walked into my office for an interview and I knew that day that you were it. But I spent the next year and a half thinking that a relationship with you was impossible." He'd smiled at Noelle. "I should've known that, once again, you'd find a way to make the impossible possible.

"I've seen it time and time again since then, and I can't wait to spend the rest of my life with you, knowing that nothing is impossible."

He'd gotten choked up hearing Jack's vows, too. Between the words, the way they were said, and the looks that Jack and Noelle had given each other, it was impossible not to.

"I wish my parents were here," Rachel had said, her words barely a whisper. He looked over at her, studying her. She hadn't talked much about them, but so many emotions filled her face. And then she'd leaned into him, putting her head on his shoulder. So he put his arm around her shoulders and he felt himself fall further.

All during the refreshments and chatting with guests, whenever his eyes weren't on Holly, they were on Rachel. Everything about her, from the way her eyes crinkled when she smiled, to how freely she laughed, to how she always seemed to have all the details of everything in her head and knew just when to check on something or get something, to how she made everyone around her feel made him feel like he was falling. Hopelessly falling.

And now that they were dancing together and all the emotions he'd been experiencing all night felt like they were wrapped in the bubble of the two of them dancing, he didn't just feel like he was falling. He felt like he'd been pushed out of an airplane. The parachute hadn't been deployed—he was just free-falling and taking in the landscape and the exhilarating feel of the wind rushing past his face.

A part of his heart had been so damaged when Clara died. But even though he'd known it had been damaged, he'd ignored it and pushed on because being a single dad was hard. Being a single dad who was grieving was even harder. Some things, like that pain in his heart, he'd just learned to live with. It had become his new normal.

But tonight, he'd felt things starting to shift and heal and not hurt so much. Just being around Rachel brought a lightness that he hadn't felt in a very long time.

He swung her out and she laughed as she twirled back into him, ending with her back against his front, and he held her for a moment as they swayed to the music. He'd seen her laughing so much tonight. That had done something to his heart, too, especially when he was the one who had made her laugh. Feeling her close to him, her breath tickling his neck did something else to his heart and made him feel things he hadn't for so long.

As they moved around the dance floor to a faster-paced song, they saw Holly making up crazy dances with Aiden and Noelle's nieces and nephews. Holly looked so happy. Maybe her heart was healing, too.

"There's so much I still don't know about you," Nick said. "And I find myself wanting to know everything."

Rachel smiled. "Me, too. What's your favorite topping on a pizza? I mean, it's not the deepest question ever, but if we're ever going to share a pizza, it's vital information to know ahead of time."

So she was thinking about the future and seeing him in it. He was smiling with his whole face when he said,

"Can it even be called a pizza if there isn't pepperoni on it? But my favorite beyond that is black olives."

"Olives? Interesting. Mine is chicken."

"Chicken? I don't understand. Like, along with the pepperoni?"

Her arms were still around his neck, but she lifted her shoulders in a slight shrug. "With or without. I like it all ways."

"Huh. Okay. If you had to play an Olympic sport, what would it be?"

She bit her lip as she thought. "Hmm. I'm going to have to go with the bobsled. I'm not the most athletic person, and for that one, it's mostly about the leaning, right? You?"

He laughed. "Um, ski jumping, maybe?" He hadn't ever done it before, but it probably felt a lot like what his stomach was experiencing now. Was he feeling all these emotions just because they were at a wedding? He'd been a sap for weddings ever since he'd had his own. Maybe what he was feeling was just because of the situation and their surroundings. It felt like more than that, though, and he had to know for sure. "Let's go on a date."

Rachel's eyebrows rose. He was hoping in interest.

"Not because we have a project or because something else pulled us together. Let's go because we want to. Just the two of us."

Rachel bit her lip as she glanced over his shoulder at where their kids were dancing, and it was killing him to not know what was going through her mind right then. Then her eyes met his again. "I would like that."

He held back the smile that threatened to overtake his face and forced himself to play it cool as they moved to the music. "I would love to take you out on a Friday or a Saturday, but I don't want to wait that long to see you again. How does Tuesday sound?" He had *just* told himself to play it cool and then he says something like that? He was so out of practice. But also, he really did want to see her.

She bit her lip and once again, he wished he could hear her thoughts. "I'll have to see if I can find a sitter for that soon. Bria has finals this week. I would ask Jack and Noelle, but the house they bought isn't ready for them yet, so they're staying in Golden, and that's probably a bit far."

"My in-laws are always free on Tuesdays. Would you like me to ask if they'd mind watching Aiden, too?"

She glanced over at where Aiden was doing a dance that looked a little like T-Rex trying not to step on Legos and failing miserably. Holly and the other two boys were trying to mimic him but were unable to because they were holding their stomachs from laughing so hard.

"I'd really like that."

After they got home that night and after he got Holly

in bed, he walked into his temporary bedroom, feeling like he was still on a high from the entire evening. He loosened his tie, unbuttoned the top button, and flopped down on his bed, opening his phone.

He swiped to the last screen and smiled at Clara's picture. "I met someone and I really like her. Her name is Rachel. I know—it feels weird to come to you to talk about this, but you were my best friend and the first person I always told everything to. You told me that you wanted me to start dating again, so here I am, dating again.

"I think you'd like her, too. She's a great mom and she is so good with Holly. If you've been keeping an eye on us, I'm sure you already know that. But I wanted to tell you that you were right—I've felt so alone since you died, but tonight, I experienced how great it feels to not be so alone. So thank you."

He turned off the phone and marveled at how excited he could be for a Tuesday.

nine

RACHEL

RACHEL LEANED in close to the mirror as she applied mascara. Aiden sat on the side of the bathtub, swinging his legs so that his heels hit the bathtub, making a reverberating thudding sound. He'd already asked questions about what she and Nick were going to be doing, what she thought he and Holly were going to do with Holly's grandparents, and if he got to stay up late.

Those questions she fielded like a pro. She'd also fielded texts from Courtney and Lucy about the date and what things she'd said yes to today like a pro. But when Aiden asked, "Is Nick going to be my dad?" she jerked enough that she swiped the mascara wand across the skin beside her eye.

After Aiden was born, she always thought that when she got serious with someone, she would have time to figure out how much she liked them and would only introduce them to Aiden once she was sure about the relationship. She didn't want him forming his own opinions before she got a chance to form her own, and she definitely didn't want him getting attached if things weren't going to work out.

But since it was through Aiden that she met Nick, that plan went out the window. Nothing about this was going as planned. What she needed to do was set some expectations and be as honest as she could with him.

She grabbed a tissue, got it a little wet, and then started wiping the mascara off. "I don't know, buddy, because I don't know how much we like each other yet. We probably won't know until we've been on a few more dates—it hasn't been nearly long enough for us to start thinking about things like that." Not that the thought hadn't crossed her mind more than a time or two or a thousand. Honestly, though, she was surprised that Aiden had gotten there already.

"But you like him," Aiden said, dragging out the word "like" as he did a little torso dance while still sitting. Then he stood to add more extravagance to his dance. "You really like him."

Her cheeks suddenly went pinker than the blush

she'd already put on as she thought about how much she did like Nick. Everything had changed Saturday night at the wedding. There had been so many moments when he'd just been thoughtful or a sweet father or had looked at her with an expression of adoration that made her knees weak. So many things he'd said all night long had made her fall just a little bit more for him.

And there had definitely been moments when a fire built in her chest that made her want to grab him by the front of his suit jacket and pull him to her so he could kiss her senseless.

They'd texted back and forth on Sunday so much and he'd been so charming and witty and fun. She couldn't wait until Tuesday to see him and eventually invited him and Holly over that night. She and Aiden had planned to do their annual snowflake creating tradition—which he'd gotten a jump start on weeks ago—and get them hung from the ceiling. Aiden was thrilled that more people would be joining in on a tradition that was one of his favorites.

She'd known that she'd love having Nick and his daughter join them. What she hadn't anticipated was watching Nick's shoulder and arm muscles flex as he climbed onto the step ladder to tape each of the snowflake's strings to their ceiling. That had brought its own joy to her world.

"I do like him. How about you?"

Aiden shrugged, looking so nonchalant, even though he hadn't managed to wipe the smile completely off his face. "He's cool."

RACHEL WALKED hand-in-hand with Nick down Main Street, both of them sipping from cups of warm wassail, looking at all the lights and decorations just as snow started to softly fall. Everything about the evening had been perfect. The dinner, the conversation, and now that they were just out enjoying the season, the feeling that there wasn't anywhere else they needed to be, the peace.

"This feels straight out of *It's a Wonderful Life*," she said.

"Except in color."

"And I'm not wearing a dress."

"That's downright scandalous." Nick pulled his phone out of his pocket. "What do you say to a selfie to remember the occasion?"

She snuggled in close to him as they both smiled at the phone camera. She had to admit that they looked pretty cute next to each other.

"You know, Jimmy is my middle name."

She looked over at Nick. "Really. Your full name is Nicholas Jimmy Stewart?"

He laughed. "No, my middle name is Buckles."

"Buckles?"

"Hey, don't knock it. It was my maternal grandpa's last name." He paused a moment. "And his first name was Jimmy."

She gave him a playful smack on the arm. "It was not."

"True story. We went to Grandpa Jimmy and Grandma Ina's farm every year growing up."

As he told about it, the feeling of peace with him settled in more deeply. She had not been expecting that emotion at all. Lately, with all she had been saying yes to, she'd been feeling rather overwhelmed. She was trying to do all the traditions that she and Aiden had developed over the years, like the snowflakes and their Christmas movie marathon. Then all the town events, like the Christmas sing-in they went to last night. And then after last year, they'd added several traditions with Noelle's big family, and every night she was coming home from work and hurrying to get Aiden ready for the next thing.

And all the Christmas shopping. She couldn't forget that.

New relationships took time, too. Time she was more

than happy to spend. Each time her phone dinged with a new text from Nick, her heart lit up like the big tree in Downtown Park.

As busy as the Season of Yes was making her, saying yes to a date with Nick was calming her stressed heart in ways she hadn't even guessed it would do.

But still, whenever she was with him, thoughts of his late wife would inevitably pop into her head. It was clear that he loved her. That he still did. Which was honestly super endearing. She was glad that he did and that he kept Clara alive in Holly's thoughts. She wouldn't want anything different from him. She just didn't know how that would affect how he felt about *her*.

"Do you mind if I ask how Clara died?" She probably should've eased her way into the question. But she'd wanted to ask for a while, and it felt like it needed to be soon. Probably not blurting-it-out soon, but it was too late to pull it back.

He didn't seem taken aback that she asked—he just looked up at the falling snow, one of the flakes landing on an eyelash before speaking. "From a heart condition she'd probably had since she was young that none of us knew about. We were completely blindsided. I only knew there was a problem when she didn't show up to the school to pick up Holly from kindergarten as she had planned."

"Oh. That must have been so hard."

"It really was."

She had an overwhelming urge to just hold him close and make everything better, but she didn't know what to say. Instead of saying something comforting, she heard the words, "I had cancer" come from her mouth.

Nick's steps halted momentarily.

"Last year," she continued, "Acute Myeloid Leukemia. It was rough, but even with as rough as it got, I never worried that I wouldn't be there for Aiden as he grew up. I always had a gut feeling that I would make it through to the very end. And I did—my scan six months ago came back clean."

She could tell he was rattled, but she didn't know what to do about that. The cancer was simply a fact. One that she worried could very well scare him away, especially after losing his wife.

"Everything is good now, then?" His voice wavered a bit, but she could tell he was trying to make the words come out strong and confident.

She shrugged. "I mean, yeah. Everything looks good so far. It was an aggressive cancer, but I had age and a good health history on my side. A lot of things really went my way, actually."

"That must have been intense. I'm very glad to hear you made it through." They walked in silence for several long moments. She stayed quiet, knowing that he needed time to process.

He must not have wanted to process out loud, though, because he changed the subject. "Do you mind if I ask about Aiden's dad?"

Rachel wondered if the question had been as burning to him as asking about his wife had been for her. It took a moment to think about how to even explain because there was so much more to it than the short version.

"That's not something I can explain in a sentence or two."

Nick gestured at all the lights and decorations on Main Street and at the soft snow that felt like it was almost glowing from the light strands crossing over Main Street. "I can walk up and down this street with you as many times as needed. Ten? A hundred? You've got it."

She chuckled and secretly swooned. How long had it been since she'd been on a date when the guy was so interested in everything she said? Long enough ago that she couldn't remember.

"Okay, then. Um, to explain, I need to go back to age eighteen when my parents died. Jack was fifteen, and the night they got in that wreck was the night I first became a parent."

That had been a dozen years ago, yet it was still hard to bring up. Probably because bringing it up always brought back the emotions she'd felt that night when the officer knocked on their door. So much had changed at that moment. More than she could comprehend. All she'd felt was the whirlwind in her mind, the stabbing pain in her gut, the ache in her heart. It took days, weeks, and months to begin to understand all the emotions that came with the news.

"But at least I'd had a lot of practice with parenting before then—our mom struggled with a lot of things and would often check out for weeks at a time. But it was different once it was only the two of us. Jack started acting out and kind of lost his way a bit."

"That's a completely understandable reaction. Losing both parents at the same time had to be tough."

She nodded, feeling the truth of that statement deep in her bones. She had been dealing with her own grief all while trying to be everything Jack needed her to be. And that was on top of simply being eighteen and trying to figure out how to be an adult and make the decisions that would impact her future so much.

"Jack didn't go to college right after high school. I think all of those first years were hard, but that one was especially tough for a lot of reasons. But then he figured out what he wanted to do and what he needed to do to get there and started college just a year late. He lived with me that year—we were both in college. That was a great year.

"Then I graduated and he moved into a dorm on

campus with some friends, and a friend moved into my place as my roommate. I just felt…" She wasn't even sure how to express what the emotions had been like that year. "Adrift, maybe? I think I had gotten so used to being the parent, the one in charge, and I didn't know how to *not* have Jack to look after. It had become a good part of my identity, I think.

"I mean, don't get me wrong— it was great to not have so much responsibility piled on me. But I suddenly no longer had school to focus on and I was working a job I hated that had nothing to do with my degree and Jack was doing great and didn't need me so much.

"After having to be the responsible one since I was young, I kind of had my own rebellious moment and made some less-than-great choices. At the same time, though, I felt a bit like…" She paused. "I don't know, like an empty nester, maybe? I think I was just really craving someone in my life to take care of. And those two things didn't mix well.

"So I dated a crappy guy. And one night, the crappy telephone customer service job I had laid everyone off the same day that my roommate announced that she was moving out of state. I was feeling extra rebellious and in need of someone. It was one night of poor decisions, and before long, I found out I was pregnant."

She glanced at Nick, almost afraid to see his reaction, but the look on his face was that of concern. Undivided attention. And something else. Understanding without judgment, maybe? Whatever it was, it made her whole chest feel warm and light even as the snow fell all around them.

"Anyway, I let the guy know, and he was mad because it didn't fit with his life plans. The day I told him was the last time I ever saw him. Eventually, a lawyer delivered papers where he'd signed away his parental rights and asked me never to contact him again. He didn't even know when Aiden was born because he never wanted to."

She looked at Nick again, and he was breathing heavily, eyebrows drawn together like he was ready to stand up to the guy right then and let him know what he thought of it all and her breath caught. She hadn't experienced a guy outside of her brother who had ever shown that kind of protectiveness of her before. He shook his head. "I can't even fathom not wanting to be there—to even know—your own kid."

She studied his expression, drinking in the look on his face that came with that statement. It was so authentic and it pulled at her heart.

"It might have been a decision I regretted making, and I definitely wouldn't have chosen the timing." She shook her head. "Those first few years were *so* hard. But in the end, I got Aiden. And he means the world to me."

"And he's a great kid," Nick said.

They stopped, right there at the winter wonderland display in front of Trove of Oldies and she just nodded as she looked into Nick's eyes. His hat and the shoulders of his coat were covered in snow—she hadn't noticed that it had started coming down so much—and the air was cold enough that each of their breaths were little puffs of clouds.

But those eyes of his were warm. Inviting. Full of all the things she'd been hoping for, both consciously and subconsciously, since the day she'd found out she was going to have a baby.

And he was looking at her like he really saw her. All of her. He wasn't ignoring any parts of her that he didn't like—he was looking at her like she didn't even have parts that he didn't like. Like she was everything just the way she was, and she'd never felt so accepted.

His eyes flicked to her lips, and suddenly she couldn't think of anything she wanted more than to have his lips on hers. She took a step toward him, and the look of longing on his face intensified. A snowflake fell right on his cheek and melted. He closed the gap between them, and suddenly the snow and the cold felt just beyond them. There was nothing between them but warmth and peace.

He reached with two fingers to brush the snow-covered hair away from her cheek, and the touch of his fingers sent a tingling warmth through her whole body.

Then she heard a buzzing sound and he looked at his watch, his eyebrows pulling together. "Oh. It's my mother-in-law." He pulled his phone from his pocket and answered it, putting it on speakerphone. "Hello?" His voice was concerned.

"I'm so sorry to bother you on your date." Rachel recognized Linda's voice from when she'd met her just before their date.

"Are Holly and Aiden okay?"

"Now don't panic."

"Linda, that's not helping me not to panic. Are they okay?"

"They were just playing in the snow and Holly jumped off the porch and landed on one of those big rocks in the flower beds—she didn't see it because of the snow—and hurt her ankle. Ben says it's not broken and it's not bad enough to need a doctor, but it still hurts. She just—"

"We'll be right there." He said goodbye and looked at Rachel. "I'm so sorry to end things early. That is not what I would have chosen."

She smiled at him, loving that he would be willing to end things early to look out for his daughter. Out of every moment tonight, that might have made her fall for him the most.

And it was also the most quintessentially parental thing that possibly could've happened tonight. So much so, that she should have known without a doubt that it would happen. But boy did she wish that the kiss that had seemed so inevitable moments ago had happened. She could almost feel how sweet his lips would be against hers.

ten

NICK

"DADDY, MY ANKLE HURTS," Holly said as they sat on a blanket on the floor of what would very soon be their dining area, having dinner with Rachel and Aiden.

"Maybe this will help," Rachel said as she took off her cardigan, rolled it up, and then placed it under Holly's ankle.

Holly looked up at Rachel like... well, like she'd found something that was lost. He understood the feeling so well.

Holly's ankle hadn't been injured too badly, but he did keep her home from school on Wednesday. Luckily, it hadn't been a day where he'd had to go into the office. His office in his in-laws' home was in the guest bedroom with him, so he had set up a bunch of pillows in his bed like a throne. Holly had felt like a princess as she colored, read, and watched shows on his tablet, Rosy by her side as he worked.

She seemed to have loved the extra attention and privileges... to a point. By that evening, she was tired of being in bed and wanted to play with Rosy. Linda had fixed her up with a simple ankle wrap, and despite a small limp, she seemed to play without any pain.

He'd taken her with him to the house every evening, and when she wasn't thinking about it, her ankle seemed to be pretty fine. He suspected that it was the attention that Rachel was giving her that was making it "hurt" tonight.

Even with Holly's ankle, he'd managed to finish the rest of the flooring and baseboard and trim Wednesday night and painted them just yesterday. He and Rachel had tentatively planned to finish the fireplace set piece on Saturday, but since the house was now ready to be moved into, he'd asked her if she could come tonight, instead.

Tomorrow, he and Holly were going to be able to move in. A full week before Christmas. He couldn't believe he'd managed to pull it all off.

As soon as they were done with the meal and got everything packed back up in the basket Rachel had brought, they let the dogs back through the gate. One of the only items in the house that wasn't a home improvement tool was a Bluetooth speaker he'd brought so he could listen to music while he worked on the house. He started it playing Christmas music and turned on the fireplace—it seemed appropriate, given what they'd be working on.

Then he and Rachel started working on the set piece. They hadn't even gotten through talking about their next steps before Aiden said, "Can me and Holly go set up the blankets for our beds?"

It would take hours to get the set piece finished and they knew they would be working past the kids' bedtimes, so they brought a huge pile of blankets and a couple of soft mats that his in-laws had so they could sleep when it was time. "Sure thing. Holly can show you which room."

The kids carried armloads of blankets away, trying not to trip on the trailing end, the dogs running around them and nipping at the corners of the blankets. He guessed there was going to be a lot of chaos and laughing and probably the wearing of blankets like capes before any beds got made. He was going to drink in every second of laughter that he heard coming from his daughter.

He and Rachel looked at the fireplace—the fake one, not the real one— which was standing but was still wood-colored. "So," Rachel said, her hand on her hips as she studied the piece, "paint from the mantle up first, so it can dry, then work on cutting and installing the brick facade? Then, hopefully, the top will be dry enough that we can paint the details and then figure out how to attach the Christmas decorations."

"Sounds like a good plan to me." He still had the floors covered with a drop cloth from when he'd painted this room yesterday, so they were able to get to work quickly. As Rachel painted the edges with the paintbrush and he painted the big areas with the roller, every time they got close to one another, he was reminded of their date on Tuesday and how they'd been moments away from kissing before it had abruptly ended. All the nerve endings firing, all the warmth spreading from his chest, all the longing that he'd been feeling that night he was feeling at full force again now.

And every time that their faces were close and Rachel's eyes would meet his, a breath of anticipation hanging in the air between them, a kid would come running into the room, usually chased by a dog, sometimes chasing a dog, and he'd be reminded how much a kiss wasn't about to happen. Holly was warming up to Rachel quite a bit, but if his daughter caught him and Rachel kissing, he worried it would be pushing her too far, much too fast.

Besides, every time he thought again about the kiss they'd almost shared, he would also start thinking again about the cancer. He knew cancer well enough to know that relapses could happen and that Rachel wouldn't fully be in the clear until she'd had scans come back clean for a full five years.

When she'd first told him, it had felt like a bowling ball hit him in the gut. He was really falling for Rachel. After losing Clara, though, could he face the possibility of losing Rachel, too? He wasn't sure.

They had gotten all the fake brick pieces cut that they would need and were in the middle of attaching them to the fireplace with the construction adhesive when Holly and Aiden came running into the room. "Can we each have one of those cookies you bought?" Holly asked.

"Yep," he said. "Just make sure the dogs don't eat any."

Somewhere in the middle of his sentence, he heard Rachel say "Oh," as an exhale.

"I apologize," he said. "I shouldn't have answered for both of us."

"No, it's totally fine. Go ahead, kids."

She might have said it was fine, but he'd seen from that initial look on her face that she wouldn't have told them it was okay. He glanced at the clock and realized that it was almost bedtime. Maybe saying yes to sugar wasn't the best idea ever.

"Yes!" Aiden pumped his fist. Then, to Holly, he said, "I told you she would say yes to anything!" Then the two of them ran over to the kitchen counter to get the cookies before racing off, the dogs at their heels.

He wouldn't have thought anything of Aiden's statement if it weren't for the way it made Rachel's cheeks redden, so he had to ask. "You'd say yes to anything?"

Her cheeks went redder and she rubbed her nose and then waved her hand. "It's just a bet with my coworkers. I'm doing a 'Season of Yes' because they think I'm too much of a planner and it'd be good for me."

Oh, interesting. He'd seen glimpses of her planning side, like when he'd seen inside her perfectly organized pantry when he and Holly had joined them for snowflake making, and anytime she opened her planner or the schedule in her phone, and when she'd unzipped her purse to grab lip balm, but he suddenly wondered how many things she'd said yes to that she wouldn't have chosen to do. "So, saying yes to helping with this set piece. Was it because of the bet?"

"I *definitely* only said yes because of the bet. I didn't have the first clue how to make this on my own."

"Going on a date with me?"

"Yes, because of the bet."

Oh.

She gave him a playful shove. "I'm kidding. That I *couldn't* have said no to."

The tension he hadn't realized had gathered in his shoulders released and a smile spread across his face.

Rachel grabbed the caulking gun with the adhesive, knelt in front of the fake fireplace, and started spreading the glue where the next faux brick section would go. Since the answer to the last question was, apparently, good for his shoulder muscles, he thought it might be fun to push it some more.

"And what about saying yes to coming over tonight? Was that because of the bet?"

She tapped a finger on her lips like she was deep in thought, and all he could think of was kissing those lips. "Well, I might not have changed plans... I was really looking forward to the wrapping presents party Aiden and I were going to have. But it turns out that going three days without seeing you is about my max."

Nick grabbed the next piece of bricks they had cut, knelt in front of the fireplace, and he and Rachel both fit it into the correct spot, both pressing on it for the thirty seconds the adhesive called for. Their shoulders were touching, their arms entangled, their knees bumping. "So what would've happened if we didn't work on this until tomorrow as we'd originally planned?"

Rachel shrugged. "I might have, say, gotten stuck in the wreaths at The Home Improvement Store and had to call for help. It's hard to say."

He shook his head, chuckling.

Aiden popped up from behind the kitchen island and

said, "Mom said that we would probably make ginger-bread cookies and bring some to you!"

Rachel put a hand over her face. "Aiden! What are you doing spilling all my secrets?" Then she looked down at her watch. "Oh, wow. I didn't realize it was that late. It's bedtime."

The kids got their teeth brushed and pajamas on, then he and Rachel worked together to get the kids and the dogs all snuggled into their makeshift beds. Aiden pulled out the Christmas book that he had packed and Rachel read it to them.

After the book, as they were both straightening the blankets on their kids, Aiden said to Rachel, "You know that paper I left for the dove in the park? I want to tell you what I wished for but I can't say it out loud or it won't come true." He paused a moment, then said, "So how about I whisper it in your ear?"

Competitive girl that she was, Holly had to whisper something in Nick's ear while Aiden was whispering in his mom's. She motioned for him to come close, then cupped her hands between her mouth and his ear and said, "I think I am ready for a mom."

He pulled back, blown away by Holly's declaration. She was? He just looked at her for a moment as she gave a satisfied smile and lay back on her pillow again. Then she and Aiden shared a look, probably because she also whispered something into a parent's ear. He took

Rachel's lead and said goodnight to the kids before quietly leaving the room.

The whole evening—having dinner, working on a project together while the kids and the dogs played, tucking the kids in bed, all of it—had just felt so... domestic. Which was especially incredible, considering that they were in an empty house that hadn't been moved into. Regardless, it had almost felt like they were a family and it stirred something in him that made him crave more of it.

It took hours after the kids were asleep to finish all the details on the fireplace and get it fully decked out for Christmas, complete with stockings hanging on the mantle. But he didn't mind even a little bit, because it meant he got to spend more time with Rachel.

They swapped stories about their lives. He told her about his two sisters and brother and all the places they'd lived when he was growing up, and she told him funny stories about her and Jack and all the crazy things they'd done as kids. There were times when they'd laughed so hard that he was surprised they didn't wake Holly and Aiden.

He glanced at his watch—just past midnight. They took a seat on the hearth of his actual fireplace and admired the work they'd done on the fake one. "I kind of wish this was staying in my house—it makes the place feel more homey and Christmassy."

He caught a slight smile from Rachel out of the corner of his eye. "Of course, you moving in tomorrow will probably do the same thing."

He laughed. "True."

They gazed at it in silence for a moment before Rachel said, "We make a good team."

"We do." His voice came out lower, huskier than he'd meant. But the words were authentic—they'd made a great team. He stopped looking at their project so he could turn his gaze to her. They'd been working hard for many hours, but she still looked beautiful. Vibrant. Full of life. Her eyes still radiated spunk and caring kindness. She'd pulled her hair up into a ponytail when they'd started working, and it exposed the most exquisite neck.

All night long and really, since their date on Tuesday, they'd had so many little touches. A brushing of their hands or arms. A bumping of their shoulders or legs. And so many times when it happened, Rachel had given him a look that started a fire in his chest. And he could tell by how often she glanced at his lips that she was wanting a kiss as badly as he was.

But between the presence of the kids and the fact that the project had to be finished tonight—the rest of the weekend would be filled with moving in and the program was on Monday—the anticipation had been building and building.

But right now, she was there with him. No kids

present, no project looming over them. Christmas music played softly from the speaker across the room, the warmth from the fire was at their backs, the sounds of fire crackling just behind them.

Rachel reached out and ran a finger lightly across his forearm and the touch sent tingles up his arm. He met her eyes, his heart racing. Not because of anything to do with Clara. Or because he felt like he shouldn't kiss Rachel—it was more because he felt like he *should*. He hadn't expected that at all.

He just studied Rachel's face and took in everything that she was. The person she was. Everything about this moment just felt right.

Like they had all night long, their legs bumped together as he leaned in closer to her and she closed the gap, pressing her lips against his. Her lips were soft and the feel of them on his made him moan. Rachel sank into the kiss, a humming sigh escaping her that made that heat in his chest burn stronger.

He stood, pulling Rachel to stand with him, and put his hands on the sides of her face, savoring the feel of her skin, the touch of her lips, the scent of her shampoo, the tickle of her breath.

He dropped a hand to her waist to cradle her close to him, and she slid her hands up to his neck, sending tingles everywhere her fingertips touched.

When they'd been dancing at the wedding, he'd felt

like he'd been pushed out of an airplane, feeling the wind brush past his face. He had that same sense now, but this time, it was as if Rachel was falling with him, hand-in-hand, and he didn't care that the parachute hadn't deployed yet. The feeling of falling so completely and totally was consuming.

He pulled away from her lips so he could trail kisses along her jaw and down that neck that had looked so striking all night. Then he trailed the kisses right back up toward her ear and breathed, "You are an incredible woman."

The sound that escaped her lips may have been a moan. Or maybe a sigh. Whatever it was, it sounded both relaxed and elated and made his chest expand. She looked into his eyes, and he realized that he could stare into her eyes for hours and not tire of what he saw.

"Wow," she whispered. "That was..." She didn't finish her sentence and she didn't need to. She just looked into his eyes for a long moment, both of them soaking in everything.

Then her gaze shifted to behind him. She squinted, her eyebrows drawing together. "When did it start to snow?"

Still with his arm around her waist, he twisted to see the window that faced his backyard. The light inside made it reflect the surroundings of the room, but he could kind of see a bit of what lay beyond the window.

Rachel grabbed his hand and pulled him toward the doors that led onto his patio, so he turned the knob and pulled it open.

Snow had blanketed everything and was still falling gently, silently from the sky in big fat snowflakes. If this house contained anything other than a fake fireplace, a bunch of tools, and the blankets that their kids used, he might have welcomed the sight. He might have even suggested that he and Rachel go out on the patio, wrapped in blankets, and enjoy the storm together.

But neither of them was staying there tonight, so the falling snow brought with it a sense of urgency. He turned and hurried across the room and down the hall toward the front door and opened it. White covered everything, shining brightly in the light of the street lamps and Christmas lights. No plows had come down the street yet, and the snow was increasing by the moment.

He closed the door, shaking his head. "It always amazes me how much more snow falls here in the mountains than it did in Colorado Springs."

"We should go before the roads get any worse."

He stepped closer to Rachel. "We should."

She closed the gap even more. "I don't want to go."

"I don't want you to go."

The reluctance on Rachel's face seemed to match his. Given the choice, he would've stayed in his empty family room, kissing Rachel for a very long time. He stepped up close to her and cupped her chin in his hand before placing a soft kiss on her lips. He looked into her eyes for a long moment, hoping she could sense how much he didn't want her to go. "I'll go get our cars started and the snow brushed off them, then I'll carry the kids out."

She gave him a smile that made him want to brave an arctic snowstorm for her, then he gave her one more kiss before he turned to grab their keys.

eleven

RACHEL

RACHEL STARED at the two-page magazine spread that she'd been working on, knowing that something was wrong with it but not being able to focus enough to figure it out. She finally gave up and swiveled in her chair to face Lucy.

"I said yes to being spontaneous on Friday."

Lucy was quick to stop trying new fonts for the image she was working on and turn her full attention to Rachel. "What? You did not."

"I totally did. Remember on Friday how I told you that Aiden and I were going to have a present-wrapping party and then I hoped he'd fall asleep quickly so I could wrap his?"

Lucy nodded.

"Nick called just as I was leaving work to say that

he'd finished with the last project in his new house and wanted to move in on Saturday, so he asked if we could meet to finish that fireplace for Aiden's school program on Friday."

"Based on how distracted you've seemed all day, I'm guessing it went well?"

She hadn't realized she'd been distracted enough for others to notice. She had to get her head in the game... *After* this conversation. She definitely needed to get it all out first. "As much as I had joked about it with Nick that night, it was actually hard! I don't love last-minute plan changes."

"But?"

"But my need to see him very much outweighed my desire to have things scheduled."

"Oh, I wish Court wasn't out of the office today—she would be so freaking proud of you right now, she'd probably have tears in her eyes! Okay, knowing Court, she probably wouldn't. She'd just act all businesslike and give you a 'good job' nod. But *I* have tears in my eyes! This is exactly the kind of thing we were hoping for when we made that bet with you."

Rachel folded her arms. "So, really, the entire bet was so that I would be spontaneous and change my Friday night plans to spend time with a guy?"

Lucy shrugged a shoulder. "Basically."

Rachel chuckled, shaking her head. She should've known.

"So things are going well?"

"Yeah. I really like him." She paused a moment, trying to decide if she wanted to share even though she knew she was going to, whether she offered it on her own or she waited for Lucy to ask. "We kissed."

"And?"

Rachel took a long, slow breath before answering. "I didn't know that kissing him could be so great. Before experiencing Nick's kisses, my brain couldn't even imagine it could be so incredible."

Lucy fanned her face with her hand.

"He was just so sweet! He kissed me like I was so..." She waved her hands, trying to find the words. "Important. Cherished. Like he was simultaneously trying to treat me with such great care, yet completely taking my breath away. The whole night was just the kind that you know you'll remember for the rest of your life." She could hear the longing in her voice, the craving to be near him. Yet, she also felt the uncertainty, and Lucy picked right up on it.

She cocked her head. "Why do I feel like there's a *but* coming?"

Rachel picked up a pen from her desk and started playing with it. "I don't know. It's all just too much. I feel like Aiden and I are busy every second of the day. Relationships just take a lot of time—especially new relationships."

"But it's a good way to spend time, right?"

"It's the best." She sighed just thinking about it. "I told him a couple of weeks ago that my mom used to leave Dove chocolates on my pillow for me and that doves at Christmastime, especially, are special to me. Even though he's been crazy busy all weekend getting moved into his new house, I got to work this morning and when I passed by reception, Shelly said a man dropped something off for me. It was a package of Dove chocolates with a note from Nick that said he hopes I have a peaceful week. How thoughtful is that?"

Rachel leaned back in her chair and looked up toward the ceiling. "We've been staying up late every night talking on the phone for hours after both of our kids have gone to bed. Sometimes he'll just text in the middle of the day to let me know that he's thinking of me." She put her hand over her heart. "It's the sweetest thing, and it just blows me away to know that someone cares about me that much."

"Oh! My heart just melted for you!"

"But do you know how little sleep I've got lately? We've been staying up so late that I completely slept through my alarm this morning."

"That was why you were late?"

She nodded. "And there's just so much to do."

"Is that what you're worried about?" Lucy asked. "Because the busyness isn't going to be an all-the-time thing. It's just crazy right now because Christmas is this week and this is our busy time of year at work. It'll get better."

Rachel looked down at the pen in her hand and then set it on her desk again. "It isn't just that. Friday night, we laid a blanket on the floor of Nick's empty dining room and had dinner sitting down with the kids. I brought cookies—"

"Homemade?"

"Lucy. Remember the part about being busy all the time? No, I didn't make them. Sugarplum Fairy Bakery did."

"Mmm. That's the next best thing."

"Right? So I got cookies, but we didn't eat them with dinner and kind of forgot about them. Then, as we were working, Aiden and Holly asked if they could have one. My immediate thought was no—it was way too close to bedtime and Aiden knew not to ask for something sweet that late at night. But in the spirit of the *Season of Yes*, I would've stopped myself before saying no and said yes. But Nick said yes without even thinking about it first."

"And this is a problem why?"

Rachel blew out a breath, feeling stupid for even bringing it up. "It wasn't a problem. It just did make me think that as much as I've wished over the years that I had a partner in the whole parenting thing and knew how much it would help, it just had somehow not occurred to me that we might not agree on parenting styles and that might be a challenge. The cookie thing wasn't a big deal at all. But it did make me wonder how many things we might run into that might be a bigger deal." It was a fear she hadn't even known she had until Friday night.

"Yeah, I can see how that would be tough."

"So, I'll worry about something like that, then *bam*! I'll get the image in my head of Nick carrying each of the kids, all bundled up in blankets, out to each of our cars as the snow fell softly, the moon and the Christmas lights casting a soft glow on them, then getting them all safe and buckled in. And then I'm just left confused and really *really* wanting him by me, his arms around me, his lips on mine."

"He carried them out to the car? Oh my goodness, I think my heart just melted again. Completely this time. It's now just a puddle."

"But here's where it gets intense. I had read a book to Aiden and Holly. When I was hugging Aiden goodnight, he was acting like he wanted to tell me something so badly that he couldn't hold it in. When we were at the Christmas Village a couple of weeks ago, he had a 'Christmas wish' that he rolled up and put in the claw of a dove. He said, 'I want to tell you what I wished for but I can't say it out loud or it won't come true. So how about I whisper it in your ear?' Do you want to know what he wished for? A dad! And, of course, Holly whispered something to Nick at the same time, and then I saw the two kids share a look."

"Oh, that's sweet."

"I don't know. What if I'm just giving him more false hope than a six-year-old can handle? That's not fair to him. Or Holly. For all I know, she was whispering about what she wanted for breakfast the next day. But if that look that I saw between them was what I think it was, it was conspiratorial. Maybe Holly wants the same thing— a second parent."

Lucy was silent for a long moment before she said, "You say you want to get married and that you want Aiden to have a dad. But do you really?"

"I do!"

"With every other guy you've started to date, you backed away pretty quickly because you didn't think he was good enough for Aiden. Now you find this guy who actually *is* perfect, yet you're still backing away."

Rachel ran her hands over her face. "I know. I don't know what's wrong with me. I'm thirty years old, and I've never had a long-term relationship." She shook her head. "Maybe I just can't handle it."

"You can handle it."

But she wasn't so sure. She didn't have history on her side.

AN AIR of excitement and anticipation filled the gym as Rachel and Nick found seats where they all had a good view of the stage. Maybe it was because the kids only had two more days of school left before Christmas break, or maybe it was just what happened when dozens of parents of first graders got together to see their little ones performing something they had been working so hard on.

Nick reached out and put his hand on hers, and she nearly moaned, right there in the middle of the crowded gym, it felt so good to feel his touch. To have his warm hand on hers, soft as a caress. She was so far gone for this man that it scared her. She forced herself to pay attention as Miss Goodrich got up and thanked everyone for coming and introduced the program.

Then the curtains opened and everyone clapped. She immediately found Aiden with all the other first graders on the risers, Holly right next to him. His eyes were scanning the crowd and as soon as they landed on her and Nick, he started waving wildly. Holly followed Aiden's gaze, and she waved, too, although much more restrained.

As she watched them up on stage, singing the first two songs they'd learned, she couldn't help but think about how much Aiden was falling for Nick, too. As they'd walked into the school, Aiden had held Rachel's hand and Holly held Nick's. Then Aiden had reached out with his other hand and took Nick's free hand, so he was between the two of them. As great as it was, and as much as it had made it feel like they were a little family of four, it freaked her out even more because she could see how much Aiden was getting attached.

When they finished singing the two songs, they started reciting the poem *The Night before Christmas* and she pulled out her phone to video it. It was impressive that they knew it so well—it was a long poem. Aiden had been practicing it at home so much that she all but had the thing memorized, too.

Then they got to the part where they listed the names of the eight reindeer and a couple of kids started saying the names out of order, which messed up more kids, and soon it was all just a jumble of reindeer names. She chuckled, trying to keep it silent so it wouldn't be on the video.

Neither she nor Nick, though, managed to keep their chuckling quiet when Aiden got extra enthusiastic with the line "Now dash away! Dash away! Dash away all," making arm motions that Holly was quick to mimic. The poor kid on the other side of Aiden nearly got knocked off the riser in the exuberance.

Then came the line, "Down the chimney St. Nicholas came with a bound," and the six-year-old who was dressed as Santa took it to mean that he needed to leap through the fireplace opening. The big, stuffed bag that the kid had slung onto his back didn't quite follow the same trajectory, and it hit the side of the set piece.

The kid yanked the bag at the same time, and as the group said in unison, "He was dressed all in fur, from his head to his foot," the fireplace started slowly tipping forward and everyone in the audience leaned in their seats, holding their breaths.

As the falling of the fireplace started to pick up speed, the kids on the risers noticed and all the ones on Aiden's side leaped from their spots and rushed to push it back to standing. Most of the other kids were gasping and pointing, but a handful of kids kept saying the lines of the poem, either oblivious to what was happening or determined to see it through to the end.

They got the fireplace righted and the audience let out a collective breath. The kids were all grinning like they'd singlehandedly saved Christmas.

"Don't worry, Santa," Aiden said, loud enough that everyone heard, "we've got your back."

"Ho, ho, ho," Santa said. "Thank you for saving my life."

"Does this mean we'll get extra presents?" A kid called out.

They were down to three kids still reciting the poem, and as they were very determinedly shouting now, "He had a broad face and a little round belly that shook when he laughed, like a bowl full of jelly."

Besides the three kids determined to finish the poem, chaos erupted. Some were peeking into Santa's bag, Santa was strutting around on the stage, the rescuers of the fireplace were giving each other high fives, and one kid was randomly dancing like no one was watching. The audience was howling with laughter as the three first-grade teachers took to the stage, trying to reestablish order.

It was tough holding the camera steady through her laughter. She glanced over at Nick. He was grinning at the whole display. Then he turned to her as the kids finally got back up on the risers and the volume in the room lessened. "What do you think? Should we head out for an after-program ice cream when this is over? I heard that *With a Cherry on Top* in Nestled Hollow is fantastic."

She was getting better at allowing spontaneity into her schedule, but it still wasn't easy. Studies had shown that kids thrived more on a predictable schedule, and she'd veered off her daily, weekly, and monthly schedules all season long. But a week ago, she would've said yes anyway, just because of the Season of Yes bet.

But today, that wasn't her biggest worry. In fact, her mind was chock full of flat-out fears. She was afraid that she was making a wrong choice and that it would impact all four of them. But more than that, it felt like the choices weren't even all up to her—she was a snowball rolling downhill, picking up size and speed as she went. She couldn't steer or stop and had no choice but to go along with it. It was all out of her control. Saying yes to everything instead of following her trusty plans didn't help.

"I don't think we better," she whispered back. "We've been so busy that Aiden hasn't been getting enough sleep lately, and I don't want him having trouble sleeping tonight, since tomorrow is a school day. And the last two days of school before Christmas break are so crazy—I don't want to add to it."

Nick nodded. "You're right." She didn't miss the disappointed look on his face, though.

She probably had a disappointed look on her face, too. But as much as part of her wanted to say yes to Nick and not care about schedules, the other part of her was completely freaking out and she didn't know how to make it stop. Or if she even should.

twelve

NICK

"OKAY," Nick said as he swiveled around in his office chair and reached for another box. "It sounds like the timeline after the break for the next release is doable." This was his last meeting of the day, on the last day he had to work before he got a full week off for Christmas and New Year's. Maybe with the time off, he'd be able to finally get the last box unpacked.

He had to admit, life was pretty great. He and Holly were settled in their own place again and he was working in his new office. It was good to have an actual space for work. He'd worked at the company office full-time before relocating to Mountain Springs, so transitioning to the folding table in the cramped guest room of his in-laws' home had been tough. But it made him appreciate his new space even more.

Plus, Rachel was in his life. And Aiden was such a cool kid. Holly had her last day of school before the break two days ago, so she was spending the day with his in-laws to help them get ready for the annual Ugly Christmas Sweater party they put on every year. He would get Rachel and Aiden and head over as soon as he was off work.

"Who do we have lined up from the UX team to do the design and layout for it?" he asked as he sliced through the tape holding a box closed. He didn't have to be on camera for this meeting. He didn't even have to be at his computer for it. So he had been wearing his wireless headphones and mic so he could move around while unpacking and organizing his office.

It had been quite a few weeks since he'd packed most of these boxes, and he hadn't thought to label them any more specifically than which room they belonged in. So the contents of each had been a surprise.

"I think it's Andrus."

"Okay, that'll be good. And Mary is confident that we can implement the new features with the current system?"

He pulled out a couple of file folders that hadn't made it into the box with the others that he'd already unpacked as Doug told him about which features the client wanted that would work out just fine and the one that they were still concerned about.

Then he reached in to grab an upside-down wooden box, turned it over, and his breath caught in his throat. It was a shadow box that Clara had made for him right after they'd gotten home from a vacation to the beach—the last vacation they'd taken. A photo was affixed right in the center of the three of them. Clara had her arms around his middle, and he had one arm over her shoulders and held a four-year-old Holly with his other arm. All three of them were grinning.

The rest of the display piece had memorabilia from the nearby museums they'd gone to, shells and colored glass they'd found on the beach, and smaller pictures of the sandcastle they'd built and of the three of them sitting at the edge of the beach where the waves came in, covering their legs. He remembered that vacation like it had just happened. They'd written messages in the sand, watched the sunset, ate lunch right on the beach, and daydreamed for hours.

All the memories came crashing in, just like the waves had, one right after another, and each came with a stab of missing Clara.

"Nick? You still there?"

Nick cleared his throat, trying to also clear out the emotion he was sure would come through loud and clear. "Can we finish discussing this after the break? I'm sorry—I've got to go."

He ended the call, pulled off his headphones, and

stared down at the picture, not even realizing that he had started crying until he felt the tears on his cheeks. Most of the time, he felt like he'd worked through his grief and was doing well. Sometimes he just missed Clara so much it hurt.

And sometimes, like right now, it felt like a wave had come in that was so large it completely submerged him in the ocean water, threatening to pull him out to sea. He ran a hand over his eyes blurred too much to see the picture of the three of them, looking so happy and so oblivious about what their near future held.

From nearly fourteen months of experience, he knew that it didn't work to just push the emotions away when they hit—they were attached to a rubber band and they'd just come back fast and hit so much harder. So he let himself feel the grief of missing someone that he'd loved so much. He let himself cry. He let himself take in that emptiness inside as everything around it felt big and heavy and crushing.

When the tears finally slowed and his ragged breathing turned smooth yet shallow, his neck muscles still tensed from all the emotion they'd been attempting to hold, he started to wonder what in the world he was doing. Clara held so much of his heart. How could he have a relationship with Rachel when he couldn't give her his full heart? It didn't seem fair to her at all.

And how could he have a relationship with a woman

whose cancer could relapse? What if he ever had to go through this again?

He tried to smile at Clara in the picture, but his lips immediately fell again. He sniffed and pressed the heel of his hand over one of his eyes. Then he whispered, "I don't know how to do this, Clara. I know you want me to find someone new and love again, but I don't know what I'm doing."

NICK WALKED up the sidewalk to his in-laws' house with Rachel and Aiden. Holly must've been watching out for them because she opened the door before they even reached it. Welcome," she said, throwing one arm wide, clearly pleased by all the party preparations she'd helped with.

Nick had texted Rachel and then his mother-in-law to let them know that he would be a little late, then he'd jumped in the shower and let the warm water wash away the tears and relax the sore muscles in his neck and shoulders. By the time he'd stepped out and wrapped a towel around his waist, he'd felt so much better. Not one hundred percent—that would take another day or so—but better enough to go to the Christmas party.

"Hey, HollyBear. How was your day?"

"*So* great. Take your coats off and come see!"

As they all took off their coats, he smiled at Rachel's ugly sweater. It was striped, but with a beach scene complete with palm trees and a flamingo, and she'd added little Christmas lights to the trees and around the neck that lit up, fading from one color to the next. He smiled. "They are going to love your sweater."

She grinned. "Thanks! Yours is..." she moved her head around like she was either trying to take it all in or find words to say, "one of the most fascinating things I've ever seen."

He chuckled and took a little bow. A friend from work had sent him the link just after Christmas last year and he'd bought it then, but this was his first time wearing it. It was also striped and looked like someone had tried to shove as many Christmas items on it as possible. A felt gingerbread man, embroidered snowflakes, a string of lights made from shiny colored fabric, tinsel was wrapped around the arms, puffy snow covered the bottom, and a sleigh and eight tiny reindeer flew across the sky. It was the most awful thing he'd ever seen and instantly knew it would be a hit.

"Mine, too?" Aiden said, puffing out his chest. His was a green sweater he'd decorated like a tree with ribbon and pompoms.

"Yours, too," Nick said. "They will all love it."

"I made it myself. Well, my mom did the glue gun part. But it's just like the costume me and my uncle Jack made for Bailey for the pet costume parade last year."

"Everyone loves mine," Holly said. She was growing out of everything so fast that he'd had to get her a new sweater this year. They'd been searching online stores together, and Holly had nearly died of happiness when they'd found a pink one with a decorated tree on it, tipped over, with a dog that looked remarkably like Rosy sitting on top of the tree.

Aiden ran ahead with Holly toward the party where, hopefully, she would introduce him to the other kids. He never wanted to squash any of his daughter's competitiveness, but he did talk to her about being nice and showing Aiden around.

"Come on," he said, putting his hand at the small of Rachel's back. "Let me introduce you to everyone."

They walked through the opening that led to his in-laws' kitchen, dining area, and family room which was fully decked out for Christmas. They'd clearly been baking all day because the place smelled of cinnamon, baked goods, and some kind of savory something that made his stomach growl.

Since they'd arrived a bit late, the place was already filled with people—most were Clara's relatives—standing and chatting, holding little plates of appetizers.

When Tanner spotted them walking into the room, he walked toward him as he called out, "May all your sweaters be ugly and bright! Hey, like yours!" He chuckled and slapped Nick on the back. "Hi, Nick. Good to see you."

"You, too." Nick turned to Rachel. "That's Tanner. He's a cousin."

Then his uncle Roger shouted, "'Tis the season for leftovers and stretchy pants!"

Nick rubbed the back of his neck. "That's... kind of a thing at this party—the random Christmas clichés turned on their sides."

He'd barely finished the sentence when Uncle Ken said loudly, "May your merry be large and your bills be small."

He led Rachel straight over to Ben and Linda for introductions, since they'd been dying to meet her. Just like he'd guessed, they were very welcoming to Rachel. His father-in-law started telling her about how he'd gotten a company to install permanent Christmas lights on his home that could stay there year round and that he could change the colors to match the holiday with his phone, right when Aunt Beverly leaned into his other side and whispered, "Is it appropriate to bring someone new *here*? At a get-together with Clara's family?"

He winced.

"Yes, it is," Linda said in her firm voice that always

sounded like a decision was final. "This is exactly where it's appropriate to bring her."

Uncle Ken was at Aunt Beverly's other side and said, "Don't get your tinsel in a twist, honey."

Linda gave Nick a reassuring smile and he glanced at Rachel, hoping she didn't hear the exchange.

As they walked away from his in-laws, Rachel said, "They're so nice!"

They were. He was relieved that she'd only been hearing what Ben and Linda were saying and not what Aunt Beverly said.

The noise level in the room seemed to rise just then, and Grandpa Hudson said in a loud voice, "Whoever wrote 'All is calm, all is bright,' clearly hasn't been here."

Nick, along with everyone else in the room, held up their drink or their plate of appetizers if they didn't have a drink, and shouted, "Ayy!" Then he turned to Rachel. "We do this every time grandpa quotes any lines from *Silent Night*. It's... kind of like a drinking game, I guess." He remembered the first time he was introduced to this group—Rachel probably thought they were as weird and eccentric as he had. She just chuckled, though.

"Who is this?" Uncle Pete said as he walked up to Rachel and Nick.

"This is Rachel Meadows, the woman I've been dating. Rachel, this is Uncle Pete."

Uncle Pete pulled his head back a little. "Oh. I didn't

think you'd be starting to date again already." Then, in a hesitant voice that conveyed how much he didn't mean what he said, he added, "Good job."

"I wasn't sure I would be, either." Nick smiled at Rachel as he slipped an arm around her waist. "Life surprises you sometimes." He hoped that Uncle Pete would get the hint not to push it any further and he hoped that Rachel would get the message that he was there for her regardless of anything anyone said.

Ken called out, "Santa Claus has the right idea to only see people once a year," and everyone laughed.

They had barely turned away from Uncle Pete when Tanner's wife, Tiff, put her hand on Nick's arm, giving him a face full of pity. "How are you, Nick?"

"I'm good. Tiff, this is Rachel, Rachel, Tiff."

Tiff smiled at Rachel and then turned back to Nick. "I'm glad you're doing well. Oh, I just miss Clara so much! I was telling Tanner that if he died young, I don't think I'd *ever* be ready to date again."

"It's definitely tough, but I bet you'd get there if you were ever faced with that situation." What was he thinking, bringing Rachel to a family event put on by Clara's parents, where so many of Clara's relatives would be present, when he and Rachel had only been together for a short time?

He was probably thinking everyone would be like

Clara's parents—super supportive of him dating again. He hadn't been prepared for this. He was especially ill-prepared after the emotionally draining afternoon he'd had.

They made the rounds to almost everyone in the group, and it was probably getting close to the games starting when a group of kids ran by Grandpa Harold, who was now leaning back in an armchair with his eyes closed. "I'm not 'sleeping in heavenly peace' here."

"Ayy," everyone called out as they held up whatever was in their hands. Rachel did this time, too.

Aiden came to stop in front of Rachel, so she crouched down to his height as he said, "There's someone whose sweater is like a fireplace, when they put their arms out straight like this, stockings are hanging down from it! Also, can you believe Christmas is in *two days*? And guess what? I told Holly's grandma that hanai means family that's kind of related but not really. Then I asked, and she said I could be her hanai, but Holly said it was only okay if Noelle's mom could also be *her* hanai. Do you think Grandma Allred would be okay with that?"

Rachel glanced at Nick before meeting Aiden's eyes again. "I bet she would."

Nick hadn't had time to process all that before his elderly Aunt Virginia pulled him toward her and patted his arm. "Are you sure you're ready to start dating again, dear?"

He took a deep breath.

"Because, you know, grief can come along and strike you at any moment."

Yep. He knew that all too well. It hit him earlier today and was hitting him pretty hard right now.

"Everyone encouraged me to start dating again a few years after Frank died," Aunt Virginia said. "So eventually, I said "Fine!" and I went on a date with a nice gentleman. The whole time I felt like I was cheating on Frank, and I kept looking around the restaurant like I was going to get caught for stepping out on him. There was just so much guilt. So I said 'I'm done.' It just wasn't worth it. I decided that I'm going to be true to my Frank always. To death, just like I said in my vows."

If that wasn't a truckload of guilt being dumped on him, he didn't know what was. He glanced over at Rachel, who was talking with Uncle Ken. He hoped she was faring better than he was.

Aunt Virginia patted his arm again. "When Clara married you and you two chose to have a child, she was choosing *you* to be Holly's dad. She didn't choose *someone else* to be Holly's mom. How would you even know if she approved of this person? Because if you find someone new, she'll be Holly's mom."

Knowing Aunt Virginia, she wasn't intentionally trying to be hurtful; he knew that, but all her words were like swords nonetheless. He took a steadying breath and said, "Clara would trust me to find the perfect person. And she would approve of Rachel."

"Hello, Virginia," his father-in-law said. "I apologize for interrupting, but can I steal Nick away from you? I need his help."

Aunt Virginia patted his arm one last time and then turned away to talk to someone else. Nick let out a long, slow breath before turning to Ben. "What did you need help with?"

"Nothing. It just looked like that wasn't the most pleasant of conversations for you, and I know Virginia will talk your ear off if given the chance."

He clapped his father-in-law on the back. "You're a good man, Ben. Thank you." He was truly grateful. He wasn't sure he could've taken many more stabs from Aunt Virginia.

Ben smiled, and then said, "Now go be with your date."

When Nick reached Rachel, he was met with a smile that faded just a bit when she took in whatever was on his face. "Are you okay?" she asked.

He said "Yes," but she was still looking at him like she could tell that something was wrong. He ran his hands over his face to try to wipe away all of it. "I'll be fine."

And he would be. After such an emotional afternoon, his nerves were just frayed because everyone was saying out loud all the fears he'd been trying to hold inside.

thirteen

RACHEL

RACHEL WAS SO glad that the Allred family had welcomed her and Aiden into their family right along with Jack because their home had become her favorite place to spend Christmas Eve. They had vaulted ceilings and a giant, gorgeously decorated Christmas tree, every area was decked out with garlands and red ornaments, a gingerbread train was moving through a mini village on a table, the long tables separating the kitchen from the family room were adorned in reds and whites with greenery down the middles, and Christmas music played over the speakers.

And this year, instead of being too sick to help, she was right in the middle of the action, cutting up vegetables with her new sister-in-law, Noelle, and Noelle's sister, Katie. She glanced over at Katie's date, who was chatting with one of Noelle's brothers-in-law, who was holding a two-year-old. "The guy you brought is pretty cute. How are things going with the two of you?"

Katie smiled as she glanced up from the cutting board to her date. "They're going fine. I mean he's not 'the one' or anything, but he's still a fun boyfriend. I don't know how much longer it's going to last, but I'm going to enjoy the relationship for as long as it's good."

Noelle, who was wearing a Santa hat with the words *Birthday Girl* stitched into it picked up a baby carrot and asked "What's he missing?" before taking a bite of it.

"I don't know," Katie said. "I'm just waiting for the guy who will just kind of grab me by the heart, you know?"

Rachel hadn't realized it until Katie said it, but that was what she'd been waiting for, too. And Nick had totally grabbed her by the heart. If only her stomach hadn't also been doing what it had been doing this week.

"How are things with you and Nick?" Katie asked.

Rachel lifted a shoulder in a shrug as she sliced the ends off some Brussels sprouts. "Nick is great. It's just that I've been feeling like a snowball rolling downhill, unable to control the speed or the direction, and after last night, it's like I rolled right off a cliff."

"What happened last night?" Noelle asked.

Rachel kept cutting the ends off the Brussels sprouts and slicing them in half. "I have daily, weekly, and monthly plans so everything will stay on schedule and be predictable and nothing will get forgotten, but I haven't been going off them much lately. Last night, after Nick's family party—well, his late wife's family, really—I went into my plans and they were all over the place. Nothing was right, everything was crazy, and it was a total mess. It made me feel even less in control of everything."

"I don't understand," Katie said as she pushed the cut cauliflower from the cutting board into the bowl. "Why did you even go look at it all if things were going fine? Why not just roll with it?"

Rachel hadn't been good at just "rolling with it" in her entire life. She thrived on plans. "Probably because I was trying to regain some control. Or maybe because of everything that happened at the party. Or a combination of both."

She glanced past the dinner tables to where Nick was playing in the family room with all the little kids, fully out of earshot. She let out a big breath and put down the knife, turning to face both Katie and Noelle. "People made so many comments about Nick and me dating last night. I mean, of course, they would—they were Clara's family, and I was just the person trying to fill her shoes. A lot of them were trying to be supportive, I could tell, but underneath, it was like they just knew that I would never be able to take Clara's spot."

And then she voiced the concern that had been growing over the past few days. "What if it's the same way with Nick? From everything I've seen, he and Clara had a great relationship and he really loved her. What if he feels like I could never take her place and he always wishes I was more like her? And what if he isn't even ready for a new relationship? It's only been fourteen months since his wife passed away. If I had a husband die, I don't know that I'd be ready to date again after just that long."

"Men get ready for a new relationship after a spouse dies more quickly than women do," Katie said.

"Really?"

Katie nodded. "Scientific fact." She pointed at Noelle. "Just like Uncle Jim."

"True," Noelle said. "He started dating like what? Five months after Aunt Tracy died? But it had been four *years* since Tracy's husband had passed, and Uncle Jim had been her first date since." She turned to Rachel. "But everyone is different. Fourteen months might be all Nick needed."

"Maybe," she said, but the worry was still there. "Look how attached Aiden has gotten to Nick."

All three of them looked over to where Nick was on the floor, kind of wrestling with all the little kids, all of them piling on top of him. The Allreds' black lab, Captain, was getting in on the fun, too.

"Oh my goodness, that is the sweetest," Noelle said.

They all just watched him. It really was the sweetest, seeing him have so much fun with the kids and they have so much fun with him. She loved that he was so willing to get on the floor with them. She had plenty of worries in her stomach, but the scene warmed her heart. He had been on his hands and knees, but then raised his torso, still on his knees, arms in the air, and growled. All the little kids squealed and then laughed.

Then Aiden went up to him, wrapped his arms around Nick's neck, and gave him a tight hug. Nick's eyes instantly found hers and she could see in that expression that he was worried about Aiden getting so attached, too, which only validated her worries.

"I'm so sorry to dump all of this on you two," she said. "And it's your birthday, Noelle! And Christmas Eve!"

Nick stood up, peeled a couple of kids off his legs, said something to them that made them all laugh, and then headed in her direction. Jack opened the last folding chair he'd brought up and came over, too, and both men joined them at the same time. Jack kissed Noelle on her cheek.

"Are you so excited to leave for your honeymoon tomorrow?" Katie asked

"Cancun!" Noelle said. "I can't wait!"

Rachel was so grateful that both women changed the subject so effortlessly.

"Thanks again for letting us stay at your house tonight," Jack said. "We're pretty excited."

Rachel nodded. "I've got the air mattress all set up for you in the living room. It's definitely worth getting excited over."

"I'm just glad that we can stay here as long as we'd like without having to think about making the drive back to Golden tonight," Noelle said. "Oh, and we just heard—our house should be ready for us to move in the day before we return from our honeymoon."

Jack smiled at her and Rachel soaked in how happy she was for her brother to have found someone that made him smile like that. "Remember when we were here a year ago?" he asked.

Noelle nodded. "It was the night that everything changed." They looked at each other with such love before they shared a quick kiss.

Rachel looked up at Nick, who had slid in right beside her, and got a sinking in the pit of her stomach, making her wonder if tonight might be the night that everything was going to change for them, too.

"Happy birthday to Noelle," Aiden called out.

Everyone shouted in return, "And to Noelle a good night!"

Aiden giggled even more than he had when they had

shouted the same phrases last year. Probably because now he knew that its inspiration came from the poem his class had memorized.

As soon as the last item came out of the oven, Mr. Allred announced that dinner was ready and they all took their seats along the long row of tables.

All through the dinner, it just felt like something was off between her and Nick, but she couldn't decipher how much of it was coming from her and how much of it was coming from him. All she knew was that it wasn't only her, and it made her stomach hurt enough that she was struggling to make it look like she didn't hate all the food on her plate. She knew from last year that every item was delicious—she just couldn't eat it today.

Then Holly said, "Grandma, can you please pass the stuffed mushrooms?"

Rachel could tell by the way Nick stiffened when he heard evidence that his daughter had claimed this family as her own that he was worried about her attachment to them. And the only way he'd be worried about that was if he didn't think their relationship was going to work out. Nick must've felt her attention on him, because he started to turn her direction, but not enough to make eye contact before glancing away.

She desperately wished that they weren't in a room with nearly two dozen people so she could just have a conversation with Nick and understand where his thoughts were. She always felt such a calm, peaceful feeling around him, and if they could talk, she knew she'd get that back.

If she hadn't thought that things were off before, she would've known they were when they sat with the Allred family to watch the Christmas Eve video that Katie made. Instead of putting an arm around her once they sat on the couch so she could snuggle into him like he would've done even just a couple of days ago, he sat stiffly next to her, his hands in his lap.

She was sure the video was great—especially with all the laughing and wiping of tears everyone around her was doing—but she was struggling to pay attention to it. She couldn't pretend that things were okay with her and Nick and she couldn't wait any longer to ask him about it. Leaning in close, she whispered, "Do you want to meet me in the living room to talk?"

He nodded, so she turned to Aiden on her other side and whispered, "I'll be right back." He was having so much fun with the other kids his age that he probably wouldn't even notice that she was gone.

Once in the living room, she looked at Nick for a moment as they stood next to the smaller tree that was right in front of the Allreds' front window. She immediately thought of that first day she'd met him when she'd gone to meet with Aiden's teacher about making the fireplace set piece. He still stood tall, showing off that great build, his auburn hair with the perfect amount of curl. She remembered thinking back then that his eyes were the color of the sea on a cloudy day, and now there was a storm of emotion going on behind them.

"You seem to have a lot on your mind." She did, too. Well, actually, she had a lot more going on in her gut. "Do you want to talk about it?"

He drew in a deep breath and shook his head as he glanced back in the direction of the family room, like he didn't want to talk about anything there. Or maybe he just didn't want to talk about it on Christmas Eve. But maybe he couldn't pretend any longer that everything was okay, either, because he gave a slight nod.

He put his hands in his pockets, and she wondered if he maybe didn't quite know what to say. She understood—everything she'd been feeling over the past few days was a jumble in her mind, too. A jumble of fears that were more intense now than they'd ever been. As intense as she was feeling everything, though, the look on his face told her that maybe he was feeling it more.

He reached a hand forward like maybe he was going to take her hand in his, but then decided against it and instead ran the hand over his face. "I am so new at all of this—trying to date again after Clara. And I don't know what I'm doing. I don't even know that I *can* do this. I kind of jumped in too quickly and didn't anticipate or think things through enough."

He paced over toward the window and then turned around to face her again. "I didn't know how I would feel about dating again until I did it. And now that I have, I'm not sure about anything. And I really didn't think about how everything would affect Holly—I was just happy that my daughter was making friends. I hadn't thought through far enough about what would happen if..."

He let the sentence trail off like he wasn't sure he wanted to say the words out loud. So she did. "If things with us didn't work out?"

He looked into her eyes for a long moment, and she felt so many things pass between them so quickly that she couldn't interpret any of them. "Yeah."

Rachel swallowed hard, the weight in her stomach feeling like it was doubling even as she started to think her next words. She said them anyway. "I've been worried about the same thing. Maybe..." She trailed off, and then just decided she should plow ahead, letting that fear that had been building up so strongly inside her take the wheel. It wasn't something she could contain much longer, anyway. "Maybe we should back away before things go any further."

He hesitated, his mouth parted like he was going to say something. His eyes searched hers, and she could see in his just what it was doing to him. How much this was destroying him. But then he brought his lips together and nodded once in agreement.

She stood frozen, just staring at Nick as the noise level in the family room rose. The video had probably finished. Had she really just ended things with Nick? Had he? Had they both decided that it was over? That this was the best thing? She felt a tear run down her cheek and she reached up to brush it away, knowing there were many more behind it, yet also knowing that they couldn't come yet.

The expression on Nick's face as she felt everything inside her crumble nearly undid her. His eyes were soft, his forehead furrowed in concern, his lips pulled down. At first, she thought in sadness, and then she realized it was the look of devastation. They should've realized all the reasons why their relationship wouldn't work earlier and ended things long ago. Before their hearts got in so deep that an ending would break them.

Jingle bells sounded just outside the house and the noise in the family room rose even more, mostly from the kids. Still, though, she didn't take her eyes off Nick until Aiden and Holly raced into the room.

"Mom!" Aiden shouted, grabbing her hand. "We have to get home and get to sleep super quickly!"

"Santa is almost here!" Holly said, grabbing Nick's hand and pulling him toward the couch that held their coats as Aiden pulled Rachel toward the family room, where she'd left her things.

She kept her eyes on Nick for as long as she could, feeling that as they were being pulled apart, he was taking her heart with him.

fourteen

NICK

A GUST of wind hit Nick as he and Holly stepped out of the Allreds' home, biting into him, making him hunch his shoulders to bring his coat closer to his ears. He felt Holly shiver through the hand he held. There was already frost on his car—he wished he would've started it ahead of time so it could have been warming up.

There were a lot of things he wished he would've done differently tonight. He started the car as Holly got in, then he grabbed the blanket in the back seat and spread it over her so she wouldn't freeze. After grabbing the ice scraper from the trunk, he went to work on the windows. The lump in his throat felt as big as the one in his gut, and his mind was a blizzard of thoughts and emotions.

He'd had doubts about having a relationship that had wound their way into his mind for quite a few days. The inner turmoil that had started with hearing about Rachel's cancer, elevated when he'd found the shadowbox Clara had made, and continued through the ugly sweater party and the Christmas Eve dinner was huge. He thought that by ending things with Rachel he'd feel relief from that turmoil. That it would be stopping it at the source.

So why did he feel so much worse now? His guts ached. His heart was filled with regrets and pangs of loneliness. His head was a clouded mess where nothing felt right. In fact, that it couldn't be more wrong.

He shook the ice off the scraper and tossed it back into his trunk before getting into his car, rubbing his hands together to give them a little warmth before grabbing the steering wheel. The entire ride home, Holly was chatting a million miles an hour about Christmas.

"This whole time, I figured I was on Santa's nice list, because I've been trying super hard to be nice to people, but as you were scraping the windows, Daddy, I suddenly wondered when Santa downloads the list."

"Downloads the list?"

"Yeah, you know, so he can print it out and give it to the elves so they can get everything ready to go. Did he download it like a month ago so they'd have plenty of time? Because a month ago, I'm not sure I was on the nice list. Do you think I'm going to wake up tomorrow and there's just going to be underwear under the tree? Because Zach S. said that one year he was pretty sure he was on the naughty list and he didn't get coal—he got underwear."

"I don't think Santa has a naughty and nice list. I think he just loves when you keep trying."

"Really? *Phew*. There are a lot of kids in my class who will be relieved to hear that. Hey, does Santa have any kids? Or are the elves like his kids?" Holly had been trying to get a satisfactory answer to that one for days.

The questions went on and on, and he did his best to answer each one, wondering how she was ever going to relax enough to fall asleep tonight.

As soon as they stepped through the garage door into the house, Rosy greeted them with as much excitement and lack of tiredness as Holly had been showing. Bedtime was sure to be rough tonight.

He went through all the motions with Holly, trying to keep a smile on his face the whole time. They placed a glass of milk and the package of Reese's Peanut Butter Cups they'd gotten for Santa on the table. When they'd last been at the store, Holly had decided that Santa was definitely a dad and that dads liked Reese's (based solely on the fact that Nick did), so they should get him that instead of cookies.

Finally, he got both the dog and his daughter tucked

into bed. He pulled the blankets up to her chin and gave her a kiss on the forehead. "Goodnight, Hollyberry."

"Goodnight, Daddy. Since this is the night before Christmas, I'm going to have visions of sugar plums dancing in my head."

He chuckled. "I can't wait to hear about it tomorrow."

"And I can't wait to go to eat cinnamon rolls at Aiden's tomorrow after we open presents."

The weight in his stomach somehow got heavier. "Actually, we are going to celebrate at home tomorrow until we go to Grandma's and Grandpa's."

She sat up in bed. "What? But no. I really want to go see Aiden and Rachel!"

"Don't worry," he said as she lay back down and he fixed her blankets again, "I'm going to make it a super special morning." He had no idea how. Making it more special than being there with Rachel and Aiden felt like an impossible task. Sometime tomorrow he'd have to share the reason why they weren't going there in the morning, once he figured out how to do that.

After he left Holly's room, pulling the door closed behind him, he wandered through his house. He'd been so happy to finally have the place finished so they could move in after being in cramped bedrooms at his in-laws. He had so much space now, but instead of feeling spacious, it just felt... empty.

He couldn't believe that he'd ended things with Rachel. Or more that he went along with her ending things without him doing a single thing to fight for the relationship. He'd felt so much turmoil leading up to tonight, but now all he could think of was everything he'd loved about being with Rachel over the past several weeks. How much he loved talking with her, texting her, doing things together with the kids, and spending time with just her.

Every memory he had with her was perfect, which made the pang of losing something that had the potential to be so great even more painful. What were the chances of a guy getting the opportunity to fall completely in love twice in his lifetime? He had it. And he threw it all away. He was feeling the pain of that loss acutely.

After mindless wandering through empty rooms, feeling as alone as he had in those first days after Clara died, he checked in on Holly. The excitement of the day must've finally caught up with her because she was fast asleep. He carried the box of presents from his room upstairs to the family room downstairs and put them under the tree.

Then he headed back upstairs, flopped down on his bed, and pulled out his phone. He swiped to the last screen, looked at Clara's face, and said, "Remember a few years ago when I was working at GilsonTech but then got offered a job at Improvementally? I didn't want to accept it, because I was perfectly happy at my job and the new job was such an unknown. I'd been afraid to take it because what if things went badly at the new job? It hadn't felt worth the risk. But you told me that you knew it was a good fit for me and that I would thrive at the new job."

He nodded. "And you were right. It was a very good change for me in so many ways. I never would've been able to work remotely and move here with the old job, either. I've definitely thrived at Improvementally."

He let out a huff of a humorless chuckle and shook his head, then closed his eyes for a moment before facing her picture again. "Apparently, I didn't learn that lesson enough the first time around and needed it again. Except for this time, I didn't choose so well. I think I messed up pretty big, actually." He looked up at the ceiling. "But everything's changed since you died, Clara, and I don't know anymore if I even can make the right choice."

He was just talking to a picture on a phone, yet he still felt bad that he was dumping that all on her. But if she was able to tune in from heaven, he knew she'd understand. He just wished she could also tell him what to do because right now, he didn't know.

RACHEL

"MOMMY!" Aiden said as he shook her arm. "Wake up—Santa came!"

"What time is it?" she asked as she pried her puffy eyes open and grabbed her phone. 6:13. It could've been so much worse. "Okay, buddy, I'm getting up. Are Jack and Noelle awake?"

"Yep! I went in and sat on their air mattress before I came in here. It bounced them so much that Noelle nearly fell off her side."

They probably loved that. She rolled out of bed and put on her slippers and bathrobe and headed into the living room. Jack and Noelle were looking as bleary-eyed as she felt, but they wore smiles on their faces.

Last night, after she'd left the Allreds' house, gotten Aiden to bed, made sure Jack and Noelle had everything they needed, and put Christmas presents out, she headed into her room to work on her Monthly Plan. Normally, she would have next year's Yearly Plan done by now, but she couldn't face it yet. The Monthly Plan, though—that, she could do.

She'd gotten the rest of December and all of January planned out. All the appointments in, reminders to do everything, and scheduling when she was going to spend time working on the goals she had for the month. As she'd worked, she'd heard the buzz of Jack and Noelle talking through the wall that she shared with the living room. It was nice. But it also made her long for someone to talk the night away with.

But she had a plan, and she stayed focused on it. Even when the buzz of talking quieted and the hour got later and later. It had felt like it was worth it, though, because she got everything in her planner all nice and neat and exactly how she liked it. Scheduled. Predictable. Deliberate.

The plan had gotten to be such a mess since Nick had stepped into her life. She'd fixed most of December's a few days ago, but it still needed help. So did the entirety of January. Scheduling everything always made her feel better, and since the craziness in her life was one of the reasons why she felt like she should end things with Nick, she figured that boost of energy and happiness that it normally gave her would be doubled.

But it wasn't. All it did was make her feel like everything was wrong without Nick in her life. And it made her get not nearly enough sleep. The two things did not combine well.

She gave her brother and his new wife a sleepy "Good morning," then took Bailey out back to do her morning duties. As she stood, shivering in the cold, she tried to keep herself from thinking about Nick and what happened last night. She had already cried herself to sleep about it and the slightest bit of thinking about it threatened to bring it on again. The puffy eyes weren't helping with the *no-sleep* look she was sporting.

But she did manage to hold things together as they all opened Christmas presents. Jack may have been a Grinch who hated Christmas up until last year, but she hadn't spent a single Christmas morning without him since the year he was born, and she was glad he was there with them. It made her house feel less lonely, too.

Every time, though, that Jack brushed Noelle's cheek with his knuckle, or she snuggled right into him, or he whispered something in her ear that made her laugh, or she smiled at him like he was her whole world, Rachel felt Nick's absence even more intensely.

As she could have guessed, it wasn't the toys that Aiden opened that he loved the most—it was the ream of white printer paper and the new set of markers that had lit up his face the most. The best part was watching him wrap his arms around them, giving them an uncomfortable-looking hug, his expression blissful.

The worst part was seeing two presents left under the tree when they were done unwrapping all of them. One for Nick and one for Holly.

"Who's ready for cinnamon rolls?" she said as she stood from the couch, ready to get some distance between her and the things threatening to make her lose her grip on her emotions.

Aiden, Jack, Noelle, and the dog all joined her by the kitchen counter, Bailey looking just as excited for food as everyone else. Rachel dished up a cinnamon roll for each of them, and as everyone sat down at her little kitchen table, she started getting the dog's food. "When do you need to leave for the airport?"

Jack looked at his watch. "Wow—it got late! We better go get the last of our things packed in the next five minutes, because we need to have the luggage in the car and pulling away in fifteen."

Rachel managed to keep a smile on her face and be happy to see them off on their honeymoon. They were on their way to a warm beach where they were going to be able to just relax and enjoy every minute together, and she was thrilled for them.

As soon as they were off, though, she and Aiden headed back to the kitchen for the cinnamon rolls. Aiden slid into his seat and asked, "Why aren't Nick and

Holly here yet? I thought they were going to have cinnamon rolls with us."

She couldn't believe that she hadn't thought to tell Aiden about the change in plans. "Oh, honey. I'm so sorry I didn't tell you earlier, but they're not coming. Nick and I decided to not see each other anymore."

"What?" Aiden slid off his seat to stand. "But my Christmas wish that I gave to the dove was for a dad! I thought it was going to be Nick. This is the opposite of the wish coming true!"

And then he was crying and she was crying and trying to comfort him and they both were a mess. Rachel couldn't remember the last time she'd cried so much in a twelve-hour period before and it hurt her heart even more that it was hurting Aiden's heart, too.

She was the mom, though, so she couldn't keep being a mess. She needed to pull herself together. "It's still Christmas, and we still have a lot of fun that needs to be had. What do you say we open that Lego set that Uncle Jack and Aunt Noelle got you and see what we can make?"

It was a good distraction for Aiden, but not so effective for her. She couldn't seem to get herself to stop thinking of Nick. She had spent the entirety of adulthood without a man in her life—she knew exactly how to do that. So why did the prospect of spending her life without Nick feel so profoundly sad? She'd never felt such an intense yearning to have someone in her life before.

It wasn't until she no longer had it that she realized it was something she'd been longing for all along—she just hadn't known she needed it. Or wanted it. Or would miss it so much when it was gone. She had been on her own for a long time. She'd been alone in raising Aiden. But she'd never felt lonely—she and Aiden had always been enough, just the two of them. So why did she feel so lonely now?

She told herself that it was because no matter how much Jack had hated Christmas most of his life, they'd always spent the entire day of Christmas together. And right now, she had no family with her outside of Aiden. Her sister-in-law, who had become one of her best friends, was with Jack, on her way to a trip of a lifetime. And her other two best friends weren't even in the state. Courtney was in Oregon and Lucy was in Nebraska, spending Christmas with their families. Her own little family felt so small.

But she knew that the loneliness she was feeling wasn't just because Jack or Noelle or her friends weren't there. It was because over the past few weeks, her family had felt twice as big with Nick, Holly, and Rosy with them.

But mostly, it was because of Nick. She missed him more than she ever fathomed that she could.

sixteen

NICK

NICK HAD BEEN SPENDING Christmas Day trying to make it happy for Holly, especially during the morning hours when they were supposed to go to Rachel's for cinnamon rolls. It had occupied him enough, apparently, that he'd completely forgotten that his in-laws were coming over until the doorbell rang.

He answered the door, still wearing his Christmas pajama pants and a t-shirt. As soon as it was open, Rosy raced to the door, and Linda said, "Well, hello, lassie-dog! I am happy to see you, too!" Then she looked up from where she was crouched giving Rosie a neck rub, to see Nick's face. Whatever she saw there made her ask, "What's wrong? Is Holly okay?"

Holly appeared around the corner just then, looking all chipper and running toward them, saying,

"Grandma! Grandpa!" and Linda breathed a sigh of relief.

After she hugged her granddaughter, she stood up straight and turned her attention to Nick. She only studied him for a moment and didn't even ask any questions before she said, "Oh, Nick. I'm so sorry."

Did his expression make it that obvious?

"Goodness, I forgot that I wanted to bring over that treat we got for Nick. How about Holly and I walk back to the house to get it."

Ben's brow furrowed. "Why don't you just give it to him when they come to our house for Christmas dinner in a bit?"

"Dear, I think we need it now." She said, putting extra emphasis on each word.

"Okay. Want me to walk back with you?"

"No, you two stay here." Ben still looked confused, so she added in a whisper that was nearly loud enough for Holly to hear, "Nick and Rachel's relationship took a hit and he needs you to talk to him."

Ben's eyes immediately flew to Nick. "I'm sorry to hear that, son." Then he turned back to his wife. "When did he tell you?"

"Oh, *Ben*, just go talk to him. Grab your coat, Holly—we're about to go on a Christmas wonderland walk!"

As soon as they were both out the door with a very excited Rosy following along, Nick and Ben headed back to his kitchen, family room, and dining area. Nick leaned against the granite countertop of his island and his father-in-law leaned against the table. They both just stood there for a moment, arms crossed, feeling awkward, looking at one another.

"So you two ended things?"

Nick nodded. "Last night."

"What happened?"

"Nothing that should've happened."

"Things didn't go so well with the woman I dated after my first wife died, either. You're new at this dating-after-having-been-married thing. You don't just automatically know what you're doing, and you're bound to make mistakes. It's not the end of the world."

"Well, I definitely made mistakes. But it was more than that." He tried to think about the events of the night before and look at them as a whole so he could figure out what went wrong. After a long moment where Ben just stayed patiently quiet, Nick said, "I think I was scared." He swallowed. "Maybe I still am."

That was so hard to admit, especially to his father-in-law, and it made heat rise to the back of his neck.

But Ben just nodded, like he understood and wasn't judging. So Nick just stayed silent and willed himself not to feel ashamed of the emotion.

"Let's talk about what you are afraid of."

"My dad was in the military, Ben. We didn't grow up

talking about things we were afraid of—we just talked about being brave."

"All right, then," Ben said. "Be brave and tell me what you're afraid of."

Nick shook his head and let out a breath of a chuckle. Then he ran his hand through his hair as he tried to think about what it was, exactly, that he feared.

"I guess I'm afraid of not knowing how to do this. To love someone new. And I'm scared that loving Rachel will..." He wasn't quite sure how to word what he was feeling. "I don't know—diminish what I had with Clara, I guess. Or that I won't be able to give my whole heart to Rachel, and she deserves my all."

His father-in-law stayed quiet for a few moments before he said, "When you love someone, you don't give a piece of your heart to them, a piece to the next person, a piece to the next. You don't have to get the pieces back to give all of it to someone—Rachel and Clara don't have to share your heart. You can love Rachel with your entire heart just like you loved Clara with your entire heart."

Could he?

"I mean, think about when Holly was born. Loving her didn't make you love Clara any less, did it?"

Nick shook his head. "It made me love her even more."

"So why would loving Rachel be any different?"

He hadn't thought about it like that. Could he honor his late wife's memory and still give his entire heart to Rachel?

"Or loving Aiden? Because loving Rachel and wanting a life with her would mean gaining a son and loving him as much as you love your daughter."

Nick nodded as he thought through everything. Before that moment when he'd let fear take hold, he'd felt like he was giving his whole heart to Rachel. It hadn't felt weird or wrong or impossible—it had felt right. Loving Aiden had felt right, too.

But there was something else that had worried him just under the surface for a while now. "Rachel went through cancer treatments recently. Her scan showed no cancer six months ago..."

"But you know she's not in the clear until she's had five years of clean scans."

Nick nodded.

"And you don't know if you can face the possibility of losing another woman you love."

Nick nodded again, not trusting his voice.

"Does Rachel seem very worried about relapsing?"

"I don't think so."

"That's a good sign." Ben was quiet for a long moment before he said, "Here's the thing about life. How long we've got here is an unknown. Someone who's terribly sick can recover and live a long life. And someone who seems healthy in every way—like Clara did—can leave at much too young of an age. It's a risk you take anytime you give your heart to someone."

Could he handle that risk?

"If you knew clear back when you'd first found yourself falling in love with Clara that she would pass away so young, would you have given up having that relationship with her?"

Their entire relationship seemed to fill Nick's mind. Their dating, falling in love, getting engaged, getting married, having Holly, buying their first house, job changes, all the time falling more and more in love. It gave him physical pain just trying to imagine that none of that happened. "No. There's no way I would give that up."

"I didn't think so," Ben said. "Here's another big question for you. Do you think Clara would have an issue with you loving Rachel?"

"No." He was sure of that. Last night, he'd "video chatted" with Clara, and then basically hung up on her after telling her his woes. It wasn't until this morning before he thought about what Clara might think of all of this if she'd been able to talk to him. And the overwhelming feeling he got was that he had her blessing and that she was happy he and Holly wouldn't be alone. He'd almost felt the breath of relief from Clara that he and Holly were loved and had someone to love.

"That's one thing my little girl always had—the ability to want for others even things she couldn't have for herself." He nodded. "I think she'd be proud of you."

Nick swallowed hard and blinked a few times to clear away the emotion that swelled up.

"And I think she'd want you to fight for Rachel."

RACHEL

RACHEL PULLED out her phone and sent a message in the group text with Courtney and Lucy.

Rachel: I said yes to something really bad.

Courtney: Oh, no. Spill.

Rachel: I ended things with Nick.

Lucy: Rachel! I wish I was there instead of being in stupid Nebraska with family so I could hug you!

Lucy: Just kidding— Nebraska isn't stupid and seeing family is great. But I wish I could be there! Why? Why would you end it?

Courtney: I think we need an emergency meeting via video call. Are you both free?

Rachel looked over to where Aiden and Bailey were wrestling on the floor and knew that they would keep each other occupied for a good ten or fifteen minutes, so she texted back *Yes*. Less than a minute later, she saw two of her best friends' faces on the phone. So she gave them a recap of everything.

"Did this all happen because of the Season of Yes?" Lucy asked.

Rachel shrugged. "I'll admit, that has been really hard."

"Why?" Lucy asked.

"I think just because I like having a schedule."

"But *why* do you? Courtney pressed. "Why does it matter so much to you?"

Rachel looked up, trying to think about why it was hard for her to not have one. "I don't know. I think because it's scary to not have one. Like if I don't, then everything will fall apart. A schedule was how I kept everything steady and consistent for me and Jack when we were kids living in an unpredictable environment. And then, as a mom, I know that it takes a good schedule and a lot of consistency if I want Aiden to thrive."

"Okay," Courtney said, "let's play a game of Worst

Case Scenario. Let's say your schedule gets unpredictable for a bit. What would happen?"

"More frequent meltdowns, for one."

"For you or Aiden?" Lucy asked.

Rachel laughed. "I was thinking Aiden, but now that you mention it..."

"And do you think you would keep it so inconsistent over time?" Courtney said. "Is that in your personality?"

Rachel thought back to the months she went through cancer treatment. Her schedule was as inconsistent as it had ever been then. And it *was* super hard on Aiden. But as soon as she got feeling better again, she was quick to get things back to that steadiness that she always craved. It wasn't just for him—she needed it, too. "No. It would only be short term." Just saying the words gave her a lot of comfort.

"Yes," Courtney said, "a new relationship can throw a monkey wrench in your schedule, but that won't be forever. And you and Aiden will bounce right back."

She nodded, completely believing Courtney's words.

"Yep," Lucy said. "Everything is not going to fall apart. When Courtney and I suggested that you read that book and then we both decided to make the Season of Yes bet with you, what we had in mind was you saying yes to things outside of your comfort zone. You are the most self-sacrificing person we know and you don't look out for your own needs. Ever."

"It's true," Courtney said. "Everything you do is in service of being a single mom. Never for you, as a woman. We thought that by you saying yes to everything, you might try some things that you'd end up liking. For you."

Lucy shook her head. "But it sounds like it backfired and just filled your plate too full."

Maybe that was exactly how it had gone. Thinking back, she had said yes to things she ended up liking. Nick was one of them. But her plate had definitely felt too full.

"My grandma Walker is staying here at my parents' house, too," Lucy said, "and I was talking to her yesterday. She said that after so many years of celebrating Christmas, one year she decided that it was all too much. So she sat down and decided what was most important to her to celebrate at Christmastime and pared everything way back. She said that she discovered that simple really was best. That all that mattered was the people you spent it with."

"Ooo, that's good," Courtney said. "Christmas doesn't have to be big to be special. Maybe you should take the day and kind of reevaluate what it is that's most important. You know, figure out what you want."

Maybe that was a really good idea. "Okay," she said. "I'll do it."

She ended the video call, and then said, "Aiden, I

need to work on my planner for a bit. Do you want to use your new paper and markers at the table with me while I do?" Since that was his favorite activity ever, she was able to sit down with him and really think.

She realized that over the years, she'd done every Christmassy thing with Aiden that came up because she grew up missing the entirety of every Christmas and didn't want Aiden to miss out on anything. So she let herself think about each thing they did and how much joy she thought it brought. She only put it on the list for next year if it truly felt integral to feeling the Christmas spirit. Then she asked Aiden what his two most favorite things to do at Christmastime were.

He said, "Making snowflakes, and..." He tapped the end of his marker against his lips. "I don't know. It's a toss-up between the hay ride and Christmas Eve."

Those were things that had landed on her list, too. She put stars by them to make sure they happened next year, but she was going to work hard to not feel like she had to do anything beyond that next Christmas unless they wanted to. She was going to spend it enjoying the people she loved.

She glanced at the window that showed her small backyard and noticed a few flakes of snow falling as the sun was setting. Last night didn't only happen because of her full schedule, though. She thought about what Courtney and Lucy said about wanting her to say yes to things so she'd find out what she really liked.

So she turned to a blank page in her planner and started writing down all the things she liked about Nick.

> *I love that he's a good dad.*
>
> *I love that he loves Christmas.*
>
> *I love that he makes everything fun.*
>
> *I love how much he shows that he appreci-*
> *ates me.*
>
> *I love the way he looks at me when he's*
> *listening to me talk about anything.*
>
> *I love the way he makes me feel.*
>
> *I love how he's willing to take on projects*
> *he's never done before and just assumes*
> *he can do it.*
>
> *I love the color of his eyes. The way his hair*
> *has the perfect amount of curl. The way*
> *he looks in a t-shirt. Actually, the way*
> *he looks in everything.*
>
> *I love his problem-solving, creative,*
> *thoughtful mind.*
>
> *I love how much he loves his daughter.*
>
> *I love how he talks about Clara with such*
> *respect and that their relationship was*
> *so great that her parents would still*
> *claim him as their son. I love that it*

> *gives me confidence that he'll always*
> *treat me with respect, too.*
> *I love how willing he was to do our*
> *Christmas traditions, like cutting and*
> *hanging snowflakes.*
> *I love how I can talk to him for hours and*
> *never run out of things to say.*
> *I love how much he can make me laugh*
> *with just a text.*
> *I love how hard he worked to make his*
> *house a home and how important that*
> *was to him.*
> *I love how safe and cherished I feel when his*
> *arms are around me.*
> *I love how great a kisser he is.*

Before long, every inch of the page was filled, even the margins. Sometime in the past week or so, she'd started focusing on what the relationship was doing to her planned-out and ordinary schedule. But as she worked on the list, she realized how much beauty and depth a relationship with Nick brought to her life and how much she had loved shouldering everything together.

Her friends had pointed out that she never did anything for herself and wanted her to figure out what she wanted. She, Rachel, had her very own wants and needs. And she was starting to understand what those were. Beyond how awful she'd felt after ending things, making the list helped her to realize that what she most wanted was a relationship with this man who she had spent this season falling in love with.

She looked over at Aiden, who was biting his top lip as he was cutting a snowflake out of a piece of paper that he'd decorated with his markers, and said, "You really like Nick, don't you?"

"Yeah."

"I really do, too. Do you want to help me think of something we can do to get him back in our lives?"

Aiden put his snowflake and scissors down and swung his legs around to kneel on the chair, leaning forward with his elbows on the table. "Yeah! Like what kind of something?"

"I don't know. We can brainstorm. Maybe something with a lot of helium balloons, or building two snowmen holding hands and then spelling out something in the snow. Or... making him giant gingerbread cookies. Oh! Maybe we could decorate that cute tree in his front yard with some kind of decorations that would, I don't know..."

Aiden was looking at her with his head cocked, his eyebrows drawn together.

"What?"

"Why does it have to be something big like that?

Holly said her dad has a picture of you from your date and he looks at it all the time when he doesn't know she's paying attention. She said he talks about you a lot, too. I think he really likes you. Can't we just go over there and you say, 'Hey I really like you, too. Let's go on dates again'?"

She just stared at Aiden. He had this simplicity thing down. Why *couldn't* it be that simple? "Aiden," she said, "you're brilliant." She kissed him on his forehead. "Go get your coat and gloves and hat. Let's go over to his house."

Aiden got his winter gear on in record time, he was so excited. Bailey was so excited. Rachel was so excited. The three of them piled into her car, and she pulled out of her driveway.

eighteen

NICK

"YOU'VE GOT YOUR COAT, hat, and gloves?" Nick asked as he grabbed his keys and the bag he'd filled and opened the door leading to the garage.

"Check, check, and check," Holly said. "But not check on my other shoe."

She hopped on one foot toward the door as she put her shoe on the other foot, then he, Holly, and Rosy all went into the garage, hopped into the car, and put their seatbelts on. He pushed the button hooked to his visor to open the big garage door at the same time he started the car. He looked into the rearview mirror as the door raised, but saw lights turning onto his driveway. Squinting at the brightness, he tried to make out whose car it was.

"Huh," he said. "I think Rachel is here."

Confused, he turned off his car and they all got out, meeting Rachel, Aiden, and her dog in his driveway. "What are you doing here?"

Rachel looked a bit... sheepish, was it? "I came to talk to you. But you're just leaving— I'm sorry. Do you need to go?"

He shook his head. "I was coming to talk to you." Did he dare hope that she wouldn't have shown up at his house today unless she had been every bit as unsettled as he was about how they'd left everything?

"You were?"

He nodded. "I wanted to tell you that I think I might have made a mistake."

"Yeah? I made a mistake, too. A really big one."

Hope started to fill him more. "Was your mistake in ending things? Because if it wasn't, this conversation is going to get awkward very quickly."

She chuckled softly. That was good. Right? "I might have freaked out because of my planner."

He nodded. "I got freaked out because of my deceased wife."

"Okay, you win."

"I guess I didn't have things figured out because dating again is so new. But then my father-in-law shared a lot with me that I needed to hear—things I hadn't considered that made me look at our relationship in a different light. And I realized that I didn't need to be freaking out about the things I was freaking out about."

"Aww," Rachel said. "Tell your father-in-law I think he's pretty great."

He definitely would. He needed to thank the man for himself again, too. "What about you?"

"Some friends set me straight. Aiden helped, too."

"Tell Aiden I think he's pretty great."

"Don't worry," Aiden said from where he and Holly stood half a dozen feet away. "I heard. Does this mean that you two are going to start dating again?"

Both he and Rachel chuckled, then looked at each other again. She was so beautiful, her dark hair falling in waves just below her red knit cap. The snow was coming down in big chunks, landing on the cap and her hair. He couldn't believe he almost let fear keep him from this woman, and he was so grateful that she was willing to talk about making things work.

"I would like to," he said. "What do you think? And don't feel obligated to say yes, even though it's still your Season of Yes."

She smiled and stepped closer to him. Their coats were brushing, their faces close enough that he could feel her warm breaths. "I would like to, also. Season of Yes or not."

"Yes!" Aiden and Holly both said, giving each other high-fives. It suddenly made him wonder how much matchmaking behind the scenes the kids had done that he hadn't known about.

"Can us seeing each other again start today? Because it feels like it's been a million years since I last saw you, and this heart of mine has been going through some serious withdrawals."

She smiled up at him. "Mine, too. And we can definitely start today."

He had thought once at the beginning of their relationship that it felt like he had jumped out of a plane. This moment felt like their parachutes had safely deployed and they were landing more or less gently on the ground.

Holly and Aiden ran off to play in the snow in their front yard as more fell from the sky. He reached out to brush a snowflake from Rachel's cheek. "So I won Aiden over, huh?"

"Yeah, but that was mostly because you showed him all the tools at The Home Improvement Store, and to a kid like Aiden, you opened up his mind to crafts on a much bigger scale." She chuckled. "In all seriousness, though. You totally won him over. All the way. I think you won us all over."

Bailey, the good girl that she was, took that moment to come over and sit at his feet, looking up at him like she just knew he was about to tell her how great she was.

"See?" Rachel said. "You even won Bailey over."

He reached down and rubbed the sides of Bailey's golden neck. "You really are a good girl."

When he stood straight again, Rachel nestled into his side, so he wrapped an arm around her shoulders, pulling her in close to keep her warm. And then they just stood there, snuggled together, watching their kids and their dogs playing in the snow, laughing, and throwing snow up into the air. He couldn't imagine a more perfect moment.

The night was cold enough to see their breath coming out in little cloud puffs, but with the low clouds, it wasn't a bitter cold. The moon was only a sliver tonight, but it still shone brightly, lighting the snow that softly fell from the sky and reflecting off all the snow on the ground, making the night seem brighter than it was.

He kissed Rachel on the temple. "You're pretty great, you know that?"

She shook her head. "Nope."

He didn't know if she meant that she didn't know or if she just wanted to hear more. Either way, he wanted to tell her how great he thought she was every day for the rest of her life. "Well, then, I better tell you."

She turned so that she was facing him, and he wrapped both arms around her waist. "I love that you're willing to try new things. I love that you're always on top of everything. That you look out for everyone's feelings.

That you always make Holly feel important and special. I love that you make a schedule. And that your purse is divided into sections."

Rachel looked down and laughed. Then she met his eyes again.

He continued. They were all coming to his mind so quickly that he couldn't stop. "I love that you make me feel like I can accomplish anything. I love the way your lips quirk up—like right now—when you're amused. I love how patient and understanding you are. I love that you've invited me and Holly into your life and that you've just as easily stepped into ours.

"I love that you're understanding about my relationship with Holly's grandparents and about Clara. I love that you bring so much joy to everything. I love that you make a point of celebrating things. People don't do that often enough and I think it's important. I love that you work hard and prioritize. And I love how you make me feel like I've come home."

The whole time, she just gazed at him like she was soaking it all in. When he finished, she said, "I am speechless. Thank you."

And then she rose on her toes and pressed her lips against his, sliding her arms around his neck, pulling them as close together as they could be in thick winter coats. Her kiss felt like a dream. Like a promise. A hope for the future.

When he'd pulled into this driveway the day he and Holly had moved to Mountain Springs, he never imagined he would be standing here on Christmas night, being so utterly and completely in love with someone he hadn't even met then. He knew that Christmas was a magical time of year, but being there with Rachel showed just how magical it could be.

He wanted to spend a lot more time kissing Rachel, but not in front of the kids, and not outside in the cold. He planted one last kiss on Rachel's lips, and then looked at the kids and dogs, who were starting to get cold.

"Should we go inside?"

Rachel nodded. "Then I can tell you all the things I love about you."

For as awful as the day had started, the ending couldn't be any better. He said, "Come on, kids," as he grabbed the bag from the passenger's seat. "Let's go inside and warm up."

"What's that?" Aiden asked, pointing at the bag.

"We decided," Holly said, "well, my dad decided but I helped, that since our parents met working on a fireplace and fell in love on that hay ride with the hot chocolate at Jack and Noelle's wedding that he should try to woo your mom with hot chocolate by the real fireplace."

Rachel's eyebrow rose as a smile played across her

lips. He should've known that Holly would tell everything.

"You fell in love with me on the hay ride?"

"And a million times since. What do you think? Should we go inside where it's warm and I can properly woo you?"

She smiled. "I'd like that."

nineteen

RACHEL

RACHEL WOULD ACCEPT Nick's wooing any day of the week. It didn't take long for Holly and Aiden to run off to see and play with Holly's Christmas presents. Rachel took the moment alone as an opportunity to tell Nick all the things she loved about him.

When she said the first thing, he placed a gentle kiss on her hand. When she said the second thing, he moved up about an inch and placed the next one. She told him everything that she could remember from her list, and he placed a kiss on her arm with each one. She even came up with new ones, because she wanted him to make it up to her neck before he stopped. With each kiss, it sent more and more tingles up her arm and so much dopamine to her brain that she could barely think.

When the kids and the dogs came back into the kitchen, dining room, and family room area, racing around and being crazy, Nick brought everyone together to play Outfoxed, a board game that they'd gotten for Christmas. Playing the cooperative clue game together was so much fun. Aiden and Holly actually worked together to solve the mystery instead of working in competition against each other. That, in itself, was a miracle.

Once the game was over, Nick left her side to go make hot chocolate for everyone while they put the pieces back into the box. He set Aiden's and Holly's mugs down on the table, where they were getting out a new game to play. When he came back with his and Rachel's mug, he nodded his head toward the couch, an eyebrow raised in question.

So they both went to the couch and she curled up next to him, the fire crackling in the fireplace, and he handed her a cup of hot chocolate. She wrapped her hands around the warm mug and inhaled. Her eyes went wide. "Is that cinnamon and ginger I smell? I can't believe you remembered that!" It was what she had put in her hot chocolate in the Allreds' yard, right before they got on the hay ride.

"Well, it was the day I fell in love with you, you know." He winked, and it did something to her heart.

She took a sip of it and savored the feel of the warm sweet chocolate and the taste of the spices on her tongue and knew that she would forever connect that taste with Nick falling in love with her.

Both dogs had followed them into the family room area and curled up just under the Christmas tree. The last time she'd been enjoying this fire with Nick, this house had been empty except for the fake fireplace that they had created. Now, the place was finished, furnished, and so inviting.

She snuggled into him even more, and he put an arm around her shoulders. Everything about this evening felt perfect. It was like all that had been missing this morning when it was just her and Aiden and cinnamon rolls was finally righted. It was all here.

Rachel placed her mug of hot chocolate on the coffee table and was resting her head against Nick's shoulder, watching the fire, when Aiden came and stood just in front of Nick, his coat in one hand. "I brought something." He reached into the pocket of his coat and pulled the object out. He let his coat drop to the floor and cradled it in both of his hands.

He stepped closer and showed them what he held. It was one of the doves from their tree. One of the ones that Aiden spent so much time running his fingers across every Christmas.

"It's a dove. It's got a little clip here instead of feet so you can clip it to a branch of your Christmas tree. Doves bring peace and happiness and they can even grant wishes!" Aiden shot a quick look at Rachel, almost like he was checking to see if she remembered that the wish he'd given to the dove in the park was for a new dad. "Can I put this one on your tree?"

Nick nodded. "I'd really like that."

Aiden carefully clipped the dove onto a branch of Nick's tree, then ran his finger along its back a couple of times, petting it. He turned and smiled at both of them before running back to the table to rejoin Holly in whatever game they were playing.

They both just looked at the bird for a long moment. Christmas really was about the people you spent it with and not about everything that was on—or not on—her planner. She couldn't believe she hadn't understood that before. She looked back at Nick. "For as long as I've gone without a man in my life, I now know that I never want to go without you again."

Nick smiled. "I came to the same conclusion."

"So what happens if one of us freaks out again and lets fear rule things a bit? I doubt we've gotten over the only hurdle we'll face."

"Well, we apparently know people we can go to for great advice." He chuckled softly, and she felt the rumble of it in his chest. "But mostly, I think we should go to each other first. Because I don't want this to ever end."

"I don't, either."

Nick's smile spread across his face gloriously, and he hadn't fully stopped smiling when his lips met hers for a kiss. She got it—she could barely stop smiling long enough to kiss him, too.

epilogue

NICK

NICK STROLLED DOWN Main Street with his gloved hand in Rachel's as they took in both the new and repeating Christmas decorations and lights all the shops had set up in their windows and in front of their buildings. It was the one-year anniversary of their first date, and they decided to recreate their date from a year ago.

They'd gone to the same restaurant. Last year, he'd just moved to Mountain Springs and had gotten the recommendation from his in-laws. Mountain Springs didn't have super fancy restaurants, but it was a nice one, the food was delicious, and the wait staff was so friendly. They'd gone several times since then, but tonight, they'd both ordered the same things they'd ordered on that first date.

Not only was it the anniversary of their first date, but it was their three-month wedding anniversary, so everything just felt extra great. This time, though, Jack and Noelle were the ones watching Holly and Aiden, and they were all at the home that Nick now shared with Rachel. He hadn't guessed when he bought the house that he'd find love again and be married to her less than a year later—he'd only known that the house had felt perfect from the moment he'd first stepped inside.

He hadn't known that it would be perfect beyond his imagination once Rachel became his wife and she and Aiden (and Bailey!) moved in. They had started the process for him to adopt Aiden and Rachel to adopt Holly the moment they got home from their honeymoon and it wouldn't be long before everything was officially official.

"I'm pretty proud of us," Rachel said.

"Oh, yeah?"

"We've done an excellent job making deliberate choices about Christmas activities this year."

Nick nodded in agreement. "I take it you've felt good about our Monthly Plan?"

"I do. It hasn't seemed like any of us have gotten overwhelmed and we've had tons of time to spend together as a family."

"Just the way I like it." He placed a kiss on Rachel's temple.

Rachel leaned her head against his shoulder as they walked, looking up at the lights that were strung from one side of the street to the other, taking in how nice everything looked.

Rachel stopped, still looking up. "I just felt a snowflake. I think it's starting to snow!" The look of joy on her face was something he would never tire of seeing in a million years.

They both stood still, watching as a meandering flake here and there made their way to the ground. And then a few more flakes started to fall. Before long, they were falling at a steady pace. Not that they didn't already have plenty of snow in their mountain town, but it always felt magical when new snow fell.

"I love that we are getting snow again, just like our date last year."

"I love that at the end of this one we won't have to go home to separate houses."

Rachel grinned up at him. "I like that, too." She cocked her head. "If we're repeating our date from a year ago... Do you think we'll get interrupted when we try to kiss this time?"

He chuckled. "I don't know. Our kids are a year older. And there aren't any big rocks hiding under the snow at our house for Holly to hurt her ankle on. But just to be on the safe side, we better kiss right now."

Rachel moved closer to him, but then said, "No, wait! We have to do our selfie first!"

He pulled out his phone, opened the camera, and flipped the screen to their faces. They were both smiling like a couple who had spent a year getting everything figured out and were loving where they were at. He snapped the picture, and then placed a soft kiss on her lips. "Happy anniversary, my wife."

"Happy anniversary, my husband."

The moment he grinned back at her, her phone rang. She pulled it from her coat pocket, said, "It's Jack," then answered the call and put it on speaker phone.

"It's time," Jack said, a note of excitement and worry in his voice.

"Noelle is in labor? Okay, we'll—"

"No, not Noelle. Everything is totally fine with her. It's time for *Bailey*. Her first puppy is already here!"

"She's early!" Rachel said. "The vet said it wouldn't happen until next week!"

"Well, I don't think that the babies heard that bit of news, because they are coming now. Remember how she didn't come running to us when we showed up? Apparently, she was hiding in the room you got ready, nesting around the box and blankets you'd set up."

Rachel turned and started walking in the direction of their car, which was parked a couple of blocks away. "I need to call the vet."

"That was the first call Noelle made," Jack said. "He's out of town—some emergency with his adult daughter. But don't worry—Noelle seems to know exactly what she's doing. And she said that more importantly, Bailey knows exactly what *she's* doing and we just need to monitor her and not interfere. So don't stress out and don't feel like you need to hurry. Everything is under control."

As he and Rachel hurried back down Main Street toward their car, talking about how they and Jack and Noelle had decided that they needed more golden retrievers in their lives, Rachel said, "If we recreate our first date every single year, do you think we'll always get an emergency call at this point in the date?"

He chuckled. "Let's hope not. But who knows? Fifty years from now, we might be walking down this path with our canes and get a call that one of our grandkids just got proposed to."

When they got home, they pulled into the garage and hurried into the house. He glanced around the kitchen, dining, and family room area that was even more decorated than it was last Christmas, snowflakes already hanging from the ceiling, just as Holly and Aiden came running toward them, their rough collie, Rosy, at their feet.

"Bailey is doing so good!" Holly said. "She hasn't needed any help at all."

Aiden nodded. "We didn't even know she was having her babies. We thought she was just tired from having that big belly and didn't want to play. But then I kept hearing weird sounds, and I found Bailey with a teeny baby puppy!"

They were trying to make their way to the small room off the kitchen that they'd just been using for storage until they cleared it out for Bailey when Holly held up a hand. "I'm going to warn you that it's gross in there."

"That's okay," Nick said.

They found Bailey in her whelping box, two little cream-colored puppies near her, their eyes closed, taking a couple of stumbling steps. Bailey's mouth was open in her signature smile, looking so proud of her babies. A very pregnant Noelle was sitting on the floor nearby, Jack at her side, and she smiled up at them like she was just as proud.

"Aren't they the cutest?" Aiden said from the doorway, where Rosy was turning around in circles with excitement. "I just want to pick one up in my hands and cuddle it."

"Soon, sweetie," Rachel said. "Right now, we're going to let Bailey enjoy them."

Two hours later, Bailey had given birth to the final puppy—number five—and they had gotten the area cleaned up, Bailey fed and resting peacefully with her babies. Not long after, they quietly said goodbye to Jack and Noelle, then read a Christmas bedtime story to Holly and Aiden before getting them tucked into bed.

Then they went back to check on Bailey and her puppies. They stood in the doorway, Rachel leaning against him as they took in the five sleeping puppies snuggled into Bailey. He put his arms around Rachel and pulled her close. They wouldn't be keeping all the puppies—they'd already promised one to Jack and Noelle and at least two to friends, but there still came with the puppies a feeling of their family expanding, just like it had when they'd joined their two little families together.

He soaked in the feeling, enjoying every moment of it. Then he kissed Rachel's temple and said, "I guess our schedule for the rest of December is going to be thrown off a bit."

"I hear that's not the most important part of the season. It's all about the people you spend it with." She twisted a bit to smile up at him. "Whatever life throws at us or our little family, we can handle."

He placed a kiss on her lips. "Yes, we can."

the christmas clause

one

KATIE

KATIE PICKED up a sprig of spruce and a few stems of berries and placed them in the centerpiece she was working on. "I want a guy who will serenade me. Even if he can't sing."

"And I want..." her roommate, best friend, and owner of this shop, Emmalee, said as she trimmed a bunch of amaryllis stems, "a guy with a sense of adventure who never gets lost."

Katie turned the centerpiece she was working on around, checking it from all angles. "And, of course, a guy who could come up with the perfect late-night snack at a moment's notice."

Emmalee stopped her trimming to give Katie a flat stare. "Really. You would sit on Santa's lap, look him straight in the eyes, and ask for a man who will make you pizza rolls at midnight."

"I'm sure he's heard more ridiculous requests."

"Okay, then." Emmalee grinned. "I want a guy who's a gourmet chef and specializes in breakfast foods."

It was ironic that Emmalee brought up the subject of qualities they'd like in a man, since it hadn't even been fifteen minutes since she said she was never going to date another man again, ever. Katie, though? She was always down to have fun casual dating. That was, of course, until the right man swept her off her feet.

And she'd made it a goal to stop wanting to date a guy based on first impressions so she could up her chances of finding that man who would do the sweeping. Usually, she found out after a date or two that a guy wasn't quite what she'd thought at first impression. Which wasn't always bad— she'd dated quite a few guys who made for interesting dates but didn't have a chance at being her happily ever after. But now, she was all-in on slowing down and finding out more first.

She just didn't really believe that getting swept off her feet would happen. At least not until she was at least thirty. Six more years wasn't that long to wait, right? Until then, she was going to keep building her videography business and helping Emmalee build her floral business.

It actually worked out well for both of them. This

flower shop was barely big enough for the two of them to work in— any customers who came had to stand outside at the window to place or pick up an order. But it was adorable and was right on Main Street in their small town of Mountain Springs. Emmalee got to do what she loved, and Katie got a part-time job that worked with the crazy schedule she often had as she worked to accommodate her clients' videography needs. Plus, it was fun to work side by side with her friend and roommate.

And okay, sometimes when there were big events, like prom, a wedding, or Valentine's day, the flower shop wasn't big enough, and her roommate's business spilled into their apartment. On the plus side, though, their apartment often smelled great.

And right now, the flower shop smelled pretty incredible. Christmas floral arrangements meant a lot of poinsettias, azaleas, roses, orchids, and pine cones. Combine it with the scent of pine sprigs, and it might just be Katie's favorite scent. Add in the Christmas music playing through a small Bluetooth speaker on the counter and their view of all the Christmas decorations that were currently going up on Main Street, and Katie was ready to dream of a white Christmas, deck the halls (or the living room) of their apartment, rock around their Christmas tree (once they got it put up) and jingle all the way to her Christmas shopping.

As well as Emmalee's business was going, it still had

its feast and famine moments. Sometimes, Emmalee could use all the help that Katie could possibly give, and at other times, there wasn't enough business for Katie to work at all. She definitely couldn't rely on working at the flower shop to cover her expenses.

Not that Katie wanted to ever have to rely on Emmalee's business for the ability to pay her bills. Especially because Katie was really good at videography. It was her passion, and every client raved about the final product. Making customers happy came easy for her. In a small town, though, word of mouth only went to so many people.

Her videography business might still be a fledgling one, but she had big plans for it. And one of those was to make enough in her busier months to not only cover the less busy months but to give her a big, "I've got this" cushion. There was nothing scarier than thinking that maybe she couldn't get all she needed on her own.

Katie sighed. "I've got to find a way to get more business. And not just soon, but on a regular basis."

"Do you have any ideas?"

"That are cheap or free until I can build up an advertising budget? Beyond trying to convince people in Mountain Springs and Nestled Hollow that they'd benefit by having a professional videographer at more events in their lives and posting about my business on social media in neighborhood groups outside of our area, nothing yet. But if I don't find a way to grow my business soon, then I'm going to be living out of my car."

"You're not going to have to live out of your car."

"I'll be living out of my car and eating those cheap packages of Ramen. Which might not work out so well, because I don't exactly have a kitchenette in my car. Oh! Maybe I could get some of those Styrofoam cups of soup that you just add water to. Then maybe I could use a convenience store's microwave or something."

"Don't be silly. Your bedroom is still the same as it was the day you moved out, right? You could just move back in with your parents."

Wait. Was that why they kept it the same instead of turning it into the guest bedroom that they said they were going to? In case her business failed? "I'm not moving back home. That would mean admitting defeat or admitting that I need help."

"And you can do neither. Okay, I'll tell you what. If your business fails and you end up living out of your car, then I will move into my car, too, in solidarity with you. We can park next to each other, open the doors between our cars, and put a big blanket over it. It can be a fort and we can pretend we are just having a sleepover like when we were kids."

"You'd do it out of solidarity? Or because you couldn't pay for rent on your own?"

Emmalee shrugged. "Call it whatever."

Katie was just putting the arrangement she'd finished in the fridge when her phone rang, lighting up the screen with a picture of her dad smiling back at her. She answered and said, "Hi, Dad. You're on speaker phone—Emmalee is here."

She and Emmalee always answered calls they weren't willing to take outside in the cold on speaker phone. If the other person in this small space had to listen to one side of the conversation, it was only polite to let them hear the other half, too. Plus, it kept their hands free for working.

She grabbed a new vase as her dad said, "Hi, Sweetie. Hi, Emmalee. Okay, so you know how I've been working on that project to rebuild the Glaciers' team image?"

Katie nodded. "Especially after all the damage that the Player Who Shall Not Be Named did." For not being a huge fan of professional hockey, Katie knew a good number of random things about Denver's team. Mostly because her dad was in charge of branding for the team. She just didn't know much about most of the players.

"Exactly. Well, my plan to have the players spread out to help out with Christmas festivities in towns all around the state is a go. My team and I have jumped through all the hoops to get it approved and everyone on board, even the players."

"That's great, Dad," Katie said as she tilted her head

at the roses she had just put into the vase, seeing if it looked like enough to create the picture she had in her head.

"I think so, too. And I am calling in an official capacity for the Denver Glaciers to offer a short-term contract to you to be a videographer for one of the players."

"Wait. For real?" The thrill of a job for her very own company with the Denver Glaciers hit at the same time as the deep-in-her-soul resistance she always had to people trying to do things for her that she could do herself. "Dad, I can't take it. I need to build my company by getting jobs because of my own merit, not because I'm your daughter."

"You did get this because of your own merit."

Katie picked up a stem with a few white azalea blooms and dark green leaves but didn't do anything with it. "I'm listening."

"We asked the players to submit names of towns they'd like to do some Christmas outreach with. Then my team and I split the state into areas and I assigned each area to someone on my team. We want videographers local to each area we are sending players— we aren't just doing this for our image, we're also doing it to help out the communities who support us, which includes supporting local videographers.

"Each of my team members scoured the areas assigned to them for the best videographers. Then they brought their list to our meeting and, area by area, we voted on which videographer to ask.

"I knew you wouldn't want me to, so I didn't say a single thing about you. My team found you on their own and had no idea at the time that there was a relation between me and KatieVid. When the portfolios of videographers in our area came up for a vote, they chose you unanimously."

"They chose me? For real? Without knowing who I am?"

"For real."

She might have squealed. Or maybe it was Emmalee. It was probably both of them. "I'll take the job!" She had filmed and edited videos for quite a few sporting events (high school games and little kids' soccer matches) and plenty of Christmas events. Lots of weddings, milestone birthdays, concerts, recitals, performances, and the occasional family reunion.

Never anything like filming a professional hockey player doing town Christmas events, though. To be able to put the Denver Glaciers on her site as one of her clients was *huge*. "When do I start?"

"Likely within the next week or so, depending on the player's schedule— I'll get you the details as soon as I can. A lot of the players are set for different locations, but ours isn't yet. I'll still get you the contract to sign soon, and then we'll get with the mayor and come up with a plan."

After thanking her dad profusely, she hung up the phone.

"This is huge for your business," Emmalee said.

"My website is going to look so great having the Denver Glaciers' logo in my client's section! I might be able to start getting business outside of the Mountain Springs area. I might be able to see some real growth." Katie had set some major goals for her business that she had hoped to accomplish by the end of the year, and she was worried that she wouldn't meet the goals. This would definitely help.

She and Emmalee just grinned at each other. Then Emmalee asked, "Which player do you think you're going to get? Oh, maybe it'll be Bradshaw."

"Which one is he again?" Katie really should memorize the players some time. She didn't need to know them as well as Emmalee did, but her dad had worked for the Glaciers for five years— she should know them by now. She just hadn't really found a love for the sport yet.

"The super hot one with the dark wavy hair. The *recently single* super hot one. I hope it's him. Ooo, maybe it'll be the bad boy, Ackerman. Although, no, your dad would never assign him to you. In fact, if there isn't a player that your dad approves of for his youngest daughter, he'll likely assign a married player to Mountain Springs."

Katie nodded. She was totally fine with that. "Maybe it'll be that one guy with the adorable wife and two little kids. The one that just had a baby."

"Davis? I'm obsessed with him and his cute family. Seriously, relationship goals there. *If* I was going to ever get into a relationship again, which I'm not."

Katie patted her friend on the shoulder. "Of course, you aren't." She totally was. "And my dad said he asked the players where they wanted to go, so I'm sure he'll honor their wishes first."

"True," Emmalee said, tapping a rose against her lips as she pondered, the top thorn getting dangerously close to her chin with each tap. "So it could be anyone. I would assign you homework to learn who all of the players are, but we both know you're not going to do it unless someone makes you. So, as your boss in this shop, for the next two hours that you'll be on duty, I am your teacher. I'm going to give you a rundown of all twenty-one players. By the time we finish today, you'll be able to recognize any of them on sight. Because girl, you need to know who is on your own team."

She really did. As someone who grew up a thirty-minute drive from Denver, the Glaciers were "her team." As Reid Allred's daughter, they were doubly her team. By blood. Plus, she needed to be prepared for whichever player she got assigned, so she nodded. "Let's do this."

CONNOR STRODE over to the aisle with shaving razors, a shopping basket on his arm, his phone at his ear, listening to his sister, Laura. She was making her way through his house, gathering things he needed.

"These contact lenses are daily-wear ones, right? I've got you a week's worth and your glasses case." She let out a big exhale and he heard the drawer shut. "I can't believe they didn't let you spend five minutes at home to pack a bag before you left."

Connor scanned the choices of razors. "There was no way I could've driven all the way home from the arena and turned around to immediately drive back to the airport— even without going inside and packing a bag— and still made that flight."

"Where are your glasses?"

"Nightstand."

"And there's really no way for you to come back home for Christmas?

Connor scanned the razors again but didn't see the brand he normally used. Maybe he would just leave the scruff. "I used in-flight WiFi any moment I wasn't fielding messages from TV analysts and reps from the Glaciers to search every airline out of Denver. I looked at the ones that were leaving from the earliest moment I could get there after my game on the night of the twenty-third until the morning of the twenty-fifth. Not only could I not find a flight, but there's a storm coming in, and they're guessing all the people who actually did find flights will be sitting at the airport, not flying."

No, he really hated the itchiness of scruff. That was something he was only willing to do when his team made the playoffs. He had to find a razor.

"This sucks," Laura said. "Did you really not have a clue that they were going to trade you?"

"None. I thought things were going well." A lot of trades happened right before the trade deadline, which was in early March this year. If trades happened earlier in the season, it was often because they didn't think a player was a good fit on the team or because the team in general was struggling.

But Connor got along great with his team. He loved the guys. Traveling with them day in and day out, battling with them, shooting for the same goals— he was willing to do anything for them. And his team was doing great. He'd been told by the management not long ago that he was in the team's long-term plans. They'd even put up a billboard featuring him six weeks ago and stocked more of his jerseys in fan stores.

"I was changing after practice when the public relations guy came in and said that the GM wanted to see me." The sinking feeling he'd gotten in his stomach at the time had immediately told him that it was about a trade.

He grabbed a razor and tossed it into his basket, then added some shaving cream.

"Okay," Laura said, "I've got your favorite pajama pants and a few shirts, including that bluish-gray one with the super soft fabric. What else?"

"Shoes." He headed to the next aisle over.

"I can't believe they would actually trade a player eight days before Christmas. Right before the Christmas blackout— which is far too short, if you ask me. No one wants to move across the country at Christmastime, let alone move with no warning."

"It's all part of the life I signed up for when I joined the NHL. At least I don't have a wife and kids I had to break the news to."

"True. But do they really have to give you zero

notice? They couldn't have just selected a later flight today to at least give you a bit of time?"

"You're really hung up on that no-notice thing. It's just part of the job. It sucks, but I've been luckier than most to have spent my entire career up until now near family. Besides, they had press interviews lined up for me, so I had to fly in quickly." He added deodorant to his basket.

"Which they lined up *after* choosing your flight."

"Laura, what's done is done."

"And moaning about it won't change anything," she said, finishing their step-dad's mantra. "I know. How did the interviews go?"

It was more than just interviews. He'd also fielded a dozen messages and calls from his new organization to find out things like his skate size, any sponsored equipment brands, and his number so they could put it on home and away jerseys. He also got calls from the team doctors and training staff to coordinate and get information, and from the Director of Services to make the transition smooth and cover all the bases. He even got a call from payroll.

And that was just the urgent stuff that directly involved him, not any of the stuff going on behind the scenes with media relations, marketing, social media, retail, community relations, and a host of other depart-ments. He wasn't through getting calls, either. Two had come in just in the few minutes he had been on the phone with his sister.

"Fine. I had my suit and dress shoes with me at the arena, of course. Oh, by the way, one of the guys is driving my car back to my place, so don't freak out if he comes in to drop off the keys while you're there. Anyway, the interviews went well, if you don't count how weird it felt to wear dress shoes without socks, which I did *not* happen to grab."

"Oh, socks!" Laura said, followed by sounds of drawers opening and closing.

"Bottom drawer," he offered.

"Got them! Who puts their socks in the bottom drawer? Weirdo. What else? Any bathroom stuff other than your contact lenses?"

"No. I'm not going to wait for that box to be delivered before I brush my teeth or put on deodorant." Tooth-brush. That's what he needed. He started walking toward the aisle with them. "You are going to ship it overnight to the hotel, right?"

"Yeah, as soon as I leave here. But in case you've acclimated to the time zone there in the past few hours and already forgot, it's ten p.m. here, so it's not going to be *tonight's* overnight." After a short pause, she added, "So, you might want to find a store where you can buy some underwear, too."

Frustration hit him and came out in a growl. He

tossed a tube of toothpaste into his basket and moved over to the toothbrushes. The shock still hadn't completely worn off yet, but grief and irritation were starting to settle in.

"You couldn't have just refused the trade?"

"Not if I didn't want to be suspended and lose my salary." Another few weeks, and he would've hit his twenty-seventh birthday, and in four months, the end of his seventh year. After hitting either, he could've negotiated a *No trade to Denver* clause in his contract.

Trades were all part of the job, and he'd long ago accepted that a trade at any time, inconvenient or not, was to be expected. It wasn't that he was angry about the timing. Although, he wished they would have waited until December twenty-seventh— when the Christmas trade freeze lifted— to take him away from his family. He was more upset that they traded him to Denver, specifically.

He chose a toothbrush and added it to his basket.

"Well, congrats on getting Mom and Max notified before your trade was officially announced."

Sometimes the players themselves didn't get notified before the media, so the congrats was well-deserved. "I knew she would *not* be happy if she found out from the Internet, so I called her as I was walking out of the GM's office."

"How did it go?"

He swallowed. "I can't say it was fun making her that sad." Christmas traditions were important to her, and he knew that all the ones he was going to miss had likely been running through her head. And he hadn't even let her know the flight situation yet that wouldn't allow him to go home during the three-day break.

"I bet."

"Hey, don't tell Mom that I'm upset about the trade or that I really didn't want to come here. I'll get over being upset, and there isn't anything any of us can do about the trade being to Denver. I don't want her to feel bad."

"I won't. This is just a new adventure, right?" He could tell that she had tried to make the sentence come out in a cheery voice, and she was mostly successful.

"Yep. A new adventure. Oh, and will you take everyone's presents with you to pass out on Christmas morning? And will you wrap Max's for me? I didn't get a chance."

"Will do. Maybe we can just video chat on Christmas as everyone opens presents." There was a small pause before she added, "Okay, I think I've got the necessities, including charging cords for your devices. I'll come back after I get this shipped off and pack more of your stuff. Any last requests for the overnight one? That cinnamon caramel hot chocolate that you love?"

Connor chuckled. "I think I can go a few days without it."

"It's weird to think that this morning when we got together for breakfast, you lived here in Charlotte, were one of the Thunderstorm, and had no idea you'd end the day as one of the Glaciers, living in Denver."

"Yep, weird." It felt like this morning had happened days ago. Waking up, going about his normal routine, going to practice, finding out he was moving fifteen hundred miles away, making that move, fielding all the phone calls, messages, interviews, and emails, coordinating with the new team, and shopping for the essentials was exhausting. He couldn't have stuffed more into this day if he'd tried.

Yet, his new team was on the ice against another team right now, and he wished he was there, playing with them. He glanced at his watch. Actually, the game was probably over by now. It would be nice to have a practice with the new team before a game, and his flight hadn't landed with enough time for him to get to the game, but it still felt strange to have tonight off. Especially because he had tomorrow night off, too— he didn't play his first game with the Glaciers until two days from now.

Someone turned down Connor's aisle, and he could tell the moment the man recognized him because the man's expression turned sour. So, either he recognized

Connor as a Thunderstorm player— and therefore was from the team that was the Glaciers' biggest rival— or the guy already saw the news that Connor had joined the Glaciers, and he wasn't happy about it. He was sure this wasn't going to be an isolated incident.

Connor had pictured being traded plenty of times, but never to Denver. The trade had completely blindsided him. He should've guessed the feelings that coming back would give him. He got it every time his team had played the Glaciers in Denver.

He glanced around the drug store to see if there was anything he needed that he hadn't thought of yet, and luckily, he noticed the shampoo.

"You might not have time to go house shopping," Laura said. "Want me to look through listings and send you the best ones? I can watch for homes with walls that resist puck and stick scuffs. Or one with a trophy room. Swimming pool? An oversized garage with goalie nets and reinforced windows that can handle a hockey puck flying at them?"

"No need. The hotel they've got me at is pretty decent. I'm thinking of living there until the end of the season, then moving back home in the off-season."

"Off-season? If your team does well in the playoffs, that's what? Three months? You can't spend the other nine in a hotel."

"Laura, I am *not* going to live here again." He was

surprised at how fiercely his voice came out. There were too many bad memories tied to this place, and he really didn't like who he was when he lived here. He wasn't about to become that person again. "I'm going to put in a trade request as we come up on the end of the season. I already told my agent."

He headed over to the self-checkout station and started scanning his items. But he couldn't seem to get his mind to go down a different path. So, he asked, "Have you talked to Dad lately? Do you know if he's living here?"

"I haven't for a year or so, but I don't think so. Last I heard, he was living in Arizona and buying a house in Spain."

At least there was that small mercy. Judging by the relief it gave him to know, maybe it wasn't *so* small. "And there's a chance I won't be living in a hotel for the whole season. I could get traded at the deadline to a team that's closer to home."

"Or to one that doesn't get a quarter of their flights delayed due to weather in the winter. Yes, I did, indeed, just look it up."

"Yes, traded to a team without winter flight delays. That'll do, too." He finished scanning the last of his items and tapped his credit card on the reader.

"Then, I'll keep my fingers crossed that you'll get

completely blindsided and have to move with zero notice again soon."

"I always knew I could count on you, sis." He grabbed his bag and noticed that there was a clothing store across the street. It was getting pretty late, but it looked like they were still open. "I've got to go. I need underwear and a shower, and I've got to be at the rink early to meet my new team who was likely just as blind-sided by the trade as I was."

"Someone on the Team Services staff can't get that for you? I thought they were there to make the transition smooth."

"I am *not* asking them to buy me underwear."

Laura laughed. "Fair enough. Okay, I'll go get this box shipped. And Connor? Fake it until you make it, right?"

He nodded and smiled. "Fake it until you make it." It was old advice, but there was something to it. Back in college, his hockey coach had their entire team read a book about how body language caused emotions, not the other way around. Slumping made you feel defeated; feeling defeated didn't make you slump. So as a team, they would do winning poses before going on the ice to pump themselves up, and Connor witnessed over and over how much it worked.

It was advice that he'd desperately needed at the time. From a therapy standpoint, if there was an underlying problem, pretending it wasn't there wasn't likely to fix it. But he'd done the therapy, yet he'd still been angry so much of the time back then. The therapy had helped, but it was taking that book to heart that had gotten him past the anger and on his way to becoming the person he was now. A person he liked.

Right now, he just needed to make his body show happiness, and his emotions would follow. So he stood with his shoulders back, put a smile on his face, then crossed the street to the clothing store.

The men's underwear section wasn't hard to find— the four full-size mannequins wearing nothing but underwear, each in a different color, led the way.

He was standing next to a table of underwear packages, finding the style and the size he needed, when a couple of people caught his attention and he glanced over. It was two boys and a girl, all about seventeen years old. One might've been her boyfriend. Or possibly brother.

Connor tried to pretend he didn't notice them as the trio discussed whether the girl should approach Connor and ask for an autograph (since she was a fan and seemed so excited to see him), or if they should maybe hurl insults at "the enemy" instead (which was apparently what the two boys thought of Connor). He wished he was doing anything other than buying underwear at that moment.

Apparently, the girl won the argument, because she straightened her shoulders as if to summon bravery— maybe she read the book, too— and walked over to him with a shy smile. "Hi. You're Connor Greene, right? The hockey player?"

He nodded, and she let out a nervous laugh.

"I think you're a great player." She pulled a Sharpie from her purse. "Can I get your autograph?"

"Sure," he said. "Um, what would you like me to sign?"

The girl looked around like a piece of paper would materialize from somewhere. When it didn't, she picked up one of the packages of underwear. "How about this?"

He hadn't fully formed in his mind the sentence that would suggest they instead ask a cashier if she had a piece of paper before the two guys must've decided that the girl had not, in fact, won the debate. They both grabbed unpackaged underwear from a bin, wadded them up, and hurled them at Connor.

The girl turned to the boys, shouted, "Losers!" then stormed off as they continued throwing underwear at him. He wasn't sure if he'd rather they hurled the insults. At least the underwear was quieter.

They were relentless, though. He turned away from the flying underwear balls to make a quick escape toward the doors and ran right into a woman. He had been in such a hurry to leave that his speed knocked them both off their feet. He wrapped his arms around the woman as they fell, twisting so that he would land on the bottom instead of landing on her.

Which wouldn't have been so bad, except that they hit a mannequin on the way down, knocking it over. And as it fell, it took out the next mannequin, which took out the next one. Connor, the woman, and each of the four mannequins fell to the ground like dominos. The landing knocked the air right out of him.

His sister was right— he really should've let someone from team services buy the underwear.

three

KATIE

KATIE PUSHED the door of the department store in Denver open and walked inside, her eyes finding the hanging sign overhead for the men's department before going back to the contract on her phone that she'd received from the legal department at the Glaciers. She was scanning it trying to find any clauses related to specific dates as she made her way back to the section where she was hoping to find some funny socks for her brother-in-law, Cory.

The spot for the name of the player she would be filming was blank, which was the source of the problem. Her dad had called to tell her about getting selected for this job weeks ago, and she really thought she'd know who her assigned player was long before now. Other videographers got their player's names right away and were able to schedule events earlier in the month when things weren't so tightly packed with Christmas.

She had even started seeing ads from the Glaciers using footage that other videographers had sent in. The ads usually cut between clips of two or three players, each being helpful with some Christmas activity in some town. Every time she saw one, it stressed her out that she didn't even know who she was supposed to be filming yet.

And she was no longer sure how she was going to fit everything in. She already had scheduled videography jobs coming up with a couple of families to film their Christmas parties, as well as her own family's traditions, and filming and editing the video she created for them.

Not to mention the stress she was feeling about the possibility that anything she filmed would get to the Glaciers too late for them to even use. And then what if it caused the Glaciers to lose faith in her and not want to use her for anything ever again? Plus, there was a player out there who wasn't going to get much screen time if things didn't start happening soon.

She was going to her parents' house tomorrow night for their annual Santa Hat activity, though, and her dad had promised that everything would be set in stone by then, and he would let her know who her player was at the activity.

She skimmed past a lot of information on what types

of things she should film, how many separate activities, and how much footage she would need to send to the team to be compiled into their campaign. There was an entire section that said they had editing rights and that anything could be cut, which she expected.

It included a player confidentiality clause that basically stated that if she discovered something personal about a player that they didn't want disclosed, she couldn't disclose it. She also couldn't film him looking like a jerk. Probably because the purpose of this campaign was to raise the team's image, not to make it worse. So, hopefully, the player she got assigned wasn't a jerk.

Something hit Katie in the chest and then fell onto her phone. She picked it up to see that it was a new pair of wadded-up men's underwear. Her head jerked up, her eyes searching for the underwear's origination, and saw a big guy standing right in front of her. Two teenage boys a dozen feet away immediately sent another wadded-up pair through the air, tagging the man in the shoulder.

He spun around to make an escape, but unfortunately, his exit route led exactly where she stood and he knocked into her. Her breath escaped with a whoosh as the two of them fell toward the floor. She wasn't sure how it happened, since he hit into her, but he managed to twist in mid-air so that when they landed, she was on top of him and was suddenly chest-to-chest with a large, muscular man.

She drew in a quick breath to replace the one that had been knocked out of her as her attention jerked to the mannequins that were crashing to the ground, one after another.

It was a moment before the shock of getting knocked down and of all the mannequins falling before it sunk in that she was laying on top of a man, his strong arms wrapped around her. And then another second before her eyes made it to the man's face. And about one more for recognition to dawn on her, and then she narrowed her eyes.

It was Connor Greene. He was the one player that Katie knew on sight even without a lesson from Emmalee. Everyone in Mountain Springs knew him—the right wing for the Charlotte Thunderstorm, which was who the Glaciers must've played tonight if he was in town. A lot of people saw him as the golden boy who went from a small-town hockey rink to the National Hockey League. Of course, those people were always the ones who *didn't* go to high school with him. If they had, they'd know he was a jerk.

Like he was at Katie's very first high school dance. She'd been wearing a dress she'd borrowed from her older sister, Noelle— a dress she'd promised she would return in the same condition she borrowed it in. Connor was at the dance, too, and decided to pick a fight with someone. Before long, more than a dozen people were involved, and Connor crashed into the punch table, sending almost the entire bowl of punch onto Katie, soaking her from head to toe in a very staining red liquid. The entire school lost school dance privileges for four months because of the brawl.

She pushed herself off the man as the boys threw a last couple of pairs of underwear before running off. Katie got to her feet as Connor was pushing himself to a sitting position. She had seen a picture or two of Connor since that day in the high school gym, but she hadn't seen him in person. It caught her off guard how good-looking he'd become.

Not that becoming more eye-pleasing on the outside changed anything. She put a hand on her hip. "Well, it looks like not much has changed. People still want to throw stuff at you."

She caught a glimpse of confusion on his face before she turned on her heel, leaving him in her dust as she exited the store.

THE NEXT EVENING, Katie pulled up in front of her parents' extremely decorated home in Mountain Springs. Even though it wasn't quite 6:00 yet, it was already dark, making the explosion of lights over the entire house, on every tree, and lighting up every decoration in every area on their big front lawn even more impressive. There was a part with a large nativity complete with all the animals, another with Santa's village, an area with giant Christmas tree ornaments, and a group of nearly life-size carolers.

Before she got out of the car, she sent a text to Emmalee.

Katie: I'm sad you're not here with me for Santa Hat night!

Emmalee: I am sad, too!

Although to be honest, I was a little intimidated by the whole thing and was kind of wishing there was someone you'd want to take as a date.

Katie: Emmalee! Did your grandpa really fall? Or was that just an excuse not to come save me?

Emmalee: He really did fall. And I really was the only one close enough to get him to the hospital. No way I would've left you high and dry without a good excuse. Are you sure there isn't someone you could ask as your date with zero notice?

Katie: Nope. I'm just going to be on my own solo team. It's going to be awesome.

It wasn't going to be awesome. It wasn't the type of thing one would ever choose to do solo. Maybe her family would give her a five-minute head start as the only unmarried, couldn't-get-a-date sibling.

She walked into the just as elaborately-decorated inside and hugged her mom, her very pregnant sister, Noelle, and Noelle's husband, Jack. Then she hugged her sisters, Becca, Hope, and Julianne, along with their husbands and a total of ten nieces and nephews. And her parents' black lab, Captain. And in the process, she confirmed at least three times that she was, indeed, there without a date.

Her dad walked out of his office down the hall, a phone to his ear, and from what she could hear over the sound of everyone, she guessed it was a work call he was finishing up. Since she had a moment, she sent a quick text to Emmalee that she'd been meaning to send. Katie had videoed a wedding proposal last night in the pine trees and snow at the edge of town and didn't see Emmalee before she went to bed. And then with the craziness of Emmalee's grandpa falling, she had somehow forgotten to tell her best friend about what happened last night.

Katie: So, I'm guessing the Glaciers played the Charlotte Thunderstorm last night? Because guess who I ran into— or, I should say, guess who ran into me — in the men's underwear section at a department store in Denver?

Connor Greene!

She pressed send, imagining what Emmalee's reaction would be just as her dad hung up the phone and called everyone to gather around. Maybe she should've waited to tell Emmalee the story because she wasn't going to get a chance to respond for a bit. She did glance at her phone when a text from Emmalee came in, though.

Emmalee: The Glaciers played the Washington Hydra last night...

Katie was still furrowing her brow in confusion at Emmalee's text when her dad started talking.

"Before we get started on our annual Santa Hat competition, I have a few announcements I need to make. Katie, this first one is mostly for you."

Katie perked up, remembering that she was going to find out which player she would be videoing tonight.

"The reason why we couldn't tell you which player was yours sooner is because the GM told me they were working on a trade. I knew you could handle getting started a little late with the player who Mountain Springs was getting, so I had the new player assigned here. The trade took longer than they expected, though, which gives you a much smaller window to get all the filming done. I'm really sorry about that."

A smaller time frame to do the filming, she could handle. But *a new player*? It felt like a stone had just dropped into Katie's stomach. She glanced at the phone that was still in her hand.

"Anyway, the trade went through, and the new player flew in last night. If any players had a connection with any particular town in Colorado, we tried to assign them to that area. I assumed that the new player we'd get wouldn't have a connection to anywhere in Colorado, but... Surprise!"

No, no, no.

"He actually does have a connection with Mountain Springs! Noelle, I think that you might have gone to school with him. It's Connor Greene!"

Julianne's husband, Ben, and Becca's husband, Corbin, high-fived each other. Cory pumped his fist and said, "Yes!" Most of the kids were jumping up and cheering, even though— except for maybe three or four of them— they had no idea what they were cheering for. They were just excited about group excitement. Jack looked to Noelle to gauge her reaction, while all five sisters looked at each other. The four of them had the same wary expression on their faces that Katie knew she wore.

Actually, hers was much more than wariness. She wasn't even sure what it was, because a mix of many emotions was swirling through her. None of them good. All of which made her feel both tense and twitchy at the same time. And, oddly enough, made her jaw feel tight.

Her dad continued talking, although a little more cautiously, as if trying to figure out the mix of positive and negative emotions he was sensing. "He practiced with the team today, and I had a good chat with him after, where I explained about going to a town to do Christmas events for a video. He seems like a good guy. I asked him about his Christmas plans, and he was really feeling bad that he wouldn't be able to go home for Christmas because of the storm coming in and the lack of flights."

Katie mentally crossed all her fingers and toes, silently hoping that the next words out of her dad's mouth wouldn't be what she could guess they would be.

"So, I talked to your mom, and we decided to invite him to stay with us over the three-day break they get for Christmas."

And there it was. The person in all of her high school — all grades included— that she liked least of all was going to be invading their family Christmas.

"So, Katie, I guess it was a good thing that your plans

for a teammate for this activity fell through because I have someone else for you to partner up with."

"What?" Katie nearly shouted as a knock sounded on the front door. "Dad, please tell me that you didn't invite him to come tonight."

"Why? I thought it would be a great chance for the two of you to get to know each other before you have to start filming him. It might make it easier to, you know, dig deep in your video and show the real Connor. Since he's new to the team, it'll give fans a chance to connect with him more. Oh, and there's the man of the hour right there!"

Katie's dad held out his arm and she turned to see the tall, muscular man who had crashed into her at the department store.

This was a nightmare come to life.

He'd started strolling into the room looking plenty confident, but as his eyes roved the room, his stride became more hesitant. It seemed like he was gathering puzzle pieces and slowly snapping them together. And then his eyes fell on Katie, and she could swear that she could actually see color leaving his face. His feet shifted ever so slightly, and she could tell at that moment that a part of him wanted to turn around and leave and that all of him was suddenly regretting saying yes to her dad's offer.

Instead, though, he walked all the way up to her dad,

shook his hand, then shook her mom's hand and thanked them for inviting him.

Her nerve endings seemed to tingle at seeing both the strong, confident walk and the slight show of vulnerability. Why? Why? Why wasn't her body getting the memo that she didn't like him? This man was a jerk in high school. Why the fluttering?

It was probably because when he knocked into her at the department store, he had twisted to make sure he fell first, protecting her. She was just feeling that. Protection appreciation. Nothing else.

Her dad started introducing him to everyone. When he got to Noelle, Connor said, "We went to high school together, right?"

"Yep. We had U.S. History together for the first half of our junior year."

Connor kept a smile on his face, but Katie could see the wince behind it, too. Then her dad motioned to her. "And this is my daughter, Katie."

Connor shook her hand, but the guy's face was pretty easy to read, so she could tell that he was racking his brain, trying to figure out if he knew her in high school.

"You don't remember me, do you?"

"From last night?"

She ignored the raised eyebrows from practically everyone else in the room. "No, from high school." She paused when there was still no recognition in his expression. "I was a freshman at that Christmas dance."

Connor didn't ask which one— they both knew which dance she was referring to. It was a low blow to bring it up, but also, it was oddly satisfying to see the look on his face.

Connor dipped his head a bit and scratched the back of his neck. "I'm really sorry about that."

Her dad didn't seem to know which dance they were talking about, and she didn't expect him to. He had five daughters, so there were a *lot* of school dances. She could tell that he sensed the awkwardness yet needed to press on anyway. "I'm glad you're here and have been introduced— again, apparently— because Katie, here, is the videographer that is assigned to you for the Christmas player promotions I told you about earlier today."

The new expression that crossed Connor Greene's face? That one was even better.

CONNOR

TODAY, Connor got to be on the ice with his new team in Denver and was introduced to everyone. Most players in the NHL had experienced either getting traded or having a teammate they were good friends with get traded. Everyone, himself included, accepted that it was just part of the game. They always embraced the new guy because they understood how hard a trade was on a player. Connor had done it plenty of times with players traded to the Thunderstorm.

But even though the Glaciers embraced him and welcomed him onto the team, he still got the sense that they weren't entirely happy about the trade. Which was probably pretty common. He'd felt the same about new players to his own team plenty of times.

He didn't know the details of their feelings about his

trade, specifically, though, and didn't know anyone well enough yet to ask. Although, one player, Erik Henderson, seemed like a cool guy. And another player, Briggs, seemed particularly unhappy about Connor's presence.

Connor reminded himself that it was all temporary. He'd get traded closer to home soon. Maybe before the trade deadline in March, but for sure by summer. He wanted to gel with the team until then, but he didn't want to get comfortable.

After practice, he met with Reid Allred and immediately liked the guy. He worked with players and their agents to discuss branding themselves and the team and each player's role on the team. So he'd be working with him off and on while he was with the Glaciers.

Then, Mr. Allred explained that they'd had a few players on the team who wreaked havoc on the team's image, harming ticket sales, especially for families. They'd traded a couple of players in the off-season, but the player they had just traded for Connor had caused a lot of damage by his actions both on and off the ice, and they were working on repairing that image.

Image repair was a pretty normal part of life for a team. So was having the players do things in the communities where they played. Being assigned to a community to do at least three activities in the week leading up to Christmas, which also happened to be your very first week on the team, was not so normal. Especially when they also had three games between now and then. It helped that the guy acknowledged that it would be a challenge for him and was apologetic about it.

It also helped that the guy recognized that Connor would be away from family for Christmas and offered to let him stay with his family during the three days he'd be off for Christmas. He probably should've guessed that there would be a problem going to someone's home if they lived in Mountain Springs.

Mr. Allred just looked so much younger than Connor's step-dad that he'd assumed the man's daughters would be younger— the ages where they'd still be living at home, not that they'd be his age.

And he definitely didn't expect to show up at Mr. Allred's house and see the woman he'd plowed into last night at the department store. Sure, she was extremely attractive and he felt like he'd connected with her a teeny bit, and not in an "accidentally crashed into her physically" kind of way. But the whole experience had been embarrassing in so many ways that he'd hoped that he'd never run into her again.

When she'd made the comment about people still wanting to throw things at him, he had assumed it was a hockey thing, especially since he came from the Thunderstorm. He hadn't recognized her from high school at all. Even after finding out he'd known her from there, he still had no flash of recognition.

His parents had a plethora of problems in his sophomore and junior years of high school, so most of his high school memories were of that. Apparently, he'd only focused on his own problems and not on anyone else at all. He might have only been in high school with two of these sisters, but by the way all five looked at him, they all knew about him.

And he had already agreed to stay with them over Christmas. Was it too late to back out?

They didn't leave any time for stewing in the awkwardness, though, before Mrs. Allred pulled out a Santa hat and said, "Are you all ready to get started?"

Everyone shouted yes, the kids most animated of all. Even the black lab seemed excited about it. Connor leaned in toward Katie and asked, "What are we about to do?" And just like last night, when they had fallen, he felt a current run through him at the nearness. A tingle of nerve endings. It was almost as if she exuded an electric charge and by getting close, he was bound to feel it.

She turned her head to him, eyes still on the Santa hat like she didn't want to miss anything, and said, "Each sibling is a team with their family. My parents are a team, too." Her eyes met his. "You're my team, by the way. We didn't get off on the right foot in high school, and we didn't again last night. But just so you know, we're going to win this."

He smiled at her conviction. He was definitely down for winning.

"We each pull out an assignment— two people get entertainment, which is a skit; two people get decorations; and two people get dinner. Except it's not that straight-forward. There are obstacles and a time limit and a money limit, and you're competing against the other team that drew the same thing."

Connor nodded. Sitting around, socializing with people who only knew him as who he used to be sounded like torture. A competition, he could handle. And as much as he didn't want to be surrounded by people who didn't have the best opinions of him, it felt good to be around a family, even if it wasn't his own, doing family Christmas things. Tonight, his family was decorating the big tree, and he was missing it.

The oldest sister, Becca, if he remembered correctly, drew a paper out of the Santa hat that Mrs. Allred held, and read, "Decorations!" Everyone reacted loudly. This was a group that really seemed to like cheering. It almost sounded like a hockey game in here.

"There are a lot of details to it," Katie continued. "We don't need to worry about all that right now. What we need to worry about is not drawing *Dinner*."

"Why do we need to worry about that?"

Another sister drew out "Entertainment!" and everyone cheered again.

"Let's just say that every other time I've drawn dinner, bad things happened."

Her sister, Noelle, the one he'd gone to school with, drew out "Dinner!" and again with the clapping and hooting, but this time with a breath of relief from Katie, probably because it just cut down their chances of pulling a dinner paper from the hat, too.

"Like what?" he asked.

"Oh, you know, just things like forgetting a pan of garlic bread was in the oven on broil until the smoke started pouring out, forgetting to put any kind of liquid in the Instant Pot when using it as a pressure cooker, a completely inedible pasta sauce. Once I forgot to turn on the burner for the eggs, realized it at the last moment, and put them in the microwave instead.

"Another time, I dropped a big pot of soup on the way to the table, sending it everywhere. And I do mean *everywhere*. Adding a bit too much salt, making everyone say 'I'm headed into the salt mines' with every bite they took. Setting a hot pad on fire. Things like that. Some of those things happened in the same year, obviously. I haven't actually drawn the 'Dinner' paper that many times."

He chuckled. "Okay then, we are crossing our fingers for 'entertainment' or 'decorations.'"

"Either one."

Another sister pulled out *Decorations*, leaving just

Katie and her parents to draw, and if he remembered correctly, that meant there was one for entertainment and one for dinner remaining. And, of course, she drew out the paper that read *Dinner*. And, of course, everyone groaned.

He watched Katie as she narrowed her eyes at the little strip of paper like she was challenging it. Then, when her dad said, "You've got five minutes to discuss with your team, and then we'll start the timer. Go!" Katie grabbed hold of his hand and pulled him to a small room off the kitchen with a washer and dryer.

She closed the door and met his eyes with her very fierce ones. She was standing close in the small space, so he got a good look at those eyes. They were blue at the outer rim with gold around the pupil, and her eyes were framed by dark eyelashes. As far as eyes went, they were rather mesmerizing. He could imagine himself getting very easily pulled in by those eyes. But he wasn't going to be in Colorado long enough for that to happen.

Besides, he didn't want to be with someone who knew him as who he used to be. It hadn't been easy for him to become who he was now, and he expected it was just as difficult for anyone who knew him back then to think of him any differently.

"Okay, here's the deal," she said. "We have a budget and thirty minutes to shop for food and get back here to meet the other team. They'll take the food we bought and we take theirs. Then we each have thirty minutes to make something out of those ingredients. The team who makes the best meal wins."

"Oof. That doesn't sound easy."

"It's not. But we *have* to win this," she said. "It's really important."

He didn't know if she was always this competitive, but he liked it. He found himself nodding and getting pumped up for the challenge. "So what's the best strategy?"

"We buy about ten items for them and they buy ten for us. The trick is to buy foods that aren't gross. Unlike the year when Julianne's team bought anchovies, wasabi peas, sprouted wheat cinnamon raisin bread, and a cheese that smelled like feet, and Becca's team made grilled cheese out of it. Because we are all going to eat what the other team makes, so we want it edible. But we also want to win, so we want to pick things that don't naturally go well together."

A smile was spreading across his face as he imagined it. They only had thirty minutes, so they'd have to race through the grocery store, but he was sure they'd be able to pick some things that would give the other team the bigger challenge. "This is going to be fun."

"Thirty seconds," they heard Mr. Allred's muffled voice call out from the kitchen.

Katie side-eyed him. "Okay, you're looking a little too

excited right now. You aren't going to start throwing any punches, are you?"

He winked. "Nah. I save that for high school dances."

Once Mr. Allred called out that the competition had begun, he and Katie raced outside and they both got into her car. She said it had been too long since he had practiced driving on snow-packed roads— even though he'd driven to the Allred's house fine— and probably didn't remember where the grocery store was. For the record: he did. But he would've been fine letting her drive if she'd simply said she wanted to.

The seven-minute drive to the grocery store was great because they spent the time brainstorming which items to get. They decided on hot dogs (after debating whether they should be considered "gross," and he thought about how they would affect his hockey performance), quinoa, spaghetti noodles, root beer, creamed corn, a can of cranberry sauce, radishes, and Greek yogurt.

Once they got there, they raced through the store to grab everything while he added up the prices on his phone. They still had a few dollars left after grabbing the final item and since they hadn't made it to ten items yet, they threw in some pretzels and gummy worms. The checkout line ate five precious minutes, but they managed to hop into the car with a full eight minutes left.

The drive back to the Allred's house was less great. No brainstorming was needed since they wouldn't know what foods they had to work with until they returned, so the awkwardness of realizing he was in a room with people who had experienced the high school version of himself returned.

And for some reason, Connor wanted to win Katie over. Why? He wasn't sure. He knew it wasn't because she would be videoing him, and it wasn't because he normally had a need to win people over. But it was there, and he decided that the only way to get past it was to address the elephant in the room— the school dance.

"Can I explain about the dance?"

"Connor, you don't need to explain about the dance."

"I know. But can I anyway?" He wasn't the same person that he was in high school, and he was pretty sure that she was still seeing him as that guy. She nodded, and he suddenly wished he would've thought through what, exactly, he wanted to share. But since he hadn't, he just started talking and hoped for the best.

"My parents' marriage started going downhill my sophomore year of high school, and I really struggled with it. But not as much as I did at the beginning of my junior year when my dad left. Just before he did, he pulled me and my sister aside and said that his leaving didn't have anything to do with us and that he still wanted to see us all the time. Typical divorce stuff, I guess. But it didn't take long before he was off, living his best life, forgetting about us completely. I didn't handle that so well and kind of became a hotheaded idiot."

That was an understatement. He'd been so bitter and angry about not only not having his dad around, but also seeing what it was doing to his mom. He was hurting and showed it by acting out a lot, catching so many people in the crossfire.

Why was he telling this to Katie? The fact that there were circumstances that led to the state of mind he was in at the time didn't change the fact that he did what he did. Maybe he was telling her so that he was more than the memory of a kid who made bad choices. So she got that there was more to him. And for some reason, he really wanted her to see the real him.

Katie kept her eyes on the road, but she nodded slightly, and he could tell that she was paying very close attention to his words so he continued. "I was in a club hockey league with other high school players in our county. Trav Donovan was in the same league, but we were on different teams. We were both captains and didn't like each other much. But I especially didn't like him when he asked my little sister, Laura, to the Christmas dance."

Katie glanced at him for a second before her eyes were back on the road. "The fight started with the two of you?"

"Yep. He came over and made a hurtful, if not clever or unique, comment about how he'd heard that my mom didn't have a big, strong man at the house anymore and asked if he needed to step in. Given the state I was in at the time, that alone probably would've been enough to provoke a fight with me. But then he said something crude about what he was going to show my sister later that night.

"Not that it was any excuse— there are plenty of kids who experience the same things with their parents that I did, and then have someone talk crap about their mom or sister, but they *don't* get their school's dance privileges taken away for four months.

"And I don't know if he was just trying to bait me or not. In his defense, I was easy to bait back then. So, I threw the first punch. Everyone kind of assumed that we were fighting as captains of two different hockey teams, so anyone at the dance who was also on one of our teams joined in and turned it into an all-out brawl."

"That was why so many people joined in so quickly?"

Connor grimaced. "Mostly. Trav and I also both played on the high school baseball team, so all those players joined in, too."

Katie stopped at a stop sign, looked both ways, then said, "And none of them thought to ask what the fight was even about?"

He chuckled. "Listen, most high school boys who are

dealing with some crap in their life need a reason to fight, but they don't necessarily need to know the reason. I don't know if I was glad for the support, or if I was just in my own troubled world so much that I didn't even care what else was going on.

"But the worst part about it was that someone gave me a good hit to the gut, and it made me back into the refreshment table. I was so mad that I shoved off that table to go after the guy, completely toppling it over. I spun around just in time to see the punch bowl go flying and dowse some poor girl."

Katie raised her hand. "Hi. That was me."

His eyes went wide. "You're joking."

She shook her head as she turned onto her parents' street. "I was soaked from the top of my head to the toes of my heels."

Connor ran his hands over his face and then around again until his fingers were steepled at the top of his nose. No way that after ten years, chance brought him into the same car with the recipient of the punch bowl that his anger had sent flying, at Christmastime, even. To add to it, that person was going to soon be videoing him as a hockey player with his new team. Was this what being mortified felt like?

He removed his hands from his face as she pulled into the driveway. "I am so sorry."

"Connor, it's okay. It was a long time ago. Besides, it

wasn't even my dress that got ruined— I had borrowed it from my sister."

"I think that makes it even worse. Okay, we are going to win this contest for you. Right now."

Katie nodded once as she put the car into park. "I'm down for that."

"What's at stake?"

"Officially? A trophy that we get to keep for a year, along with bragging rights. Unofficially? A curse lifted and future smack talk about me drawing the 'Dinner' paper abated."

He glanced over at Noelle and Jack, the couple who were competing against them, as they pulled into the driveway next to them. Then he turned back to Katie. "Okay, we're doing this."

KATIE

THIS WAS PROBABLY the seventh time that Katie had done the Santa Hat activity with a date as her partner. But as they hurried to grab out the bags of groceries, laughing and bumping shoulders with Noelle and Jack as the four of them all tried to go through the door first, she realized it was the first time she was going into it with confidence that her teammate was as dedicated to winning as she was. Maybe they actually had a chance.

For a moment, she internally rolled her eyes at the thought. She'd chosen the *Dinner* paper, after all. Maybe if they'd drawn anything else. She never would've guessed that Connor Greene, of all people, would make her feel like she had someone who was very solidly on her team.

They laid out the groceries they bought for Jack and

Noelle to use on one end of the long table. It had all the leaves in it, ready to seat all twenty-two of them. Jack and Noelle set out all the food items they'd bought on the other end. Then they swapped sides to see what they had to work with.

Both she and Connor started moving items around on the table, pulling things together that seemed like they fit, and it didn't take long to see a theme. There was a turkey breast, a big can of pumpkin pie mix, heavy cream, cranberry sauce, and mini marshmallows, like the kind they always put on top of yams. Did Jack & Noelle think they could make a Thanksgiving dinner in — she looked at her watch— twenty-seven minutes? The turkey breast was thawed and boneless and the ovens were both pre-heated, but still, twenty-seven minutes wasn't enough time.

Katie and Connor had chosen for Jack and Noelle a bunch of random ingredients that they didn't think would go together. But Jack and Noelle seemed to be leading them along a theme that they couldn't possibly pull off in the amount of time that they had.

She picked up a head of cauliflower and a bag of Lay's potato chips and, loudly enough to be heard at the other end of the table, said, "Really? Are we supposed to mash potato chips into cauliflower to make it taste like mashed potatoes?"

Noelle patted her pregnant belly and said, "What can

I say? The baby loved Thanksgiving and wants it again. But we're not telling you what you have to make at all. Besides, can you really complain when you gave us..." she picked up two items, "Hot dogs and gummy worms?"

"Fair enough," Katie said, and couldn't help the smile on her face. She was pretty sure that she and Connor had bought some pretty difficult ingredients to use together.

Then, in a quieter voice meant only for Connor, she said, "Seriously, though, how are we supposed to make Thanksgiving dinner in such a short amount of time?" She pulled together the other ingredients that didn't seem to fit the theme— red and green bell peppers, Reese's Puffs cereal, flour tortillas, and a can of pineapple chunks. She couldn't even imagine how to use them.

Connor just looked at the ingredients for a small moment, hands on his hips, a focused expression on his face. Then he said, "The theme is just to throw us off. To keep us from thinking of other things."

Katie eyed her sister and her brother-in-law. "Clever."

He started moving things around, putting them in different groups. "We have pineapple and peppers. Can we use any additional ingredients besides what's here?"

Katie nodded. "Yes. Salt, pepper, seasonings, oils, and

condiments. But we have to use *all* the ingredients they bought for us."

"Okay, we have pineapple chunks. We could make something similar to sweet and sour chicken but use turkey instead. Then we can cut it into small enough chunks to cook in time, and maybe use the cauliflower as rice. To make the sauce, we can use marshmallows instead of brown sugar, some of the juice from the pineapples, and I'm sure your parents have ketchup, soy sauce, and cornstarch."

"Oh, wow," Katie said, feeling a bit impressed and in awe. "You're actually pretty brilliant."

"I can't say that is the most frequent compliment that hockey players tend to get."

Katie picked up the box of cereal, thinking, then grabbed the marshmallows. "Rice Krispies treats!"

Connor paused a second before he grabbed the can of jellied cranberry sauce. "We can use this in the sauce for sugar instead of the marshmallows." Then he grabbed the potato chips. "Maybe crumble some of these up with the Reese's Puffs? It could be a sweet and salty treat."

"I'm not sure if that will make it awful or awfully tasty. I say we find out."

Connor pulled the final two ingredients toward them — the pumpkin pie mix and the flour tortillas— and Katie gasped. "We can make mini pumpkin pies in a muffin tin! We'll use the tortillas as a crust, and we can whip the cream."

"That's perfect." As they quickly gathered all the ingredients into their arms to haul them over to the counters, Connor said, "But we need a side. Our plan gives us one main dish and two desserts."

"We can call the pumpkin pies a side." When Connor shot her a look, she said, "What? Pumpkin is a vegetable, right?"

They were down to twenty-three minutes remaining, so Katie hurried to put a skillet on the stove and turned the burner on, and they quickly divided up who was going to work on what item first. Connor cut the turkey into cubes, dredging them in corn starch and putting them into the skillet as he went, while Katie cut up the peppers on a second cutting board beside him as fast as she could.

"Coming up with what to make out of random ingredients is one of the hardest parts of drawing the *Dinner* paper." She glanced at him as she worked. She had to admit that the guy was creative. "Yet you came up with something pretty great."

"Wow. A second compliment in three minutes." He didn't look away from his slicing— which was good, because they were in a hurry— but said, "I guess when your parents start to have a falling out that lasts the better part of a year, then your dad leaves completely and your mom is left dealing with a myriad of struggles, you tend to get plenty of opportunities to figure out how to make things from random ingredients that resemble meals."

Katie did actually stop slicing peppers for a full five seconds to just look at Connor. She wasn't sure what she thought of him, exactly, but she was definitely intrigued. Plus, he had that strong jaw and the hair that curled over his ear just a bit that was rather attractive.

Stop being attracted, Katie, she reminded herself. She had a plan and was going to stick with it.

She finished cutting the peppers before Connor finished the turkey, so she started grating the cauliflower. Her parents had two ovens, but they had to share the stove with Noelle and Jack, so they only got two of the burners. Things were going to get tricky, so she got out another pan to cook and slightly toast the cauliflower.

Before long, Katie found herself cutting the tortillas into triangles and working to get them to sit right in the muffin tin right next to where Noelle was layering Greek yogurt, gummy worms, crushed pretzels, and a drizzle of cranberry sauce in nearly two dozen clear cups at one end of the long island counter. Connor was at the other end, mixing ingredients into a bowl for the sauce, taste-testing it, and then making adjustments. Jack was keeping an eye on... Katie wasn't sure exactly what on the stove while mixing stuff in with the spaghetti.

Without glancing up, Noelle nodded her head toward Connor. "Things between you two don't seem as tense as when he first got here."

Katie used the back of her hand to rub her forehead and took a quick look at Connor. "I can forgive the guy who ruined the dance and my dress."

"*My* dress."

"*Your* dress. It was a very long time ago. What matters is what he's like now."

A bit of yogurt fell from the spoon as Noelle was scooping it, falling onto the apron covering her big belly. Noelle just looked at it, sighed, and kept going. "And what is he like now? Dateable?"

The old her would've said yes. The new her didn't. "I don't have enough info yet."

"But you do think he's very attractive, right?"

Katie smiled. "That, he is." She glanced at him again as he took the sauce to the stove, gave both the cauliflower and the turkey a stir, then added the peppers to the turkey skillet. "As far as the rest goes, though, I'm withholding judgment for now. I'm sure I'll find out what he's really like as we're filming."

"Come on, Katie. He's been great while he's been here. You can't tell me that you haven't been thinking about what it would be like to date him, even if it's only for fun and not for anything long-term."

"Okay, I have." Because he kind of got her heart fluttering quite a bit. She placed the final tortilla triangle in the last of the two muffin tins and grabbed the can of pumpkin pie mix and a can opener. "And I also haven't. I decided I make decisions too quickly when it comes to men to date, and I made a goal to be more skeptical. Now, I slow down and get more information first. I don't use my initial gut reaction anymore. That thing can't be trusted."

She exhaled as she opened the can of pumpkin. "Besides, even if he does end up being great, when would I ever fit in dating? Christmas is in a week. I have to film Connor at three activities. Then I have to edit all that footage and get it sent in."

As she put dollop after dollop of pie filling in each spot in the muffin tin, moving as quickly as she could, all the things she needed to do outside of tonight moved just as quickly through her mind. "I need to finish filming our family's video and edit it, and I have to do one for the Waldrops' Christmas party in a few days, edit that, work at my other job because this time of year is always crazy for Emmalee, and finish last minute shopping. On top of all our regular family traditions. Plus, I don't even really know what he's like yet. And I'll only see him through Christmas, anyway."

"You're right. It's good to know when to admit defeat, call it quits," Noelle said as she drizzled the last bit of cranberry sauce on her crazy creations in a flourish.

"You'll never get me to admit defeat. Like everything, I'm in this to win it." She was pretty sure she was talking about the dinner competition now.

Katie put the mini pumpkin pies in the oven, and then Connor dipped a spoon in the sauce on the stove and held out the spoon. "Taste this. Does it need anything?"

"Oh, wow," Katie said, wiping a bit of sauce off her lip with her knuckle. "That is amazing." He seriously made that using random ingredients and cranberry sauce. Was she impressed? Maybe. Was she going to let herself be attracted, based on that impressiveness? Nope. She was going to stick to her plan.

"What's left to do?" Connor asked.

"Whip the cream and make the Rice Krispies treats." She glanced at her watch. "And we've only got seven minutes left!"

Without discussing what they were each going to do, Katie got out a pot and started melting the butter and marshmallows, and Connor pulled out a bowl and started measuring Reese's Puffs cereal and crushing the potato chips into it. As she mixed the melted marshmallow mixture into the cereal, he whipped the cream.

When she reached for something in his space, he leaned away the perfect amount. When one of them needed a utensil that was closer to the other, they handed it to the other person before they even asked. Almost like they'd rehearsed everything ahead of time.

And it was extra surprising that they were working so well together given the fact that they were working against the clock. She had done the Santa Hat activity with plenty of different dates over the years, so she knew how much the time limit could bring out not only the stress but annoyance with each other.

(Unless they drew the *Entertainment* paper. It was easy to go with the flow when it came to a skit, because no one knew if you were following a script or making it up as you went, anyway. *Dinner*, though? That was a completely different beast.)

As Noelle tended to whatever hotdog concoction they had going on at the other burner, from the corner of her eye, Katie saw that Noelle was smiling at their in-syncedness. If she felt the need to bring it up, Katie could always bring up the "loading frosting bags and getting some on my cheek so he has to wipe it off" incident that happened in this very kitchen between Jack and Noelle that Katie had a front row seat to.

Wait. That eventually led to the two of them getting married, so maybe it wasn't the best comeback.

They were down to almost no time left when she

dumped the Reese's Puffs treats into a pan and the two of them pressed it out together. Katie pulled the remaining bit of it from the spoon she'd used, divided it in half, then put half in her mouth and half in Connor's. Her eyebrows shot up just as Connor said, "Oh! This is actually quite good. I didn't think it would be."

She playfully punched him in the shoulder. "Weren't you the one who suggested it?"

"Yes. I like taking risks. It doesn't mean that they always work out."

With less than a minute to go, they hurried to cut up the treats, which were still too warm to be cut in a pretty way, so it took a little finessing, pulled the mini pies from the oven, and barely had time to get everything on a sample plate to show before the air horn sounded from where her parents were coming up the stairs from the basement. All her siblings, their spouses, and their kids descended on the room that was a combination kitchen, dining room, and family room, all seeming pretty excited about whatever they'd prepared.

Katie took a deep breath and stood next to Connor, but the nerves that had popped up the moment that horn had sounded stuck around. While she and Connor had been cooking, she'd forgotten about her curse when it came to the *Dinner* card. There was one other time she had, too, and that was when she and her partner had spilled the pot of soup everywhere. She leaned in closer to Connor. "If anything needs to be picked up and moved at all, I need you to do it."

He didn't question it— he just nodded and lifted one of the arms crossed over his chest enough to form a fist, so she bumped it with hers. "We've got this," he said.

When she'd leaned in to bump his fist, they'd gotten close enough that her entire upper arm was pressed against his, and she didn't move. It made it feel like they were an unstoppable team. She could really get used to having a teammate who was as dedicated to winning as she was. And had she ever enjoyed a teammate this much before? The same fluttering happened in her chest again.

But maybe it was just the nerves.

Once everyone was gathered, her dad announced that it was time for both teams to present their meals. She and Connor presented their sweet and sour turkey over riced cauliflower, the "vegetable" side in the form of a mini pumpkin pie, and the Reese's and Lay's treats for dessert.

And then Jack and Noelle presented their grilled and sliced hotdogs smothered in a root beer reduction glaze with a touch of honey mustard, served on a bed of quinoa, with radish garnishes cut to look like flowers, a side salad of spaghetti noodles tossed with creamed corn and topped with crumbled pretzels, and the layered dessert in a glass. Which kind of still sounded gross, but looked pretty good, somehow smelled tasty enough, and was definitely impressive, given the ingredients she and Connor had bought for them to use.

As everyone sat down to try the foods, Katie pulled out her video camera to get everyone's reactions for the family Christmas Eve video.

After eating her fourth bite— surprisingly— of the glazed hot dogs and quinoa, she leaned closer to Connor and said, "Theirs wasn't nearly as bad as I thought it would be. And judging by the fact that you've finished yours, I'm guessing you felt the same."

Connor nodded. "And ours is better than I guessed it'd be."

"It's the sauce," Katie said, taking another bite. He should seriously submit the recipe to a cooking blog.

"I don't know," he said, picking up their dessert. "The Reese's / Lay's treats are pretty tasty. We made a good team."

As everyone finished eating, she managed to pull a couple of people to the side for interviews, like she did every year. Then they all gathered on the couches to watch the skits, and she filmed some more of everyone laughing and *aww*-ing.

Which was totally warranted, because her parents performed a skit about Christmas in space, with her dad wearing a colander as a helmet and her mom wearing slinkies on her arms like a space suit. They wandered a new planet to try to find a Christmas tree but ended up wrapping some flashing Christmas lights around a "space rock" that was really an upside-down bucket.

And then Julianne and her family pretended to be on a Christmas cooking show, with their seven-year-old as the host, the baby as the audience, and Julianne, her husband Ben, and her four-year-old all pretending they didn't realize they were using a collection of tools that would be more at home in a garage instead of the ones meant for a kitchen.

She filmed some more as Hope and her family presented their three-foot-tall Christmas tree decorated with a lollipop-theme, and Becca and her family presented theirs decorated with the aquamarine and navy blue of the Glaciers, complete with popsicle stick hockey sticks and hockey pucks made of chocolate Oreos as decorations.

Then they all voted on the winners, and she was looking through the video camera when her mom said, "And the trophy for *Best Dinner* goes to... Katie and Connor!"

She nearly dropped the camera. "We won?" She turned to Connor and shouted, "We won!" He picked her up and swung her in a circle with her fist held high in the air. When he set her back on the floor, she still felt like she was floating. And, well, connected to Connor in a way that she hadn't experienced with any previous

Santa Hat date. She wasn't going to let herself think about that, though. She gave Connor a high-ten, which was a medium-ten for him because the guy was seriously tall. "I can't believe we won!"

Her dad handed her the trophy, and she hugged it tight to her chest for a moment. Not only was their dinner edible, but they had won *Best Dinner*! Her curse was lifted. She passed the trophy to Connor so he could hold it, too.

He looked at the trophy, which had a wooden base with a slightly charred, very worn oven mitt, painted with gold spray-paint, and mounted on the base along with a very mismatched salt shaker and pepper shaker just in front of it. The front of the plaque read "Best Dinner." "*This* is the trophy we were competing for?"

"Hey, don't knock it. It has lots of history and stories and sentimental value."

"Do you have a special place on the mantle all picked out for it?"

"You know it."

As everyone was getting ready to leave and Connor was thanking her parents for inviting him, she noticed Becca's two oldest kids, nine-year-old Erika and seven-year-old Sadie carrying between them the Glacier-themed Christmas tree.

Once Connor finished talking to her parents, the girls approached him, and Erika said, "Our mom said that your hotel room is probably sad because it doesn't have any decorations, so we want you to take this Christmas tree with you so it'll be happy."

Connor immediately crouched down so that he'd be closer to the girls' heights, told them how much he loved the tree, how touched he was that they would let him take it with him, how amazing it was going to make his hotel room look, and how honored he felt to be able to put the tree in his room.

Her nieces were absolutely beaming. When Katie glanced at her sister and brother-in-law, she saw that they were, too. She looked back in time to see Connor stand again, checking out the details of the tree, looking like he genuinely appreciated it.

Was she being swept off her feet? Seeing hearts? Maybe a little. He had been pretty fantastic today. But anything could be faked for a day. Her feet were going to stay firmly planted on the ground and the hearts brushed away from her vision because she was determined to keep that skepticism in place for a little while longer.

six

CONNOR

IT SNOWED A BIT. The big storm hadn't come in yet— this was officially the "warm before the storm," and left just enough snow on the roads to really slow down traffic and make the drive between the arena to Mountain Springs that would normally take forty minutes take Connor nearly twice that long.

His nerves were getting more and more frayed the longer past one o'clock— the time he was supposed to arrive at Mountain Springs Elementary— that the clock climbed. This was his first town activity, and he was going to be late. He hated being late. And beyond that, he had some unexplainable need to impress Katie, and being late wasn't going to do it.

Okay, maybe it wasn't so inexplicable. At some point last night, he had to admit that he wasn't just enjoying the competition— he was enjoying Katie. He was attracted to her and wanted to impress her. All while not wanting to get involved with her, of course, since he'd be gone by the end of the season.

Because he'd been traded to the Glaciers so late in the Christmas season, many of the activities they probably would've asked him to participate in if he'd been there all month were past. He didn't know much about today's activity other than it was at the elementary school, which was fine. He liked kids.

He just wished he didn't have to go there today. It was a home game day, so most of the team started off the day with a workout before their mandatory team meeting, followed by a morning skate. This morning was only his second time practicing with his new team, and tonight would be his first game with them. He'd usually try to get a workout in after the morning skate, but had to skip today.

When he got into his rental car to head to Mountain Springs, most of his teammates were heading home for a pre-game nap because that was what they did to play their best. Outreach stuff like this usually only happened on non-game days. Adding it in today was hard, but with the short timeline they had to work with, it had to happen.

Whenever he wasn't focused on how slow traffic was moving, he was thinking about tonight's match-up, and thinking about plays— the ones he used on his own team and the new ones that he would be using with the Glaciers. He had excited nerves before every game, but it was different this time. He didn't have any past experience with being traded— he'd been with the Thunderstorm since he'd been drafted. It was strange to think that he'd be on the ice with a different team tonight. The Thunderstorm's rival, no less. He needed to be getting his head in the game.

No, he needed to get his head on this town activity.

"Oh, good, you're here," said the anxious woman with brown hair cut into a bob and an ID badge on a lanyard that read Ms. Messina when he finally made it to the school's front office. She didn't even have him sign the *Visitors Sign Here* clipboard on the counter— she just ushered him into the hall and said, "Let's get you to the stage quickly."

"Uh, the stage?"

"Oh, don't worry— we aren't having you perform or anything like that. That's just where we've got your costume. And my, you're a rather big guy. We didn't know which player we were getting until yesterday so we had to guess on the size, and hopefully we guessed right."

On the way down the hall, with her short heels clacking twice for every one step he took, she explained that the students had been collecting donations for a toy drive and that the older three grades were already in the gym, wrapping them. "You brought your jersey, right? Good, you can wear it while you're with the older kids."

For the younger kids, she informed him that he was going to be listening to their Christmas wishes. While dressed like Santa's elf, so he could relay the information to Santa.

"Oh, and expect the kids to be a little... rowdier than normal today. It's the end of the day on the last full day of school before Christmas break. You know how that gets." No, no he didn't. Not unless she counted the time when he was a third, fourth, or fifth grader himself. She led him to a storage closet on the stage where he could change out of his suit and into his jersey while she left to check on something with the younger grades.

Once he changed, he went down some stairs at the side of the stage, opened the door leading to the gym, and was immediately hit with a wall of noise and chaos. The stands at the game tonight weren't likely to be this loud. Luckily, his eyes quickly fell on Katie, who already had her camera up, filming, and he smiled in relief. It was incredible how much of the stress from the day melted away simply by seeing her.

Then she put the camera down and came over to him. Her smile seemed a little hesitant, like it had been a huge problem that he wasn't on time or because she was worried he wasn't up to today's task.

"It looks and sounds more chaotic than it is. That's just the sound of so many kids talking at the same time in a room where every sound echoes. For the most part, they're wrapping presents, like they should. They told me they want you to just grab a gift from one of those bins, find a spot at one of the tables, and wrap it while chatting with the kids around you. Then grab another present and find a spot at a different table. Easy enough?"

He nodded.

She studied him for a moment before asking, "Are you doing okay?"

He nodded again. "Great." Being here was practically the same as being back at his hotel, curled up in his bed for an energizing nap before a big game.

Katie put a hand on his forearm, a touch he swore he felt through his whole body. His eyes went to her hand first, then to her eyes. Once their eyes met, she said, "You've got this." She lifted the camera and started filming again.

Connor could go blade-to-blade with any player on the ice. So, he could wrap a simple present with a bunch of 8-11-year-olds. He grabbed one— a craft kit that looked like an easy box to wrap— and then went to a table where a group of boys who looked like they were probably fifth graders were waving him over. He introduced himself, and things seemed like they were going okay.

Until about thirty seconds in. He'd barely gotten the wrapping paper cut before one of the boys said, "My older brother's favorite hockey team is the Thunderstorm."

That... he wasn't expecting. Especially this far from Charlotte. He smiled. "They're a great team."

"Yeah. He says you're a traitor."

He might have been able to salvage the conversation at that point, but before he could, another boy said, "My uncle said he went to high school with you and that you've basically been a traitor your entire life."

The comments went downhill from there. And Katie was not only witnessing them all but getting them— and his reactions to them— on video.

The moment he was done wrapping the craft kit, he quickly left that table, put it in the bin for wrapped gifts, and grabbed a new one from an unwrapped bin. He decided to go to a table with a completely different demographic: third-grade girls.

They seemed a lot happier about having him join their table. In fact, the girl to his right really wanted to help him put the tape on his present. As the group chatted about books and gymnastics classes and gossip and what games they were going to play at recess and what presents they thought they were getting, he worked on wrapping presents. The girl next to him sometimes put the tape where she should, but more often tried to tape his fingers to the present, making everyone laugh when she did.

Then, when he turned his attention to a girl on his left who was talking about her brother, the girl on his right started placing the pieces of tape right onto his arms.

"He looooves hockey."

"Oh, yeah?"

"Yeah. He's twelve. He plays right wing, too. He thinks he's pretty good, but he doesn't get nearly as many assists as you do." Then her eyes shifted to the tape on his arm and she said, "Hey, Shaylie, that's mean!"

Then she, along with the girl across the table from him, both leaned in to help pull the tape off, and pretty soon, he had four hands pulling tape— along with all the arm hairs they were stuck to— from his arms.

He couldn't guarantee what expression was on his face, but he didn't yelp. He didn't curse. He didn't say any bad words. That had to be worth something.

The third group he visited didn't seem interested in hockey at all and only talked about Minecraft. He tried to join in their conversations, but he didn't speak the lingo. He didn't know what piglins and griefing and spleen meant, or what an Enderman, a creeper, or skelly was. The more he tried to join in, the more they looked at him like he was just another out-of-touch adult in their world.

What was he even doing there? Not anything good or helpful at all. He should be at his hotel in Denver, preparing for his first game day with the Glaciers.

He should have been glad when the teachers finally had the students line up to head back to their classrooms, except that meant that it was time for Ms. Messina to lead him back to the storage room on the stage where there was now an elf costume hanging from a hook, waiting for him.

An elf costume that was much too small. He came out of the room wearing green pants that were super tight and about eight inches too short, pointy-toed slippers that slid on over his own shoes— barely— and a green button-up shirt with a red zig-zag collar that would only button up if he sucked in and then didn't breathe. The sleeves only came halfway between his elbow and wrists. Luckily, he'd been wearing a white t-shirt underneath his jersey, because if he didn't have it to wear under the elf costume, he'd be showing a good three inches of his stomach.

He opened the door to see Katie waiting, and she immediately tried to stifle a laugh.

"Katie, what do I do? I can't wear this." She brought her video camera up to film, which just annoyed him. "Seriously, what do I do?"

"Maybe I can check with some teachers, and see if any of them have a green cardigan or something stretchy that you can wear over it."

"Or I can just change back into my jersey. Tell the kids that Santa lets hockey players act as elves, too. Maybe make up something about us spending so much time on the ice as the reason."

But before he could even take a step back toward the room, Ms. Messina appeared and said, "Oh, my, that really doesn't fit. Well, there's nothing we can do about it now— the first class of Kindergartners is already here, and they are extra squirrelly today. Come quickly. We've got a throne ready for you to sit on and everything."

She led him to the front of the stage where there was indeed a throne. Maybe one they'd used for a school play. Katie had positioned herself on the other side of the kids, ready to film their interactions. She gave him a thumbs up with the hand not holding the camera along with a smile, which looked more like a grimace.

He couldn't take a deep breath, not in this shirt, but he took a shallow breath and then greeted the kids and told them he was one of Santa's elves and that he would let Santa know about their Christmas wishes. Ms. Messina placed the first kid on his lap, a five-year-old girl who kept poking at his shirt that was showing in the spaces between each button as she told him her mile-long list.

When she hopped down, Ms. Messina didn't place the next kid on his lap. The little boy just walked right up to him. So he reached down to pick the boy up, and as he was lifting him, the seams on both of his sleeves tore open at both the front and back, leaving only a few threads at the top and bottom to hold it on.

"Oh, my!" Ms. Messina said. "Um, children, it looks like Santa's elf has been eating his vegetables and has grown big and strong. We need to take a short break while we get a new shirt for him."

Connor breathed a small breath of relief— he hadn't popped any buttons, so a huge breath of relief wasn't exactly possible— and set the boy on the ground as he stood. The motion made one of the sleeves fall completely off, though, and it fell to the floor. Without thinking through the likely consequences first, he bent to pick it up, completely tearing the seam in the rear of his pants from top to bottom. And because they were so tight, he hadn't put a pair of shorts or pants on underneath them.

The entire class of Kindergartners immediately burst into stomach-clenching laughter. He had been booed at enough stadiums in locations away from home before, but even that wasn't exactly like a bunch of Kindergartners laughing because they could see your underwear.

Nor was it like having a vice principal who was probably old enough to be your mom take off her cardigan and tie it around your waist to hide said underwear and usher you off stage as your second sleeve threatens to burst free at the slightest move.

Or to have the woman you felt like you really connected with and are attracted to strongly enough to maybe forget your rules filming all of it.

WHEN CONNOR finally got back to his hotel, he didn't have long before he needed to leave to head to the arena. The front desk stopped him, though, and gave him a package that had arrived. He looked at the label and saw it was from his sister— it was the package she had put together the day he'd gotten traded and mailed to him. He took the elevator up to his room and opened it as soon as he walked inside. Items from home was just what he needed after the debacle at the school.

He smiled when he saw that his favorite cinnamon caramel hot chocolate mix was right on top, even after telling his sister that he didn't need her to send it. The contact lenses were a huge relief to find. He'd been wearing the same daily lenses for three days, and his eyes were dying for some new ones. Same with the socks. One of the t-shirts she sent was a greenish color, which would've been a life saver today.

The charging cords were a relief to find, too. He'd

been relying on charging his phone during practices by borrowing from other players. He laughed when he saw his pajama pants, though, and picked up his phone to call his sister.

The moment she answered, he said, "Really? The pajamas with the flamingo hockey players are my favorites?"

"Well, yeah. They're from your favorite sister."

"I should've seen that one coming."

"You really should have. I shipped off a bigger box of your stuff— you'll get it in a couple of days."

"Thank you. For both. And thank you for the hot chocolate mix. It's been a rough day, and it was a nice thing to find."

"Okay, hot chocolate doesn't usually warrant that much gratitude in your voice. I've got a few minutes before my next meeting. What happened today?"

He told her the entire frustrating and embarrassing story, from showing up late, to Katie being there to film everything, to the vice principal tying her cardigan around his waist. Not just handing it to him— actually tying it on.

"I've had two embarrassing experiences related to underwear since I got here, and Katie was there for both of them."

"Well, at least it wasn't the fifth-grade boys who witnessed this one."

He laughed. "True."

Now he needed to apologize to Katie for his frustration at the elementary school that probably ruined every bit of footage she filmed when he had just apologized yesterday for his behavior at the school dance. She was going to start thinking this was normal for him— act poorly, apologize, repeat.

He was quiet for a minute, and so was Laura. Then she said, "You miss home." It wasn't a question, just a simple statement.

"Is it stupid that I'm a twenty-six-year-old man— almost twenty-seven— and I do?"

"No. Missing the place that you love, the people you love, and the team you love has nothing to do with age and everything to do with the strength of your connections."

It also didn't help that Charlotte had been where his family moved to get a fresh start. That was where he'd flourished after everything had hit rock bottom. Maybe if he had gotten traded to anywhere other than the place where his dad had left their family, at the same time of year as when he'd left— the place where he'd actually hit rock bottom, things would be different.

"Hey, sis. I've only got about ten minutes before I have to change and head to the arena, and I'm not in the right head space to go play my first game with the Glaciers. I need you to pump me up."

"Okay," she said, and he could hear the squeak of her office chair as he was sure she was leaning all the way back, putting her feet up on her desk. "Tell me about the ice."

"The ice?"

"Yep. Talk me through what it's like the moment you first step a skate onto the ice. Don't think about where the ice is, just that you're on it. How do you feel?"

He closed his eyes and pictured it. The stands could be completely full with a raucous crowd, but the moment he stepped on the ice, everything always seemed to quiet. Knowing that his sister might razz him about a lot of things but never would about this, he was willing to talk through it out loud.

"From the first step onto the ice, I'm relaxed. But somehow energized, too. It's a feeling... I don't know. Like coming home. No matter where the ice is, the scent of the cold, the gleam on the ice, the expanse of white spread out before me always feels *right*. Like I'm in control of the space and even of time.

"That first glide is almost... sacred. Untouched by chaos. Smooth. The sound of the blade slicing across it is like music. It's a whisper, but so full of possibilities and potential. And gliding forward on it is powerful. Like *I'm* powerful. As I pick up speed and then make a tight turn, the centrifugal force pulling at me, it's like there's a trust, an agreement between gravity, the ice, and me. When I come to a stop, the side of my blade cutting across the ice, sending a spray of white ice in an arc, it reminds me that we're all working together to make something beautiful.

"The ice is where I'm most alive. Most myself. Most free. And as the crowds come back into focus, they energize and exhilarate me. They give me fuel to work with the ice, the gravity, and my team to pull off something amazing."

As I talk while picturing it, a calmness seeps into me. It gets me into the head space that I need to be in before a game. It grounds me and gives me energy I know I didn't possess when I first walked into this room.

Laura is quiet for a moment before she whispers, "Wow. Keep talking like that and I might become a hockey player."

He chuckled.

"Ice in a rink in Denver is the same as ice in a rink in Charlotte. Focus on your love of the ice wherever it is, and I can tell you that you'll be just fine."

"Thanks, sis."

"You're welcome. Sean and I have a date tonight, so I won't be able to watch, but call me tomorrow and tell me how the game went?"

"Will do."

"Oh, and tell me about this videographer who has caught your eye."

"What? How?" he sputtered. He'd said one sentence to Laura about Katie. And he'd kept it neutral.

"You give away much more in the tone of your voice than you realize. Now, I helped you today, so tomorrow, you tell me all about her."

seven

KATIE

KATIE WAITED for Connor in Mountain Springs' Downtown Park, standing right between a snow sculpture of an alien wearing a Santa hat while decorating a Christmas tree and a pirate ship with Santa as the captain. Connor wasn't late yet, but still, she wondered if he was going to show up after how things went yesterday.

Things at Mountain Springs Elementary School yesterday had been a disaster. The only genuine smile he had the entire time might have been the one he gave her when he first arrived and saw her. (Which was, admittedly, pretty fantastic and might have sent her heart a buzzing.) Yes, he also wore a smile when he went up to the first table to wrap a present with the fifth-grade boys — before they started smack-talking— but even that smile had seemed forced. Like he just hadn't wanted to be there.

She'd expected him to be good with the kids, especially because he had been so great with her nieces when they'd presented him with the Christmas tree to keep in his hotel room. An average response to her nieces would've been to thank them, tell them they did a great job, and then set the tree down. But he got down to their level, made them feel like they'd decorated the tree the best he'd seen in his life and that they'd given him the greatest gift ever.

Where had that Connor been yesterday? Yes, the boys had been rude. But he could've just joked with them about their comments instead of acting like they were being serious. Laughed with them about it. Pretended to be having a great time, even if he wasn't, so she could've at least turned off the audio and replaced it with something else.

As it was, she had no usable footage. The one part where he genuinely smiled at her? That shot had included no other people, and it was at an angle where it was impossible to tell that he was even in a school. She did try playing it in slow motion, though, just out of curiosity to see how it looked. His walk, complete with that smile, was amazing and looked epic. And, okay, she may have watched it through at least a dozen times.

Other than that, there really wasn't anything she

could send to the Glaciers. Her choice of footage would've been limited, anyway, because not all the parents had given permission for their child to be in the video, but she didn't have *any*. She'd spent the night tossing and turning and spent this morning wondering how she was ever going to pull off this job.

She hoped that yesterday was an anomaly. That he wasn't actually closer to being the kid who ruined the school dance back in high school than he was to being the guy she'd cooked a meal with at her parents' house two days ago.

But if nothing else, at least she validated her decision to not just go on initial impressions of a guy and to wait for more evidence to know if he was someone worth being interested in.

She shook out her gloved hands and stomped her feet in the snow a bit to get more circulation and warmth to them. And to help her nerves. Maybe she just needed to pull Connor aside often tonight and do what it took to get him in the right mindset so she could get some genuine smiles out of him.

Or... maybe not. From the moment she first spotted him walking toward her from a parking stall, there was a great smile on his face. When he glanced around the park, it didn't even fade. She didn't realize exactly how stressed she'd been until she felt relief at that smile. Maybe today wouldn't be the disaster that she feared.

When he reached her, she said, "So, I heard you won last night. Congratulations." It didn't explain yesterday, but maybe that was why he was smiling today. She pulled her camera from its case so she could get some footage of that smile in case it wore off.

"Thank you. It was a great game." He glanced again at all the snow sculptures lit by landscape lights before his eyes were back on her. "You're not a hockey fan?"

She looked at him, confused.

"You say you 'heard' we won."

Yeah, she "heard" it from the announcers. And from Emmalee's screaming. "Nah. I don't usually watch." Which was true, even if it wasn't true last night. She hadn't planned to watch, but then Emmalee brought home a bunch of flowers so she could watch on their TV in the living room while working. Katie had been at their table, attempting to edit the footage she'd shot during the day, trying to keep her attention off the game.

But she was curious. She had seen how Connor had acted at her family thing and had seen how he'd acted with the kids at the elementary school. Since the two glimpses she'd gotten of him didn't match up, she wondered which version she'd see at the game. That curiosity won out, so she brought her laptop to the couch to watch while she worked.

She couldn't really compare the Connor she saw on TV to either one. Although she did see the competitiveness that had come out during the cooking competition. And he did seem to truly love what he was doing when he was on the ice, even while in a fierce battle with another player over a puck. There weren't any interactions with kids, of course, so she had nothing at all to compare there.

"Hey, um," Connor said, rubbing the back of his neck, "I'd like to apologize for yesterday. It was a hard day for a lot of reasons." He looked like he wanted to say more but then changed his mind. But he added, "I imagine that made your job pretty tough."

She just blinked at him. He apologized *and* acknowledged the position it put her in? If she was keeping score, that would've earned him some extra points. And not that she'd give extra points for attractiveness, but his nose, which was now red from the cold night air, made his hazel eyes pop. And that 5 o'clock shadow along his jaw looked rather touchable.

"Thank you. Here's hoping tonight goes much more smoothly."

Like every night in the weeks leading up to Christmas, there were plenty of people in the park. Some were walking around, looking at the sculptures. Others were admiring the elaborate setup of Santa's village or riding the small train that circled the village. Some were looking at the life-sized nativity, and some were lined up at the hot chocolate gazebo.

Connor glanced at Santa's village and said, "Please tell me that I'm not here to put on an elf costume to help Santa."

Katie tried to hide a smile as she turned and started walking, Connor joining her. "I heard that the town's one and only costume was completely destroyed by a barbarian. No— we are going to that building just between the hot chocolate gazebo and the nativity."

"The community center? What's in there?"

How had she forgotten even for a moment that he used to live in Mountain Springs? He knew where everything was. It was his eyes. They distracted her. "All of the gingerbread houses that were submitted for the competition. *You* are going to judge them."

"Oh. I wish someone would've told me— my Gingerbread House Judging Certification has lapsed and I didn't get it renewed."

"I've heard the renewal process is a real bear," Katie said.

Connor nodded. "So many classes..."

"And so many terms to memorize..."

"And the certification test takes hours."

"And there's only so many hours in a day," Katie said.

"I feel like you really get me." He gave her a look that was part teasing, part something else. She wasn't sure what, just that it made her suddenly aware of her own heartbeat.

"Don't worry." Katie patted him on the shoulder. "That NHL jersey with your name on the back came with an honorary certificate."

"Whew!" He brushed the back of his hand across his forehead. "That's going to save me some embarrassment here in a minute."

Katie snuck a peek at him as they walked and smiled. She liked a guy who didn't take himself too seriously.

When they had almost reached the community center, a boy who looked like he was probably five years old came running up to Connor and said "Are you number seventeen?" It surprised her that Connor was already being recognized since he'd only been on the team for three days, but he was wearing a Glacier's coat, so maybe that helped.

Connor stopped and gave all his attention to the little boy, who was dressed in a puffy coat, gloves, and a knit hat with a big pom on top. "I am."

Katie immediately pulled her video camera out, just in case. She held it up just a bit, wordlessly asking the boy's mom for permission to get the exchange on video, and the mom nodded quickly, her focus going back to her young son. She started filming from behind the child, so she was getting Connor's face and not the kid's, but the more the little boy talked, the more she moved to his side so she could get all his animated expressions and gestures.

"I watched you last night and you did awesome! 'Specially that one part where you got that pass and took the puck down the side going *swish, swish, swish* back and forth, and that defender was right on you, so you turned around backward! *Swish, swish* with the puck, and he couldn't keep up and went *down*! And his skate nearly took out you, too, but no. You just turned around and *swoosh*!" He threw his arms up into the air. "Right into the net! It was so awesome! And the crowd was screaming so loud. We were only watching it on TV, but I'm pretty sure that we were screaming louder."

The boy's arm motions as he told about the play and his excitement were pure gold. So were the expressions crossing Connor's face as the boy talked. And all the Christmas festivities in the park were the perfect backdrop. She couldn't have planned a better composition for the shot.

"Wow— you really know a lot about hockey. Do you think you'll want to play?"

The boy puffed out his chest. "I already do."

"I bet you're pretty good at it."

As they talked, Katie noticed a second, much quieter boy who was holding back from the conversation a bit. He looked like he was about twelve years old, and if she had to guess, he was the animated boy's brother.

She was surprised at how quickly Connor noticed the boy and pulled him into the conversation. "Do you play, too?"

The boy immediately lit up and stepped forward. "I do. Right-wing, just like you."

She suddenly wondered if the boy was the older brother that the girl at the present wrapping station yesterday was referring to. If she was his sister, she didn't see her nearby, though.

Connor chatted with the two brothers, and when the older one asked for Connor's advice about what he should do if he wanted to play in the NHL someday, Connor gave it. He told him to focus on the fundamentals, not get caught up in complaining, work hard, and get the best grades possible. Yes, as a way to get into a college where he had a better chance of being drafted, but also because hockey was about a lot more than skill on the ice, and getting good grades helped prepare for all of that. Katie was pretty impressed by his answer. When she glanced at the boys' mom, she saw the woman was not only impressed, but grateful nearly to the point of tears.

This was the Connor she'd hoped she'd find for her videos. *And this is the kind of man I had hoped to find for me*, a voice in her head whispered.

I am working! she hissed back to the voice. But it

didn't stop the fluttering that was going on in her heart and the buzzing in her mind.

The boys sounded like they were finishing up, so she quickly asked their mom if she could call her about using the footage.

As she and Connor neared the community center building, she said, "You're really good with kids."

"You said that with an awfully straight face for someone who saw me in all my frustrated glory yesterday."

Katie lifted a shoulder in a shrug. "This feels more authentically you than yesterday did."

Connor studied her for a moment, but she couldn't read the expression on his face before he opened the door and they walked inside. The mayor and his eleven-year-old daughter, Breanna, were waiting to greet them and walked them to the room with the gingerbread houses. He explained that one of the tables had entries from elementary school-aged kids, one from middle school, one from high school, and two tables contained entries from adults. Connor needed to pick a winner from each age group.

Without even getting closer, an obvious winner from each table stood out as being way more impressive than the others. If he wanted to, Connor could've pointed out those four, been done in thirty seconds, and headed back toward his hotel in Denver moments later. She could kind of picture the Connor from the school yesterday doing exactly that.

But he didn't. He listened as the mayor explained Mountain Springs' tradition and how hard everyone worked. The mayor gave him a stack of cards that he could write on if he wanted to take notes on an entry to refer back to.

Connor looked down at the cards. "And what happens to these after?"

"We typically give them to the person who created that gingerbread house."

Connor tapped them against his hand a couple of times. "How long do I have to judge them?"

"We announce the winners at eight-thirty, but the doors open for people to come in and look at them at eight. So..." he looked down at his watch, "you have about thirty-seven minutes."

"And how many entries are there?"

"Forty-one."

Connor looked up at the ceiling for a moment. "Okay, so about forty-five seconds each, and that still should give us a few minutes at the end." He pulled out his phone and went into something. Then he turned to the mayor's daughter, who had been looking kind of bored but was trying valiantly to patiently wait for her dad, and held his phone out to her. "Do you mind being my timer?"

"Sure!"

"Okay, when I get to the first gingerbread house, push this button. When the timer goes off, say 'Next!' and press the *repeat* button. It's up to you to keep me on track to get through all of them. Are you up for it?"

"I sure am."

The moment Connor got to the first one, Breanna pressed the timer, and he spent a few seconds studying it, then he wrote the entry number on the card and started writing something about the gingerbread house. When Breanna said, "Next!" he moved on to the next one and did the same thing. Was he really going to write a note about the gingerbread house to every person who entered?

Yep. It looked like he was.

She'd thought she'd gotten a good sense of who Connor was that night at her parents', but everything at the school made her question it. Was this who the man really was? He did seem at home, natural, outside with the kids just a few minutes ago and now as he wrote on each card, where he hadn't at all yesterday at the elementary school.

She got some good footage of the houses in focus in the foreground with Connor blurred in the background and plenty with the focus on Connor as he studied the gingerbread houses, noticing details, and writing on cards.

A few times as she was filming, he looked right at her and smiled, and she wasn't entirely sure if it was a smile meant for the camera or for her. It wasn't just a happy smile or an "I'm enjoying helping out in this community" smile. If she read it right, it was an "I like you and I'm glad you're here" smile. Maybe even an "I'm attracted to you and really want those lips of yours on mine" smile.

But she could be imagining it. She would definitely be spending time rewatching some footage tonight.

When he had finished the final one, the mayor said, "Well, did you decide which ones are the winners?"

"I guess. There are four that definitely could be called 'the best.' But look at this one over here. It arguably isn't 'better' than that one, but look at all the details they put in. All the creativity. And check out the backside— there's a ladder leaning against the house, with the string of lights hanging off, like they weren't quite finished yet. And look at this one over here. Same thing— so much uniqueness and so many fun details. This one, too. There's a second one in each category that also deserves recognition."

Katie owned a business in a creative field. She worked part-time for her roommate in a creative field. Watching Connor notice creative details and appreciate them was doing things to her heart that she couldn't explain. Maybe because she'd never quite had it do that.

All she knew was that she was glad she had the camera rolling at this moment because she would definitely be watching it over and over.

And when he offered to personally donate prizes so that a second "Creativity Award" could be given to the entries that were clearly showing it in abundance, the buzzing in her heart and the buzzing in her mind seemed to click into sync.

CONNOR

MOST OF THE gingerbread houses had been picked up by their owners, leaving only a handful behind. Except for the tables and half a dozen folding chairs that were placed randomly throughout the space, he and Katie were all that was in the room. Yet, Connor wasn't ready to leave.

He probably could've left as soon as he was done judging, but he'd had fun hanging out with all the people from town who came to look at the gingerbread houses before the winners were announced. He loved seeing them notice the same details that he had noticed when judging them and seeing if their reactions had been the same as his. He chatted with them quite a bit, too. And it was a lot of fun to help the mayor hand out the awards to the winners.

The whole time, he hadn't thought about the fact that he was back in Mountain Springs, about his dad, or even about hockey. And he *always* thought about hockey. Everything tonight had just been about being in that moment. It had been a long time since something had captivated him so fully. Since some*one* had captivated him so fully.

Instead of walking out to his car, as he should have, he walked over and sat down in one of two chairs close together and stretched his legs out in front of him. It only took a moment before Katie sat down next to him. Possibly because she felt like she couldn't leave until he did, but he hoped it was because she wasn't quite ready to leave, either. He was so drawn to her, and he hoped that she was having a hard time walking away from him, too.

"So," Katie said, "it looks like that honorary gingerbread judging certificate really kicked in."

"It definitely came in handy. Would you have chosen the same winners?"

"Oh, I'm not here to judge. I'm just here to document it all for the masses."

He nodded toward the video camera still in her hands. "What got you into videography?"

She shrugged. "I noticed that when you are in the middle of experiencing a memorable moment, it can be too much to take in all at once, you know? Like if you're dribbling a ball down the court and making a game-winning basket, your focus at the time is on the other players, the ball in your hands, the basket. It can't be on everything else, too, so you don't experience the moment all the way. If you're at a family Christmas party and are focusing on your ninety-eight-year-old grandma's delighted face when the tree is lit up for the first time, you probably aren't noticing the look of wonder on your nephew's face.

"But if you also have it on video, you can experience other parts of it later. Just like if you re-watch a TV show or movie, you catch different things the second time through. And re-watching lets you relive those same emotions you enjoyed the first time around. I like being a part of that."

"I have never thought of it that way."

"I started doing it to catch those moments for people, and by doing it, I kind of found out that I'm good at capturing the emotion of the event. Of knowing what to focus on."

Connor studied her, wondering if her camera would catch the sense of wonder on his face that he was feeling just by talking with her. He had known since that moment when she said they were on the same team in her parents' kitchen that he liked being around her. The more he learned about her, the more he realized why. He liked the way her mind worked.

He nodded at the few gingerbread houses that were left. "Did you ever enter a gingerbread house into this competition?"

"Oh, yeah. I was nothing if not up for a competition. Plus, we made them together as a family every year." She chuckled. "I was probably six the first year I entered one. I was always pretty independent, so even though I didn't exactly have the skill to make a gingerbread house without help, I was adamant that I do it myself. Of course, the walls kept falling down before I could even get a third one attached because I was working with two little hands and not a lot of patience or coordination.

"Eventually, I got one of those square boxes of tissues from the counter and just glued the walls to the side of that with the icing. But I'd had so many struggles leading up to it that the gingerbread was covered in icing smears and fingerprints, so it wasn't the prettiest thing ever."

Connor chuckled, too, as he imagined it.

"The roof was a different story, though, because I couldn't glue it to the tissue box. It was the most askew roof ever. I came across a picture of it a couple of years ago and was surprised that it somehow stayed put. Anyway, I finished, decorated it, and since I didn't think to empty the box of its tissues before commandeering it, I reached with my little fingers in between the roof pieces and tugged a tissue halfway out, and said it was the smoke from the chimney."

Now, he was fully laughing. "That's genius."

"It didn't win, of course, but I was so proud of that house!"

"As you should be."

"Did you ever enter a gingerbread house?"

Connor shook his head. "If we lived here when I was in elementary school, I totally would have. We used to make them together as a family, too. I always tried to see how creative I could get— building it unconventionally, using candies in less obvious ways, and putting in lots of details. I loved it. But we didn't move here until the middle of my freshman year. And by then..."

Katie nodded. "Things just get so much busier once you hit high school."

"Yep. It gets a little crazy. Besides, my family wasn't really doing family things by then."

That last part was something he wouldn't normally share. With anyone. Yet, it had just come out. And when Katie responded with an "Oh?" that was clearly an invitation to share more, he didn't change the topic like he normally would have. He realized that he felt not only comfortable enough around Katie to share, but felt like he could trust whatever response she'd have to it.

He took a deep breath. "I think maybe my parents decided we should move to Mountain Springs as kind of a last-ditch effort to save their marriage. Spoiler alert: it didn't work. I think that they wanted to get away from everything that was making them so busy in the city and move somewhere that had more of a community feel. Like maybe a change was what they needed to start over.

"But it didn't really fix anything. My parents were still there for me and my sister, Laura, but just not at the same time as each other anymore. Then they decided they were going to get divorced, and my dad gave us the speech about how he was still going to be there for us.

"I believed him. And at first, he was. He lived in Mountain Springs for the first little while, and we saw him all the time. Then he moved to Denver, and it got less frequent. He started loving that newfound freedom, I guess. It was harder to get him to come to things that were important to me or Laura. Then he just stopped coming around altogether.

"We'd been pretty close, too! He may have said it didn't have anything to do with me, but it was hard not to get your feelings hurt when he didn't seem to want to see you."

"I bet. I am so sorry you had to go through that." Katie reached over and placed her hand on his forearm, and it sent a tingling warmth radiating out from it. He just gazed at her hand for a few moments until she asked, "Is that why your family moved? I don't remember seeing you again after that dance."

He flinched. He did every time he even thought of the dance because it had been the culmination of everything bad. "It was. My mom knew something big needed to change for me. She literally let me throw a dart blindfolded at an NHL teams map and we moved to the one closest to where the dart landed. We started completely over there— everything we'd known was in Colorado."

"Wow," Katie said. "I can't imagine the bravery that required of your mom. Of all of you."

"And I love her forever for it."

"It was a good move? You didn't miss home?"

"It was exactly what I needed— I thrived there. It's coming back here that is hard." It wasn't a place he wanted to be. But he couldn't bring himself to tell her that he was going to request a trade.

"Well, I guess we need to change your memories here into good ones."

He smiled.

"You have an away game tomorrow, right?"

"Yeah. Minnesota."

"All right, on Friday, your third event to fulfill your contract is a hay ride. We'll make sure it's full of good memories."

nine

CONNOR

CONNOR STEPPED off the ice and headed down the hallway toward the visitor locker rooms after the game against the North Star in Minneapolis. It had been a hard-played game that left him frustrated and exhausted. They'd managed to squeak out a win in the end, but it wasn't pretty.

Normally, nothing except the game was on his mind for hours afterward. But he was barely off the ice and Katie popped into his mind. Yes, she'd been spending a lot of time in his head lately, but her coming into his mind right now was unprecedented for him. Maybe it was because he wanted to talk with her about the game. He loved every chance he got to talk to her— their conversations were easy and natural and made him feel like he could be himself.

Last night had been fun. Outreach was a big part of the NHL, and he didn't usually mind doing it at all. But it was tough having to do it while trying to gel with a new team, during Christmastime, and with such a tight window to fit everything in. But unlike the previous activity that had gone so disastrously, he'd really enjoyed every bit of last night.

And even more than the gingerbread judging, he enjoyed talking with Katie after. He always felt a strong connection with her whenever they talked, but last night, it had gotten stronger. After he spilled so much about his dad, they'd talked about random things, laughed, shared goals, and just chatted until the people closing up the building kicked them out. Then they got ice cream at an all-night convenience store and talked more.

And now, he really wanted to talk with her about the game. To work through what was going on. He had played hard— they all had, but things just weren't coming together with this team.

Although it wasn't super common, fights happened in the NHL. It was an intense game played by driven players, and sometimes emotions and frustrations spilled over. Sometimes it was during a game with a player on the opposing team. Sometimes during practice with a teammate. When you spent so many hours a day with the same guys over so many months, traveling together and rooming together, you could get on each other's nerves.

But fights with a teammate during a game rarely occurred. And it wasn't exactly what happened out on the ice tonight, but Briggs lifted his stick with both hands a few times like he wanted to cross-check Connor, and once looked like he'd much rather grab him by the jersey and give him a punch. That time was right after Connor had scored a goal, which made zero sense.

Connor missed the comradery he had with his old team. He couldn't get traded quickly enough.

He got the sense that if he talked with Katie about it, she would be level-headed and help him to see things more clearly. He liked the way he always felt after being with her, too, and had been all but counting down the time until he got to see her again.

But he shouldn't be wanting to talk more with her or to see her more. Not when he was doing what he could to be traded far from Denver.

Since they all still wore their gear, they mostly walked single-file from the ice to the locker room, and he had guys behind and in front of him. He heard the distinct muffled rhythmic clacking noise of walking with hockey skates on foam padding speed up right before Briggs knocked his shoulder into Connor's as he passed by him.

"Hey!" he called out to his teammate.

Henderson was just behind Connor and said, "Just ignore him."

"What is his deal tonight?"

"He's just agitated because we played the North Star, which is who Thompson got traded to at the same time as you. They were pretty good friends."

"It's not like I replaced him," Connor said, then used his teeth to undo the strap on one of his gloves. "Or that I had any say in it even if I had."

"I know. And he knows. He'll get over it."

After he showered and changed, he was at his locker when his phone rang. It was Vaughan— his old team captain and best friend on the Thunderstorm— so he stepped out into the hall to take the call.

"I caught the tail end of your game," Vaughan said through the line. "Sorry it was rough."

"Eh. It happens." Connor said, acting like it was no big deal when he was still very much feeling the full strength of the frustrating game, even if they did manage to pull a win out of it.

"I saw Briggs sizing you up like you are a Thunderstorm and the rivalry is still as strong."

"It was that evident, huh?"

"Pretty much."

"How's the new guy on your team?" He was the one whom Connor was traded for. He wanted only the best for the Thunderstorm, but a part of him didn't want the guy to be so amazing that they forgot about him.

"Let's just say that we're trying to not be like Briggs is to you."

"Oh?" He was pacing the hall as he talked, but he came to a stop.

"I mean, he's great on the ice, but he kind of sucks as a person. We've all been missing you over here."

"Believe me when I say that the feeling is very mutual."

"It was hard to see you go."

"I'm guessing it wasn't hard for the GM, but it's good to be missed."

"That's actually why I called. The GM pulled me in for a meeting after the trades went through to get the pulse of the team— thought you might like to know what he said."

Connor went back to meandering down the hall as they talked. "All right. Shoot."

"The Glaciers *really* wanted you. Apparently, they've been wanting you for quite a while, but the Thunderstorm didn't want to give you up."

"You're making that up."

"I swear on my grandmother's grave that it's true. But we needed a goalie— you know how badly we did— and we apparently had our eye on North Star's goalie, but they weren't willing to give him up. And Thompson is great. You know— you played against him tonight. Even scored against him.

"The Glaciers have a second goalie— the one you're using now— who is practically as good, so they went to the North Star and said they'd give them Thompson if the North Star would give us their goalie. Solving our biggest problem was a good move on the part of the Glaciers because it was the only way they could get us to give them you."

Suddenly, everything with Briggs made sense. Thompson was his goalie up until five days ago. And his friend. As a hockey player, it was your job to protect your goalie. In warmups, you never shot above your goalie's waist. But in a game, you were playing against the opposing team's goalie, and you got the puck in the net any way that you could. Thompson was unprotected, and Connor had shot high. And he scored.

Earlier in the game, the puck was in the crease, and Connor went into the crease after it and may have had some incidental contact with Thompson. He knew how much he hated it when the opposing team made contact with his goalie. Knowing that Briggs was still seeing Thompson as his teammate made his reactions understandable.

Connor stopped walking and leaned his back against the wall. "They gave up two players to get me?"

"Yep. Apparently, it took a while."

He didn't know if it made him feel better to know that he was wanted and that the trade wasn't as casual as it felt, or if it made him feel worse, knowing that there were four players who all got traded a week before Christmas.

After he and Vaughan hung up and Connor went back into the locker room, he decided that if he was being real with himself, he had to admit that maybe things hadn't been gelling between him and his new team because he hadn't been trying hard enough. All he'd been thinking about since he arrived in Denver was how to get back out. And if he played with that in mind, he couldn't play his best. And that wasn't the kind of player he was.

He needed to acknowledge that Erik Henderson had been a good friend and teammate since the first time Connor had met them, too. As they all headed out to the team bus that would take them to the airport and the plane back home, he decided that he was going to give everyone on this team his all. They deserved better than what he was giving them.

And as he made the decision, he wondered if he had come to the conclusion partly because of Katie. She didn't seem to ever be far from his thoughts lately, so maybe by deciding to give Denver a better chance, he was deciding to give the two of them a better chance, too.

KATIE

THINGS KATIE DID *YESTERDAY*: worked most of the day at Emmalee's flower shop, where they watched Christmas movies as they put together so many arrangements for people's Christmas tables.

Saw several ads from the Glaciers with footage that she knew came from other videographers, and then stressed about the fact that she didn't even have all of hers filmed yet and had sent in exactly zero clips so far.

Stopped by a shop in Mountain Springs to get a present for her brother-in-law, since she never got anything after Connor knocked into her at that department store in Denver.

Texted Connor several times about random things, including a picture she took of a life-size gingerbread man costume she saw at The Crafty One, suggesting that next year, he try it instead of an elf costume if he visits any schools.

Spent an hour editing the footage she'd gotten from the gingerbread house judging last night.

Spent way too much time replaying the parts where Connor talked about the creative details on the gingerbread houses that should be recognized and his advice to the five-year-old and twelve-year-old boys about hockey.

Went to the Waldrop home to film their big extended family Christmas party, where she caught their Aunt Martha accidentally setting her festive hat on fire with a candle, while their Uncle Bob dozed off and snored loudly into the microphone during karaoke.

Wondered how Connor was doing and how his flight was.

Looked up the score for his game. Several times. In between thinking about yesterday and how great it was to just chat with him for so long afterward.

Stayed up way too late editing more footage from the gingerbread house judging until she had something (but not everything) to send to the Glaciers, answered some emails, and worked on editing as much of her own family's Christmas video footage as she could.

Things Katie had done so far *today*: laid in bed, thinking about how tired she was and how she wished she hadn't stayed up so late last night. Although she wouldn't have changed anything about how many times she re-watched the parts where he smiled at the camera and she wasn't sure if it was an "I want to kiss you" smile or not. (She came to the conclusion... okay, *strong suspicion*, that it was, in fact, an "I want to kiss you" smile.)

And she thought about what she needed to do today — work a half day with Emmalee, edit a lot more footage, and then go on a hay ride with her family and one incredibly good-looking hockey player who also happened to be a great conversationalist.

The second she tossed off the covers and got out of bed, she wanted to get back in. Why was it so cold? Once in the hallway, she saw that Emmalee's bedroom door was open and she wasn't in there. Same with the bathroom. That was unusual. She walked toward the kitchen and living room area, where it only got colder.

As soon as she turned the corner to the living room, she saw an explosion of red, white, and yellow flowers and winter greenery. Flowers spilled out of boxes and containers, and greenery was spread across their coffee table and couch. Vases, pots, and containers were stacked up in the corner and in front of their TV. Rolls of satin ribbons, floral tape, and bags of cranberries were overflowing from a box onto the floor. Every available surface from their front door all the way through the living room and half of the kitchen table was swathed in blossoms and leaves.

Emmalee hurried over from where she'd been getting something out of the fridge. "I'm so sorry for taking up all the space! And sorry about it being so cold in here. All this really should be in a fridge, so I had to open the windows."

"Emmalee, what— " She noticed for the first time that Emmalee looked ready to walk out the door. She quickly looked at her watch— they weren't usually at work for another hour and a half— before she met her friend's eyes again. "How did this happen?"

"I know. I'm such a sucker. I said I wasn't going to take any more orders, but then a friend who's a florist in Nestled Hollow Facetimed me from the hospital. She's getting an emergency appendectomy, but she was supposed to do the flowers for a wedding tomorrow. She and the bride were desperate, so what was I supposed to do? They didn't have other options. So, I told her she could send everything here. I, uh, really wasn't expecting it to be quite this much."

Katie ran her hands through her hair and just kept them there, holding her hair away from her face, taking in the sheer mass of flowers— while trying not to shiver to death. "How are we going to do all this?"

Emmalee shook her head. "No, this is not on you. I am the one who said yes to this. You've got your own massive deadlines to worry about."

Yeah, this was Emmalee's problem, but Katie was her

employee *and* her roommate *and* her best friend. She had a responsibility to help her, so this felt like her task, too. "But seriously, Emmalee, how is this possibly going to get done by tomorrow?"

"I don't know. I'm going in to work now to get started on all the regular orders we still need to fulfill there. Plus, lots of people are going to be picking up orders all day. Then I'll have to find a way to do this after work and just... not sleep?" She grimaced. "Energy drinks for the win!"

"Okay," Katie said, "I'll hurry to get ready so I can start on it. Will I be more help working here or at the shop?"

"No, you can't. You have your own crazy deadlines today."

Katie shook her head. "I had already planned on working a half day. I'll help out for as long as I can." Maybe she could edit faster. Or stay up longer. Emmalee was going to need as many hours of her assistance as she could spare.

Emmalee let out a huge breath of relief. "You are a godsend. Working here would be better. I'll email you the list— it also has pictures of what the centerpieces and bridesmaid bouquets and boutonnieres and a few other things are supposed to look like." She pulled out her phone and forwarded Katie the email as she headed back into the kitchen, and Katie followed.

"I'll get right on it," Katie said as Emmalee sliced a bagel in half and started spreading cream cheese on it.

"Before I go, you have to tell me how things are going with Connor Greene. Was the gingerbread judging event any better?"

Katie leaned against the counter. "Last night was amazing. I even got that feeling of buzzing in my mind. You know the one where there's that excitement of possibilities and, I don't know, endorphins or whatever it is that makes you happy and hopeful and kind of swoony. I might have gotten some flutters with guys lately, but it's been so long since I've had the buzzing in my mind."

"Oh, wow— you're falling for him! I figured you'd get a crush because the guy seems super crush-worthy in every way, but wow!"

"I know. Is it crazy? I mean, I might only see him until the day after Christmas."

"Then you make sure to enjoy every moment of the next four days." She squealed, gave Katie a hands-free hug where she just squeezed with her arms since her hands each held half a bagel, and then said, "I've got to run. Call me with any questions, okay?"

And then she was out the door, *not* taking the cold with her, sadly.

Normally, Emmalee's advice to enjoy the next four days would be speaking Katie's language, because she was always up for dating someone who was going to make life more fun. But she wasn't sure she could be so casual with Connor. She'd been waiting for someone to come along who would just kind of grab her by the heart, and Connor felt like that someone. And when someone had your heart and just left, that leaving wasn't painless.

It took nearly an hour just to get everything organized and to figure out which flowers went with which arrangements, which bases to use, what ribbon, and to get it arranged in an accessible location. It took another thirty minutes to figure out how many flowers went in each centerpiece, boutonniere, corsage, and bridesmaid bouquet, and which ones to put aside for the floral swags.

It didn't help that the place was so crowded that she could barely move through the forest of flowers, or that she was wearing a coat, gloves, sweat pants, and a knit hat like she was outside in the winter. Which she practically was.

She was sitting at the table, working on one of the mothers' corsages when she got a text on her phone and leaned over to look at it.

Connor: What should I wear tonight?

She smiled and picked up her phone.

> Katie: Well, we'll be outside, so I would probably suggest wearing something warm over, say, flip-flops and swim trunks.

> Connor: Bummer, because I have new flip-flop socks I was hoping to show off. So, an outfit like this would be more appropriate?

Then he texted a selfie at an angle where it got most of his body, and she could see that he was wearing the hockey gear he must practice in, with the edge of the rink in the background.

> Katie: That's perfect. I'm a little unsure about the skates, though. Can you go up porch steps with those? I'd hate to see Glacier's prized new player break an ankle.

> Connor: True. We're going to be on actual hay, right? Maybe I'll ditch the skates and wear my farmer boots instead. I think they'll go pretty well with these padded pants and shin guards.

She sent the laughing emoji in response.

> Katie: So are you starting practice right now or just finishing?

Connor: Finishing, and about to head in to work out. Maybe get a massage.

Katie: Ahh. The life of a famous hockey star.

Connor: Yep. Nothing but massages, treatments, and food. Lots of food. What are you up to today?

Instead of responding with words, she sent a picture of the floral tornado surrounding her, making sure to get as much of it as possible in the picture.

Connor: Is that your apartment or the backstage of a flower show?

Katie: My apartment. Does it look cold? It's a giant fridge in here. My roommate owns a little flower shop on Main Street, and a floral emergency landed in her lap. I had plans to edit footage today, but until the hay ride tonight, I think this is all I'll be doing. She needs all the help I can give her.

Connor: Oof. Best of luck to you both.

A little over an hour later, as she was working on one of twenty— yes, twenty!— boutonnieres, a knock sounded at her door. She extricated herself from the mess of buds, greenery, floral tape, and ribbon that was on the table and her lap and went over to the door. She opened it to see Connor, holding a paper bag, smiling. She just blinked a few times, not registering how and why Connor was there, at her apartment.

"Hungry?" he asked, holding up the bag. "I brought lunch."

eleven

KATIE

KATIE DEFINITELY WAS HUNGRY— she had meant to get breakfast at some point but had been too focused on working. "What are you doing here?"

He stepped inside, closing the door behind him. His eyes widened as they scanned all the flowers in the room before they met hers again. "Well, after your stories about not wanting to accept help even when you need it, I figured that if I asked if you needed help with the flowers, you would say no."

She scratched her forehead. "Yeah, I totally would've said no."

"And you clearly could use help. I mean, I'm no expert, but this feels like a lot of flowers. So I figured I should just show up ready and willing to help."

"I don't even know what to say." She wasn't sure what to even think. It was hard to accept help, but this was help for Emmalee's thing, not hers, so it made it easier. And as much as she would've said no if Connor asked if she wanted help, she was so glad that he made the drive from Denver to Mountain Springs and showed up without asking. She *did* need his help. And it would be so much more fun with him there. "Thank you. Really."

"Anytime," he said as he walked over to the table, gently pushed some cuttings away from a couple of spots, and set the bag down. He gave a little involuntary shiver. "You're right— it does feel like a fridge in here."

"Wait. How did you know where I live?" Her eyebrows were creased in confusion yet she couldn't help but admire his strong face, the piercing blue eyes, the scar that ran along his jawline on the right.

"You said your roommate owned a little flower shop on Main Street, and there happens to be only one. So I went there, introduced myself, and asked for your address."

And, of course, Emmalee recognized him, because she would recognize any hockey player, and she was probably ecstatic to know that one would be helping with her business.

"Extra points to you for being so thoughtful and resourceful."

"Don't forget bonus points for bringing food."

"I never forget to award bonus points for food. How many, though, depends on what you brought."

"Sandwiches and soup from The Cozy Cabin."

"Are you serious?" Katie hurried to the bag, opened it, and did, indeed, smell the comforting goodness of The Cozy Cabin's butternut squash soup. She hadn't realized exactly how hungry she was until her stomach growled just knowing the delectable food was so close. "How did you know?"

"When we left the community center, you glanced over at the building. Your eyes widened just a bit and I heard a faint rumble from your stomach."

She just stared at Connor. "For real?"

Connor chuckled softly. "No. I asked your roommate what you would most appreciate, and then I went there and got it."

She smacked his shoulder playfully with the back of her hand. Then she pulled the items out of the bag. "Have you ever eaten at The Cozy Cabin before?"

He shook his head no.

"Oh, you're in for a treat. Sit."

As they ate lunch, Katie moaned a couple of times at just how good the food was. She might have been a little hungrier than she realized. But she was pretty sure she heard Connor moan a few times, too.

Katie told him about all that needed to be done— six

more boutonnieres, eight bridesmaid bouquets, and a dozen centerpieces, and that wasn't even counting all the pieces that Emmalee needed to do herself, like the floral swag and arches.

Once they finished eating, she taught Connor how to make a boutonniere, and they both started working on them. Katie couldn't help sneaking peeks at Connor. This tall, muscled man normally glided across the ice in padded gear, fending off other players as he hit a puck with a stick.

Today, he sat at her kitchen table, surrounded by flowers, holding small, delicate ones in his big hands, trying to gently hold them while intently wrapping floral tape around a small stem. If she didn't think that it would ruin the moment to pull out her video camera, she would've tried to capture it. Instead, she attempted to burn it into her memory because it might just be one of her favorite things she'd ever witnessed.

They had finished four of the six remaining boutonnieres when Connor said, "There is no way the two of us can do all those things you listed before we have to meet at your parents tonight. There's a guy on my new team, Erik Henderson, that I'd like to become better friends with. Do you mind if I text him to see if he's free to come help?"

The words "no way" sounded like a challenge. And

she was always up for a challenge. The words "more help" were something her very core wanted to say "no" to.

But this wasn't help for her; it was for Emmalee. There was only so much help that Katie could offer herself, and Emmalee was really never going to be able to go to bed tonight if she didn't have lots and lots of help. It might not even be possible for her to pull it off before the wedding tomorrow. Besides, she liked the idea of playing a small part in Connor making friends with a teammate. "That would be great."

When they finished the last of the boutonnieres and got the boxes of them moved to the kitchen counters, they worked side by side to clear the table of all the debris and get everything gathered for the centerpieces. She was just about to start explaining what they needed to do when there was another knock at the door.

This time, Connor was the one to answer it. And instead of a hockey player on the other side of the door, it was four of them. The one with sandy blond hair at the front, who Katie was pretty sure they called Henderson, said, "These loafers weren't doing anything productive, so I convinced them to come, too. Can we all help?"

Connor turned to her with an eyebrow raised in question and a grin on his face that made her suddenly wish she knew what he looked like as a ten-year-old.

"Of course! The more the merrier."

One of the guys gave an exaggerated shiver and said, "Feels like a hockey game in here."

A second added, "Except for the flowers."

"Nah," the first one said, "it just means we played well. Like when fans throw flowers on the ice after figure skaters do their thing."

It wasn't long before she had five— *five!*— NHL hockey players around the table in her little apartment. Katie filled the short but wide, clear, circular vases for the centerpieces with water, plant food, and cranberries. Then she set it on the table where she showed one player how to cut and place floral tape in a grid pattern over the opening to support the flowers they'd be putting in.

Three players, Connor included, were taking a stem at a time, removing extra and damaged leaves from the stems and any damaged petals from the buds, cutting the stem diagonally at the base, then placing them in a big bucket of water with flower food in the middle of the table.

The fifth player was preparing the spruce and eucalyptus stems for the base.

As they worked, Katie grabbed her phone and took a picture of the five of them hard at work and texted it to Emmalee along with the words *More help showed up.* Emmalee texted back a gif of someone screaming with unrestrained enthusiasm.

Emmalee: I'm closing the shop at four.
Sooner, if I can get the last person to
pick up their arrangement earlier.
Please, I beg of you, DO NOT LET
THEM LEAVE BEFORE I GET THERE.

When they finished the prep work, Katie gave them each a vase and moved the extras to the counter. Then she taught them how to make a centerpiece based on the picture that the florist sent. She started with the base of greenery— the spruce and eucalyptus— then added five focal flowers, which for this, were red and white amaryllis that were striped like a candy cane. Then she added the red roses and dahlias, giving tips on how to arrange them and when to cut the stems. She finished it off with some fern pieces and a few pine cones.

They watched with amazing focus. Was that an athlete thing? And then they all got to work. She took the moment to grab her video camera and started filming. They worked so intently that she wasn't sure they'd even noticed that she'd pulled out the camera.

A smile tugged at the corners of her mouth as she captured these five big, strong, athletic men who were known for their brute strength and relentless aggression on the ice as they hunched their broad shoulders over her kitchen table. They all had their brows furrowed in focus as they tended to delicate petals and stems with their big, calloused hands, choosing with great care where to place each one. These titans of the rink were doing such a gentle task. The sight of it was disarmingly charming. It was a dance of contrasts, and it was absolutely beautiful.

One of the players, a guy they called Calloway, placed his final amaryllis and said, "My mom would be so proud of me right now!"

Then one she was sure was named Bradshaw said, "Mine, too." Then he brought two fingers to his lips, kissed them, and held them high in the air. "Love you, Mama!"

Connor was the closest to him, and he glanced over and said, "Oh, did you lose your mom?"

Bradshaw shook his head. "No. She just told me when I was a kid that not only did she have eyes in the back of her head, but she had eyes in the back of *my* head, so I better make her proud whenever she wasn't around."

Henderson, the player that Connor had texted to come help, reached over and ruffled the back of the guy's hair. "Is that why you have this shaggy mullet? To cover the eyes?"

Bradshaw smoothed it back down. "You know it."

Katie was chuckling right along with them and trying very hard not to shake the camera as she did.

Davis studied his centerpiece, which was looking

pretty good, and said, "I think I'll take my little girl with me to get some flowers so we can make a centerpiece for Christmas dinner. My wife will be blown away."

It hit Katie that all these men were used to having cameras on them, so even once they did notice that she was filming, nothing changed. They continued to make jokes and rib each other over floral choices. The tough veneer of the hockey players seemed to melt away.

The more she filmed, the more she could tell that beneath everything, these were people with depth that went well beyond anything in the rink. They were brothers. They were friends. Even though Connor was new to the team, they had a shared experience as elite players who were at the top of their sport that bonded them even before they became teammates.

Since Connor was the player she was assigned to film, she spent a good amount of time zooming in on him, focusing on the way he bit his bottom lip when he concentrated. The way his left brow raised. The look on his face of... what was it? Focused contentment? The way he would put a flower stem in the vase and then look at it from the right and the left, adjusting it in small amounts before deciding that it was right.

After a good long moment of filming him, he looked straight at the camera— at her— and smiled. One side was raised just slightly more than the other, and he had a little sparkle of amusement in his eyes. His expression was mesmerizing. He picked up a flower by the stem and held it out toward the camera. She had been zoomed in enough that the auto-focus switched to the flower, bringing it momentarily into crisp clarity and blurring him, before she put the focus back on his face, blurring the flower.

That, combined with the expression on his face was perfection. She couldn't wait to pull this footage up on her laptop later.

She didn't know if the Glaciers could use footage like this, especially since it wasn't one of the scheduled events she was supposed to film and it included more teammates than just the player she was assigned to film. But this moment with five professional hockey players making floral arrangements felt like something that needed to be documented, regardless.

About the time they all finished their second centerpiece, which meant that all twelve were finished, Emmalee came bursting through the door, like too many things had been keeping her back and she was finally free. As soon as she flicked the door shut with her foot, her hands flew to her face. "Oh, I don't think I've ever seen a more beautiful sight. Thank you so much for coming to help!"

She went around the table, looking at each arrangement, complimenting them on what a great job they did. Calloway pulled out his phone. "I'm putting this on social media!" He switched the camera into selfie mode and twisted it so he could get both his face and the floral arrangement in the shot. The other four did the same.

"The bride and the groom are huge hockey fans," Emmalee said. "They are absolutely going to go nuts for this! Can I tell them that you guys made them?" They all said yes, so she had them write their names and jersey numbers on a piece of floral tape that they stuck to the side of the vase so she could make a card to go with it on the tables tomorrow.

By the time Emmalee finished complimenting them, they all seemed more than ready to take on making a bridesmaid bouquet each. She suspected that it would give them additional bragging rights that they were all strangely excited to have.

At some point, she ordered pizza, and it showed up as they finished their bouquets. They all ate as they admired their work, bragged about their new skills, and smack-talked about whose was the best. Even though the temperatures in the room made the pizza go from perfectly warm to "fresh from the fridge" cold much too fast, the mood in the room was light. Fun. And something she wished could happen every day.

Especially the Connor part of it. As they all talked and laughed, his eyes kept finding hers, and he kept giving her that same smile. The one that told her that her heart was definitely in trouble.

After Emmalee thanked everyone profusely, Connor's teammates said goodbye, and Connor asked Katie if she wanted to ride over to her parents' for the hay ride in his car. Even though her head was telling her to pull back, her heart was saying "Grab every extra moment you can with this man!" So she told him yes.

As they walked out to his car, he said, "I'm really glad you let me come help today, even though you probably would've chosen to do it by yourself."

She definitely would've chosen to do it by herself, for sure, but she wouldn't have *preferred* it. "Today was fun. And the help lifted a huge weight from my shoulders."

He stopped walking and studied her before holding his hand out flat near the top of her head, squeezing one eye shut like he was trying to gauge her height. "I can tell. You're taller now than when I arrived."

She chuckled, then met his eyes. "Thank you for everything today." Her voice seemed to come out with all the sincerity she was feeling.

He held her gaze for a long moment. Long enough that something really sparked between them. And something was happening to her heart. She was falling hard. And then the man glanced at her lips and something happened to her stomach, too. And suddenly, all she could think of was kissing this man. Grabbing him by the coat and planting her lips on his.

But then he reached into his pocket, pulled out his keys, and pressed the button to unlock his car. Then he gave her that smile that was melting her just a bit more each time and opened her door. So she gave him a smile right back and got inside.

twelve

CONNOR

CONNOR WALKED with Katie onto her parents' front yard, which was not only covered in a layer of crunchy snow but was filled with decorations. In the midst of the decorations sat a couple of tables, and people in coats stood around, socializing. At a quick glance, it looked like everyone who was at the Santa Hat activity earlier in the week was present, plus a few extras.

"I'm sorry that I'm having you go from spending all day in a cold apartment to spending all evening in the cold outdoors."

"You do remember that I hang out on ice for a living?"

Katie laughed. "So I guess you're used to it."

"Yeah, don't worry about me."

"Still, we should get hot chocolate first."

As they neared the hot chocolate table, Katie sucked in a quick breath. "I did tell you that caroling is part of the hay ride, right?"

"No."

She grimaced. "Sorry about that. Can you sing?"

"*Well*? No. *Enthusiastically*? Yes. Mostly, I've learned that if you do anything enthusiastically, people will forgive it not being done well."

She smiled. She'd asked the universe for a man who would serenade her, even if he couldn't sing. It sounded like the universe answered. "You and my gran-gran would've gotten along well."

Mr. and Mrs. Allred were behind the table, ladling hot chocolate into cups. Connor shook Reid's hand and thanked both he and Elizabeth for inviting him, once again, into their family traditions. He also verified that it was still okay that he come to spend the three days he had off hockey for Christmas with them. The closer it got, the more grateful he was to have a place to go. Before long, he had a cinnamon caramel hot chocolate in his hand that was even better than the stuff that Laura had overnighted to him along with his essentials.

As another family walked toward them, Katie said, "I think you've met all of my family. And this is my brother-in-law Jack's sister, Rachel, and her husband, Nick. These are their kids Aiden and Holly. And this sweet little girl," she said, bending down to ruffle the fur at the sides of the neck of a rough collie that looked like she could be Lassie, "is Rosy."

"Oh, hey," Aiden said, "I saw you on TV!" He looked to his mom. "He was the one on TV, right?" Then he turned and called out louder, "Grandpa, is this guy on your team?"

"He sure is, buddy."

"Hi," Connor said, holding his hand out to the little boy. "I'm Connor Greene."

Aiden, who looked like he might be seven, grinned at him. "I liked watching you play. It made me want to play hockey, too."

Forget making it to the playoffs. Comments like that made him feel as though he had the best job in the world. "That makes me happy to hear."

The big black lab that he'd seen at Allred's home during the Santa Hat activity came over to Aiden, and Aiden started rubbing the sides of her neck. Then Katie asked, "How is Bailey doing?"

"She's doing so good," Holly said. "She had five of *the cutest* little puppies. I'm talking like the cutest puppies on the entire planet."

"They really are," Katie said to Connor. "I got to see them a few days ago." Then she pulled out her video camera. "I better start filming."

She shadowed him as he chatted with everyone for a

bit. The day was already long, but it had been a good one. He bonded with some of his teammates more this afternoon arranging flowers, of all things, than he had since he'd first stepped foot in Denver.

He felt like he'd bonded with Katie more, too. He never would've guessed he would've liked making floral centerpieces or bridesmaid bouquets, but he'd had fun doing something so out of the ordinary with her. He suspected he would have fun doing pretty much anything with her.

He could tell as they'd stood outside his car that she wanted to kiss him, and he really wanted to kiss her. He nearly did. But he really liked Katie. Possibly more so than anyone he'd ever dated. And he didn't want their first kiss to be right after she thanked him for his help as if he expected something in return. He didn't want it to feel like a "You're welcome"— he wanted it to be something much more than that.

They all made their way to the hay ride, which was two flatbed trailers hooked to Mr. Allred's truck. They both had hay bales stacked in ways that gave plenty of seating options on both trailers, with blankets covering them. As soon as he and Katie took a seat, Aiden said, "Okay, I'm sitting right here," and sat down next to him. Holly sat on Aiden's other side.

"Do you like hockey?" the boy asked.

"I do."

"Is it cold on the ice?"

"It is at first. But we dress warm, and once we start really playing, it kind of keeps us from getting too hot."

"That's cool. Do you like scoring goals?"

"It's my favorite part."

"Are you in love?"

"Wh— what?" Connor stammered.

"My uncle Jack fell in love on this hay ride two Christmases ago."

"Oh, yeah?"

"Uh, huh. And my mom fell in love—"

"—with my dad," Holly cut in.

"—last Christmas. Well, maybe they didn't fall in love on the hay ride there. Maybe it happened at Jack and Noelle's wedding because that's where the hay ride went last time."

"But they for sure fell in love on the hay ride back," Holly said. "Maybe *you* can fall in love this year."

"Wow. This sounds like a really magical hay ride."

Both kids nodded, then Aiden said, "It is."

He glanced at Katie, who looked like she was trying not to chuckle audibly, and gave her a smile, keenly aware that she had the video camera on the whole time and likely caught whatever reaction had been on his face.

He quickly got into the groove of the hay ride. They *oohed* and *ahhed* at every house they went past that had lights and/or Christmas decorations in their yard. When Mr. Allred pulled over at someone's house, they all hopped off, including the dog, Captain, went up to the door, and started singing a Christmas carol. He made sure to sing enthusiastically. Mostly because it seemed to make Katie happy.

In between the stops, Katie filmed quite a bit, including several interviews with her family members for the video she was preparing for them. She even interviewed him. She filmed the caroling, too, which he was pretty sure was part of what she would send to the Glaciers.

Mr. Allred had driven them in a big loop through Mountain Springs, making a lot of stops for them to sing, including several houses where they were having big family parties. When they were a couple of blocks away from the Allred's home, Katie said, "I've been sitting too much and my legs are cold and getting numb. Do you want to walk the rest of the way back with me?"

Of course, he did. As Mr. Allred came to a stop at a sign, they hopped off the trailer, then gave him a wave, and he continued on without them.

A few stops back, snow had started to gently fall. It wasn't the bigger storm they were supposed to get— just a gentle snow before the storm. Enough to look beautiful as it lazily fell, making the night a little less dark and a lot more quiet.

"Thank you for being such a good sport about all this," she said. "I've had nightmares of being assigned a player who was a grump, and I ended up having no good footage to turn in."

"Oh, like our first filming session at the school?"

She chuckled. "Exactly like that."

"Did I ever apologize?"

"You apologized *and* acknowledged that it made things rough for me as the person under contract to turn in the footage. But you didn't apologize while dressed as Santa's elf, which would have made it even better."

"I'm pretty sure that costume is in the landfill now."

"Bummer," she said, her breath making little cloud puffs with her words. "What I wouldn't give to see a *smiling* Connor Greene wearing it."

Why did that make him want to go out and buy an elf costume?

There was only maybe half an inch of snow on the sidewalks and roads so far, but everything else still had several inches from a previous storm. The new snow softened everything. It reflected the light of the moon, making it feel almost like it glowed from a light within, casting everything in a faint, bluish light.

As they came under the warm golden glow of a street light, Katie stopped and looked up. The light caught each of the snowflakes, highlighting their meandering path to the ground. "It's so pretty!"

So was his view. She tilted her head up, opening her mouth to catch snowflakes on her tongue. She caught several and grinned, and he just gazed at her, bathed in the golden light, snow falling all around them. Those blue-with-gold eyes held the perfect mix of determination and optimism. Her knit cap was pulled down over her ears, and her light brown hair peeked out just enough to frame her face, showcasing cheeks and a nose reddened by the cold and a smile that could melt an entire rink of ice.

During the hockey season, he never kept his eye out for someone he might want to date. In the off-season, sure. He'd found plenty of people to go on dates with, but none who ever felt right. None who pulled at his heart the way Katie had from that first moment at her parents' home. Or really, since that moment he had knocked into her at the department store, making them both fall to the ground.

How, when he moved to the one place in the country that he least wanted to go, did he manage to find the one person who would capture him the way that Katie had?

A snowflake fell onto her eyebrow. He pulled off one of his gloves and reached out to brush it away with his knuckle. Another one fell on her eyelash and she blinked a few times, never taking her eyes off of his.

Until her eyes fell to his lips. They came immediately back to his eyes, searching. He moved a bit closer to her, a signal that if she wanted a kiss, he wanted it, too. With everything in him. She leaned in slowly at first, then she slid her arms around his neck and pulled him close, pressing her lips against his.

Her lips were cold from the night air, but as soft as the falling snow. They moved against his carefully as if she was testing for his reaction. He put his still gloved hand at the small of her back, pulling her close, his other hand sliding to the back of her neck, his fingers, still warm from being in a glove, tangling into her hair.

Her lips responded by moving more purposefully, more sure, as she pressed against him and the soft snow fell all around them. When she ended the kiss, she did by only pulling back the smallest amount, keeping her body still pressed against his, the warmth of her breath mingling with his, their cold noses touching.

"Oh, my," she said. "You, Connor Greene, are an amazing kisser."

He smiled into her lips, then gave her another kiss. "Feel free to make sure that's still true as many times as you'd like." He hoped she wanted to take him up on it often. It wasn't like he hadn't experienced some decent kisses in his life. But he was pretty sure this kiss just changed his world. Nothing was ever going to be the same.

thirteen

KATIE

SINCE KATIE, Connor, Connor's teammates, and Emmalee were able to get so many of the wedding floral arrangements done yesterday and after she got back last night, Emmalee was confident that she could get everything set up at the wedding today without Katie.

Which was good, because editing videos was a very time-consuming process, and Katie had so much work to do. She really needed to spend every second of the day doing it.

She was glad that it was work she enjoyed doing. She might even like the editing more than she enjoyed shooting the videos themselves. She got to see everything again when the emotions of the event weren't currently happening and gauge whether she was able to capture that same emotion in the video.

And if it wasn't quite there, by cutting out parts and placing other parts next to each other, she was able to pull that emotion through. Especially when she added just the right music. Editing was the part of the process when she could look at it most objectively.

What made it hard to be objective? When you kissed your subject the night before editing all of the video footage he was in. Especially when it was a kiss that took the bar she had set, flung it clear up into the clouds, and stayed there. She had never experienced anything like it and hadn't been able to stop thinking about it since.

Was it because Connor was just so much better at kissing than any other guy she'd dated? Or was it because he, as a person, was so much better? Because she had fallen for him so much more? Because he was exactly what she'd been waiting for all along?

Whatever it was, it meant that, as she edited, her eyes were drawn more to things like his lips. To how she could pause it at any moment and study the exact expression on his face, guessing just how he was feeling in the moment. She was working at her desk today, where she could connect her laptop to a much bigger monitor to have more space to move things as she edited. So she got to see him in crystal-clear, ultra-high-definition resolution on an expansive screen.

She'd bought the monitor earlier in the year to increase her productivity, but she couldn't exactly say it was helping her today. But stopping to smell the roses was an important thing to do, right? A healthy thing. That was basically what she was doing.

Her phone lit up with a picture of Connor's face that she'd taken just a couple of days ago, and it made her heart leap and get all giddy just at seeing it. She swiped to answer the call and put it on speakerphone so she could still work while they talked.

"Well, hello there. What are you up to?"

"Oh, just looking at the video of you smiling at the camera on repeat. You?"

He chuckled, and the sound made her smile ridiculously big.

"I am getting my suit on..." there was a slight pause before he continued, "because I need to be down at the team bus in about fifteen minutes to head over to the arena." A few of his words had sounded a little muffled and she was pretty sure it was because he had just taken off his t-shirt. And now she was imagining what that big, strong, athletic body of his looked like without a shirt.

To stop herself from letting those thoughts continue and distract her even more, she asked, "Are you required to always wear a suit to the arena?"

He had an away game today— against his old team, actually— so she'd spent the morning thinking about him as he was getting on the team bus to head to the airport. As the plane was in the sky. As he was landing and heading to the arena for a practice skate. The fact that he'd texted her several times during the day made it that much easier.

"Yep. On home game days, we wear a suit to the arena. When we get there, we change into our practice gear to skate. Then we change into workout clothes, exercise, shower, and change back into a suit. Then we leave and go get lunch or go home for a pre-game power nap and change out of the suit. Then we change back into the suit, go to the arena, change into our uniform, play, shower, change back into the suit, have media interviews, head home, and then change out of the suit again. At away games, it's not too different."

Katie couldn't help but laugh. "Wow, you're a pro hockey player *and* a pro clothing changer. I'm pretty sure that makes you a part-time fashion model."

Connor's laughter echoed through the phone. "Well, I do like to think I look pretty good strutting down the runway, also known as the arena corridor. But it does feel like we waste a lot of time just putting things on and taking them off. I'm still waiting for quick-change Velcro suits to be invented."

"Now *that* would be a fashion statement. They might ask you guys to make a calendar of you in your suits instead of in your team uniform."

"You do photography as well as videography, right? Maybe we could hire you to make us look good."

She gazed at his face in the video that was paused on her big screen. "Oh, believe me— you don't need my help to look good."

"I think I need to call you before every game to pump me up. You're quite good at it."

Katie grinned.

"We had a bit of a break before the game, and I got to see my mom, stepdad, and sister. They met me at the hotel we're staying at."

"Oh, that's fantastic!"

"Not the same as seeing them at Christmas, but still pretty great."

"Did your mom have a hard time saying goodbye?" She had heard Connor talk about his mom enough to know that she probably did.

"Yep. Since this was our last game before the break, she really wanted me to stay for Christmas instead of flying back with the team. She gets that the storm coming in will cause delays in Denver for days and would compromise my ability to get back for our home game on the twenty-seventh. And that I'm expected to make travel decisions that align with my professional commitments, but that doesn't make it easy."

"Well, it's Christmas, and you're her son. She has the right to be sad that you won't be there, even if she does support the reason why."

"She says she thinks she'll love you. If she just heard you say that, she'd be convinced of it."

Katie was grinning, just knowing that he told his family about her. Knowing that his mom liked her without even meeting her was icing on the cake.

"Are you going to watch my game?"

"I will be editing, but you better believe I'll have it playing beside me as I work."

"Then I'll give a little wave to you at faceoff."

"I'll be watching for it."

"I'll see you tomorrow?"

"Yep, tomorrow," she said, and they told each other goodbye. When she first found out that her dad had asked the guy who had spilled punch all over her dress at her first high school dance to spend his three-day Christmas break at their home, she hadn't been happy. Now, though, she was very grateful that her dad had that kind of foresight. She chuckled. He would probably say it was "a Christmas miracle!"

Things were going so well with Connor. So well, in fact, that doubts had started creeping in. Could something this good last? Since her dad not only knew way more about hockey than she did but also worked for the Glaciers and therefore often had inside information, she called him this morning. She had never been too interested in hockey, but since she'd grown up in her family, she'd heard a lot of things even if she hadn't been trying to.

So she knew that there was a trade deadline. Google told her that it was just before the playoffs and that a lot of teams traded players then. That was just a couple of months away. She had already fallen so deeply for this man and knew that with him, she had the potential to fall so much further than she'd ever fallen. She needed to know how much she should worry about him being traded away.

Her dad had confirmed that players were often traded at the deadline. "But sweetheart," he'd said, "they really wanted Connor and worked hard to get him. They aren't going to trade him away anytime soon." It had been a huge relief.

She got to the part of the footage where she'd had the camera on Connor while he and his teammates were arranging the centerpieces, and he'd looked straight at the camera.

At the time she'd shot the footage, she'd known it was something special. The expression of joy mixed with contentment on his face. The amusement in his eyes. The way one eyebrow raised just slightly. The smile quirked up more on one side. What that smile did to the little crease at the side of his lips. The unblemished amaryllis that he held out to the camera. The lighting had been perfect. The chill in the room had given his cheeks and nose a color reminiscent of his look while skating on the ice.

She paused the video and just took in his face. It was unmoving, yet still conveyed so much emotion. But it wasn't just that his emotions were recognizable on him — it was that his emotions could be felt, experienced, just by looking at him. It was mesmerizing. The longer she looked, the more depth of emotion came through. The more she felt everything.

She wanted to take the still frame image and blow it up large enough to cover an entire wall in her room. She wanted to wake up every morning to that face. To experience that sense of wonder and happiness that he exuded. To look into those beautiful eyes and feel that same bliss, comfort, and contentment.

It wasn't exactly the footage that the Glaciers had been asking for, but she was going to send it to them, and she hoped that they would show it. If they wanted fans to fall in love with their new player, this was going to do it. Yes, Connor was good-looking, and this was a shot that captured that, but they were going to fall in love because of what it made them feel. This image and this seven seconds of footage had the potential to go viral. If it did, it wouldn't just be Glaciers fans who would fall in love with him— the whole country would.

When she finished all of her edits of Connor and his teammates working with the flowers in her apartment, she had taken her thirty-two minutes of footage and gotten it down to three files to send to the Glaciers. A ninety-second version that included all five players, a two-minute version of just Connor, and the seven-second clip of him holding out the flower. All three videos captured the mood in the room as the big athletes tackled a delicate project that wasn't so common for them to tackle, experiencing joy and a sense of fulfillment doing it that maybe they hadn't expected to experience. It made them relatable. It showed their vulnerability. It captured their humanness.

It was, quite possibly, her best work.

She sent it off to the Glaciers, her chest buzzing with the thrill she always got when she created something, multiplied so many times by what it was that she created. That Connor was the focus of her creation.

She took a moment to stand and stretch, and then she got started on the hay ride footage. Once she finished that, she needed to edit her own family's video with the activities they'd done this season and the interviews with her family members— the one they'd watch tomorrow, on Christmas Eve. She'd have to work quickly to finish all of it in time and still go to bed at a decent hour.

And she had a hockey game to watch.

fourteen

CONNOR

A STRONG MIX of emotions hit Connor as the Glacier's team bus pulled into the parking lot of the Thunderstorm stadium in North Carolina where he'd spent his career playing. Loss and longing, a bit of regret, some sadness and exclusion, happiness at the memories he'd made in this place. Plus so many things he felt intensely but couldn't begin to name. Counting back the days, he realized it had only been a week since he'd last been there. It was simultaneously as if no time had passed and that weeks had. Maybe even months.

It didn't help that all day long, the sports commentators had been donning their Santa hats and talking about this final game before the league's three-day Christmas break. They played up the rivalry between the Glaciers and the Thunderstorm and how the Thunderstorm's D-

Man, Ackerman, was very recently on the Glaciers' team and that the Glaciers' right wing was quite recently on the Thunderstorm's.

They kept talking about how Ackerman had been a big source of the rivalry between the two teams, especially after last year's playoffs and wondered how it would all turn out. Were the two of them going to go easier on their old teams? Harder? Make mistakes? Play their best to show their old teams what they gave up? Had they gotten a chance yet to bond with their new teammates? Was swapping players going to be like an olive branch to soften the rivalry between these teams? The only thing they could all agree on was that emotions were going to run high on the ice.

The commentators also talked about the fact that since Ackerman was on defense and Connor on offense, and that they played on the same side of the rink, they were going to be matching up a lot. They were no strangers to playing toe-to-toe against each other; they'd just never done it before with their jerseys swapped.

Connor wanted to call Katie and talk it all out with her. He knew she would keep a level head, bring out the best in the situation, keep him grounded and focused on the right things, and leave him pumped up and ready to take on the world. Not only would the guys razz him and his coach get after him for it, but it was Connor's job to ignore all the voices outside of his team and to get his head in the game.

So he did, even though the response of the fans toward him being back in town seemed to be a mix of support and resentfulness, leaving him feeling like he'd lost a sense of home and belonging. He got off the bus with his team, grabbed his gear, and headed inside. It felt strange to head to the visiting team lockers instead of the home team ones.

It was strange to put on a different team's jersey inside this particular arena.

It was strange to go onto the ice and warm up on the opposite half of the ice.

And it was strange lining up at center ice for the faceoff against his friends and very recent teammates.

He made eye contact with the Thunderstorm's new goalie. He gave the player a nod— an acknowledgment that they both got traded to new teams and had to move eight days before Christmas and that it was hard.

He found the camera, sent a little wave and a wink to Katie, and then turned his focus to the game.

It was clear from the moment the puck was dropped onto the ice that it was going to be a tough game. And it was clear from the moment Ackerman body-checked him into the boards— a short twenty-three seconds into the game— that his opponent was going to play hard and that the game would get physical. Any time Connor had the puck, Ackerman hit into him. It was all a legal but exhausting way to play.

As the game went on, Ackerman's hits became even harder and of the less legal variety, including a penalty for boarding, when he came from behind and hit Connor in the back, pushing his face into the boards when he didn't have the puck, slashing at his stick, and, in the third quarter, grabbing him by the jersey and punching him. They both spent time in the penalty box, but Ackerman got three times the number of minutes that Connor did.

Connor gave his all at every single game he played. But knowing that Katie was watching made him give more of himself than he thought he could. It was a hard-fought game from every single player on the ice— not just from Ackerman and Connor— from beginning to end. It was as if every one of them was looking to be at the top of the leaderboards on body checks. As hard as every one of them played, though, when the end-of-game horn sounded, the scoreboard showed the Glaciers down by a goal.

Connor and his teammates headed off the ice and toward their locker room. As soon as they were away from the view of the cameras and the fans, Calloway took off his helmet and chucked it down the hallway, letting out a string of swears. Connor got it. The loss felt personal.

Even still, he couldn't pass up the chance to see his old teammates off the ice once the meeting with the coaches to review the game was over. He headed toward the Thunderstorm's locker rooms, his body already aching from the beating it had taken. He was about to text Vaughan to see if he could meet him in the hall so he didn't have to risk a possible incident with Ackerman when he rounded a corner in the corridor and saw his friend walking toward him.

"Hey," Vaughan said. "I was just coming to find you." He and Vaughan greeted each other with a half-handshake, half-hug and chatted about the game for a few moments, just like they used to after games. It was bittersweet to talk to him in the same way they did when they saw each other daily, knowing they were going home to separate states tonight and he wouldn't see him again until their teams played each other again in April.

"I have an old teammate who plays for the Explorers now," Vaughan said, "and he told me there are rumors that they're looking to trade their right wing."

Connor's eyebrows raised.

"Ohio's only an hour-and-a-half flight from here, and they're a great team. You should consider talking to your agent about that possibility."

He imagined what that might be like all the way back to the locker room. It would be nice to be closer to home. But today only left him feeling pulled between conflicting desires. He missed Charlotte. He missed this stadium, this team, these fans. At the same time, though, he couldn't wait to get back to Colorado to see Katie again.

IT WAS LATE when the team's plane landed at Denver International, and even later by the time Connor finally got back to his hotel. He fell asleep quickly and didn't wake nearly as early— or as pain-free— as he had hoped. He had a bit of shopping he wanted to do before he headed to the Allreds' home to spend the next three days, though.

He stretched his shoulder muscles a bit to ease the soreness as he walked out of the store and into the snow, pulled out his phone, and called Katie. Last night's game had been a punishing one, and he was aching and sore all over.

"Good morning!"

It was so good to hear her voice, especially after the exhausting trip to Charlotte. "I didn't wake you, did I?"

"Connor, it's eleven o'clock. That would be ridiculous if you did." She paused. "I've been up for a good ten minutes."

He laughed. "I'm glad I didn't call you when I first wanted to, then."

"When was that?"

"The moment I woke up." It was a confession he was surprised he said out loud, given the amount of time they'd been dating so far. But things with Katie were just different from anything he'd experienced before. "But since you were still working when I called you on the drive home last night, I figured I better wait. Did you finish?"

"I did." He could hear the smile in her voice. "I got the footage from the hay ride— which was the last of it — sent to the Glaciers, and I got the video for tonight's Allred family party finished at about four a.m."

"Congratulations! You didn't drool on the keyboard, accidentally edit in your snoring as the soundtrack, or leave a trail of Z's in the captions, right?"

"Nope," she said rather proudly. "I had enough caffeine in me up until the end. Of course, I can now hear colors and see sounds, so there's that."

"Then I will make sure to only wear the most melodious shades when I see you today." He reached an intersection and pressed the button for the crosswalk. "I am just heading to my car right now, then I've got to stop back at my hotel to grab a bag with the few clothing items I have until my package from Laura shows up." If he'd known it would take so long to ship during the holiday season and with weather delays, he would've just had her pack him a suitcase to take home with him last night.

"Has it already started snowing?"

The light for the crosswalk turned green, and as he started walking, he looked up at the snow that had been lazily falling from the sky when he'd first gone into that store but was now falling with a bit more enthusiasm. "Yep. It's not too crazy yet, but I want to get up the mountain before the roads get bad."

He was most of the way across the sidewalk when he noticed a family that was walking toward the crosswalk. Two kids— a boy and a girl who were both teenagers— and a mom who was holding hands with a dad. *His* dad. "I've got to go. I'll call you when I get close." He hung up the phone and put it in his pocket just as he reached the other side where his dad had stopped in his tracks, as surprised to see Connor as Connor was to see him.

It had been ten years since Connor had last seen him, and all the pain of his dad not only moving out but deciding that he didn't need them anymore hit him fresh.

"Connor," he said, letting go of the woman's hand and taking a step toward him. "It's good to see you. I heard you were traded to the Glaciers."

Connor hadn't known where his dad was living for years. But he knew that Connor was back in Denver? So many questions filled his mind. More than he could take in, making the moment feel overwhelming enough that he couldn't even manage to say anything.

"I, uh, got remarried about a year ago."

Connor's eyes flicked to the woman and then to who he presumed were her kids. A boy and a girl, just like he had the first time around with Connor and Laura. Somehow, this felt like an even bigger betrayal.

"I've wanted to tell you."

"Tell me what? That you found a family to replace us?"

"No, that's— "

"I'm sorry," Connor said. "I've got somewhere I need to be before the roads get bad." Then he turned away from them and hurried toward his car, not even pausing long enough to see the expression on his dad's face. Whatever it was, it was more than he could handle right now.

Why did he have to get traded to *Denver*, of all places?

He felt the buzz of a text and pulled his phone from his pocket. It was a text from his agent.

I caught the game last night. You played well. Sorry, you weren't able to pull a win out of it. That was rough, buddy. Just let me know when you're ready for me to submit that trade request. It could cause strife between you and the GM, especially since they just worked so hard to get you, but it's also good to give them a heads-up that you want to leave so they can keep an eye out for a beneficial trade. But it'd probably be best if you kept it from your teammates. If you don't end up getting traded until the end of the season, you don't want it causing ripples before then.

Connor didn't respond to the text. He just turned his phone off, shoved it into his pocket, and kept on walking.

KATIE

KATIE STOOD beside her mom in their big kitchen, cutting up apples for the pies while her mom rolled out the pie crusts. Three of her sisters had arrived with their families, so the place was already filled with a lot of action, a lot of noise, a lot of delicious scents, and enough Christmas decorations that everything felt exactly like Christmas Eve.

A couple of her nieces were folding the red napkins that went with the Christmas place settings into origami shapes based on some "YouTube research" they'd done, while all the littler cousins were either playing with a car set just under the big Christmas tree or piling on top of a couple of her brothers-in-law.

"You know," Julianne said, leaning in to point at the

apple Katie was slicing, "if you slice along there first, then— "

"I've got this," Katie said. She could do something as simple as slicing an apple without instruction.

She glanced toward the hall leading to her dad's office, waiting for him to come out. And waiting for Connor to arrive— she really thought he would beat her there.

She heard the front door open and looked over to see Jack and Noelle come into the family room. "We just got to see the puppies!" Noelle said while holding up her phone, and Katie rinsed the juice from the apples off her hands and hurried over to see.

"Holly's grandparents are over for Christmas Eve," Noelle said, "but they let us come play with them for a bit."

Katie leaned in to look at pictures of the little fur babies as Noelle swiped through them, several of her nieces and nephews coming in close to see, too.

"Three of the five of them already have their eyes open," Noelle said. "Oh, see this one? She's the one that's going to be ours when she's ready."

"I'm impressed you two are willing to take on training a new puppy so soon after having a baby," Katie said.

"Yeah," Jack said, "we might be a little crazy. Funny story— we were babysitting Aiden and Holly when

Bailey went into labor. When I called them to let them know, they thought it was Noelle who was in labor."

"Oh, I wish I was," Noelle said, putting a hand on her belly. "I'm ready to pop."

"Happy birthday to Noelle," her six-year-old nephew, Porter called out in the cadence of the poem *The Night Before Christmas.*

Katie, along with everyone else in the room called back, "and to Noelle a good night."

She had just made it back to the kitchen to continue with the apple slicing when her dad came out of his office and headed straight toward her, a big smile on his face. She started grinning even before he got there. "You, my daughter, did an excellent job on those videos!"

As the head of brand management, her dad was one of the people who she knew would be the first to see the videos she submitted. "You like them?"

"When I first told you that you were being assigned the player who was traded, do you remember that I assigned them to you because I didn't want to dump it on someone else last minute? That I didn't think it was professional but that I knew you'd be forgiving of that?"

She nodded.

"That wasn't the actual reason why. I didn't want to tell you at the time because I didn't want you to feel the pressure of it, but we assigned the new player to you because out of all the videographers we hired, you were by far the strongest at bringing out the emotion of an event through your videos."

"I was?"

"The franchise is really excited about getting Connor, and they wanted a video that would really sell him to the hearts of the fans. And you knocked it out of the park, just like we guessed you would."

She smiled widely as she took in a big breath that made her feel like she had grown an inch or two.

"It's not my call what gets aired— Advertising and the GM get the ultimate say on that, but I'm betting they'll love it and see the brilliance behind it. I also spelled it out for them just in case."

"Thank you!" she said and gave him a tight hug. She was so deliriously thrilled that it was making her light-headed. She heard the front door open, and she looked over to see Connor as he rounded the corner into the family room. She practically skipped over to him, wrapped her arms around him, and gave him a kiss.

"Wow, you are beaming."

"My dad just watched the video I sent the Glaciers of you, and he loves it."

"Of course he did. You're very good at what you do."

She grinned at him. Creating something that others appreciated gave her a high unlike nothing else. Her smile faltered just a bit, though, as she took in Connor's face. "Is everything okay?"

He smiled, but it didn't feel quite as genuine as his smiles normally did. "Yes, I'm fine. Everything is good. I'm just a little sore from yesterday's game. I'm sorry for taking so long to get here— I decided to get chains on the tires of my rental car. And with the snow that has already fallen, I-seventy was moving painfully slow."

"Happy birthday to Noelle," her nine-year-old niece, Erika called out, and everyone else, including Katie, joined in to say, "And to Noelle a good night."

"Oh, yeah," Katie said, noticing the confused look on Connor's face. "That's a thing here."

He nodded and grinned. As they were all working on dinner and socializing, Katie watched Connor with her family. Katie liked dating, so she'd had plenty of dates at family things over the years. Usually, they kind of hung back, being a spectator on the sidelines. Or stuck to her like glue. Or found one of her brothers-in-law to chat with. How was this man, who had only been in her life and in her family's life for the past eight days, already fitting in with her family so well? Sure, it felt like much more than eight days, but it was still only eight days.

Since he'd arrived, he'd stood side by side with her, cutting vegetables for roasting, racing some teeny cars with the littler kids, playing a board game with the older kids, and chatting and joking around with all of her sisters, their husbands, and her parents.

She hoped that advertising and the GM of the Glaciers would decide to air the footage a lot. And that everyone would see the man that she saw and fall in love with him, too. Then, there would be no way that the Glaciers would ever trade him to another team, and he'd be around for a good long time. Because she wanted this man to be in her life always.

As they set all the dishes of food on the table and everyone made their way over, she wrapped her arms around his waist and smiled up at him. "You are pretty perfect. Do you know that?"

It was Christmas Eve *and* it was Noelle's birthday. The conversations could've revolved around those two subjects as they ate prime rib and maple bacon Brussels sprouts. But since Connor was there, they revolved around hockey and what Katie was like as a kid— one of her family's favorite subjects whenever she brought someone new to the family table.

"When Katie was born," her oldest sister, Becca, said, "I was nine. Me, Hope, and Julianne are each only a year-and-a-half apart and Noelle is three years younger than Julianne. So she had a lot of sisters who really wanted to smother her with help."

"'Smother' was definitely a good word for it," Katie said, and her parents, especially, laughed.

"She tolerated it well enough until she was, what? A year-and-a-half?" Her mom looked at her dad and he nodded, so she continued. "Then one day, Hope was helping Katie to put on her shoes and Katie said, 'No, I do it.' And from that point on, she had to do everything herself."

"And she does mean *everything*," her dad confirmed.

Was that really so bad? She got to be pretty independent and capable at a very young age.

Julianne pointed at Katie with her fork. "I'm pretty sure her first words were 'No, I do it."

Noelle nodded. "It kind of became her anthem."

Katie grimaced and snuck a peek at Connor. He was chuckling along with everyone else, then said, "It's probably why she's so good at everything she does."

"Thank you!" Katie said, feeling vindicated and giving pointed looks to her siblings. "Also, thank you for telling that story instead of the story where I got into the penguin habitat at the zoo that you told the last time I brought a date to Thanksgiving."

"Oh, that was a good one," Corbin said.

"No," Ben said, "it was the chaos caused by getting her back out that made the story great."

As everyone laughed, reliving probably both their enjoyment at hearing the story and at seeing her date's expressions as they all told the story in detail, Connor leaned in close to her ear, tickling it and sending a happy shiver straight to her heart as he said. "I'm going to want to hear that story later."

"And deprive my family the joy of telling it to you at some future family dinner?"

He chuckled. "Fair enough." But something still seemed off, and she didn't know what it was.

After dinner was finished and cleaned up, all twelve adults, ten kids, and her parents' dog, Captain, made their way to the couches or the fluffy rug in front of it so they could watch Katie's annual Christmas video. It was her favorite part of their celebrations because it brought everything together. All their activities, gatherings, and everyone's thoughts. She could see how much it made their family bonds stronger and helped everyone to realize how grateful they were for each other.

She woke her laptop that sat on a shelf by the TV, turned on the TV, and went into her laptop's settings to connect to it. It gave an error that it couldn't connect using WiFi, and her brother-in-law Cory started to get off the couch, saying "I can help."

"I've got this," Katie said, a little annoyed.

"No, I do it!" Becca said, and everyone laughed.

Katie had just forgotten that she had put her laptop into airplane mode to minimize distractions while she'd been editing, and it only took an extra two seconds to turn the WiFi back on, and then everything worked.

In Katie's defense, she kind of had a right to get bugged by everyone always wanting to help. They always assumed that since they were older, they knew more.

And since she was the youngest, she needed extra help with everything, like she was incompetent. *She wasn't.*

She brought up the video, made it full screen, pressed play, then hurried to her spot on the couch closest to the laptop, and snuggled in right next to Connor.

Since Jack and Noelle were about to become parents, she started by showing an interview she'd shot with the two of them a few weeks ago when they had decorated the gingerbread cars for the train at the side of the room.

"We are so excited because this is the first Christmas that we'll be spending in our new house!" Noelle said. "We probably won't be able to say that it's our first Christmas with a new baby, but you never know when this little one is going to come."

"But whenever he does," Jack said, "we are ready. The house is all ready. His nursery is ready. We are... well, we're not exactly ready, but we're excited and as prepared as we can be."

Noelle gave him the sweetest smile, then said, "And the timing couldn't be more perfect if we had planned it. We fell in love this time of year, we got married this time of year..."

"Noelle's birthday is this time of year..."

"Happy birthday to Noelle," her dad said loudly, and everyone, including Connor, replied back with "and to Noelle a good night!"

It was bound to happen at that point in the video, so

Katie had included a few seconds of Jack and Noelle just smiling at each other, not saying anything, so her family wouldn't miss words while they said it.

And then, with almost perfect timing, if she did say so herself, Noelle said, "And now our baby is going to have a birthday at this time of year, too."

The next several clips were of her nieces and nephews and her sisters and their husbands. She liked sitting in the spot at the edge of everyone so she could see all their faces as they watched the video. It was how she determined whether she hit the mark on what she chose to include, and seeing them enjoy it was the best kind of payment for all her work.

The clip came up that she'd gotten of Aiden sitting next to Connor on the hay ride, with him saying. "My uncle Jack fell in love on this hay ride two Christmases ago," and she felt Connor chuckle at the memory. Then it cut to Jack and Noelle all snuggled up together, Jack kissing Noelle's temple. Then she had the part where Aiden said, "And my mom fell in love" with Holly interrupting to say "with my dad" before Aiden finished "last Christmas," and showed Rachel and Nick sneaking a kiss as they walked from the hay ride toward a house they'd be caroling at.

She had debated including the part where Holly said, "Maybe you can fall in love this year," followed by a clip of her and Connor together. But they hadn't actually said the L-word to each other yet. She wasn't sure why because she definitely felt it. Maybe it was because eight days— even if it felt like it was fifty— just seemed too soon.

Plus, if she had included every clip of Connor in this video that she wanted to, a good fifty percent of the video would be just him. To keep herself from doing just that, she put all those clips in a separate video to enjoy later.

Instead, she went to a clip of her parents saying how much they enjoyed seeing their family grow and find love and happiness and watching everyone figure out what they were really good at.

She also included a clip she got of Holly saying that Bailey had five of the cutest puppies, then showed those puppies. She figured that since Jack and Noelle were getting one of those puppies and that Rachel and her family were keeping at least one, those puppies were going to be in family Christmas videos for years to come.

Her stomach started getting fluttery as one of her favorite parts came up— all four of her sisters standing side by side, near the end of the Santa Hat activity. Hope said, "The most surprising thing about this year's Santa hat activity was that Katie drew dinner *and it was really good!*"

She grinned at Connor and he grinned right back and then gave her a quick peck on the lips as everyone in the room laughed. She was already enjoying that trophy sitting on a shelf in her living room, and she was going to proudly display it all year.

She also included an interview she'd gotten with Connor. It was right after Erika and Sadie had presented him with the tree their family had decorated so he could have it in his hotel room. Connor had a very wide, very genuine smile on his face, and he was clearly thrilled about the tree he was holding.

"This might be the coolest thing anyone has ever done for me. Thank you for making such an awesome tree and for giving it to me." Katie glanced at Becca and her family and could see that they were all beaming, just like they had that night. "And I would like to thank Reid and Elizabeth and every single member of the Allred family for inviting me into your home and into your family's traditions before you even knew me. It means a lot to have a family to celebrate with when I can't be with my own."

A chorus of *Awws* sounded in the room. Connor put his arm around Katie and pulled her close, kissing the side of her head. Every time Katie watched this part while she was editing and as she was watching it now, she felt the same emotions she had felt when Connor had gotten down to Erika's and Sadie's heights and thanked them— like she was being swept off her feet.

She had only known Connor for a few hours at that

point, and she was already more gone for him than anyone she'd ever dated. Did she know that night how hopelessly in love she was about to fall?

She always included in the video an interview with herself, and in this clip, she had taken on the hay ride, she'd handed the camera to Noelle, who aimed it back at Katie. "One of my favorite things this year has been how Connor sang so enthusiastically while we were caroling that it inspired Captain to do the same."

And then she showed a clip of Captain caroling, seeming to pour his soul into it. At hearing it, Captain sat up from where he was nestled among the kids on the floor and sang right along with himself. Everyone's laughter made her smile. That was what she went for in these videos— a trade-off between the laughter and the *Awws*.

"That," she said in her interview, "and being with everyone as we watched the skits at the Santa Hat activity." She cut to a clip of Julianne and her family pretending to be on a Christmas cooking show, just as Ben "stirred" his dough using a battery-powered drill, their four-year-old's eyes going wide as he stirred his with a socket wrench. Everyone laughed now and in the video clip, and in both places, she could easily pick out Connor's laugh the most. She loved that laugh.

She ended with her parents saying how much they loved spending Christmas with everyone and got a hearty applause. *This* was why she made videos. Not because she got praise, but because it led everyone to feel all the emotions that compelled them to clap enthusiastically. They weren't clapping for her; they were clapping for the experience that they enjoyed. And that was everything she hoped for.

All the little kids had bedtimes soon, so her dad slipped out to grab the sleigh bells he kept in the garage and ring them in front of the house, causing all the little kids to jump up and scramble to gather everything they had brought, put on their coats and shoes, so they could hurry home and get in bed before Santa arrived at their house.

Connor pulled Katie close, his arms wrapped around her, and she snuggled into him. She was still feeling the high of her dad watching the videos she'd submitted to the Glaciers of Connor and of her family watching the Christmas video. But the last few days had been insanely busy, and she was exhausted. It was wonderful to just relax and melt into him, feeling the strength of his arms. He kissed along her jaw, and when he got close to her ear, he breathed, "You truly are incredible at what you do."

His words sent goosebumps all over her body. "Thank you," she said and pressed her lips against his.

AS EVERYONE WAS GETTING ready to leave, Katie's dad looked out the living room windows, and everyone else crowded around to look, too. A good amount of snow had fallen. A foot, maybe?

"It looks like the snow plows are keeping up just fine." He turned to look at everyone. "But they're expecting it to keep dumping for quite a while. Will you all text the group chat when you get home and let us know you made it safely?"

Katie's sisters said yes and they, along with Katie's brothers-in-law and her nieces and nephews, all said their goodbyes. He was sure he heard at least twice as many callouts of "Merry Christmas!" as there were people present.

And then they all shuffled out into the snow, leaving

just Katie, her parents, and Connor in the home. Without everyone's shoes and coats strewn about, Katie noticed his bag. "Oh! I didn't even think to show you to your room when you first got here!"

He picked up his bag and followed her down the hallway and into a bedroom. He had kind of expected a typical guest bedroom— white or cream-colored walls, a queen bed with a comforter in a neutral color and pattern, a dresser, maybe a generic piece of art hanging on a wall, but not much else. Instead, this was a bedroom filled with personality and items.

The walls were painted lavender. The bed was queen-sized, but the comforter was teal and purple and had a handful of fuzzy throw pillows. A dozen square, black-and-white framed photos hung on the wall above the bed. Inspirational quotes about dreams and creativity were on the walls and on objects on the dresser and shelves. A few trophies stood tall on shelves.

"Was this your room?"

"Yeah," Katie said, scratching the back of her head. "My parents kept it the same because I stayed here on weekends and summers when I came home from college. I don't know why they didn't change it into a legit guest room when I got my own place like they said they were going to." Then she laughed. "Maybe because I haven't come to pack all this old stuff up yet. I kind of forgot they asked me to." Her eyes went wide as she flipped a frame on the dresser to face down. "I probably should have."

He dropped his bag on the floor and wandered around to check everything out. The place might not have been Katie's for a while, but it still felt like the spirit of her was here. Like he was getting a glimpse into the younger version of her.

The pictures above the bed were a mix of beautiful landscapes, candid shots of family and friends, and close-ups of nature's intricate details. All proof that she'd been good with a camera for a while. More photos, some sentimental notes from friends, a teacher's scrawled encouragement torn from the corner of some kind of assignment, and a few fortunes pulled from cookies lay under the glass on top of the wood on the bedside table.

He walked over to the shelves and saw a few things he hadn't noticed when he first walked in— a snow globe, probably from a family vacation, a ceramic hand-print she'd made as a child, framed photos of her with her sisters, and a few photography and videography books. And right next to that, something that he was pretty sure was a photo album. He put one finger at the top of the spine. "Can I look at this?"

"Um, sure. I don't really remember what's in it, but I guess we'll find out."

The two of them sat on the edge of her bed and he opened it up. In the first picture, she was maybe ten and had a butterfly on her finger that she was holding out to the camera. A quick glance at the other photos on the page told him that this was a mix of random pictures from throughout her childhood.

He asked plenty of questions, and she told him story after story. It was mesmerizing to hear about her childhood. Seeing how she looked at the world. Hearing about what was important to her. He didn't even realize that it was getting late until she tried to hold back a yawn in the middle of a sentence. He grabbed his phone. "It's nearly midnight!" He couldn't believe how fast time flew whenever he was with Katie. Why couldn't it slow down instead?

Katie nodded. "And I'm betting Santa passed right by us." She stood up and studied him, her hands on her hips. "When I was a teenager, I felt like a queen being able to have a bed this big— it was one of the perks of being the youngest— but I'm betting you won't feel the same. You're used to what? A Texas king-sized bed?"

Connor laughed, then flopped himself onto the bed, linking his hands behind his head. "This one is going to do just fine."

"Your feet are hanging off the end."

"That's perfect because my feet get hot when I sleep. Plus, I'll get to lay here and wonder what you were like as a teen. If I have any trouble sleeping, I can look at the pictures on your walls, the things on your shelves, and maybe come to a few conclusions."

Katie ran her hands over her face. "I really should've come and packed stuff up before now."

Looking through the photo album had taken his mind off everything. Talking about her as a high-schooler, though, got him back to thinking of when he was, too, and the school Christmas dance where he ruined her dress and caused countless other problems.

One of the many reasons why he arrived later yesterday than he had planned was because after seeing his dad, he decided he needed to spend some time with the standing punching bag in the hotel's gym. But even that didn't help keep his mind from going right back to his teenage years when he realized that his dad found his new life so much more interesting than a life with his family.

The shower after and the painstakingly slow drive up the mountain didn't take his mind away from it, either. So once he'd gotten to Mountain Springs, he'd taken a detour and driven past the house his family had lived in back then. He didn't know why— he wasn't expecting it to give him closure or anything. And all it did was re-open old wounds.

"Are you sure you're okay?" Katie was studying him intently.

He nodded. "It was just hard being back in Charlotte,

seeing my old teammates, talking with my best friend on the team. Things like that."

She placed a hand gently on his shoulder. "Do you want to talk about it?"

He shook his head.

But at the same time, between Vaughan bringing up the rumor that the Explorers were looking for a new right wing and his agent asking when he wanted to submit the trade request, all of the trade stuff was working its way through his head, too.

Did he want to have his agent put in the trade request? Eight days ago, if he had known his dad was in Denver or if he had run into him then, the answer would've been a resounding yes. He couldn't keep having those old wounds opened. He had told himself that he could make it here because he thought his dad had moved on far from this place. Like to another country, as Laura had last heard. But now, he knew that he could possibly run into him anywhere. His dad always liked hockey— he could even be at his games.

He was surprised it affected him so much. After that incident in his junior year, his mom got him into a great therapist. He thought he'd worked through everything. But apparently, working through issues didn't mean they couldn't resurface when unexpectedly facing them again. And he felt like every time he saw his dad, he would be sent right back to that place where he was angry all the time. When he hated who he was as a person.

Yes, his dad was in Denver. But Katie was, too.

And he could really use her level head and logical thinking to help him work through everything.

"Actually, I would." He stood, and she took a seat on the edge of the bed. "When we moved away from Denver, I never wanted to come back. In the NHL, you can't have a No Trade clause in your contract until you are twenty-seven or have played seven seasons. I had planned to have my agent negotiate a *No Trade to Denver* clause in my contract the moment I could. But then I got traded just a few weeks before I could have.

"So, I told my agent the day I got here that I was interested in putting in a trade request. It's not the same thing, and it doesn't guarantee anything— it just lets the franchise know that I'm not happy here and want to leave. They don't tend to love having a player who doesn't want to be on their team, so they'll usually look to trade them.

"He hasn't put in the request yet, though, because it can cause friction, but he texted me earlier today to ask when I want to." He paced over a little rectangle of her floor, looking down at the carpet as he tried to put it all into words.

"And I do like the Glaciers. It's a great team. Good teammates, a coach who knows how to push us, supportive management, and an incredible fan base. I'm just not sure if I can play my best here. There are too many things I keep running into that take me back to that person I hated being."

He let out a long breath, stopped pacing, and looked up at Katie. "But I don't know— what do you think?"

He had been so focused on trying to put all that was swirling around in his head into words that he hadn't even noticed what his words were doing to her. And right now, she had an incredible amount of pain on her face. Slowly and carefully, she said, "I think that if you're so unhappy here, you should put in the trade request."

Taking two steps toward her, he knelt down just in front of her knees. "Katie, listen. You know this isn't about you at all, right?"

"Yeah, I get that it's not about me. I didn't before this conversation, but I do now." She stood. "Listen, it's late, and it's probably still snowing, so I should really go."

He hadn't even been thinking about the snow. He pulled out his phone to check the weather and road conditions as he followed her out of the room. All of the lights in the house were off except for the one nearest the front door, so her parents must've already gone to bed. Which wasn't surprising, given the time.

"The snow plows are no longer keeping up," he said as they reached the living room, still scanning info on his phone. "It says that emergency vehicles can't get to people who are stuck, and they recommend not driving."

She was still putting on her coat, though. The feelings of comfort and bliss that had surrounded them as they'd looked through the photo album were gone, replaced by an uneasy tenseness.

"You should stay," he said. "You can sleep in your old bed— I can sleep on that giant sectional couch in the family room."

She finished zipping up her coat and turned to him. "Connor, my parents offered you a place to stay. Not only if there was any 'room at the inn.' You have a reserved room. I do not."

He stepped closer to her. "I really don't mind."

Instead of closing the gap between them even more, as he had hoped, she turned and grabbed one of her boots and put it on. "Connor, I'm not staying."

He wanted her to stay because he wanted to know that things between them were okay. But even more than that, he wanted her to be okay. And going out into the snowstorm wasn't the best way to do that. He walked over to the window and moved the curtains to look out. While they'd been talking and Katie had been telling him stories about her childhood, the amount of snow on the ground had doubled. It always amazed him how the skies could dump so much snow and do it without making a sound.

He turned to face her. "Would you like me to drive you home?" He grinned, trying to lighten the mood enough that she would take him up on his offer. "I have chains on my tires now."

"I don't need my hand held. I've been driving on snow-covered roads since I was sixteen. I am not inexperienced."

They sometimes got snow in Charlotte, but it was rare and never more than just an inch or two, so she definitely had him beat in experience. He'd spent a couple of winters living in Mountain Springs, though, so he knew how bad the roads could get. He motioned toward the window. "But that's a lot of snow. There's probably close to a foot of fresh stuff on the roads. How about you at least take my car?"

She just gave him a look before tugging on one of her gloves.

He held up his hands. "I know, I know. You've got this."

"I do," she said firmly and got out her keys.

He knew enough about Katie to know that trying to convince her even further would only backfire. "Will you at least text me when you get home to let me know you made it safely?"

She nodded and said, "I will," which at least lightened the heaviness of his heart just a bit. She turned to leave but then turned back. "And Connor?"

"Yeah?"

"Merry Christmas," she said, then took a couple of steps toward him and gave him a kiss on the cheek before turning and walking out of the house. He couldn't help but feel like his heart was leaving with her.

seventeen

KATIE

KATIE'S HEAD was a jumbled mess as she walked out of her parents' house, leaving Connor behind. She got a text from her dad a couple of hours ago saying that they were going to bed, but if much more snow fell and she wanted help shoveling the driveway so she could get her car out, to just call or knock on their bedroom door. Or to feel free to not deal with the snow at all and just stay the night.

She didn't knock or call. But when she got outside, she saw that her dad had already shoveled around her car and all the driveway behind it. Several more inches had fallen since he had. She got into her car to find a plate of food with a note from her mom taped to it.

Leftovers! Your car is at least as cold as the fridge, so I figured I'd bring them out so you didn't forget them.

Maybe she should start wearing a pin to family things that said *Just because I'm the youngest doesn't mean I'm still a kid.* She squeezed her eyes shut for a moment as a little voice in her head said, "Your parents would do those things for any of their kids." She ran her hands over her face, then pulled out of the driveway and started heading toward home. She was just upset because of what happened with Connor.

Why did she have to fall so fully for a guy who had one foot back in Charlotte and the other foot looking for a place away from Denver to land? It had only been eight days since he'd run into her at that department store, yet she already knew him so much better than she'd known any one of her past boyfriends. She already loved him more than any past boyfriend. How much more would she have a month from now, a year from now, if given the chance?

With every previous guy that she dated, there was always a moment when she thought, "Do I want to continue dating him? Or am I ready to move on?" Connor was the only guy who had ever stepped into her life that she'd had thoughts of spending her life with.

She had recently edited the part of his videos when they'd been heading to the community center to judge the gingerbread houses, and the five-year-old boy stopped to ask him questions about hockey. It was one of her favorite clips, and as she re-watched it several times, she realized that somewhere along the way, she had started imagining a life with Connor.

Maybe they'd get married and live near the arena for the first while so he didn't have far to commute, and she would expand her videography business to Denver. On home game days, he'd go to practice in the mornings while she edited videos, and then, he'd come home in the afternoon for a nap to power up for the game. On days when she didn't have too many deadlines, she would crawl into bed and snuggle up in the covers with him. And then she would go to his games in the evenings, taking Emmalee with her, and she'd cheer for him until she lost her voice.

And then, after a couple of years, they'd decide that it was time to start a family, and she'd get pregnant. And maybe they'd decide that they wanted to raise their child in a smaller town, and they'd head back to Mountain Springs, and maybe add a couple more kids to the mix. Because he was so great with kids, he would be an amazing dad. They would buy them little hockey uniforms and teach them how to skate so they could experience the sport that their dad loved so much.

It was a life she really thought she'd love. It wasn't a dream she'd had for long, but it was so vivid and felt so right. And so new. She'd never been able to picture herself having a life with anyone before. Maybe because she'd never met anyone who was so giving and fun and up for anything. Or so thoughtful and helpful and a good cook. Or have a face that she could never tire of staring at.

Her tires slipped a little as she slowed for a stop sign, so she pumped the brakes several times to slow down but didn't come to a complete stop out of fear of not being able to go again. They slipped at the next turn, too. She might have had a ton of experience driving in snow, but she wasn't actually sure she'd driven in this deep of snow before. It was slowing her enough that she probably hadn't gotten over 10 miles per hour since she left.

She turned onto a road where the snow was a little deeper, and she worried that her little car wasn't going to make it. But she just took it slow and was able to keep moving. She was squinting to try to tell where the edge of the road was since everything was covered in white, then saw a little something that wasn't white. In fact, it was moving. She squinted a little more, trying to see it through the snow.

It was a dog! He was crouched under a small bush in an area with empty lots and no houses around. The bush had gotten completely covered in snow, leaving only a small window between the snow on the ground and the snow on the bush for him to peek out of. She pulled her car to what she thought was probably the side of the road and put it into park but left the engine running. Then she trudged through the snow to the snow-covered shrub.

The poor little pup was trembling. Maybe from the cold, maybe from being alone in a storm like this. Maybe both. She pushed the snow out of the way and reached in to grab the small dog. "*Shh. Shh*," she said as she wrapped it in her arms and carried it to her car. "Everything's going to be okay. Oh, you must be so cold."

Once back in her car, she blasted the heater, grabbed some of the napkins she kept stashed in her glove box, and dried off the little guy's fur as best as she could. The longer he was on her lap, getting warmer, the more he stopped trembling. She put him on the passenger's side floor, then pulled up the plastic wrap from the corner of the plate her mom had made for her, took out a piece of the meat, put the rest of the plate in her back seat, and started tearing the meat into chunks.

The dog devoured it. "Wow, you must've been so hungry. Let's get you someplace warm, and I'll get you some more food."

She put her seatbelt on, put her car into drive, and gave it a bit of gas. The tires just spun. *Don't panic.* She gave it the tiniest bit of gas, took her foot off the pedal, and then gave it the tiniest bit more. She kept repeating the process, getting the car to gently rock, giving it slightly more gas each time. For a moment, she thought it was going to work. Until the wheels spun again and made her slide a bit.

"It looks like I'm going to have to dig us out. You stay in here and keep warm, okay?"

She popped the trunk of her car and rifled around for anything she could use as a shovel. There wasn't, but if she wanted to go hammocking or roast some marshmallows, she was set. She did have a blanket, so she got back into the car, made a little nest with it on the passenger's seat, and put the dog in it. Then she opened the back door, flipped the plate of food upside down onto the plastic wrap, then removed the plate, and wrapped the plastic around the food. A paper plate wasn't the best shovel ever, but it was better than nothing.

Using the plate was only a little bit helpful. But really, using her foot worked better. She cleared a path around the tires as best as she could, then got in and tried again. It moved an inch or two, then seemed just as stuck.

She just needed to warm up and then she could try again. She pulled the dog onto her lap, and he snuggled right into her, so she grabbed the blanket and wrapped it around them both. Her phone binged with a text, so she picked it up from its spot in front of the gear shift.

Connor: You never texted to let me know you made it home safe. Is everything okay?

She couldn't say that she got stuck. Not after he warned her about the conditions of the roads and practically begged her not to go. She would get herself free and make it home soon. She looked down at the dog in her lap and the blanket wrapped around them both.

Katie: Sorry! I'm snuggled up all nice and warm.

Connor: So good to hear. Sleep well.

The moment she was warm, she got out and tried to clear away more snow from the front of the car. But it was just falling so fast that it was undoing her work. She cleared the snow from around the exhaust, too. She knew better than to let it get high enough back there to cause problems.

Still, the car wouldn't move at all.

After blasting the heater for several minutes to warm back up, she got out and cleared away more snow with her feet and her gloved hands. This time when she tried to drive away, the tires just spun from the start until they started to slide, taking her car off the shoulder of the road, and getting it more stuck. She hit the steering wheel with her palms and let out a shout of frustration that scared the dog. "Oh, I'm so sorry." She gathered it into her arms. "It's going to be okay. I promise."

She turned the car off to preserve the gas she had. She would just turn it back on whenever she got too cold. She wrapped the blanket around her again and tucked the dog into her lap. Then she picked up her phone and texted Emmalee.

Katie: Are you awake?

About two seconds later, her phone rang, showing Emmalee's face. "I am, actually. Can't sleep. I think it's leftover from days of trying to wait up for Santa, I guess. Probably because I'm back home in my old room. Why are you awake?"

"My car got stuck in the snow on my way back to our apartment."

"Oh my gosh! Have you called for help?"

"No. Emergency services already said they can't help motorists because the conditions are too bad. You know how it is when there's a big storm here. They'll slowly get dug out and will eventually get around to everyone who needs help. I just need to wait out the storm."

"You can't just wait it out in your car overnight!"

"Sure I can. I had a spare blanket in my trunk. My parents sent me home with leftovers, so it's not like I'm going to starve." Even though Emmalee couldn't see her, she motioned to the food in the back seat and noticed that the dog must've gone back for more while she was outside clearing away snow. The plastic was open and the food was spread all over it and her back seat, and the rest of the meat was gone. She gave the dog a scolding look, but she couldn't really be mad at the cute thing. "And I still have a fourth a tank of gas, so I can turn my car on for heat now and then."

"Until the snow gets higher than your exhaust pipe and you accidentally carbon monoxide yourself to death."

"Not going to happen, because I just keep going back there to clear it away. Plus, I have a little dog to keep me company. We're keeping each other warm."

"What dog?"

"*The* cutest little honey-colored cairn terrier. He was trapped in the snow and freezing, so I helped him."

"You got stuck in the snow because you were trying to save a dog?"

"Listen, Emmalee. He was so scared and cold that he was trembling!"

"Our apartment doesn't even allow pets!"

"Oh, he already has an owner. He's got a collar with one of those tags where there's a chip and they can scan it to see who the owner is. So I can't call them to say I have their dog. But Emmalee, he was lost in the snow! He probably belongs to a family with kids. Come morning, they're going to get a call saying that their dog was found and it's going to be the best Christmas present ever.

"If I didn't save him, then they were going to wake up Christmas morning to find out that their dog died. *On Christmas Day.* They'd be scarred for life. I had to save him. I don't know what his name is, but I decided to call him Biscuit."

Emmalee was quiet for a moment, then said, "I probably would've done the same." She paused a moment, then added, "When I said 'the same,' I meant rescuing him. I would've named him Zamboni."

"Of course you would have."

"Okay, then, we need to get both you and Biscuit rescued. Call your parents! They might know someone with a snowmobile or even a Sno-cat."

"It's the middle of the night— I'm not going to call them. Especially because I made such a stink about not wanting help."

"Katie."

"And if I did, they'd have to call around for help. Again: middle of the night. And not just that, but the middle of the night on Christmas Eve."

"Then call Connor."

"When I left, things weren't exactly going well between us. He told me that he had already asked his agent about putting in a trade request and his agent was just waiting on him to say when." She rubbed Biscuit's fur by his ears, and the dog laid his head in her lap, closing his eyes.

Emmalee gasped. "He did not."

"He did. Here I am, completely falling for him and thinking that he feels the same about me. But if he was considering *asking* to leave, then he wasn't. I don't think he cares about us nearly as much as I thought he did."

"How is that even possible? The man made bridesmaid bouquets for you! Are you so heartbroken right now?"

"I am. I really thought he was the one."

"I can't believe he would just send you out into a storm, though, and not even care."

"Oh, he cared." She was getting really cold again, so she turned the car on to let the heater run for a bit and ran the windshield wipers a couple of times so she could see.

There was a slight pause before Emmalee said, "He offered to drive you home or follow you to make sure you made it, but you told him no."

"Something like that." It was stupid. She had just been bugged by everyone offering to help with things she could do herself. And then when she found out that Connor wanted to leave, it was just too much, and her agitation made her react in a way that she'd known had been stupid at the time. Still, though, she did it.

"Did he at least ask you to text him when you made it home?"

"Yep. And when I didn't and he texted to ask if I made it, I told him I was snuggled up all nice and warm."

"You *lied* to him?!"

"It wasn't a lie! I was snuggled up all nice and warm with Biscuit."

"Did you purposely make him believe something that wasn't true?"

"Okay, fine, I lied and it was a really stupid choice. Listen, Emmalee. I didn't call to worry you or make you feel like you needed to solve this. I just called to see if you would commiserate with me. So... commiserate with me?"

There was a long pause. "Emmalee?"

Still nothing, so Katie looked at her phone. The screen was black. She tapped on it a few times, but it still didn't light up. She pressed the power button, but nothing. She held it down, and the *No battery* symbol lit up. "No!" How could it have died without her noticing that it was getting low on power? Then she remembered that freezing temperatures drained a phone battery faster.

It was okay. She would just keep getting out every thirty minutes or so to make sure the area behind the exhaust was clear of snow. Then she'd try to wait fifteen minutes between each time she turned the car on to blast the furnace so the gas would last as long as possible. It would be a very long night, but she could get help in the morning.

It turned out that she couldn't wait fifteen minutes between each time she turned on the car, though. Her boots, socks, the bottom half of her pants, her gloves, and the bottom half of her coat sleeves were so wet from trying to clear the snow, and it made her so cold. Her hood was pretty wet, too.

Why had she not just called Connor while she had the chance?

She shivered as she pulled the blanket tighter, and then she petted Biscuit again. "We're going to make it through this, little guy. We'll be okay." She just needed to keep saying it, and it would be true.

eighteen

CONNOR

CONNOR COULDN'T BELIEVE how dense he'd been to ask Katie her opinion on him putting in a trade request. He should've expected that she would look at it through the lens of the two of them. When he'd said that it wasn't about her, he'd meant that his wanting to go had nothing to do with her. Now that he was looking at it from her perspective, he understood that she took it to mean that she didn't make a difference in his wanting to stay.

He wished he could rewind the night and try again. Actually, that he could rewind the previous day and a half. Between going to Charlotte, playing such a rough game against his old team, and seeing his dad again in the same city where he was living, he had been just throwing so many things in the "Why I should leave" column in his head.

Of course, he put Katie on the "Why I should stay" side. But his focus had been on the longer side— the one with the fresh emotions he'd been experiencing in quick succession. What he should've been asking himself was "Could I handle being traded away from Katie?" The answer to that was an unequivocal *No*. He had no interest in being away from her. If he hadn't lost perspective so much and just asked himself that question from the start, he wouldn't have dwelt on everything else. It all would've fallen away as insignificant.

He stayed up and worried about Katie until he got the text from her saying that she made it home. But as much as he tried, he still couldn't fall asleep. At one point, he considered calling Vaughan, or even Erik, just so he could talk through everything. But he wasn't about to call them in the middle of the night. Especially on Christmas Eve, and especially because they both had wives whom he would also be waking up with his call.

Eventually, he must've fallen asleep because he woke from dreaming about ice melting under his skates to the sound of a phone call. He reached for the phone, disoriented and clumsy. But he managed to pry his eyes open to see that the screen showed a time of 3:11 a.m. and a phone call from the name *Emmalee*. It took a moment for his brain to wake up and realize it was Katie's friend.

When he'd stopped at the flower shop to get Katie's address, they had swapped phone numbers in case he couldn't find their apartment.

As soon as he answered the phone, Emmalee said, "Katie is stuck in the snow."

He sat up straight. "What? Isn't she home?"

"Nope! She's stubborn and stuck on the side of the road with a dog."

'With a dog?" He put the phone on speaker so he could start changing.

"Apparently a really cute one that she rescued and is calling Biscuit. We have our locations shared with each other, so when she first told me she was stuck, I went in to see where she was and took a screenshot. I'm texting it to you now. Before our conversation was over, the line went dead. I don't know if there's a problem with cell reception because of the storm, or if her battery died, or what. And I'm at my parents in Lakewood and I-seventy is closed, so I can't get there to help."

He'd changed into pants, put on socks, and checked to make sure that he got the screenshot. Then he said, "No, stay where you are. I'm going to go to her. I'll keep you updated."

After taking two steps toward his door, he went back and grabbed the pajama pants he'd just taken off and an extra pair of socks. Then he rushed to the home's front door and put on the boots he bought just a day ago in anticipation of this storm, tucking his pants into them. Then he put on his coat, gloves, and hat, grabbed his keys, and went outside.

A snow shovel was leaning against the garage door, so he grabbed it, tossed it into his back seat, and started driving toward where the map said Katie was.

The roads were so much worse now than when Katie had left. Even with chains on his tires, he worried he wouldn't make it through some parts. It was just so deep. The going was slow, but he made sure not to come to a complete stop anywhere.

The road he was coming up to hadn't been plowed as recently as the one he was on, and he worried about the extra depth. He glanced at the map to see if there was any alternate road he could take to get him from where he was to the dot where Katie was, but he couldn't see any other options. So he turned onto it.

His car felt so much more bogged down. He kept his speed steady, making sure he wasn't pushing on the gas too much. His tires were still turning, likely only because of the chains.

And then suddenly they weren't.

He tried giving the car a little bit of gas and then tried to get it rocking back and forth to compress the snow around the tires enough to get some traction, but it was no use. The snow was just too deep. After putting the car into park, he pulled off a glove, grabbed his phone, and looked at the screenshot. Katie had to be only about a block and a half away from him. He could walk to her, but simply getting to her wasn't enough. She needed to be someplace warm, and there was no way to drive.

There weren't any houses nearby, and this area didn't seem familiar to him at all. It could be because everything was covered in snow so nothing looked normal. He switched out of the screenshot and went into a GPS map on his phone where he could look at a bigger area or zoom in.

He looked between the map and his surroundings. Currently, he was about a block away from a cross street, and Katie was not far from the corner going right. Going left at that corner and about a block down, though, was the rink he used to practice at as a teen when he lived in Mountain Springs. He swiped over to his phone's contacts— maybe he still had the owner's contact information. The man used to let him practice in the early mornings before they opened and just hid a key outside for him.

He did! He tapped to call him. After several rings, a man's groggy voice came on the line. "Hello?"

"Knox? This is Connor Greene. I don't know if you still remember me from when I used to skate— "

"Connor! Of course, I still remember you." His voice was sounding much more alive, the grogginess slowly falling from it. "Remember how I had all the jerseys from the current Glaciers' team up on the wall in the rink?"

"I do."

"When the Thunderstorm signed you, I was one of the first people to buy your jersey. It's been hanging next to them ever since. I tell everyone who comes in that you used to skate here."

"Really?" The man remembered him? And not in a bad way?

"Yep. And you better believe that I have a Glaciers one with your name on the back on pre-order already."

"I am really touched. Thank you." He glanced out at the white landscape and the snow that was still falling at the same relentless pace. "The reason I'm calling you is that I'm stuck in the snow."

"Oh no. Do you need me to come rescue you?"

"No. The roads are too bad to help. I was actually driving to rescue someone else when I got stuck. A woman that I've realized I'm in love with, right after foolishly causing some damage to our relationship that I'm hoping isn't irreparable. She's not far from where I am, which is close to the rink. I'm wondering if you still keep a key outside."

"Oh, for sure. It's in the same place, actually."

"In the broken grout between the bricks right below the window near the back?"

"That's it. When you get her there, take her to my office. It should be unlocked. It's the warmest place in the building, and there's a space heater."

"Thank you so much. I really appreciate it."

"You're welcome. Oh, and Connor? I'm still rooting for you."

Connor could tell that the man was referring to more than just hockey, and his voice came out a little choked as he said, "Thank you."

He stuffed the pajama pants and socks into the front of his coat, put his glove back on, grabbed the shovel from his back seat, and started shoveling his way toward Katie. The snow was deep, and not only was trudging through it going to be difficult, but he needed to keep from getting so wet that he wouldn't be as helpful to Katie.

He wanted to run to Katie, yet he was making his way toward her so slowly. To distract himself from the anxiety of needing to get to her quickly— she had been out there for hours already— he named something he loved about her with each shovelful of snow. *She's competitive.* Shovel. *She's creative.* Shovel. *She believes family is important.* Shovel.

Shovelful after shovelful, he thought about her. *She is a good friend. She's talented. She's skilled. She helps out others. She makes me laugh. She helps me to see the good in everything. She keeps me grounded. She's tenacious. She has strong convictions. She's thoughtful. She's strong-willed and persistent. I like the way her mind works. She makes me feel like I can be myself.*

Why did he ever think that leaving this place was something he could possibly do? It wasn't. If he'd gotten his head away from the negative things that had bombarded him in such quick succession, none of this would've happened.

Finally, he neared her car. It had slid off the road and was sitting on an angle, so it would likely take a tow truck to pull it out. And there was so much snow on top of it that she must feel like she was inside an ice box.

He went up to her door and wiped away the snow from her window. She sat in the driver's seat, wrapped in a blanket, hunched over and shivering. She didn't seem to notice him at first, so he knocked on the glass with the knuckle of his gloved right finger. Her head immediately spun toward the sound, and he watched as recognition and then relief washed over her face, followed by a smile. It was an exhausted smile, but that smile lifted his spirits like nothing else.

She was okay. Not great, obviously, but she couldn't have managed a smile unless she was at least okay.

He shoveled the area in front of her door, then opened it, and she said, "Connor, you came!"

Oh. She looked *very* cold. He gave her a smile he hoped was encouraging and didn't show the worry he felt. "My car got stuck, too, but I know somewhere warm we can go to wait for help. It's just over a block away, maybe a block and a half. Do you think you can walk?"

She nodded, then unwrapped the blanket and handed him a dog. It was a little thing, with soft creamy fur, who looked like he was very content to lay on Katie's lap. He tucked the dog into one arm, then offered her a hand. With muscles that seemed either sore or frozen— or both — she stepped out onto the space he had shoveled.

"We are headed down this way to an ice rink I used to skate at. I'll have to shovel the snow as we go, and you'll need to follow behind me holding the dog." He raised an eyebrow, asking if it was something she thought she could do in her current state.

"I've got this," she said.

He nodded. "Of course you do." He handed her the dog and then helped to get her blanket situated around herself and the dog, clutching it tight at the front. Then the two of them started making their way toward the rink. They walked with their heads down, trying to keep the falling snow off their faces.

It was cold and he was exhausted, but he had to admit that the landscape was pretty incredible. White blanketed everything, leaving only mounds indicating that a rock, or a shrub, or a mailbox was present. Even the sky was white. The kind of bluish-white that could only happen in the middle of the night during a snowstorm.

The most striking thing, though, was the silence. With no cars, no people, and just the steady fall of snow that seemed to mute every sound, the silence was a profound, enveloping quiet. As destructive as the snow was, it also brought with it a calm sort of peace.

"Connor," Katie said, her voice almost a wheeze. "Can we stop and rest? I'm just so cold, and my feet hurt so much, and I am so tired."

They were maybe twenty feet from the corner. Then they needed to cross a street, then cross the ice rink's parking lot to the front door. They were so close. They couldn't stop now— he needed to get her warm. He shook his head. "That's a really bad idea, especially with as cold as you are." He leaned the shovel's handle against the trunk of a tree, then scooped Katie up in his arms. The little dog yelped in surprise but then burrowed into the blanket at Katie's stomach.

"Are you good?"

She nodded, so he trudged his way through the snow, counting each step as he went to help him stay focused. He counted to the end of the sidewalk. Then he counted as they crossed the road. Then he counted to the front doors of the building. A small awning kept most of the snow away from the space nearest the doors, so he set

Katie down there and headed alongside the building to retrieve the key.

As he was walking back to the door, it was evident in the hunched way Katie stood that the cold had drained her of all her energy. She probably hadn't been able to sleep at all. And Katie wasn't someone who would just sit and wait for help— he could only guess how much energy she had expended trying to free her car. She looked ready to collapse at any moment.

Once inside, he helped Katie as they went around the rink to the backside. Knox was right— his office was unlocked. He, Katie, and the dog went inside, and he shut the door behind them to help hold in the heat. Then he found the space heater and turned it on. Katie whimpered in relief as the warm air started coming out.

"We need to get you into dry clothes." He had her sit in Knox's office chair while he pulled off her wet boots and equally wet socks. Then he pulled the pajama pants and socks out of his coat and said, "Change into these." He smiled at her. "They come pre-warmed. I'll turn around."

He turned his back to her until she said she was finished. Then he took off her coat, put it on the back of the office chair, then slipped out of his coat and helped her into it. His wasn't exactly dry on the outside, but it was dry on the inside, and the sleeves were much drier than hers.

"But what about you?"

"You do remember that I hang out on ice for a living?" When she gave a weak laugh, he said, "Don't worry about me."

He went to the corner of the office where Knox had a half-empty case of bottled water and grabbed a couple. He handed one to Katie. "Drink. Dehydration can lead to hypothermia much more quickly."

She guzzled the water, so maybe she had already been well on her way to hypothermia. Then she looked down at the floor for a moment before deciding to just lay down on it. He looked in the little closet in a corner and found a zippered hoodie. He rolled it up until it was roughly pillow-shaped and placed it under Katie's head, then spread the blanket over her.

He got the dog some water and got him settled just above Katie's head, snuggled into the dry part of her coat. He pulled out his phone and texted Emmalee to let her know that he found Katie and that they were sheltering at the ice rink. Then he lay down on the floor next to Katie. They were both lying on their sides, facing each other, him using one arm as a pillow.

He reached out and brushed Katie's hair away from her face, saying, "You're okay" and "We're going to be okay" until she fell asleep.

nineteen

KATIE

WHEN KATIE WOKE UP, all she knew was that she was gloriously warm and that her hip hurt. It took a minute of blinking at her surroundings to remember that she was on the floor in the office at the ice rink. She vaguely remembered Connor lying on the floor beside her as she fell asleep, but he wasn't there now.

She thought of Biscuit and found him curled up in her coat near her head. He looked so blissfully asleep. She gave him a little pet on the head, then stood up and stretched. Then she laughed when she saw the pajama pants she was wearing. She did remember changing into them last night, but she hadn't noticed that the fabric print was of pink flamingos, dressed in hockey gear, playing a fierce game of hockey.

It was so unbelievably sweet of Connor to brave such

a bad snowstorm to find her. She wasn't even sure *how* he found her. Or how he got them into this place. She spotted her cell phone that had been in her coat pocket — it was plugged into a charger on the desk of whoever's office this was.

She unplugged it and scrolled through her notifications. There were several texts from Emmalee, starting from when her phone had shut down during their conversation, asking if she was okay. They got increasingly panicked until the last one.

> Emmalee: I called Connor. Don't worry. He's got you.

Don't worry. He's got you.

Things got so much worse than she ever could've guessed they would. But he showed up when she needed him most. Just like when he showed up to help with the flowers. He was there when it mattered, even when she told him not to be. He somehow seemed to understand when she genuinely didn't want help with something and when she truly did need help but either didn't want to ask for help or really didn't want to accept it. She just kept finding new things about him to fall in love with.

She sent Emmalee a text thanking her for being such a great friend, and then she slid the phone into the pajama pants' pocket. She ran her hands over her face to help her wake up, then drained the rest of the water bottle that Connor had given her last night.

Then a thought occurred to her, and it felt ridiculous that it hadn't occurred to her sooner. Connor didn't say that he was leaving Denver, just that he was thinking about asking. It wasn't a done deal. She could fight for him; let him know how she really felt, because it mattered to her. He mattered to her. If he was going to leave, he wasn't going to leave not knowing how she felt.

She finger-combed her hair, then headed out of the office wearing Connor's socks and no shoes, in search of him. This was a small-town rink, so there weren't many places he could be. Sounds led her to the ice, and she found him skating in big lazy circles on the ice, looking at the ice like he was deep in thought.

He hadn't noticed her yet, so she just watched him. Hockey may be a hard-fought sport played by big, strong athletes, but this man was nothing but graceful on the ice. Every movement flowed. Even with the meandering nature of his turns, everything looked perfectly controlled. Effortless.

It was clear the moment he noticed her because he was suddenly alert, upright, focused. "You're awake already." He skated over to her with just a few strides and skidded to a stop right at the waist-high wall that separated the aisle where she stood and the ice, his skates spraying a small arc of ice. "It's still early."

She shrugged. "Probably because it's Christmas morning. It's the day you're supposed to wake up the earliest, right?"

He chuckled, but his eyes were searching hers, checking to see if she was okay.

"Or maybe it was because I could sense in my sleep that I was wearing awesome pajamas." She took a step back and motioned at the flamingos in all their glory. Then she met his eyes. "And the fact that I was so toasty warm. *Thank you.*"

He gave her a smile. "I'm just glad you're okay." He moved his hand, like he wanted to reach up and maybe cup her cheek but then decided against it.

"I need to apologize."

"No, I do."

She held up a hand. "Hold on. I really need to. I could tell last night that it was probably a bad idea to head out into the storm and that I was just being stubborn about it and not listening to reason. I was on edge from finding out that you wanted to leave and apparently decided to react by making a phenomenally bad decision. I'm very sorry that I made a choice that caused you to get into a bad situation to save me. And I'm also very grateful that you did."

"I don't want to be traded."

She froze. "You... don't?"

He shook his head. "No. I mean I did the day I was

traded here. But then I met you and everything changed."

"It did?"

He met her eyes. "Everything." And then, after a long moment, he put his hands on his hips and looked up, his feet skating him in a small, tight circle. "And then, after getting home from a hard game in Charlotte, I ran into my dad yesterday morning."

Her eyebrows shot up. "Oh?" She didn't know where his dad lived, but she had gotten the impression that it wasn't close.

He nodded. "We didn't talk for long. Just enough for me to notice that he had a new wife, a son, and a daughter, and to make a comment about him replacing us."

Katie winced.

"Yeah, I didn't handle it well. And then, apparently, because I'm a glutton for punishment, when I arrived in Mountain Springs yesterday, I drove past the house we used to live in."

"You mean the place where you lived when your parents' marriage imploded— "

"— and I became an angry teen. Yeah, that one. It was stupid, I know. It was like everything in a twenty-four-hour period started taking me down. First, smaller things, then bigger and bigger, and I decided to finish it off with a bang. To fully bury myself in every hard thing."

"Connor, that sounds awful. Why didn't you tell me? I could've helped." She paused for a moment. "Okay, I recognize the contradiction in wanting you to come to me for help when I didn't go to you for help. But I would have listened."

"You are really good at that. And at helping me to see the bigger picture." He tried to hide a smile and added, "As long as I don't lead with 'I want to be traded away from here.'"

She looked down, laughing quietly. "Yeah, probably best not to lead with that."

"Anyway, it kind of all got into my head and I started only looking at that, which wasn't so helpful. If I had looked at the whole picture, I'd have known exactly what I wanted. I want you."

A warmth and light filled her whole chest at hearing his words. "You know," she said, "I was fully ready to come out here and do everything I could to convince you to stay. Even with hair that has spent way too much time in a hood and while wearing hockey-playing flamingo pants."

"You definitely convinced me to stay." He reached out and placed a hand at the side of her neck, his thumb lightly brushing the skin just in front of her ear, and she leaned into his touch.

Then he wrapped his other arm around her waist, pulling her close, and gently pressed his lips against hers. There was something about this kiss that was different from any other they'd shared, and it wasn't just the waist-high wall that was between them. It felt more sure. More confident. She wrapped her arms around his neck and sunk into him, soaking in the feel of being cherished by this man that she couldn't imagine loving more, yet knowing that every day, she would love him more than she had the day before.

Eventually, they ended the kiss, and she looked out over the ice. "So... Do you think they have skates here that are my size?"

His eyebrows rose. "Do you skate?"

She shrugged. "Kind of. I haven't for years, but I went with friends for fun when I was a kid. I never had a teacher or a coach or anything. But I'd like to try."

He took her to the skate rental area and she put on a pair, walking over to the ice with wobbly ankles. With one hand on the short wall, she stepped onto the ice, and one skate slid more than the other. She had to hurry to try to pull her feet together. She went a little way on the ice, moving slowly and with tiny strides. Still holding onto the wall, Connor at her side.

"Are you good?"

She nodded. "I've got this."

"Of course you do."

She tried to let go of the wall but nearly fell. "No, no, I don't have this!"

In a second, Connor's strong arm was around her waist, supporting her. Her ankles were still feeling wobbly, but she dared let go of the wall, trusting in Connor's strength and balance. He skated around the rink with her, as slowly as she needed while she worked to find her balance and figure out how to move her legs. The further they went, the more she figured it out, and the more Connor loosened his arm, turning control over to her.

During their second time around the rink, she was doing so much better that he dropped his arm from her back and slipped his hand into hers. She grinned at him as she found that she could do it. She could stay upright and skate forward with only his hand as a failsafe.

The third time around, she was so proud of how well she was doing. It hit her that relationships were about helping each other. Supporting each other. Not feeling like she needed to be so independent that she pushed him away. It was about finding that beautiful interdependence where they helped and supported each other as they both fully became who they were supposed to be. She hadn't really understood the concept until now.

By the fourth time around, she had gotten to where she could skate a bit faster. As they went down the long straight part, she tipped her face up, feeling the wind from their speed blowing across her. She closed her eyes for a moment, knowing that he had her hand and would keep her going in the right direction. She felt free. Like a bird flying down low to a lake, skimming just above its surface.

As they reached the curved part of the rink at the end, Connor grabbed her other hand and spun the two of them in a circle before coming to a stop. She laughed at the joy of it. "I can see why you love this."

He grinned at her. "It's pretty great, isn't it?"

She grinned right back.

"Are you hungry?"

"Why? Are we going to walk to the nearest restaurant, find a hidden key, and go inside? Are there hidden keys everywhere? Do you know where they all are?"

Connor laughed an unrestrained laugh that she loved. "No, but Knox, the man who owns the rink, called a bit ago to see if we made it safely and to make sure that we are doing well. He said he keeps snacks in his office and told me where. Do you want breakfast?"

"I sure do," she said, realizing how hungry she was.

As they took off their skates and headed back to the office, he said, "Oh, and I texted your parents to let them know where we are."

Her eyes widened. "Thank you! I didn't even think of that— they're probably waking up about now."

In the office, Connor gathered protein bars, snack-sized bags of crackers and chips, and a couple of little cups of mandarin oranges. Biscuit woke up at hearing them, so Katie bent down and gave him a good rub on the sides of his cute face. She turned to Connor. "Do you think it's still snowing?"

"It stopped a bit ago." He put the snacks into the middle of her blanket, added three water bottles, then gathered the edges of the blanket up and put it over his shoulder. "Come with me."

Katie scooped up Biscuit, and then she walked with Connor along the aisle that separated the ice from the bleachers, and around to the front doors, which were in the middle of an area that made a big half circle with floor-to-ceiling windows.

The view beyond the glass was incredible. Deep snow covered everything, making it a sea of white. The sun was getting close to rising, and the sky was turning a beautiful pink that reflected on the snow below. "Have you ever seen anything so beautiful?" she asked.

She felt his eyes on her as he said, "Yes, I have."

Connor spread out the blanket, and the two of them sat down on it and ate a Christmas breakfast that wasn't exactly the traditional cinnamon rolls that her mom made, but it was now her favorite Christmas breakfast. They ate and played with Biscuit and chatted as the sky changed from pink to a light blue.

The moment the sun poked its head over the mountain, it lit up the snow, making it shine like it was made of silvery-golden glitter. She wasn't sure she'd seen anything so incredible.

"Katie?"

She looked over at him.

"Merry Christmas," he said and kissed her on the cheek.

twenty

CONNOR

CONNOR AND KATIE stayed in front of the big windows for a long time, just chatting and hanging out with Biscuit. The lack of sleep during the night was catching up with him, so Katie was sitting on the blanket, and he was lying with his head in her lap as she played with his hair. It was the most relaxed he'd been for as long as he could remember.

"Wouldn't a little Glacier's jersey look so cute on him?" Katie asked.

He chuckled. "It would." Biscuit yipped in a way that he was pretty sure meant that he agreed.

He thought about what his plan had been for Christmas before he got traded. It was so different from how he was spending Christmas morning, but he wouldn't have exchanged this morning for anything.

Katie's phone rang, and she answered it on speakerphone. It was her mom. "Merry Christmas! Are you two doing okay?"

Katie looked at him and smiled. "We are. We're staying warm and everything."

"Oh, I'm so glad to hear that. What a scary night you had. You're at the ice rink, right?"

"Yep."

"Okay, well I've got some news— Noelle's water broke and she went into labor!"

"Really?" Katie grinned at Connor, happiness all over her face.

"They managed to track down someone with a Mini Ripsaw and a sled to take them to the hospital." She chuckled. "Jack was a little freaked out that he might have to deliver the baby himself."

He heard Katie's dad say in the background, "I don't blame him!"

"Anyway, her labor is progressing well, and they are guessing that she'll have the baby soon. They're sending the Mini Ripsaw around to get everyone, and it should be to you before long."

They immediately stood and started gathering everything into the blanket. After they hung up, Katie turned to him, practically bouncing in excitement. "Noelle's about to have her baby!" Biscuit seemed just as excited, so he was barking and turning around in circles.

Connor had put their boots, socks, and Katie's pants in front of the heater last night, so they were mostly dry. He'd put her coat in front of it, too, once Biscuit was no longer using it as a bed. Sadly, Katie changed from the pajama pants back into her jeans. With her wearing them, he'd decided that they were, indeed, his favorite pajamas.

Once they were all ready to go, it didn't take long before the guy driving the Mini Ripsaw showed up. It was basically an ATV that had tracks like a tank instead of wheels, and it was pulling a sled with seats that could easily fit four people. He locked up the rink, returned the key to its hiding spot, shook the driver's hand, and then climbed into the sled with Katie and Biscuit.

The vehicle seemed to have no problem at all traveling on top of the snow. "Has this been a busy morning for you?" he asked the driver.

"Oh, yeah," he said, grinning. "All night long. I live for storms like these."

The route to the hospital took them down the same path they had taken last night. The snow shovel he'd left by the tree was still there, but it was so covered in snow that it was almost unrecognizable as a shovel. When they went past the cross street where his car was, he looked in its direction, and even though he'd seen how much snow had fallen everywhere, he was surprised at how buried his car was.

Then they spotted Katie's car ahead, and she gasped and grabbed his arm. It was so covered in snow that its color almost couldn't be seen. "I can't believe I had just planned to wait out the storm." Her eyes were wide as she took it in. "Look at how much is on top! And on the sides! I probably couldn't even get my doors open right now." She brought her gloved hands up to cover her mouth as they drove past it, just staring at it.

Then she turned to him. "Did you see how much snow was in front of the exhaust? I would've had to get out so many times to clear it! And I would've gotten wetter each time. And that's only if the gas I had in my tank would've lasted through the night."

He wrapped an arm around her, pulling her close. "I'm so glad that Emmalee told me you were stuck." It made him sick to imagine her being in there all night long.

She turned her head to meet his eyes. "Thank you again for coming to save me after I made a really stupid choice."

He smiled. "And thank you for saving me from almost making a really stupid choice."

"What do you say we keep saving each other?"

"Deal," he said. "And what do you say to always asking each other for help, too?"

"Deal."

They were about a block past Katie's car when there

started being houses again, and they heard some kids calling out, "Glacier! Glacier!" He wasn't sure why, but as they neared, Biscuit's ears twitched and he stood on Katie's lap, then started barking.

"Oh!" Katie said. "Are those your owners?"

When they reached the kids and their dad, who were all outside in snow gear, looking for their dog and calling out "Glacier!" she held up the little dog. "Is this him?"

"Glacier!" the kids shouted. The dad tromped through the snow that was well past his knees over to them. The little dog looked like he wanted to run to them but was afraid to jump into the snow. Good. Because if the little guy did, he'd probably sink and be completely buried.

Katie handed off the dog to the dad, and he said, "I cannot thank you enough for bringing him to us. I was really worried we wouldn't ever find him."

As the dad took the dog over to the kids, Katie said, "Look how happy they are!"

He gave her a squeeze and kissed her hair as the kids shouted, "Thank you!"

She turned to him. "He was a pretty cool dog, wasn't he."

"He was." This morning had made him imagine more than once the two of them sharing a life together and having a dog just like Biscuit. And kids. He really wanted to have kids. They thanked the driver when he dropped them off at the hospital before he left to go help other people in the snow.

When they got inside, Mr. Allred met them and walked them to the labor and delivery wing. "She had the baby not too long ago," Mr. Allred said. "Elizabeth is in there with them right now. They're about to move her to her room, and after seeing the crowd of us, they said they'd get her the biggest one they could. We should be able to see them and the new baby soon after that."

At labor and delivery, they found Katie's entire family, along with Rachel, Nick, Aiden, and Holly. They all hugged Katie and Connor and said, "Merry Christmas!" and they all shared with each other their stories about Christmas morning and the crazy snowstorm. Everyone treated him just like they did every other member of the family. This big family had all welcomed him with open arms from the very start. He'd never felt a part of another family so quickly before.

It hit him that maybe he didn't need to feel so bad that he was far from family. He had family here now, too.

Elizabeth came into the waiting room and said, "Okay, she's in her own room and ready for you now. You won't be able to hold the baby or get too close, but you can come in and see."

They followed her down the hall and filed into Noelle's room. Noelle was lying in the bed, the swaddled baby in her arms, and Jack was seated in the chair right next to Noelle, the baby's little fingers wrapped around one of his. Both parents looked tired but were beaming.

Everyone talked over one another as they told Jack and Noelle how beautiful their baby was, and he really was. Seeing their little family just made Connor yearn for the same. Katie looked up at him and smiled in a way that told him that maybe she was thinking the same thing.

"What are you going to name him?" Holly asked.

"Since it's Christmas," Nick said, "I vote for Nick."

"I think you should name him Dasher," Aiden said. "There's a kid in our class named Dasher."

"You can name a kid Dasher," Katie's brother-in-law, Corbin said, "but I'm not sure you can name a kid who was born on Christmas Day 'Dasher,' or people will only think of the reindeer playing games."

"How about Joseph?" Julianne offered.

"You can't name him Jesus's dad's name," Holly said, "he's *the baby*!"

Then everyone started giving their helpful suggestions.

"How about Cole?"

"Like what you get in your stocking if you're naughty?"

"Oh, Douglas! Because Douglas Firs are Christmas trees."

"Name him Winter because he was born in a snowstorm!"

"*Winter Meadows*? That's kind of a weird mental image."

"No, it's not. Meadows get snowed on, too."

Noelle, who was gazing down at her baby, said, "We've decided to name him Gabriel."

Katie looked up at Connor and smiled, and he pulled her into a hug. "Isn't he the sweetest?"

"He really is."

Katie turned back to look at the baby and her hands fluttered like she was having a hard time not going over to Noelle. "Oh, I can't wait until I can hold him!"

And he couldn't wait until she could hold one of their own.

KATIE

One Year Later

"The rehearsal went pretty well, don't you think?" Connor asked Katie as they walked into the room with the tables all set for the rehearsal dinner.

"If you consider how many kids are part of the wedding party," Katie said, "I think it went *very* well." Family had been a big part of their wedding plans, and she was glad that it was as important to Connor as it was to her.

Her nieces and nephews were going to be flower girls and ring bearers, or had tasks of greeting guests, taking gifts to the gift table, handing out wedding favors, and being junior bridesmaids and groomsmen. Aiden and Holly had been calling Katie's parents "grandma" and "grandpa" for the last couple of years, and somewhere along the way, they had just become part of the family. Katie considered them her niece and nephew every bit as much as she did her actual nieces and nephews, so they had assignments at the wedding, too.

Besides Emmalee, Katie's bridesmaids included her four sisters and Connor's recently engaged sister, Laura, whom Katie had become good friends with over the past year, despite living in a different state from her. Connor's groomsmen were Katie's four brothers-in-law, his best friend, Erik, a few of his other teammates, and Vaughan — his team captain from the Thunderstorm.

The Thunderstorm played the Glaciers in Denver last night, followed by two days without a game for both teams. With as perfectly as that lined up, they couldn't pass up the opportunity to plan their wedding for tomorrow so that his old teammates could be present, too. The fact that the date was almost a year to the day since Connor ran into her at that department store the night before they first met officially was a happy bonus.

Tonight, with all their closest family and friends surrounding them, they were going to have a much more casual dinner before they got married tomorrow. And Connor's dad was even present!

She'd been so proud of Connor for reaching out to him. There had never been abuse in his family, and before things between his parents got bad and his dad just disappeared, the two of them had been quite close. Connor seemed to feel that it was a relationship he really wanted in his life, so she supported him in moving forward at whatever pace he wanted to go. He and his dad weren't back to the same level of closeness they'd had when Connor was young— they still had a long way to go in repairing their relationship— but they had made enough progress that Connor really wanted him there.

As they made their way toward their seats at the tables in the room, Noelle and Jack came up to them, their one-year-old in Jack's arms. Noelle said, "Well, what do you think?" She spun in a circle, then struck a pose, showing off her dress that was a gorgeous deep blue.

"You picked out a good one," Connor said. "It looks beautiful on you."

Noelle grinned. "Thank you. For the compliment and for the dress."

"I'm sorry that it took me nearly eleven years to replace the one I ruined when Katie was wearing it at that dance."

"I'll forgive the delay— this one is definitely an upgrade. But I vote we keep this room a punch bowl-free zone for tonight."

Connor laughed and said, "Deal."

When Noelle, Jack, and little Gabriel turned to take their seats at the table, Katie turned to Connor, straightening his tie. "And what are you going to do to make up for my dance being ruined all those years ago?"

Connor leaned in closer to her, his breath tickling her ear. "I'm going to give you such an amazing time dancing at our wedding tomorrow that you will no longer even be able to remember another dance."

A smile spread across her face. "Oh, yeah?"

"Or we can start tonight if you'd rather. Out there on the patio, after the dinner."

Katie glanced toward the patio. "It's snowing."

Connor shrugged. "It's Christmastime and it was at a Christmas dance, so it feels appropriate."

"And I do remember a pretty amazing kiss in the snow."

"Maybe we can recreate that while we're at it."

Katie grinned. She felt tingly and breathless just knowing that tomorrow, she got to marry this man. "Come on," she said. "Let's get to our seats."

She loved that they got this more casual chance to enjoy the company of everyone they loved before the wedding tomorrow. And it gave all of those people plenty of opportunities to give them plenty of roasts.

"We joke about how speedy Connor is on the ice," Vaughan said. "We just hadn't expected him to go from meeting someone to marriage this quickly."

Connor sat up straight. "Was it fast? Because I was

ready to marry her back in April when I proposed. I didn't think this day would ever get here."

"It's a good thing you like things to go quickly," Katie's brother-in-law, Ben, said, "since you'll only get the three days over Christmas break for your honeymoon!"

"If you get to go at all." Laura held up her phone. "I saw that there's a big storm coming in that's going to shut down the airport."

Connor pointed at his sister. "Okay, that's not even funny. It's not true, right?"

By the look on Laura's face, it really wasn't. "Don't worry," Katie said. "We're taking a long, slow, luxurious honeymoon in the off-season."

"And we're going to enjoy every minute of it," Connor said, then lifted her hand and placed a kiss on the back of it.

"A year ago," Noelle said, "everyone our age in Mountain Springs knew Connor as the guy who started a fight at a school dance, making us lose our dance privileges. Some in town knew him as the kid who used to play hockey at Mountain Springs' rink. Others knew him as the kid who moved away and then became an NHL star."

Aiden piped up, "And everyone at my school knew him as the elf who tore his pants!" and they all laughed.

"As great as those memories are," Noelle said, "I'm

glad everyone in this area now knows the real Connor. And I'm especially glad that we get to." She held up her glass. "Welcome to the family, Connor."

Katie loved the smile that overtook Connor's face. He gave her hand a squeeze and held up his own glass.

The Christmas outreach program had gone so well for so many of the players that quite a few continued going to the same areas they'd been assigned at Christmastime throughout the year. Connor did the same, helping out with lots of town projects and celebrations. He was around enough, helping, that everyone in the Mountain Springs, Nestled Hollow, and Copper Mountains area knew him well. Half of them would be coming to the wedding tomorrow.

The rest of her sisters got in on the roasts, too. Becca did a whole bit about Katie's "I do it!" tendencies that got the group roaring with laughter. "Luckily," she said, "we talked her out of being the videographer for her own wedding. Seriously, though, Katie has come a long way since meeting Connor. Now she saves 'I do it' for things like beating everyone at board games, challenging Connor to ice skating races, and arguing with GPS directions."

Katie laughed. The part about her wanting to be her own videographer was an exaggeration. She wanted *her company* to do it. Or, more specifically, the assistant she now had. Her business had exploded over the past year.

Enough that she was no longer worried about living in her car and eating cold Ramen. The Glaciers had loved her work and had since asked her to do several other projects for them. And with how much they had shown her footage of Connor in ads, she was getting clients left and right, both in the Mountain Springs area and in Denver and its surrounding cities.

"Katie might have gotten past a lot of her need to do everything herself," Emmalee said, "but I think she gave some of it to Connor."

"Not just to Connor," Bradshaw said, pointing between him, Connor, Erik, Davis, and Calloway. "We *all* wanted to make the centerpieces."

And then all five men high-fived each other and nodded and talked about how they were basically professional florists now and how much everyone was going to love their centerpieces tomorrow. Katie loved that they were all not just willing but excited to do it again. They even thanked Emmalee several times for letting them. Of course, it put Emmalee on a high that she still hadn't come down from.

Plus, Katie was pretty sure that Emmalee had a crush on Bradshaw. And after covering for her florist friend with the last-minute wedding a year ago, especially since the centerpieces and bridesmaid bouquets were made by NHL players, Emmalee's business had exploded, too. Katie was no longer working for her friend, but

Emmalee had been able to hire two assistants in her place.

Erik said, "I know you'd never guess it by looking at Connor now, as he wears his Denver colors with pride, but there was a time when he actually wanted to leave this great state."

Several people gasped in mock shock.

"Seriously, though, you two. Congrats on buying your new place. I hope you have many happy memories there."

Katie looked at Connor, and he had an expression of serene happiness on his face. His eyes were lit up just like they always were when something made him excited. She was excited, too. They just closed on the place, and she couldn't wait to start living there with him. It was so cute and so exactly their style. It was halfway between the arena and Mountain Springs, so it would be easy for her to meet with clients in either location, and Connor wouldn't have to go far to go to practices or a game.

They knew that Connor could get traded at any time to any team in the U.S. or Canada. If that happened, they would go wherever the NHL took them. It'd be an adventure. And if they did move away, they hoped that eventually, they would find their way back to Mountain Springs and raise a family there.

Katie's dad stood and said, "You know, from the

moment these two met, we could tell there was something special between them. And it wasn't just because their last names were Allred and Greene and it was Christmastime."

It wasn't the first time they'd heard the "all red and green" comments. They decided to embrace it. In fact, the sign at the door to their wedding ceremony was a play on ones they'd seen before. It read, *Just like Christmas colors, Allreds and Greenes belong side by side. So pick a seat anywhere— you're loved by the groom and the bride.* It might be a little cheesy, but Katie loved it.

"And since they fell in love at Christmastime," her dad continued, "getting married right now feels perfect."

She smiled and thought back to a year ago when they were on the hay ride and Aiden asked Connor if he was already in love, and Holly suggested that maybe Connor could fall in love on the hay ride. She'd heard the two kids telling people that they had, indeed, fallen in love on that night. They may have been right.

"I wish you two all the best life has to offer," her dad said. "You already have each other, and that's all you really need." Then he held his glass high, and everyone else did, as well.

She and Connor looked at each other, smiling. Then she leaned against him, laying her head against his shoulder, and he kissed her hair. Tomorrow, she was going to put on a beautiful dress, walk down that aisle, and say "I do" to the man she'd been falling more in love with every single day over the past year. If she got to spend her life with him, that really was all she needed.

At the end of dinner, as everyone was getting into their cars and heading home or to a hotel for the night, she and Connor shared a moment together just outside the building as light snow fell softly from the sky.

He brushed a snowflake from her forehead, just above her eyebrow. His fingertips were soft and gentle, like always. His face was full of so much love, anticipation, and hope for their future together. She felt the same buzzing in both her heart and mind.

"Tomorrow," she breathed.

"Tomorrow. I feel like I've been waiting my entire life for this moment."

"You're not getting cold feet?"

He chuckled. "You do remember that I hang out on ice for a living? I'm impervious to cold feet. You?"

"They've never been hotter."

"Katie," Emmalee called from where she stood at the open driver's door of her car, "come on. We've got to get home so you can get beauty sleep before the big day!"

Connor's eyes shifted for a moment toward Emmalee, and then his eyes returned to hers with a longing that had become very familiar. "Tonight's the last time that 'going home' means going to separate places."

Tomorrow night, they'd be leaving to go to *their* home. Hers and Connor's. Heading home had never sounded so wonderful. A smile overtook her face. "I can't wait. See you tomorrow, my soon-to-be husband."

Connor's smile was every bit as big as hers. "Tomorrow, my soon-to-be wife."

series epilogue

NOELLE, RACHEL, KATIE

Five Years Later

Noelle

Jack put the car into park after pulling into the driveway at Noelle's parents' house, and then they all started getting out of the car. Gabriel, her son who was turning six tomorrow, started running up the curved sidewalk toward the door.

"Gabe, honey," she called out, "will you come back and help your sister so she doesn't slip on the snow?"

Her four-year-old daughter, Evalena, had just gotten out of the car, put her hands on her hips, and said, "No, I can do it by myself," just as Gabriel said, "It's not slippery."

"Can you help carry in the presents then?" Jack asked, which were apparently the magic words, because Gabe was back in a flash to help, begging his dad to load them up high on his arms.

Noelle opened the back door and helped her one-year-old, Leo, out of his car seat and into her arms. He was the sweetest little boy with the softest curls. She gave him a kiss on the cheek as Jack got their dish of freshly roasted cinnamon butternut squash out of the trunk. He came over to her, wrapped his arm around her shoulders, and placed a kiss on her temple. "Happy birthday, sweetheart."

She smiled and gave him a kiss right on the lips. Christmas Eve— her birthday— got busier with the birth of each of their three kids, but Jack never ceased to make her feel like she was worth the sun, the moon, and the stars every time.

Actually, he never ceased to make her feel like that every day, not just on her birthday.

As they went around the car and to the sidewalk, Evalena was still standing in the same spot, just gazing at all the decorations that covered the front lawn. She looked up at them with her big eyes and said, "They're just so beautiful! Don't they make you want to cry because they're so pretty?"

Noelle loved that Evalena thought so. All of her kids loved Christmas. She made sure they were all growing up enjoying the same traditions that Noelle had loved doing with her gran-gran. And she made sure they knew all about the woman she'd loved so fiercely so she wouldn't ever be forgotten.

"They are beautiful," Jack said, and he leaned down to hold her hand with the hand that wasn't holding the baking dish and walked with her up to the front door.

Noelle followed behind with Leo, taking in how adorable it was to see her husband holding her little girl's hand. She would never tire of seeing that. Or of seeing him care for and play with any of their kids. She had known Jack would be a great dad by seeing the way he interacted with his nephew, Aiden, when they were first dating, but it had grabbed hold of her heart like nothing else to see him with their own kids.

They went inside and greeted and hugged her parents, Becca and her family, and Hope and her family, and then she got Leo settled and playing with some blocks that her parents had placed near the Christmas tree.

When the front door opened, she leaned forward to see around the wall toward to see Nick and Rachel come in with Aiden and Holly. Holly must've had a hockey game or practice because she was wearing her team's jersey, looking pretty proud of herself. Aiden walked beside her, holding a present in his hands.

She couldn't believe how tall the two of them had

grown! They were both thirteen, so she guessed it was to be expected, but they had just shot up in the past little while. Aiden might have passed her height, even.

She got up off the floor to greet Jack's sister and her husband. Then Jack put an arm around Noelle, gave her a squeeze and a kiss to the temple, and said, "I'm going to help out in the kitchen. Have a seat on the couch and socialize. You've had a long day and it's your birthday—kick your feet up."

"You're the best, you know that?"

Jack gave her that smile she loved so much. "I try to be."

Rachel

In the festive home where Rachel and her family now spent every Christmas Eve, she hugged all her brother's in-laws who had become her family as well. She loved this place and she loved these people.

Nick went up to their nephew, Gabriel, and, crouched down, said, "How's my favorite six-year-old?"

"Great!" Gabe said. "Because not only is it my mom's birthday, but Santa is coming tonight, and I really hope — and I mean crossing-all-my-fingers hoping— that he brings me this Lego set I'm really wanting. And not only that, but tomorrow is *my* birthday! This really is the greatest time of the whole entire year."

"It sure is," Nick said. Then he turned and chatted with their niece, Evalena, his "favorite four-year-old," and then he told Leo that he was as cute as ever.

Gosh, she loved this man. She loved seeing how great he was with kids, especially with her brother's kids, and she loved seeing him with their own kids. Even now, as Aiden and Holly were entering their teenage years, he was still great with them. Even when they really tried to test exactly how much patience he had. So far, Aiden and Holly had learned two things— that they still hadn't seen the limits of their dad's patience, and that he loved them unconditionally.

As soon as Julianne and her family came in the house, their ten-year-old, Tommy, called out "Happy birthday to Noelle," and everyone else replied with "And to Noelle a good night!"

Aiden, present in hand, sat down on the couch next to Noelle. He might be an official teenager now and had been growing like crazy lately, but he still never lost the way he sat down with a bounce anytime he took a seat on the couch. He handed the gift to Noelle and said, "I made you a birthday present."

"You have a present for me? Aww! And you made it?"

Aiden's smile was wide as his Aunt Noelle opened the package. It was a ten-inch square piece of art that was maybe two inches thick and made of resin. He had poured the resin in layers, carving parts of the intricate lines of a snowflake into each layer with a little tool before adding the next layer. Each of the layers was a slightly different shade of blue or silver, and the end result was a beautiful masterpiece. The artist that her little boy had turned into never ceased to amaze her.

Noelle was pretty amazed, too, and so touched. It warmed her momma heart to watch their interaction. Nick came up behind her and wrapped his arms around her shoulders, hugging her. She reached up to place her arm on his and leaned her head into his arm.

Then her eyes caught her daughter in the kitchen as she went up to Connor. Connor had been cutting Brussels sprouts but stopped when she neared and came around the counter to talk to her. "Did you win?"

"Still undefeated!" Holly said with a grin on her face that hadn't left since the game yesterday.

Connor put out his palms and she slapped them with hers, then put out her palms and he did the same, and then they bumped fists. "Right on! Did you score?"

Holly folded her arms, looking pretty satisfied. "Twice."

"We've got some pretty great kids, don't we?" Nick said, his breath warming her ear.

"We do," Rachel said. "And a pretty great life."

Nick had been able to continue working four days a week at home, only going into the office one day a week, for their entire marriage. It had allowed her to do really well at her job, knowing that he was able to take care of things on the home front as needed.

Plus, she had passed the five-year mark of being cancer-free over a year ago. Which meant that she no longer had to have that deep down, constant worry that it could come back. She hadn't realized how big a part of her had been worrying without her even realizing she was doing it until that threat was gone and she experienced the freedom of living without it.

She looked around at everything. At this big, beautiful family. At Aiden and Holly. At her husband, Nick. All of them together, celebrating Christmas. All of this wasn't anything she was sure she would *ever* get. It made having it all the sweeter, and she would never stop being grateful for every single bit of her incredible life.

She turned so she was facing Nick and wrapped her arms around him. She gave him a kiss on the lips, then said, "Thank you for being part of what makes my life so great."

Nick grinned, not entirely following her train of thought, but clearly enjoying it.

Katie

Katie and Connor had been trying to get pregnant from pretty close to the day they got married five years ago. In the beginning, it was fine that each month they found out that they weren't. The extra time they had with just the two of them gave them a chance to really bond as a couple and to figure out who they were separately, who they were together, and how to best support each other.

And it gave her time to figure out life being married to a hockey player who had 82 games a year, all while her company was growing at a rate fast enough that she was constantly having to figure it out anew.

But as the years went on, it became a lot harder. They both just really *really* wanted children. As much as she loved holding each of her new nieces and nephews, the emotions she experienced as she did were so much more complex and difficult when they wanted so badly to have their own.

And now they were. The fertility treatments they'd been doing for what felt like an eternity had finally worked. Not only had they worked, but they were going to be having twins. She was now thirteen weeks along, and things looked fantastic and the babies were so healthy. After their last doctor's visit, she and Connor decided that they were ready to share the news with everyone.

And because it was Christmas Eve and she was going to be showing the annual Allred Family Christmas Video that she made every year, they decided that they would make the announcement part of the video. She'd made a lot of these videos over the years, but none of them had been as fun— or made her tear up as much— as this one.

Since she filmed events for a living, she made sure to have the camera rolling at all the important parts of their lives. The video tonight had clips of them with their eyes glued to the pregnancy test that Katie held, waiting for the results, and the jumping up and down, cries of joy, and hugging when it revealed that the test was positive. The doctor's visit where they confirmed it. The looks of surprise, joy, and lots of shock during the ultrasound when they found out that two little babies were growing inside her.

Her stomach was getting all fluttery just thinking about pushing play on that video tonight and watching everyone's reactions to the news.

It had been a long, hard journey to get to this point. But after facing all the emotional, physical, and mental struggles of infertility together, she and Connor were so much stronger as a couple than they ever could've been without. Katie was sure they could face absolutely anything together, side by side. Connor could be traded to another team across the country, or even Canada, the day before she gave birth to her twins, and they could handle it.

She looked over at him from where they were cutting up vegetables next to each other in her parents' kitchen. After making sure no one was close enough to hear, she said, "Please don't get traded to another team the day before I give birth."

He chuckled. "I won't."

She knew he wouldn't. Her due date was in the off-season, so if he did get traded, it wouldn't be rushed like it was when he was traded to the Glaciers. At least she expected the births to happen in the off-season. But the Glaciers could go to the playoffs, and she could have the twins early. Twins usually came early.

"But even if you did, we could handle it, right?"

He gave her a kiss. "Together, we can handle anything."

"Even twins."

He nodded. "Even twins. *Especially* twins." He cut a few more carrots, and then paused before adding, "Maybe even a move."

Katie's eyebrows rose. "A move?"

He lifted a shoulder. "What do you think? We've always talked about moving back here when we have kids. I don't think we should hold off just because I might get traded to another team someday. I might stay with the Glaciers until I retire from hockey. And it'll probably be easier to get the house before the babies come because then we can get it ready for them."

Katie let go of the knife and the cauliflower she'd been cutting and turned to face Connor, putting her hands on his cheeks, and pulled him toward her, planting a kiss on his lips. She hadn't even realized that a happy tear had escaped her eye until she felt its wetness as it made its way down her cheek.

She pulled back just a bit but kept her hands on his face. "I think we're ready for all of it, Connor. The house, the babies, and whatever life throws at us."

"I think we are, too," he said and kissed her again.

Want to read more Christmas romances by Meg?

Get *Stockings, Snow, and Mistletoe* —two full-length Christmas romances to snuggle up with and swoon over. Both are full of heart, humor, hope, and all the magic of Christmas wrapped up in one holiday-filled collection.

Start reading today

Meg Easton is the *USA Today* bestselling author of contemporary romances and romantic comedies with fun, memorable, swoon-worthy characters, and settings you'll want to pack up and move to. She lives at the foot of a mountain with her name on it (or at least one letter of her name) in Utah. She loves gardening, bike riding, baking, swimming before the sun rises, and spending time with her husband and three kids.

She can be found online at www.megeaston.com

Sign up to receive her newsletter and stay up to date with new releases, get exclusive bonus content, and more.

If you liked this book please leave a review. Your review can help other readers find books they might fall in love with.

youtube.com/@megeastonauthor
bookbub.com/authors/meg-easton
instagram.com/megeaston_author
facebook.com/MegEastonBooks